SPUN YARNS UNWOUND: VOL. 4

URBAN FANTASY FOR ALL AGES

DEBBIE MUMFORD

DEB LOGAN

WDM
Publishing

URBAN FANTASY FOR ALL AGES

This volume of Spun Yarns Unwound contains urban fantasy stories written by WDM Publishing's authors.

Deb Logan loves to write contemporary fantasy that edges into urban fantasy. While she usually writes for middle grade and teen readers, these twelve tales include a few that move into the "new adult" category.

Debbie Mumford enjoys reading urban fantasy and is fascinated by writing stories that fit the genre. She was thrilled to be invited to join the Uncollected Anthology. A group of talented authors who specialize in urban fantasy. Three of her UA stories are included in this volume.

So sit back, relax, and let these paranormal tales of our modern world whisk you away!

COPYRIGHT

12 STORIES BY DEB LOGAN

I

DEMON DAZE

DEB LOGAN

AUTHOR OF *FAERY UNEXPECTED*

DEMON DAZE

SPUN YARNS
A Dani Erickson Short Story

A shiver of anticipation raced along my spine as Allie and I ducked inside the fortune-teller's tent. My parents didn't approve of psychic nonsense, but they'd allowed me to come to the carnival with Allie's family as a pre-birthday treat. The even bigger treat? Not a single one of my older brothers was tailing me. If the Erickson boys were at the carnival, they were enjoying their own night out, not watching over their baby sister.

Turning fourteen had its advantages!

The inside of the tent lived up to all my expectations. A thick Turkish rug covered the brittle, brown August grass and swags of colorful silk festooned the sidewalls and ceiling, ropes of twinkling LED lights camouflaged within the folds. A small table draped in blood-red velvet sat in the center of the small enclosure. A single intricately carved high-backed chair occupied the far side, while two folding chairs waited for us.

Allie glanced at me as if seeking reassurance. The corners of her lips curved in a timid smile and her eyes widened. "Are you sure we want to do this?"

I grabbed her hand and pulled her to the folding chairs. "This was your idea, remember? We're here. We're not backing out." I plopped onto a chair and waited. Allie lit on the very edge of hers, muscles tensed for flight.

A figure disengaged from the draping silk and approached the carved chair.

"I am Madame Simone. Welcome to my den of enlightenment. This place is hallowed, serving as a threshold to the great beyond."

The olive-skinned woman was swathed from head to toe in a rainbow of silk. Small golden discs dangled from her headdress, gracing her forehead and calling attention to dark, liquid eyes. She studied my best friend for a moment and then turned her attention to me.

"You have come at an auspicious moment," she said, and lowered herself gracefully into the high-backed chair. Leaning forward, she placed long-fingered hands upon the velvet tablecloth. "Tell me what you seek."

Allie uttered a nervous squeak and huddled back in her chair, moving as far from the fortune-teller as possible without jumping and running.

I glanced at Allie and then faced the psychic. "Aren't you supposed to tell us what we need to know?" I don't like people intimidating my friends.

"What you need to know," the woman murmured, holding my gaze and refusing to allow my escape. "Are you sure you're ready for that? Wouldn't you rather I told you silly tidbits about boys and kisses and who to dance with at homecoming?"

I straightened my shoulders, but didn't look away. Her sarcastic tone bugged me. Allie and I might be young, but we were paying for this woman's time.

"Look, just do your thing, okay? We paid for a reading, so read."

Madame Simone's smile could've frozen Boulder Reservoir. "As you wish." She inclined her head, breaking our eye-lock, and turned to Allie, "Your hand, my dear."

Allie placed her right hand in Madame Simone's left and shuddered slightly when the woman traced the lines in Allie's palm with a perfectly manicured nail.

"I see a long life if you sever your relationship with dangerous friends," the psychic said, spearing me with a pointed glance. "You will dance on the stage to the acclaim of millions. Beware the company of demons."

Allie snatched her hand back the moment Madame Simone released it and cradled it to her chest.

The fortune-teller cocked an eyebrow at me and held out her hand.

Time slowed. My heart thumped wildly, but the air had thickened, making it hard to breathe. Something moved just beyond my peripheral vision, and a desperate desire to flee seized my soul.

And then the moment passed and everything snapped back to normal. I sat in a stuffy little tent with too many silk drapes and a middle-aged woman who looked at me expectantly.

"Sure. Whatever." I placed my hand in hers...and a jolt like electricity convinced me I'd made a huge mistake. My hand jerked reflexively, but she held on tight and smiled an enigmatic little grin.

"As I suspected," she murmured, drawing her index finger along my palm and studying the lines like they spelled minuscule words. "You are the seventh ... the child of a seventh ... and you stand at the cusp."

She closed her eyes and held my hand open between both of hers. A sharp intake of breath and her eyes widened and sought mine. Fear glazed her eyes.

"Tomorrow a great burden will descend upon you. Have a care lest it crush you...and all who care for you."

With that happy thought she released my hand, sprang from her chair and melted back into the shadows.

"That's it?" I yelled after her. "Whatever happened to you're going to meet a tall, dark, handsome stranger?"

Anger mixed with a heavy helping of fear and roiled in my stomach. I wanted to hit someone. Instead, I grabbed Allie's hand and the two of us sprinted from the tent.

"What a load of ..."

"Hush, Dani," Allie said, glancing over her shoulder. "Let's go find my folks."

I huffed, but allowed my pretty little ballerina of a buddy to drag me into the throng of people wandering the midway. Alejandra Chavez had been my best friend since preschool. She was everything I'd ever wanted to be; everything my whole family still hoped I'd become. Dainty, graceful, feminine to the core, Allie was a lady, in all the best senses of the word. She played the piano with finesse and danced like a rose petal on a summer breeze. Of course, grace came more easily to her five-feet-two-inch frame than it did to my towering five-feet-ten-inches. At least, that's how I consoled myself. Whatever my talents were, I'd yet to discover them. I just kind of bobbed along in Allie's wake, never quite measuring up to her shining example.

She pulled to a stop when we spotted her parents tossing rings over bottles at a nearby booth. "Okay. Listen, we don't want to upset Mom and Dad, so let's pretend we never went in that psycho's tent."

I inhaled lungfuls of crisp night air, doing my best to calm my breathing and make my sprinting heart slow to a peaceful crawl. Alarmed parents would only ensure a quick trip home. Besides, there were still plenty of rides and games to explore that didn't involve weird middle-aged women wrapped in silk.

"Gotcha." I nodded. "Everything is peachy. We're having a grand time."

Allie stared at me, a small frown creasing her flawless brow. "Are you alright, Dani? She didn't scare you, did she?"

"Of course not," I scoffed, wishing my stomach agreed. "Tomorrow's my birthday. What kind of great burden hits someone on her fourteenth birthday? I mean, it's not like I'm turning sixteen and Dad's gonna give me a car I could crash. Get real."

Allie smiled a knowing little smile, one that said she saw right through my bravado. She patted my arm and said, "I knew you'd be okay with it. Let's see if we can help Dad win that stuffed tiger for Mom."

I grinned and we joined Mr. and Mrs. Chavez, but I had to force myself not to turn around and study the crowd. Someone was watching us. I could feel their focus ... and my skin tingled in response.

2

Fists pounding on my bedroom door startled me awake. I lunged upright, glanced wildly around the room, and managed to comprehend the chorus of, "Wake up, Birthday Girl!" that echoed from the hall.

Brothers! You gotta love 'em. It's the law; at least it is in my family. From the sound reverberating through my skull all six of them must have come home for the big celebration. Flattering...except it meant I'd have to spend my big day pretending I was Allie.

I grabbed a shoe from the floor and hurled it at the already besieged door. "All right, already. I'm up! Give it a rest."

Chortles sounded on the far side of the barrier, followed by a deeper bass shushing.

"Get a move on, Kitten," Mike commanded. The eldest of seven and a medical student to boot, Mike was accustomed to seizing control of a situation. "Mom's making French toast for breakfast. If these guys devour it all before you make it downstairs, she'll be in a mood all day."

I sprang from bed, leaped the intervening distance, and jerked the door open. Half a dozen boys in various states of early morning dishevelment blocked my path, while the sweet scent of maple syrup and frying bacon wafted through the air. "Outta my way!" I bellowed, elbowing my way into the hall. "No one's eating my birthday breakfast."

A race for the sugar erupted. We scrambled across the hall and down the stairs, barely making it to the kitchen with everyone still on their feet.

"Halt!" Dad's shout brought us all to attention, a ragged line of teens and twenty-somethings with straight backs and squared shoulders.

"Happy birthday, Dani," said Mom, turning from the griddle with a spatula in her hand. "Now, if all of you would be so kind as to march back up the stairs, wash faces and hands, and comb your hair, we'll have a civilized breakfast in a few minutes."

As one, the Ericksons deflated. We turned and my brothers tromped back up the stairs.

"Dani," called Dad, halting me in mid-step. "A moment, please."

I turned around wondering what I could've done. I couldn't be in trouble yet, I'd just woken up. Besides, it was my birthday.

"Yes, sir?"

Dad crossed the sunlit kitchen and wrapped me in a bear hug. He ruffled my still messy hair and smiled down at me. "Happy birthday, kiddo. Take your time in the bathroom. Nobody's eating 'til you get back."

I grinned, wriggled out of his arms and raced back upstairs. French toast! And the guys had to wait for me. Maybe I should take my time. Get dressed. Fix my hair. Would make-up be too over the top? I sniffed again, savoring the delicious aromas of non-store-bought delicacies.

Nah. Not worth the wait.

My mouth watered for French toast NOW!

Boulder Reservoir sparkled in the afternoon sun, inviting the people on shore to step into its cool water. Our extended family's annual end of the summer bash was underway. Partly my birthday party, partly an excuse to barbecue, swim, and laze in the sun before everyone went back to school. And I do mean everyone.

Several of Dad's brothers and sisters were teachers, everything from preschool to university professors, but not Dad. My dad was an architect, a partner at one of Boulder's most prestigious firms. Mountain lodges designed to withstand Rocky Mountain snow loads were his specialty. Too bad we lived down on the flats.

One of the great things about family gatherings was that they grounded me in reality. Sometimes being the youngest of seven weighed on me. I mean, none of my friends came from such humongous families. Two, three, even four kids, that was normal, but seven? What were Mom and Dad thinking? Then we'd have a family gathering and I'd realize that in Dad's world, a family of seven kids was kind of minimalistic. Dad fell right smack in the middle of thirteen — seven boys and six girls. Now that's a family!

Anyhow, I was lazing under a tree with a couple of my cousins, having had enough sugar and exercise for my lifetime, when my vision went wonky. Everything kind of twisted and blurred. I rubbed my forehead, blinked a few times, and focused on Jamie. My youngest brother — who was still three years my senior — was entertaining some of the younger boys by walking on his hands. I could see him, right down to the goofy grin on his face, but he was encased in a deep purple haze.

I blinked again and shifted my gaze to Mike. The doctor-in-training sprawled in a lawn chair a few yards away, a cell phone held to his ear and surrounded by a pale blue fog. Though the hand touching the phone glowed lime green. I closed my eyes and stretched out on the tartan picnic blanket.

I'd obviously had too much sun. A few minutes' rest would put me right as rain.

I could say something to Mom, but who wanted to be treated like an invalid on her birthday? Certainly not me! Sure, fourteen wasn't a big deal. I wouldn't be getting my driver's license or even a learner's permit, but still ... a birthday is a birthday. You take your celebrations where you find them. Especially when you're the youngest of seven, and the only girl.

"What's wrong, squirt? You look a little green."

I squinted up to find Jamie peering at me. He knelt beside me, looking all buff and tan from a summer of lifeguarding at the local pool, but he was still covered in that weird purple haze which was quickly modifying to a rich blue. Actually looked quite good with his ice-blue eyes and sun-bleached chestnut hair.

"Gee, thanks!" the corners of my mouth twitched, but it was hard to smile when your brother looked like he'd been cocooned in blue silk. "It's nothing. Something's weird with my eyes. Stuff is ... hazy."

Jamie scowled. He turned to Mike. "Hey, lover-boy! Get off the phone and come over here. Something's wrong with Dani."

Mike turned, eyes dark and irritable, ready to yell at Jamie ... and stopped. His jaw slackened and his eyes widened. He mumbled a few words, snapped the phone shut, and sprinted to my side.

"What's wrong, Dani? Did you eat something bad?" Mike scrutinized my face, his eyes narrowing. Cool fingers encircled my wrist as the physician-to-be assessed his little sister. He dropped my hand and scowled. "Tell me you're not stupid enough to be messing with drugs!"

"Wha-" That was the extent of my snappy comeback. My jaw locked and no further sound passed my lips.

My heart slammed against my ribcage like a passenger in a speeding car that had braked too suddenly. Panic clawed at my throat, but not a sound escaped. I was locked inside my own skull looking at everyone through silky gauze layers. Could Mike be right? Had someone drugged my potato salad?

"MOM!" Jamie scrambled to his feet and fled to the pavilion on the other side of the park.

Mike moved into Jamie's position, a worried frown replacing the scowl. His pale blue fog deepened to purple and pulsed in a rapid beat. The visual assault dizzied me, so I closed my eyes again. At least my eyelids still obeyed.

A flurry of voices rode the wind off the reservoir, alerting me to the imminent arrival of my parents, buoyed by a wave of aunts and uncles. With the familiar chatter of family came a decidedly unfamiliar sensation: awareness. Each person who approached was heralded by a distinct bubble pushing against the boundary of my conscious mind.

Though my eyes remained closed, I could identify each and every person in our quadrant of the park. I knew exactly where they stood in relation to me, could judge their level of agitation by the color of the bubble. Worse yet, other blips appeared on my psychedelic radar. Not the comfortable, concerned, well-rounded bubbles of my extended family, but twisted, dark blips that oozed like malignant wounds.

My eyes popped open. Each family member stood right where I expected, but the blips weren't visible. No. That wasn't true. The air shimmered where the blips should be.

"What is it, Dani?" asked Mom, her voice soft and soothing. She slipped to the ground beside me and searched my face with a concerned gaze. "Tell me where it hurts."

A shimmer intensified and I shifted my gaze from Mom to the anomaly. Maybe if I squinted...

A creature sprang into existence and eyed me with curiosity.

I recoiled, horrified by its scaly maroon skin, long filthy claws, and sharp, protruding teeth. The vaguely humanoid being stood erect and wore a torn, brown tunic. Its eyes, black and dangerous, glittered with intelligence, and something else — some dark amusement.

I shuddered and closed my eyes, but my awareness only heightened. More blips accumulated, surrounding my family. Drawn like sharks to blood. But what drew them? And why could I see them when my family obviously couldn't?

"She started to say something," Mike explained, "then, I don't know. It's like she seized. I think we should call an ambulance. I don't want to move her, but she needs help."

Mom stroked my hair and murmured reassurances while my brain scrambled to make sense of the unbelievable. What was happening to me?

A new bubble converged upon my family and drifted to my side, a shining white beacon tinged with radiant gold. Warmth and comfort emanated from the newcomer.

"Excuse me," the being said in a voice filled with authority. "May I have a look at her?"

My family drew back, except for Mom. The stranger laid cool hands on my head, one covering my forehead, the other supporting the nape of my neck. "Relax, child. Don't fight it," he murmured. "Acceptance is the key. I can and will explain, but not now. Right now, you must accept the unacceptable."

He continued to cradle my head and energy poured through my mind. I haven't got a clue how to explain what happened, but synapses fired, my emotions sorted, my understanding cleared, and my body relaxed. I opened my eyes and stared into the face of the man who had promised to explain my destiny to me. Blue-green eyes stared back at me from a hard, chiseled face. A mustache and short, well-trimmed beard provided the only softening to the planes of his face.

He released me, extended his hand, and helped me sit up. I shivered in the late afternoon heat and glanced from family member to family member. "I'm okay now."

A collective sigh of relief whispered through the ranks, but I knew the next indrawn breath would release a barrage of questions. My self-proclaimed mentor forestalled them.

"Nothing to worry about," he said, rubbing his hands together and backing away from the tartan blanket. "Just a bit too much sun and exercise. Happens all the time around here."

Jamie frowned and glanced at me, eyebrows lifted. My lifeguard brother knew something was up.

I shook my head, and he shrugged. We'd talk later.

Dad was shaking the man's hand. "I don't know what you did, but thank you, Mister..."

"James. Warwick James, but everyone calls me Wick. Don't think a thing of it, sir. I'm just glad I could be of service." He looked at me, and our gazes locked. He smiled, and I nodded and closed my fist around the slip of paper he'd palmed me when he helped me sit up.

I was still aware of creatures that shouldn't exist, but the members of my family were no longer shrouded in colored fog. Whatever was happening, I could deal with the remnants for the rest of the day, but tomorrow Mr. Warwick James and I were going to have a come-to-Jesus meeting.

4

The next morning I hitched a ride downtown with Jamie. That sounds a lot more exciting than it was. Downtown Longmont was a nicely renovated street of Mom and Pop stores, but most of the action was on the west edge of town at the mall. However, the piece of paper Warwick James had slipped me the day before specified a Main Street address, so that's where I headed.

"Are you sure you're all right?" Jamie asked for about the forty-fourth time. "Maybe I should stay with you."

"Jamie, please. Do you think Mom would've let me out of the house if there was anything to worry about?" That stopped him. Mom was one of those old-fashioned women whose career was home and family. Nothing slipped past her where her children were concerned.

"Okay. You win. I'll pick you up in front of Perks A Plenty at noon. Don't be late."

I slammed the car door, leaned back in the open window, and blew him a kiss. "Not to worry. I'll be there."

He shook his head, waved me off the car, and pulled away from the curb.

I glanced at the slip of paper and strode south down the wide sidewalk. The address was about a block south of the renovated portion of Main Street. Not yet to the train tracks, but beyond the well-groomed shopping district. I halted in front of what appeared to be an abandoned storefront. Wide display windows covered with brown paper stared back at me. Chipped white paint above and below the windows shouted the building's need for repair.

A small, hand-lettered placard announced a budding business:

Coming Soon!
Longmont's Own Martial Arts Academy.
Classes Enrolling Now!

I shivered, but reached for the doorknob. What choice did I have? Warwick James had promised to explain things, and I desperately wanted information. I hadn't seen any more monsters, but my newly acquired weird-o-meter told me they were still there, lurking just beyond my field of vision. I wanted them gone. I didn't want to know that the monster under the bed was real or that his cousin really was hiding in the closet.

Pushing open the door, I stepped into a large, dimly lit room. My footsteps rang against ancient linoleum floors and echoed off walls in need of a fresh coat of paint. The paper-covered windows washed the room with a diffused amber glow, causing the glare of an electric bulb from a half-open door in the back wall to stand out like a flashing neon sign.

"Hello. Is anyone here? Mr. James?" I listened as the echoes of my voice died away. No response. Much as I wanted answers, my sense of self-preservation refused to allow me to walk to the back of the room and step into that well-lit doorway. I turned toward the front door. Warwick James had found me once; he could find me again.

"I'm glad you came, Miss Erickson."

I nearly gave myself whiplash, jumping and turning in a less than smooth movement. Warwick James stood just a few feet from me. How had he gotten so close so fast? I frowned and studied the strange man who had appeared out of nowhere to release me from yesterday's spasm. Tall, trim, with good muscle tone. Definitely not a guy who lived on pizza and beer. Short brown hair and neatly trimmed mustache and beard, his blue-green eyes sparkled with humor. All in all, a good-looking guy, if you're interested in middle-aged men. I'm not.

"How do you know my name?"

"I know your family well, Miss Erickson." He raised an eyebrow and waved an arm in the direction of the back room. "Would you join me in the back? We can sit down and discuss this in more comfort there."

"No thanks. I'd prefer to stay near the door." I glanced over my shoulder, gauging the distance to the sidewalk outside. Not far. I could sprint it easily. Exit plan decided, I turned back to Mr. James. "How do you know my family? I've never seen you before."

"As you wish," he said with a shrug, thrusting his hands into the pockets of his jeans. "You misunderstand. I said I know your family well. I didn't say I was a family friend or even an acquaintance. You see, Miss Erickson, yesterday was the first time I've ever spoken to a member of your family, though I've been studying them for years."

A shiver ran down my spine and I backed a step closer to the front door.

"Please don't run away. You need to understand what's happening to you and why."

"So get to the point," I said continuing back until the doorknob was within easy reach. To my immense relief, Warwick James remained in the middle of the room.

"You had, shall we say, visions, yesterday. You saw things that can't possibly exist. Things no one else in your family saw. Am I correct?"

I nodded.

"That ability is the reason I've been observing your family. I've been watching, waiting for your power to manifest."

Silence descended on the room. A heartbeat, two ... fifteen or twenty passed. Neither of us spoke. Finally, when the pressure of words waiting to be released was palpable, I caved.

"You were watching ... me?"

"Not at first. Your father's family first drew our attention. Thirteen children is uncommon in this day and age. The stage was set, the potential for your ability to manifest existed. So we waited, checking back each year. Noting new members, new births. Updating the genealogical records. Do you know what we were waiting for?"

My shoulders relaxed, the knot in my stomach eased, and I snorted. "Don't tell me. You're one of those 'seventh son of a seventh son' fanatics. Well, I'm sorry to disappoint, but one: I'm a girl; two: you've got the wrong branch of the family. Uncle Gus is the seventh son, and unfortunately for you, he and Aunt Ellen can't have kids."

The jerk had the nerve to smile.

"I'm not disappointed Miss Erickson. Not in the least. Your family's understanding of the ability is incomplete. Yes, a seventh-seventh is required, but gender is not an issue. We were never interested in your Uncle Gus — though we were amused by your family's delight in producing a seventh son. Your father was always the object of our study."

I jumped and grabbed the doorknob for support. "My father?"

"Yes. Your father. The seventh child in his family. Only the fifth son, but the seventh child. And you, Miss Erickson, what does that make you?"

I swallowed and tried to speak, but my tongue felt swollen and the inside of my mouth was too dry to function.

He nodded. "That's right. You, Dani Heleen Erickson, are the seventh child of a seventh child. *You* are the hereditary Demon Hunter."

5

I wanted to rip open the door and run for my life, but I couldn't. My knees wobbled, my lungs seized, my heart pounded like my brother Seth's drums, and a series of cold chills played tag on my spine. And you don't want to know about my stomach. Trust me. Too much information doesn't begin to cover it.

But sooner than I would've expected, my racing brain calmed. A serene acceptance washed through my mind and I knew, absolutely, positively, with no question of doubt, that whoever Warwick James might be, he'd spoken the truth. I was a born and bred Demon Hunter.

I slipped sideways away from the door and leaned against the peeling paint of an interior wall. One by one my pieces parts returned to normal until I found the strength to speak.

"I'm a demon hunter." A simple statement of fact, and once the words were out, I straightened away from the wall, stronger and more sure of myself than I'd ever been in my life. I made eye contact with Wick and nodded. "I'm a demon hunter."

Concern fled from his face and he smiled like a proud father presented with his first-born. "Yes, Miss Erickson. You are a demon hunter, and I am your guardian."

A small frown pulled at my eyebrows. "Why would a demon hunter need a guardian? Besides, I already have a father and six brothers."

"True, but can they teach you to fight? Can they see demons? Can they watch your back while you learn the skills you'll need to survive?"

I chewed my lower lip and prowled the room, keeping my new awareness centered on Wick. "You can see demons? You can train me?"

"I can and I will. That is my purpose: to find demon hunters and protect them while I train them to protect mankind."

"I'm missing something here. If you can see demons and already know how to fight, why do you need me?"

He pivoted slowly on the spot, keeping me squarely in the center of his vision despite my pacing. "I'm not a demon hunter, Miss Erickson. I don't have your, shall we say built-in radar? I can fight them and make a nuisance of myself, but I cannot kill them. That power is reserved for your kind." He bowed his head in acknowledgement of my superior abilities.

"I will be your mentor and trainer, but you, Miss Erickson, are the demon hunter."

I stopped pacing, faced him, and planted my fists on my hips. "What is this place? Why did you bring me here?"

He held out his arms and completed a slow circle. "This is my new business, a martial arts academy. I will teach Tae Kwon Do, Karate, Judo, and Kendo. You will learn a blend of all of them while developing your own unique style."

"Doesn't look like much," I muttered.

He threw back his head and laughed so loud the room echoed with his mirth. When the explosion of sound died back, he wiped his eyes and said, "Give me a chance, Miss Erickson. Madame Simone and I have barely had time to set our plans in motion. She only confirmed your burgeoning power on Saturday night. I think I've done well to find a Main Street location on such short notice."

My eyes widened and my jaw dropped. "Madame Simone? Do you mean that wacko fortune teller from the carnival?"

"Language, Miss Erickson. Madame Simone is a gifted psychic. She and I have been with the carnival for years. The perfect cover for traveling around the country checking up on families that might possibly produce a demon hunter. Now that we've found you, we will settle in Longmont and other members of our clan will make the rounds." He shook his head. "Possibles are far too few these days."

I filed that comment away for future consideration and wandered back to the door. "Okay. So let's assume I buy this crazy story," I said, all too aware of the lie implied. I believed him and he knew it. How could I not? Even now I sensed three demonic entities roaming Longmont's peaceful streets ... and they were just the ones in range of my newly awakened weird-o-meter. "What do you expect me to do?"

He strode to the door, reached for the knob and opened it for me with a small bow. "I expect you to assimilate your new knowledge. Rest tonight. Think about what you've learned, and come back tomorrow ready to begin your training."

I stared at him for a moment and then stepped out into the late August sunshine. "I've got to meet my brother."

"I'll look for you around ten," he said, joining me on the sidewalk. He glanced up and down the street before continuing, "I'll shadow you back to your brother. For your own safety, go straight home and stay there. The home of a hunter is sacrosanct. You will always be safe there, as will anyone else within its walls. Be vigilant, Miss Erickson. You are now aware of demons; they are also aware of you."

With that cheery thought, I headed north to meet Jamie, Warwick James following at a discreet distance.

6

I spent that evening trying to convince myself Warwick James was
a scam artist or a serial killer. Anything to erase the exceptionally
abnormal future he'd outlined for me. What did I know about
demons? Why would I want to hunt them? As far as I knew, no demon
had ever harmed me or mine. Wouldn't Mom counsel me to live and
let live?

And what about Mom and Dad? How were they supposed to take the
news that their only daughter would never be the epitome of graceful
femininity they desired? That she was instead destined to be a warrior
charged with protecting the human race? They didn't want a guard
dog; they wanted a pampered Pomeranian.

I stalked from room to room of our comfortable home, unable to
settle anywhere. The kitchen taunted me with visions of the girl I'd
never be. If I were more like Allie, I'd be warm and welcoming like its
terra cotta red walls and pale lemon curtains, nourishing like the
contents of its hickory cabinets, accomplished like the woman who
ruled the heart of our home: my mother.

The great room, usually my retreat of choice, repelled me tonight. My brothers and their friends had gathered to watch a pre-season football game on Dad's awesome eighty-inch high-definition television. I could fit in with a roomful of guys, no problem. I'd been fitting in with guys since birth. But tonight I needed to think, and the guys' rowdy antics would kill higher brain function.

The formal living room mocked me. Every piece of furniture in that room knew its place and function better than I did, same with the elegance of the rarely used dining room. One of the bathrooms? No. Unless I wanted to settle in for a soak, someone would be beating on the door in a matter of moments. Bedrooms? All were off limits except my own, and I felt like a caged animal pacing round and round my bed. I briefly considered sitting on top of the washer in the laundry room, but the white enameled metal looked cold and uncomfortable.

My restless wandering finally drove me outdoors — not far out, I remembered Wick's warning — onto the wide, covered porch that wrapped three sides of our two-story home. I settled on a cushioned patio chair and stared across the street into the familiar shadows of Loomiller Park.

Big mistake.

On an ordinary night, I could've stared for hours at the well-known tree shadows, the mirror smooth lake that was really little more than a pond, the winding walkways and seen no more than the outline of an occasional Canada goose. Heard no more than the peaceful chirping of crickets or the breeze sighing through the foliage. But tonight was no ordinary night. Tonight I possessed the senses of a demon hunter, and the normally quiet park teemed with life of a type I hadn't known existed until yesterday.

Demons of all shapes and sizes crowded the edges of our property. They crawled across the streets, climbed on the kiddie play equipment, splashed in the shallows of the lake, and hung from branches of the evergreens. But mostly, they stared at me. Hundreds of pairs of eyes gleamed in the darkness of the still August night.

A paralyzing chill clenched my spine in an icy fist. An impulse to jump and run seized my brain, but my feet and legs refused to act. Like a rabbit charmed by a swaying snake, I stared into their eyes and drowned in fear. I was no demon hunter. I was prey. How could one untrained teenage girl hope to survive when the night teemed with such ... such ... filth?

Filth? I shook my head, breaking eye contact and laughed. Not a happy giggle, but a terrified, ironic chuckle. Something deep inside had challenged the thought the demon horde had tried to plant. Yes, I was young and untrained, but an unacknowledged spark in my soul recognized them for what they were, filthy vermin to be hunted from the face of the earth.

"Thanks, guys," I murmured, rising and walking to the door with a newborn calm. "You've convinced me. I'm a demon hunter in need of training." I smiled, waved a salute to the unholy creatures only I could see, and strode to the great room to join my brothers. "See you in the morning, Mr. James," I murmured to myself as I grabbed a handful of popcorn from Jamie's bowl.

Settling into my favorite chair, I smiled as the buttery goodness of popcorn melted on my tongue. I finally knew who I was. Never again would I see myself as a clumsy, too-tall imitation of Allie. No, I was exactly who I was meant to be.

Dani Heleen Erickson: Demon Hunter Extraordinaire!

II

SCHOOL DAZE

DEB LOGAN

AUTHOR OF *FAERY UNEXPECTED*

SCHOOL DAZE

SPUN YARNS

A Dani Erickson Short Story

1

I see demons, and they're not pretty, but since I discovered my destiny within hours of starting to see the little monsters, I don't let them faze me. I'm a demon hunter, and my training was about to begin.

"Bye, Mom," I called as I raced through the kitchen, snatching a cold protein shake from the refrigerator.

"Halt!" Mom commanded, and I stopped dead, hand on the doorknob. "Where do you think you're going, and why are you going so fast?"

Busted! Well, I hadn't really expected to get past Mom that easily. The woman was wise to the ways of teens, seeing as I was the youngest — and only girl — of seven.

"I'm headed over to Allie's. I'm going to shadow her for her ballet lesson this morning." I shrugged and tried to look embarrassed.

Evidently guilty passed pretty well for chagrin, because not only did she buy it, she smiled radiantly, wrapped a piece of toast in a paper napkin and handed it to me. "What a great idea! Maybe you'll decide to join Allie. I'm sure you'd enjoy ballet."

I held the grimace inside ... just barely. Yeah. I'd love ballet. All five-foot-ten of me lumbering around among the petite five-twos of Allie's crowd.

"Yeah. Well. Don't get your hopes up. I'm just checking stuff out."

Mom laughed, kissed my cheek, and waved me off. "Have fun, sweetheart."

I nodded and launched myself out the door before I confessed all. My mom is not the kind of parent you lie to with impunity.

As soon as I was off our property, my newly acquired weird-o-meter started pinging like mad. I glanced around, mindful of my trainer-to-be's warning. Warwick James, Wick to his friends, had promised my home was sacrosanct, but once I stepped off my property all bets were off. Fortunately, there were no demons close enough to be a problem.

Nevertheless, I didn't saunter down the street, I hoofed it to Allie's house, scarfing toast and chugging protein as I went. I hadn't totally lied to Mom. I was going to Allie's; I just had no intention of visiting her ballet class. While she danced her little heart out, I planned to train with Wick. Allie would provide my camouflage.

I dusted toast crumbs off my lime green tee shirt and rang Allie's doorbell. Her mom answered.

"Why, Dani, how nice to see you," she said with a smile. "Allie didn't tell me she was expecting you."

I grinned. "That's because she's not. Is it okay if I come in for a minute?"

"Of course, dear, but you'll have to make it quick. We're about to leave for Allie's ballet class."

"No problem," I said, sliding past her into the entry hall. "I'll just go on up."

I paced to the stairs and took them two at a time, calling, "Hey, Allie! You decent?" Below me, I heard Mrs. Chavez chuckle as she closed the front door.

Allie opened the bathroom door, toothpaste foaming through her lips. She ducked back to the sink, rinsed, spit, wiped her mouth and rounded on me. "What's up? What are you doing here?"

I gave her a significant look and murmured, "Remember the fortune teller? Well, we need to talk." The night before my fourteenth birthday, Allie and I had gone to a carnival where we'd had our fortunes told. That silk-clad woman had provided the starting point for a couple of really weird days. I needed to catch my best friend up on my new reality.

Allie's eyes widened, but she nodded and we raced to her bedroom, closing the door firmly behind us.

"I've only got a minute," she said.

I nodded. "I know. Ballet. I'm going with you."

"You're what?" Allie knew the extent of my undying non-interest in tutus and pink tights.

Quickly I outlined the high points of my recent experiences, ending with, "So you're going to be my cover. If anyone asks, I'm with you at your ballet class. And the great thing is, if my mom asks your mom, your mom can truthfully say she took us both to ballet."

I beamed at the brilliance of my plan, until an awful thought hit me. "Wait a minute! She doesn't stay, does she? Tell me your mom doesn't stay to watch your class!"

Allie rolled her eyes, grabbed my arm and pulled me out into the hall. "What do you think I am? Six? Of course she doesn't stay. Come on. We need to be in the car."

I stopped dead in my tracks, forcing her to pause, too. "You mean you'll do it? Just like that? You believe me?"

Allie cocked her head and looked at me like I'd lost my mind. "Of course I'll do it. You're my best friend, right? Why wouldn't I help you? As to believing you, well, I'll need to hear all the details, but we don't have time right now." She yanked my arm and we clattered down the stairs and into the kitchen. Well, I clattered. Allie descended gracefully. As always.

Mrs. Chavez plucked car keys from a rack by the back door. "Good. You're ready. We'll see you later, Dani," she said, opening the back door.

"Dani's coming with us, Mom."

"If that's okay, Mrs. Chavez," I said, elbowing Allie for her rudeness.

Mrs. Chavez glanced back in surprise, but kept moving toward the car. "Of course it's okay, Dani. I didn't know you were interested in ballet."

I shrugged and slid into the backseat. "Mom would like me to take lessons. I thought I'd check out Allie's class."

"I'm sure you'll like Allie's teacher, but remember, Allie's been training for years. You'll need to join one of the beginner classes, so don't get discouraged by what you see."

"Oh Mom! Dani knows about all that. She'll be fine."

Yep. My morning was off to a great start. I'd deceived two of the best mothers in town. Not to mention embroiling my best friend in my schemes.

2

The ballet studio where Allie studied occupied the second floor above a downtown furniture store. Her mom dropped us off at the curb and waved as she pulled away. Allie and I headed to a door sandwiched between two display windows. We stepped inside and huddled in the tiny space at the base of the stairs leading up to the second floor.

"Okay," Allie said, stepping onto the bottom stair. "We're here. Now what?"

"Now I follow you upstairs and you introduce me to your teacher. It's Mrs. Jennings, right? I want her to remember me just in case anyone checks up on us. I'll hang around for a few minutes and then duck out and head to Wick's place."

Allie frowned. "Are you sure this is safe? I mean, what do you really know about this guy? Will there be anyone else there? How do you know he's not some kind of pervert?"

I held up my hands to stop the flood of questions. "Whoa! Slow down. No, I'm not sure it's safe and I don't know much about him. But, and this is a big 'BUT,' I'm seeing demons and he's the only one who seems to have any answers for me."

Another girl stepped into the narrow space behind the door and glared at us for blocking the entry. A typical ballerina dressed in pale pink sweats, her blonde hair pulled into a severe knot at the nape of her neck. She edged past Allie and ran up the stairs, giving us a final withering look before disappearing through the door to the studio.

Allie grimaced, but held my gaze. "This isn't the time or place to discuss your delusions." She bit her lip and then blurted out, "Do you want me to skip class and come with you?"

"First, they're not delusions. There's a perfectly nasty little guy about three feet tall crouching in the shadows just outside that door." I nodded to a shaded spot just past the glass door.

Allie paled and moved up another couple of steps. I followed, staying one step below her, my gaze flitting back and forth between the demon and my best friend. No way was that little monster getting past me if he came through the door.

"Second, no, I don't want you to come with me. I want you to help me establish my alibi. Are you going to help me or not?"

Allie eyed the shadows where the demon stood, shivered, and turned her attention back to me. "Of course I'm going to help you. I just don't want you to get hurt, and this whole ... story ... makes my skin crawl."

I nodded. "Believe me. I understand. I wish I could give you proof, I really do, but for now, you're just going to have to trust me."

She cocked her head, studied my face, and nodded. "Come on. We're going to be late, and Mrs. Jennings is really strict about punctuality. We want you to make a good impression."

She turned and ran lightly up the stairs. I followed, feeling more like a lumberjack than a ballerina. Of course, considering the demon just outside the door, a lumberjack might be the more useful of the two.

Fifteen minutes later, Allie's class was in full swing, and I was hoofing it down the street to Wick's dojo. The demon had moved on, but I did my best power-walk anyway. I swept the area with my gaze as I practically ran down the street. My goal? Get to Wick before any more of the nasty little monsters showed up.

Allie planned to meet me at the dojo as soon as her class finished. She wouldn't be happy until she'd met Wick for herself. Her mom wouldn't pick us up until we called — she wanted to give me plenty of time to audition for Mrs. Jennings — so we had time to spare.

I stopped just outside the dojo's entrance and took a deep breath. Did I really want to do this? Did I really want to step into this building and put my life in a stranger's care?

A small noise distracted me and I glanced toward the railroad track in time to see a bloated green ghoul leering at me from beneath a parked car.

Yeah. I not only wanted to do this, I needed to do it. If I was a demon hunter, and not just a teenage loony, then I needed to learn to fight. I grabbed the doorknob, twisted and pulled. I'd rather be a fighter than a psycho.

Wick looked up as I stepped through the door. He was arranging thick red mats in the middle of the floor. The kind we used in gym for floor exercise, or the guys used for wrestling.

"You're right on time, Ms. Erickson. Good. Timeliness speaks of a disciplined mind. You'll need that for our training.

I grinned. "I learned early to be on time," I said. "It's the only way to survive with six brothers. Besides, my dad insists on arriving early, not late."

Wick nodded. "A wise man. Come in and let me show you around."

I walked toward him, outwardly calm, but inwardly on guard. Too aware that I was alone in a deserted building with a man I barely knew. Not that my being on guard would save me if he turned out to be a pervert. He was a martial arts instructor, after all. But still, better safe than sorry. And I fully intended to be safe.

Wick noted my wariness and nodded. "Good. You've decided to trust me, but not yet wholeheartedly. You have excellent instincts, Ms. Erickson. I assure you, you are safe here, but you are wise not to fully accept my word so early in our acquaintance.

"Now, there are locker rooms in the back, still in need of remodeling, but functional. Eventually we will have individual lockers, but for now there are clean cubbies where you can stow your belongings while we train." He walked toward two doors at the back of the spacious room and held one open for my inspection.

I glanced in, nodded, and moved to one side of the main room. "I'm fine for today. I'll just drop my backpack over here."

He let the door swing closed and nodded. "As you wish. You've chosen your clothing well," he said, approving my navy sweat pants and lime green tee shirt, "but I will provide you with a gi for future workouts. You'll want to come prepared to change, and you'll undoubtedly wish to shower before you leave. But that is for another time when you are more comfortable with this place, and with me."

As he spoke, he moved to the middle of the mats. "Please, remove your shoes and socks and join me on the mats."

Once I stood before him barefoot, he continued, "Today we will concentrate on some basic forms. I will show you how to control your breathing and how to move with strength and economy."

We spent the next hour doing what felt like a slow motion dance. He demonstrated each movement, and then watched to make sure I had copied him precisely. Insisting that I bend the knee exactly so, or that my arm be extended at just such an angle. Who knew you could work up a sweat moving at a snail's pace? But it was hard work holding the positions once he was finally satisfied with the placement of each of my limbs.

I was nearing the end of my patience — not to mention endurance — when the door opened, flooding the room with bright sunlight.

I straightened my back and shook my cramping arms, to find Allie silhouetted in the doorway.

Wick frowned. "I'm sorry. This is a private class. You'll need to come back during regular business hours."

I laughed. "You have regular business hours?"

Wick scowled. "Don't be impertinent, Ms. Erickson."

Allie giggled, and I grinned in delight. "You'll need to find a different student if you don't want impertinence. Come on, Allie. He doesn't bite."

At my invitation, Allie closed the door and stepped closer to the mat.

Wick's eyebrows rose as he looked from Allie to me, and back to Allie. "You should have told me we were expecting a guest, Ms. Erickson."

I shrugged. "Insurance. If you didn't know she was coming, you couldn't set a trap for her."

Wick nodded, but Allie looked startled.

"Allie, this is Warwick James, but you can call him Wick."

Allie nodded and whispered, "You're all right, aren't you?"

"Just great. He's a strict teacher, but he doesn't seem to be a serial killer," I answered in a stage whisper.

Wick rolled his eyes.

"Wick, this is Alejandra Chavez, my best friend and co-conspirator."

"Oh? And just what does Ms. Chavez conspire with you about?"

"In this case, Allie's helping me with my cover story."

Wick eyed Allie's sweat suit, duffle bag, and hair-do and asked, "Ballet?"

Allie nodded. "I just finished a class up the street."

"I see." He turned to me, "So, if anyone asks, you are studying ballet with Ms. Chavez?"

"You got it in one!"

He frowned. "Obviously you have given this more thought than I have. I assumed you would simply tell your parents you were studying martial arts with me."

I shook my head. "You don't know my family. Ballet is girly. Martial arts are manly. I'm the only girl out of seven. I'm supposed to do girly things."

"But many women study martial arts," Wick countered. "I fully expect my classes to be co-ed."

"Great, but I repeat: you don't know my family. Trust me. This subterfuge is necessary."

Wick raised an eyebrow and glanced at Allie.

"She's right, Mr. James. Her parents will be thrilled that she's studying ballet, but they wouldn't be happy with this." she gestured around the room.

"It will look better soon," he said, a touch defensive.

Allie smiled, and when Allie smiled, who needed sunshine? She simply radiated peace, good will, and happiness. "No, I didn't mean your studio, I meant your entire field of study. Dani's family wants girly-girl stuff for her, nothing that smacks of tomboy. I swear, I'd like to slap them some days. Tell them to wise up and appreciate the diamond they have instead of wishing for a pearl they don't."

My jaw dropped and I stared at Allie. "Really? You think I'm a diamond?"

Allie's eyes widened and then relaxed. "Well of course. You're my best friend! I certainly don't think you need to be more like me. I think you're fabulous just the way you are."

My face flamed and I dropped my gaze to the mat at my feet. My cheeks probably matched that red.

"We are in agreement then, Ms. Chavez. Dani is exactly who she needs to be. You and I will work together to prepare her for the destiny that awaits her."

I glanced up to find Allie chewing her lower lip. "About that," she said. "Are you serious about the demon hunter thing?"

Wick stepped toward Allie, took her right hand in his, and stared into her eyes. "Totally and completely, Ms. Chavez. Demons exist, and far too few demon hunters are being born in this modern age of small families. Much of the world's present ills are caused by demon activity, which flourishes in the face of too few hereditary demon hunters. Ms. Erickson will need all the help and support we can give her."

Just then the front door opened again, and a woman swirled inside. Though she was dressed in jeans, a button-front shirt, and a bolero vest instead of flowing skirts and gauzy scarves, I recognized the fortune-teller instantly.

"Am I late, Wick? Ahhh ... I see the friend has accompanied our little huntress."

"You!" exclaimed Allie, recognizing the woman as well. "What are you doing here?"

"Come in, Simone," Wick said, dropping Allie's hand and moving to usher the fortune-teller inside. "I don't think you three were properly introduced. This is Dani Erickson, our demon hunter, and her friend, Alejandra Chavez."

The woman nodded to each of us.

"Ms. Erickson, Ms. Chavez, permit me to introduce my colleague, Simone Dalca. You may address her as Madame Simone."

Allie and I stood perfectly still, shoulder to shoulder. Us against the world.

Wick and Simone faced us, their expressions serious, but friendly. Finally, I broke the silence. "Nice to see you again. I think."

Madame Simone inclined her head. "I'm sorry if I frightened you at the carnival. Better to be on guard when you can't yet be aware."

A chill raced down my back, but I refused to shiver.

"Madame Simone will also assist you, Ms. Erickson. I will teach you to fight and guard you while you learn. Simone will instruct you in demonology, Tarot, and runes. She will help you make sense of the supernatural world you now inhabit."

"You're going to teach me to tell fortunes?"

"No, Dani. I'm going to teach you to read signs and portents so you are prepared to face the creatures who will stalk you as you hunt them. You must be skilled in more than just fighting techniques if you are to survive against demonkind."

I swallowed. Survival sounded so ... intense.

I glanced at Allie and our eyes met. She looked like a frightened bunny. Then she nodded and the bunny suddenly had nerves of steel.

I made eye contact with each of my new friends. I was a demon hunter, and these three would be the keys to my success. Silently, I extended my hand, palm down. One by one, the others laid a hand on mine. Just like the four musketeers: all for one and one for all.

3

The next few days passed quickly. Using the ruse of ballet class and practice with Allie, I met with Wick every day. Training went well. Actually, it went beyond well, right into the realm of unbelievable. I discovered that the forms and exercises he taught me resonated on an almost biological level. It wasn't so much that Wick taught me martial arts as that he reminded me of forms I'd known forever. My body completed the exercises with glee, relishing both the activity and the movements themselves.

Studying with Madame Simone required yet another deception on my part. In order to make time to learn about demonology and other arcane knowledge, I joined Allie for singing lessons.

Yeah. Right. Songbird that I am (NOT!) I tagged along to her lessons, met Ms. Lawson, and then scampered over a block and down two to Madame Simone's newly set-up psychic counseling business. She had rented a small home on the edge of the business district and she and Wick lived in the back. Handy.

Demonology, Tarot and runes also came scary easy to me. Who knew I was such a reservoir of arcane facts about forgotten species? I learned the hierarchy of demons and discovered that the ugly little beings I'd seen so far were only the lowest rungs on the ladder. Fabulous. Bigger bad guys to come.

While I stuffed my brain and strained my muscles, I also prepared for school. A big deal as this year Allie and I were moving from middle school to high school. We'd made it to the big-league, but I didn't have time to be nervous over rubbing shoulders with juniors and seniors. I was too worried about which class of demons I might meet in the halls.

Wick shadowed me around Longmont, making sure I moved securely through what I'd always considered a safe town. As my fighting skills grew, he relaxed, but he didn't desert me. He seemed surprised, maybe even disappointed, that we hadn't yet encountered any demons bold enough to try to take out the new hunter.

The day before classes were to start Wick presented me with two gifts: knee-high boots and a backpack.

I stared at the gifts in disbelief and then glanced up at Wick. "Uh, hmm ... wow, Wick. I don't know what to say. I mean, who knew you were a fashionista?"

He grimaced and aimed a slap at me, which I dodged effortlessly. "A bit of respect, if you don't mind, Ms. Erickson." He nodded at the boots. "Try them on."

With a dramatic sigh, I grabbed the boots and dropped to the exercise mat. The black leather was supple, but oddly stiff along the side seams. And they were heavier than expected. I frowned and examined them more closely. Along the outside seam of each boot I discovered a cleverly concealed pocket, and inside each pocket was something long and thin. Who sewed staves into the sides of high-fashion boots?

Wick watched, a slow smile spreading across his lips.

I arched my eyebrow at him, and he nodded his encouragement.

Exploring the right boot stave a bit more closely, I found a handle and pulled. The stave slid from the boot, but it wasn't a piece of whalebone for shaping and reinforcement. It was a needle thin, sharper-than-my-mom's-best-kitchen-knife stiletto.

I almost dropped it in surprise, but my training took over and I examined the blade for balance. Flipping it end over end a few times, the handle returned unerringly to my hand. Perfectly balanced. Like it was made for my fingers alone.

I grabbed the second boot and extracted its mate. A matched set. I was armed and dangerous.

I leapt to my feet and ran through a few forms. The blades were extensions of my fingers. They fit. More than that, they felt right.

Finishing the form, I crossed the blades in front of me and bowed to Wick. "Thank you, sensei. They are perfect."

Wick nodded, satisfaction plain on his rugged features. "Sheathe the stilettos. We'll move on to the backpack, but before you go, I want you to put the boots on and practice drawing the blades while you're moving."

I nodded and did as instructed. Wick handed me the backpack.

It looked like a pretty standard piece of teenage school equipment. A main compartment, padded shoulder straps, a couple of pockets on the flap of the main section, rugged black fabric. But when I hefted it, I knew that like the boots, it harbored secrets.

Dropping back to the mat, I examined every inch of the pack, from the padded leather handle on the top to the durable leather bottom. The pack guarded its secret well, but I was determined, and once I found it, I held my breath. Running down the back of the pack was a concealed scabbard. When I wore the pack, the scabbard would be snug against my back. The leather handle at the top of the bag was actually an extension of the grip of a short sword. Carefully I withdrew a gleaming blade.

"You do realize you're going to get me expelled before I even make it to my first class in high school," I said, glancing up at Wick.

He shrugged. "Better expelled than dead. Besides, you're smart enough not to be flashing those around unnecessarily."

I nodded, but my attention was back on the sword. Several narrow grooves ran the length of the blade and etched besides the grooves were runes I'd only recently learned to recognize. I stood and took a couple of swipes at imaginary foes. The blade swished satisfyingly through the air, the handle fit my hand like they were made for each other.

"It's perfect. How can a sword be light as a feather? Who made it, and how did they make the grip fit my hand so well?"

"Those grooves are called fullers or flukes. They lighten the sword and increase its flexibility. As to the grip, well, let's just say that my people have some magic of their own. That blade was made for you. It will never perform as well in another's hand, and the runes are spells to ensure it won't be used against you by demonkind."

"It's beautiful, Wick. They all are. Thank you."

"You're welcome, but the best thanks will be hard training with your new weaponry. I want them to become extensions of your body. So natural in your hands that you don't even think about them. Obviously, that will take time. So let's get started."

We spent the next two hours working up a sweat as Wick taught me the basics of my new blades. I worked barefoot. I worked in the boots. I learned the knack of pulling stilettos on the run and re-sheathing them without cutting myself. That last was trickier than expected, but by the time Wick released me, I was comfortable with his gifts. I was far from expert in their use, but I wasn't in danger of maiming myself.

"I won't be able to shadow you at school," Wick said when I emerged from the locker room wearing my new boots and shouldering my backpack, "but don't be surprised if you see me on campus. I have an appointment with the principal tomorrow morning to discuss teaching a self-defense class as part of the physical education curriculum."

"Sweet!"

"It'll give me an excuse to be nearby. Just in case."

A shiver ran down my spine, but I controlled my reaction. "So, when do I start, you know, hunting demons?"

"Patience, Ms. Erickson," he said as he walked me to the door. "For now, leave them alone unless they threaten you. I'd like a solid month, preferably two, of training before you have to use your new skills. I doubt the truce will last that long, but I can hope."

"No problem on my side. I'm not anxious to fight."

"Good. Come by after school. I'll want to hear about your first day."

I nodded, grabbed the doorknob, took a deep breath, and left the security of Wick's dojo.

.

4

High school. What can I say? Demons changed all my expectations.

I'd been looking forward to high school for years, but I'd only anticipated dealing with upperclassmen. The recent changes in my perceptions had radically altered my worldview. When I stepped through the front door with Allie by my side, a bizarre sight greeted me. The entry teemed with students, but a few humanoid demons lurked in the shadows and quite a few of the students carried not a chip on their shoulder, but an actual tiny demon! Who knew the demonic species was so varied?

Madame Simone had described these personal demons to me, but somehow I'd thought she meant them figuratively, not literally. I mean, people talk about this or that person having a lot of baggage, but you never see anyone dragging an actual steamer trunk around the streets.

I thought personal demons were like that, just a figure of speech, psychobabble to explain away someone's bad attitude. Nope. Not so much.

Take Jason Davis. My brother Jamie would love for someone to take Jason — the further away, the better. Jason had been bullying and backstabbing Jamie for years. Now I understood why.

Jason strode past, sneered at me, and said, "Great. Another Erickson. This place really is going to the dogs."

"Nice to see you, too, Davis," I responded, but without the fire I'd usually have put behind the words. It's hard to despise a guy who's got a demon riding on his shoulder and doesn't even know it.

The nasty little creature, a rat-faced being about the size of a scrawny house cat, had its claws sunk deep into the base of Jason's neck and was licking bright drops of life-energy as they oozed from the puncture wounds.

I couldn't stand it. I didn't like Jason, but nobody deserved to be victimized by a creature they couldn't even see. I followed Jason a step or two, grabbed the demon's tail and yanked. The being yowled in surprise, leaving severe gashes in Jason's neck as its claws disengaged.

Everything happened at once.

The little cat-demon spun in my hand and tried to attach itself to my wrist.

Jason turned and charged at me, bellowing, "What the hell did you do to me, you little bitch?"

The humanoid demons emerged from the shadows and moved to encircle me.

First things first. I shook the personal demon loose, dropped it on the floor, and stomped it beneath my boot. It yowled and squirmed, but I put my weight on that foot and held it in place.

Turning my attention to Jason, I raised my hands to keep him at arms' length, but the motion was unnecessary. He'd already stopped. He just stood there with his mouth open, staring at me and rubbing his neck.

"What's your problem, Jason?" I asked with as much innocence as I could muster while pinning a squirming demon to the floor.

He closed his mouth, opened it again, and glanced around, a look of total bewilderment on his face. His handsome face. Now that his features weren't screwed up in pain and menace, I was amazed to see that Jason was a really good-looking guy. Blond, blue-eyed, even features, strong jaw. Without the demon, Jason might not be so bad.

"N-nothing," he finally managed to croak. "I'm, uh, I'll see you around, Dani." With that he turned around again and rushed down a hall.

Allie appeared at my elbow. "What was that all about?" she asked, staring after Jason.

"Not right now," I said eyeing the tightening circle of demons. I gave her a push toward the freshman wing. "Go to class. I'll find you in first block."

She flashed me a worried look, but walked away.

The larger demons continued to close their circle. How was I supposed to handle all those demons without freeing the one under my foot — or being expelled for bringing weapons to school? Because I sure couldn't defeat them all without drawing my blades.

Just when I was starting to sweat, radiant warmth washed over me. The demon horde faltered and stepped back a pace. I glanced over my shoulder to see Wick leaving the main office and walking in my direction. Relief flooded my soul. Whatever happened, I wasn't alone.

Wick glanced from the little demon under my boot to my face, a sly smile twitching the corners of his mouth. "What happened to leaving them alone unless they threatened you, Ms. Erickson?"

"You didn't warn me that people I knew would be demon-ridden," I whispered, glancing at the encircling demons. "How do I get out of this?"

Wick grinned. "This is why untrained hunters need guardians. They get themselves into the worst messes." He stooped as if to tie his hiking boot, whipped out a pocketknife and beckoned me to join him at the floor. Palming the blade, he handed it to me and muttered, "Finish it."

I stabbed the evil little creature and watched it disappear in a belch of grimy smoke. Returning the knife, I straightened to standing; my feet now free to find a fighting balance.

Wick rose as well, glancing casually around the entry. "Now, Ms. Erickson, we wait. Whether or not we fight will depend on the actions of the horde."

I nodded and turned so that my back was to Wick. My breathing slowed and I focused my concentration on the ring of nasties. They glanced at each other before slowly melting back into the shadows. Their gazes lingered, like hundreds of midges biting my skin, but the moment of danger had passed.

"Looks like they've decided to live another day," Wick said quietly.

I turned to face him and whispered, "Thanks for being here."

He nodded and said in a normal volume, "It's nice to see you again, Ms. Erickson. I hope you'll consider signing up for the self-defense class I'm going to teach."

I smiled, relaxing a bit. "I'd like that. See you around, Mr. James."

He inclined his head and waved one hand in a graceful gesture for me to leave. "Have a good day, Ms. Erickson."

"You too, Mr. James." I replied, striding off down the corridor where Allie had disappeared. "You too."

High school was so not what I'd been expecting. But then, I'd never expected to be a demon hunter, either. School days were going to be far more interesting than I'd imagined.

Whoever said high school was full of kids waiting for their lives to start had been dead wrong. My life was in full gear, thank you very much. My eyes were open, my weapons razor sharp, and my training well underway. I intended to scour the demon scum from my school — and then I'd get to work on my town.

Demons beware. Dani's on the prowl!

III

FAMILY DAZE

DEB LOGAN

AUTHOR OF *FAERY UNEXPECTED*

FAMILY DAZE

SPUN YARNS
A *Dani Erickson* Short Story

1

I see demons and they're not pretty. Take the goblin hovering behind Ms. Hockinson's chair for example: scaly, maroon skin; long filthy claws; sharp, protruding teeth; only vaguely humanoid. The nasty creature stood erect, clothed in a torn, brown tunic. His eyes, black and malevolent, glittered with intelligence, and something else, something truly disturbing ... dark amusement.

A shiver of anticipation zinged along my spine. I was born to battle demons. Me. Not one of my six older brothers. I might be the youngest child and only girl, but I was also the one heredity had chosen — and this idiot had wandered onto my turf. He had no clue how dead he was. Yet.

I weighed my options while I sized up my opponent. A glance at the institutional clock clinging to the wall above the chalkboard behind Ms. Hockinson's desk informed me that the school day would end in five minutes. Classmates squirmed in their desks, surreptitiously gathering their belongings in anticipation of the longed-for final bell.

The demon examined the class, his gaze moving from student to student while one clawed hand encircled my teacher's throat. He smacked his lips and a long thin tongue darted between his teeth to lick Ms. Hockinson's ear.

She cleared her throat and flicked a hand toward his face as if warding off a pesky fly.

The clock ticked nearer the hour, and then the unthinkable happened. The second hand stopped, suspending time.

Every person in the room stiffened, frozen in mid-action just like the clock. Everyone, except the demon and me. No way was I going to be stuck in Ms. Hockinson's social studies class until the end of time! That demon was going down.

The demon grinned, and I launched my attack. Sliding out of my chair, I jumped to the top of my desk, flipped over Jeremy Brody's head and landed in a crouch before Ms. Hockinson's desk. On the way to standing I yanked twin stiletto blades from the concealed sheaths sewn artfully into my favorite high-top boots.

"Well, well," said the demon. "What have we here? A human immune to the ravages of time?" He licked Ms. Hockinson's ear again and stroked her neck. "You must wait a bit, my tasty morsel. One of your students needs my attention."

He released my teacher and hurtled across her desk.

I skipped sideways, letting one stiletto trail across his midsection.

The stroke surprised him. He glanced at his bloodied belly, roared, and lunged.

I danced away, using my knives as I'd been trained — like a picador with a bull. Wounding him with small, precise cuts designed to sap his strength and enrage his ego.

We scuffled briefly, but silver blades and sacramental preparation gave me the edge. I leapt and rolled, bounced and twirled, and each time a hand passed his flesh, my blade left a mark.

At last, he staggered toward Cynthia Larrabee, intending to take a hostage to shield his escape. He had waited too long.

I raced past my desk, exchanged stilettos for backpack and withdrew the sword from the concealed scabbard running down its back. With an aerial leap that would've done a ninja proud, I landed between the demon and his target, momentum carrying my sword arm through a perfectly timed arc. The demon's head flew to the opposite side of the room while his body crumpled at my feet.

I leaned over the remains, cleaned my blade on his tunic and, pulling a vial from my pocket, sprinkled holy water over the body. Moving quickly, but carefully, I made my way back to my desk, stowed my stilettos, sheathed the sword, straightened my hair and resumed my seat. I looked up just in time to see the demon fizzle out of existence, along with all traces of his blood. The second hand resumed its circuit around the clock face and the final bell of the day rang.

Ms. Hockinson dabbed her handkerchief across her neck, looked up with a frazzled sigh, and called, "Class dismissed!"

I smiled to myself, stood and shouldered my backpack. Sometimes, being a hereditary demon hunter rocked. Too bad Grandpa would never know that his self-imposed breeding program had worked. He hadn't attained his goal of a seventh son of a seventh son, but he'd gotten his ultimate desire: me.

Dani Heleen Erickson.

Mom and Dad didn't know it, but they'd given me truly prophetic initials: D. H. E. — Demon Hunter Extraordinaire.

2

I reread the entry I'd just made to my ultra-secure, my-eyes-only computer journal:

I may be a hereditary demon hunter, but that's nothing compared to the trials of being a teenage girl with six older brothers. I'd rather battle undead, soul-sucking monsters than try to keep secrets from my family, but that's just what I have to do every single day because they don't want an Amazon warrior princess; they want a delicate little lady.

Well, you don't always get what you want, and I'm living proof. Deal with it.

Pity party, much? Well, yeah, but I figured I was entitled. Fresh from battling — and defeating! — a demon in Social Studies, I arrived home only to be smacked with the news that my ballet teacher had complained that I'd skipped out on three lessons in a row.

Mom was steamed. The family was paying good money for my lessons in dance, not to mention grace and deportment. Gag!

Did anyone ever ask me what I was interested in learning? Did they bother to clue into the fact that I was rapidly approaching black belt in not one, but three disciplines of martial art?

Of course not.

Delicate little ladies don't beat the crap out of demons, or their older brothers. I trained with my sensei Wick — Warwick James to the rest of the world, in secret because my family would never tolerate me practicing martial arts. To quote the standard line, "Act like a girl, Dani. We've got enough boys in this family."

Someone banged on my closed bedroom door. "Come on out, Dani," yelled Brent, my next-to-the-youngest older brother. "We're having a family council in the kitchen." He stomped off down the hall, while I considered escaping through the window.

I could do it. I was getting really good at scaling walls, climbing roofs, and running lightly across ledges that were never designed for transit. But I'd pay in the end. The parental units were strict about family councils.

Reluctantly, I signed out of my journal, closed my laptop, and scrambled off the lacy pink and white coverlet that was just one more indication of how little my family really knew me. I mean, take this room. Please! Take it! My retreat from the testosterone pervading our home, and Mom had to decorate it so that it was practically uninhabitable. Pastel pink walls, gleaming white trim, eyelet curtains, and a four-poster bed complete with pink and white canopy. Over the years I'd managed to put up enough Goth posters and sports banners to somewhat subdue the pink, but still, who did they think lived here? When had I ever expressed the desire to be an animated princess?

"Dani! We're waiting." My dad's voice carried right through my bedroom door. Time to face my doom. Who'd have believed Mom would call a family council over a few missed ballet classes? Certainly not me.

I squared my shoulders and ran down the back stairs into the large family kitchen, my favorite room in our sprawling, comfortable home. Sunny yellow curtains and terra cotta counters balanced rough hickory cabinets and cool stone floors. All heads turned as I entered the room. Four of my six brothers ranged around the scrubbed oak table; Mom and Dad stood close together near the back door. Worry etched the parental units' faces.

"What's up?" I asked, taking my place beside Brent and noting Jamie's absence. Mike, the eldest of our tribe, sat across from me, with Evan and Seth flanking him. Pat was absent, but since he didn't live at home, that wasn't unusual. I was actually surprised Evan and Seth were there. Both of them lived on campus at the University of Colorado, Boulder. Mike was a doctor, a resident actually, and lived at home because it was simpler than maintaining an apartment when he was so rarely away from the hospital.

Dad gave Mom a quick squeeze around the waist and the two of them joined us at the table. "We're concerned about Jamie," Dad said. "He didn't come home from school today and he hasn't called."

That was a major breach of family protocol. Everyone had cell phones and we were all expected to keep the parents apprised of our where-abouts. They weren't Nazis or anything, but they did insist on knowing our plans. Reasonable for parents, a big pain in the butt for me as a demon hunter, but I managed.

"Dani, did you see him after school?"

Hearing my name snapped me back into focus. "No. I walked home with Allie." That's Alejandra Chavez, my best friend in the whole world and the only person besides my trainers, Wick and Simone, who knew my secret identity.

A little knot of fear bloomed in my belly. Jamie knew the house rules and played by them. Always. I zoned out of the family discussion, tuned into what I thought of as my weird-o-meter, and concentrated on Jamie. Ever since my fourteenth birthday when my demon hunting powers had manifested, I'd had this uncanny ability to sense demons. As a side effect, I could also sense my family, those who shared my blood and heritage.

No one else in the family had my abilities, but we were all connected, so I could sense them if I chose to. I homed in on Jamie's bat-signal now. A sigh of relief whispered out as I found the rich blue blob that represented my youngest brother, and then caught in my throat nearly choking me as I widened my vision and found him encircled by demons, and not the little guys either. Wherever he was, Jamie was in the company of some very dangerous beings.

Guilty terror tingled along my nerve endings and the contents of my stomach — why had I eaten that gooey cinnamon roll and washed it down with a huge glass of milk? — threatened to spew themselves across the table. This was my fault! Demons wouldn't have kidnapped Jamie if I hadn't been hunting them.

Then another thought struck. A truly terrible possibility. One that froze my heart and made my vision swim. When I rescued Jamie, he'd learn my secret. And once he knew my secret, my demon-hunting days were over. No way would he keep quiet. Not Jamie. Not the pain-in-the-ass brother who was always looking for ways to get me in trouble.

And once Mom and Dad knew the truth, I'd be grounded for life.

I closed my eyes and drew a deep breath, pulling my priorities into order. Of course I had to rescue Jamie. Major pain he might be, but he was still my brother and I loved him. That and the inescapable fact that I was a demon hunter. I existed to protect humans from demons.

So the order of business: rescue Jamie; deal with the consequences later.

Pushing back from the table, I jumped to my feet. All eyes turned to me. "We need to find him," I said, loudly and firmly. "We need to find him right now. Let's go out and search. I'll get Allie and we'll check the school parking lot and the ball field. Brent, you call all his friends. Find out if they know where he went..."

"Whoa!" Brent shoved to standing, hands on hips. "Who appointed you Supreme High Commander?"

I was about to give him a shove and a smart answer when Mike interrupted. "Easy, you two," he turned to Dad. "We can't go to the police yet. He hasn't been gone long enough. I think Dani's idea is sound."

Dad nodded. "It's essentially what your mother and I had already decided to ask you to do."

"Good enough. Dani, go get Allie. If you two find anything, call home. Dad and I will hand out the rest of the assignments."

I stuck out my tongue at Brent and dashed through the door before he could retaliate with something more physical.

I had no intention of dragging Allie into this. She might be my BFF and have the inside scoop on my demon fighting abilities, but she was also the epitome of female delicacy. The ideal my family would love for me to attain. No way would I pit her flawless pirouette against demon slobber. Instead, I yanked my cell phone out of my pocket and tapped Wick's icon.

My trainer answered on the first ring. Technically, Wick was my guardian. He was part of an ancient race who studied bloodlines and waited for hereditary demon hunters to manifest. He'd been onsite the day my powers bloomed and had been helping me adjust ever since. The guardians could see and fight demons, but they couldn't kill them. They needed my kind for that.

"Miss Erickson," Wick said. "Is this a social call or are you in danger?"

See? That's one of the many things I loved about Wick. Quick on the uptake and not one to waste words.

"We've got a problem. My brother Jamie is missing, and when I checked my radar, I detected a ring of high-level demons surrounding him."

Wick sucked air, the sound assuring me he'd heard my report. A moment passed and I could almost hear the wheels in his brain turning, even through the cell phone. "Where are you?"

"Crossing the street to Loomiller Park. Can you pick me up? I'll meet you in the high school parking lot."

"I'm out the door. Meet you in ten."

I disconnected, jogged across the park's green grass — no time to follow the meandering sidewalks — past the picturesque pond with its fleet of Canada geese, and down the street to the high school. When I arrived, I settled on a stone bench near the flagpole and tuned in to my weird-o-meter. Might as well get a sense of where the demons had Jamie stashed.

Images of my youngest brother, who was still eighteen months older than me, strapped to a table with demon claws flaying skin from his arms flashed into my head. My belly did a queasy little dance, pushing bile up my throat. I gagged, swallowed, and forced the image from my mind. Those high echelon demons would *not* play mind-games with me. I refused to participate.

Instead I pulled a vision of my healthy, happy, rival-for-the-parental-units'-attention brother into my mind and concentrated on finding him, on *knowing* his location. The image fought me. It buckled and morphed, trying to show me horrors. But I held on. I concentrated on the information I sought, refusing to allow anything else mind-space.

Sweat beaded my forehead and trickled over my temples, seeping into the corners of my eyes and making them burn, but I held on. "Come on, Jamie," I whispered through clenched teeth. "Where are you?"

The image solidified just as Wick's Jeep Wrangler whipped into the school's loading zone and screeched to a halt in front of me.

I jumped to my feet and ran forward as Wick leaned across the passenger seat and opened the door.

"Get in," he called. Once I was safely buckled in beside him, he revved the motor and peeled out. "Where are we heading?" he asked as he screeched to a stop at the street.

"Turn left," I said. "They've got him in the old turkey factory."

Wick nodded. "Makes sense. Abandoned building. Private. Could even be where they've located their portal."

"Portal?"

"Yes. The gateway from their universe to ours."

I shifted in my seat and stared at him with open-mouthed disbelief.

He glanced at me, grinned, and turned back to the road. "Come now, Miss Erickson. Surely you've figured out they're not normal creatures. Otherwise everyone would be able to see them. What has Simone been teaching you?"

I forced my mouth closed, swallowed, and re-engaged my brain. "We're studying tarot, runes, and demonology," I said, "but she never mentioned other universes. I would've remembered that. She's always talking about their realm, like it's a neighboring kingdom or something."

He smirked, but kept his eyes on the road. "I suppose it is. It's just that they neighbor us from an alternate universe. Without getting into the science of it, which I don't understand, the best anyone's been able to guess is that they're from a parallel dimension and are able to open gateways where our realities touch."

"Wow," I said, shaking my head as if that would help the thoughts settle more firmly into my brain. "So, I'm really killing aliens."

"More or less," he agreed. "But don't go getting sentimental about them. They're still life-sucking parasites attacking innocent people who don't have a clue they exist. Normal people don't stand a chance against them. Hard to protect yourself from something you can't see and don't believe exists."

I nodded, suddenly picturing Jamie as a dried out husk. A mummified horror. How would I ever explain that to Mom and Dad? I licked my lips. "What do you think they're doing to Jamie?"

Wick glanced at me, a quick assessment of my emotional status. "Not much, yet," he said. "They're not interested in your brother except as bait for you."

I nodded. "Do they know about my weird-o-meter? That I can home in on him because he's family?"

"Undoubtedly," he answered, "but that's a good thing for Jamie. If they kill him, you won't be able to locate them, and they lose their ability to lure you into a trap."

"Great. So Jamie is safe so long as we walk into their clutches."

"Pretty much."

I stared out the window at the passing neighborhoods. Houses filled with families who had no clue they were being stalked by demons capable of sucking the life-force right out of them. Innocent people who fell ill, went to the doctor, and were treated for maladies that had nothing to do with bacterial infections or viruses or cancers. Who were in fact having their health and well-being sucked from them by personal demons who fed on their life-force.

Well, not on my watch.

We were going to rescue Jamie and send those demons right back where they came from.

Wick turned into the parking lot of the abandoned factory and pulled around to the back of the building. After killing the motor and tucking the keys in his pocket, he turned to face me.

"How do you want to handle this?"

I'd been thinking about that, running scenarios through my mind, but I wanted his take.

"What do you recommend?"

"Well, I figure we've got two basic options. One, we march in together and assess on the fly. Two, you go in the front and I sneak in the back. All their attention will be on you, so I should be able to move without interference."

I nodded. He was thinking pretty much what I was.

"Agreed. If we go in together, I'll have the security of having you by my side," I said, giving my thoughts voice and therefore validity, "but it'll be a false security. We can be trapped too easily if they know where we both are."

I paused, licked my lips. Part of me hoped he'd disagree.

He nodded.

Damn! My stomach churned and then quieted as resignation turned to acceptance, acceptance to determination.

"If we go in separately," I continued, "you might be able to get Jamie out of there while their attention is on me."

"That's my thought," he agreed, his gaze going steely. "You do whatever you need to in order to distract them. I get Jamie out, and once he's on his way home, I'll come back. We'll fight our way out at that point."

I tuned in to my weird-o-meter and gave a low moan.

"What is it?" Wick asked.

"There must be a portal in there," I said, panic edging my words. "There's easily twice as many demons as the last time I checked."

Wick paled. "How many?" he whispered.

"Hard to get an exact count — they're milling around, but I'd guess two dozen of the regulars and five or six of the high-level types."

Wick nodded. "Okay. We need to do this now, before it gets worse. First priority, rescue Jamie and get out alive. Second goal, find the portal and close it."

"Can we do that?"

"You can," he said with a nasty grin. "Think about Simone and what she's taught you about thresholds."

Wick gave me a push and then turned to open his door.

Understanding dawned, and my mouth formed a surprised, "Oh!" I yanked my door open, jumped from the Jeep and ran to join Wick at the back end. He had the tailgate down and was rummaging in a concealed compartment.

"Gear up," he said.

I grabbed a sheathed sword and strapped it across my back. I couldn't believe I hadn't brought my backpack, which held my usual weapon. At least I was still wearing my high-top boots with their concealed stilettos.

Wick strapped on his own sword and tucked several throwing stars and a couple of daggers into belt and pockets.

He glanced at me, eyebrows quirked in a question. I nodded.

"Let's do this."

He secured the Jeep, and we strode toward the building, separating before reaching the entrance.

I watched Wick disappear around a corner and then took a deep breath, reached for the door and tugged. It opened without so much as a squeak. So much for having to scrap the mission for lack of a way in.

Evidently the demons wanted me inside.

Inhaling deeply, I drew my stilettos and stepped across the threshold into a dimly lit, cavernous room. The door swung closed behind me, shutting out the bright sunlight of the normal world, and increasing the gloom of the musty, abandoned factory. I strode forward, my booted footsteps echoing against gray cement walls and floors. My eyes adjusted to the dimness. Everything was gray. Walls, floors, even the light filtering through grimy windows had an unhealthy gray tinge. Forgotten bits and pieces of the working factory littered the floor. A box here, a broken board there, the occasional bit of metal, remnant of a piece of machinery.

But my demon hunter senses also recognized another leftover from the building's former occupants: the stench of death. I shuddered, not wanting to dwell on how many turkeys had died in this place to provide food for families just like mine.

I bit my lip and moved further into the room, my heartbeat sounding as loud in my ears as the reverberations of my footfalls. Had that pervading sense of death and gloom attracted the demons to this place?

I approached a patch of deeper darkness and found myself at the opening of a corridor leading further into the monstrous building. I sniffed the air. A new scent mingled with the pervasive mustiness of disuse, the foul odor of demon. I'd learned to recognize that smell over the last year, though I still had trouble classifying it. Decay, yes, but not the normal, healthy scent of the compost heap Dad turned on a regular basis to provide mulch for the garden. No, this was nasty, unnatural. A stench that gagged and made the eyes water. Demon.

But mixed with it, floating above it, I caught a whiff of Jamie. His personal scent of warm skin, soap, and testosterone, mingled with the unmistakable smell of fear. I stepped into the corridor, ready to follow that scent to my brother.

"Dani!" Jamie screamed my name. His voice more strident than I'd ever heard it. "Go back, Dani! There…there are monsters here!"

A sharp crack split the air, followed by Jamie's cry of pain and a hoarse, guttural laugh.

I steeled myself and ran forward, stilettos at the ready, but my mind whirled. Jamie knew he was surrounded by monsters. How was that possible? Normal people couldn't see demons, and even though he shared my blood, Jamie was normal.

The corridor opened into another cavernous room, twin to the first. Gray light filtered through grimed windows, allowing me to see my brother huddled on the floor a hulking figure looming over him. Dozens of demons of all varieties roamed the room. Slowly, all movement stopped as every demon turned his attention to me.

"Ah, the demon hunter arrives." The largest demon, the one standing over Jamie, sneered at me. He was massive. Easily twice the size of the one I'd fought in Ms. Hockinson's class. Yellow cat-slit eyes glowed in the gloom, but the general grayness of the room leached the color from his skin. He blinked and I tore my gaze from his curved horns and deadly looking teeth.

"Good of you to accept our invitation," he growled. "I'm sure your brother appreciates your sacrifice."

"I'm sorry, Dani," moaned Jamie. "I don't know why I came to this building."

The big demon kicked him in the ribs. Hard. "Silence, human. The demon hunter and I have business to discuss."

I ignored him and focused on my brother. "It's okay, Jamie," I said, keeping my voice as calm as my racing heart would allow. "They lured you here." I turned my gaze on the spokesdemon. "What I don't understand is why you can see them now."

Jamie looked confused, but for once my smart-alec, always-ready-with-a-wisecrack brother kept his mouth shut. A movement at the far end of the room caught my peripheral vision, but I resisted the urge to look. Wick had arrived.

My heart-rate steadied and my breathing eased. Jamie was alive and I had back-up. Time to put my training to work.

The spokesdemon's rasping laugh grabbed my attention and held it. "Even normal humans can see us this close to a portal," he said. At a gesture, his minions parted revealing a softly glowing tear, a rupture in space, that hung suspended about a foot above the cement floor.

I nodded. "Wow. You must have really had to work to get through there," I said, putting as much sarcasm behind my words as a lifetime of banter with brothers could provide. "Did your little friends have to drag you through?"

As hoped, he roared and lunged at me.

I skipped past him, grabbed Jamie and pulled him to his feet, then pushed him past two startled, lesser demons to Wick. "Get him out of here," I bellowed and turned to cover their retreat.

Demons exploded into action all around me. I danced back and forth, my blades flashing, intent on assuring none of them followed my fleeing brother. After an eternity that might have been only seconds Wick appeared at my side.

Together we fought like the well-oiled mechanism he'd insisted we become.

Heredity and a year of Wick's hard training burned the fear from my system. A fierce joy seized my mind and I reveled in the strength of my arms, the agility of my body as I leapt and twirled, stabbed and parried. I was a human whirlwind, dealing death and destruction to the enemies of my race.

At last, all of the lesser demons had been either vanquished or driven back through the portal. Wick lay on the floor, a slice to the back of his left knee having taken him down. I dropped my stilettos beside him and drew the sword from the sheath on my back.

Only the massive spokesdemon remained.

"You and your friend have fought well, little demon hunter," he said, the words grinding together like stones in a rockslide. "Now it is just the two of us, and you are tired, your strength sapped. I will kill you without effort."

I laughed, circling him, drawing him away from my wounded guardian. "You forget, I'm wise to your mind games. You can't defeat me with words, so don't even try."

I lunged at his chest, but he slipped sideways with an agility, an almost artless grace I hadn't expected from such a massive creature.

We circled each other, slashing and parrying, neither connecting. A soft shuffling penetrated my concentration, but I ignored the noise. Wick had undoubtedly shifted position. I kept my focus on the monster before me.

He dove at me with curved horns, and in the same movement swiped sideways with taloned hands. I bounded away, but not quite fast enough. A single claw slashed my side, ripping sweatshirt and grazing the flesh beneath.

A scratch, nothing more, but the wound seared with white hot pain and I wondered what poisons the demon's claws carried.

My training held. I clamped the pain and fear in a corner of my mind and continued my death-dance with the demon.

We circled and fought, danced and slashed, leapt and parried. I landed a few non-lethal blows, but nothing seemed to slow him down. He continued to wear me down, whispering aspersions on my strength and dexterity, maligning my skill and Wick's training.

Almost I fell prey to his words. Almost I allowed them to burrow into my mind and take up residence. Until he uttered Wick's name.

My guardian was no slouch. He'd trained me well. He'd fought beside me valiantly, though he lacked my inborn abilities. No one, no sleazy, back-stabbing demon was going to disrespect Wick!

Immediately my mind snapped back into focus and I recognized my peril. Snake-like, he'd been charming away my will, sapping my concentration. I shook my head, sealed away my pain, and scrutinized my enemy.

He lunged at me again, head down, horns aimed straight for my chest. But I was awake now. I leapt lightly to one side and found my opening. His arm was up to swipe at me again with those deadly sharp claws, leaving his side vulnerable.

I stepped into the opening and stabbed my sword deep into his flesh.

I don't know if demon anatomy is anything like human, but I'd caught him between the ribs and sliced straight for the heart ... if he had ribs ... if he had a heart.

Whether he did or didn't, he dropped like a boulder, my sword stuck in his flesh. He shuddered for a moment, then went still. I dropped to one knee beside the body, wiped sweat from my forehead with my sleeve, and sprinkled him with holy water. A moment later, the remains vanished and my sword clattered to the gray cement floor.

"The portal," Wick gasped, pain evident in his tone, "seal the portal."

I nodded without looking at him. Grabbing my sword, I staggered to the rip in the universe. Drawing myself upright, I lowered the tip of the silver sword to the wound, dribbled holy water down the blade so that both elements touched the portal together and then sketched the rune of protection across the opening.

The portal blazed with white light and then disappeared, leaving me alone in an abandoned warehouse with my guardian.

Well, almost alone.

When I turned to make my way back to Wick, I froze. There, kneeling beside my guardian, holding his wadded up shirt against Wick's bloody knee, was Jamie.

"What are you doing here?" I yelled when my brain kicked back into gear. "You were supposed to go home. We came here to rescue you!"

"What?" Jamie asked, his eyes flashing with belligerence. "You thought I was just going to run away? Leave my baby sister and some guy I don't even know alone in a building full of monsters?" He jumped to his feet, hands fisted on hips, bare chest heaving. "What kind of a coward do you think I am?"

My shoulders drooped. My strength abandoned me and all my worries and fears flooded in. I shuffled over and dropped to the floor beside Wick.

"I don't think you're a coward," I said without looking up at him. "You're just not equipped to battle demons."

He crouched on Wick's other side. "And you are?"

Wick laid a hand on each of us. "She is, and you've just seen proof of that."

I glanced up and met Jamie's gaze.

"Yeah. Okay," he said after a pause. "You were amazing, Sis. Really. Where'd you learn to fight like that?"

I nodded at Wick. "From him."

Wick shrugged. "I merely honed skills made manifest by her heritage and destiny."

Jamie frowned. "Destiny? What destiny? I don't understand."

Wick grimaced with pain and shifted position. "I know you don't, Mr. Erickson, but now is not the moment for a treatise on demonology. If you would be so kind as to help your sister get me to my Jeep, I believe you can drive us to my associate, Simone. Dani can direct you."

"What?" Jamie asked, then glancing from Wick's pained expression to his knee, he caught on. "Oh. Right. Are you sure you wouldn't rather go to the hospital?"

"And try to explain a knife wound? No, thanks," he said, groaning as Jamie and I pulled him to his feet. "Simone is a skilled healer. She will tend to me and disinfect that rather nasty scratch of yours, Miss Erickson."

3

———

Miraculously, Jamie kept his questions to himself while I guided him to Simone's small house. Half carrying Wick up the walk, Jamie did raise his eyebrows as we passed the sign proclaiming Simone's business: *Piercing the Veil: Psychic Readings, Tarot, and Runes.*

"Interesting company you've been keeping, Sis," he whispered as Simone threw open the front door and ran down the steps to help Wick inside.

Once Wick's knee had been bandaged and my scratch tended to, Simone went to the kitchen to make tea.

"It's time you two called your parents," Wick said. "You should have them pick you up a block or two away. Perhaps on Main Street. And you'll need to think of a cover story."

Jamie nodded and pulled his cell phone from his pocket.

I squirmed in my chair, my heart thudding and my belly churning with despair. I should be elated. I'd won a major victory and sealed a portal, and considering the odds, our casualties had been light. I should be dancing on the ceiling.

Instead, misery ate at my soul. Jamie would tell my parents everything and they'd forbid me to ever see Wick or Simone again. My demon hunting days were over. My whole family would clamp down on me and try to force me into an Allie-mold.

I mean, I love Allie, but I'm so not a perfect little lady! I'm a Rottweiler, not a pampered Pomeranian.

Wick smiled at me. "Before you make that call, Jamie, I think you should reassure your sister."

"About what?"

"Dani?"

I stared at the pine floor boards, swallowed the lump in my throat and whispered, "Are you going to tell on me? Are you going to get me in trouble with Mom and Dad?"

Jamie moved to the window and stared out at the green grass of Simone's front lawn.

I bit my lip and waited to hear my fate.

Finally, he turned and met my gaze.

"Dani, I don't have a clue what's up with you, but I do know you saved my life today. I won't tell if you don't want me to."

I expelled a sigh that sounded suspiciously like a sob and blinked back tears.

"But that doesn't mean you're off the hook," he said with a scowl. "I still expect the whole story." He glanced from me to Wick and back. "And, well, you're going to have to convince me that Mom and Dad don't need to know."

I nodded. My secret was safe ... for now.

IV

CHALLENGING DAZE

DEB LOGAN

AUTHOR OF *FAERY UNEXPECTED*

CHALLENGING DAZE

SPUN YARNS
A Dani Erickson Short Story

1

High school. It's a totally different world than what I expected when I first stepped through the glass-paned front doors last year. Back then I'd just discovered my destiny as a demon hunter and was still focused on the mundane issues I'd always anticipated when entering the big-leagues of public education. You know what I'm talking about: bullying upper classmen; cute boys who didn't know I existed; cliques of mean girls; cute boys who would break my heart; teachers intent on writing tests filled with the most tedious details imaginable; cute boys who wouldn't return my affection. The normal problems of a teenage girl's life.

What I hadn't expected to find were kids just like my six older brothers who were demon-ridden. Literally. Teens with small, rat-faced demons riding their backs, claws firmly embedded in necks and scalps, draining their victims' life force while whispering evil suggestions into their psyches.

That was then.

Now, my high school was a much happier place. I'd defeated hundreds of personal demons and enough of the larger, humanoid demons that the vermin were wary of stepping foot on my territory, and Longmont High was very definitely *my* territory. Consequently, kids were kinder, more gentle than the national average. Teachers — many of whom were also demon-ridden when I arrived — were more inclined to be helpful, more willing to explain difficult concepts multiple times, seeking alternate examples to get their points across.

Now, I'm not claiming that my school was a utopia once I'd exterminated the demon pests, but it was, on the whole, a calmer, more civilized environment than anyone had a right to expect … and that was largely due to me.

Even my youngest older brother said so. Jamie had been at Longmont High for a year or two before I arrived. He definitely noticed the difference. Of course, he also knew all about my demon-hunting abilities. He'd learned my secret when I rescued him from a horde of demons who were using him as bait last spring. And to my eternal surprise, he'd kept my secret.

For a price.

"You want what?" I asked, my eyes bulging and my face heating. "Wick doesn't do charity work."

"That's my price." Jamie folded his arms across his chest and stared at me with familiar belligerence. "You want me to keep your secret. Fine. I'll risk the Wrath of Mom, but I expect something in return. I want Wick to teach me how to fight. If you can do it, so can I."

I shook my head and stomped onto the little bridge in the center of Loomiller Park. We'd needed privacy for this conversation, so we'd headed to the park where we could see anyone approaching long before they could hear what we were saying.

"And just what are you going to do with said fighting skills," I asked, not bothering to keep the sarcastic tone out of my voice. This was Jamie, after all. The closest brother to my age. We were rarely civil to each other, even without the excuse of personal demons.

He frowned, but his jaw jutted out at a stubborn angle. "Once I'm trained," he said, "I'll help you fight demons. Make sure you don't get yourself killed, 'cause if you did and Mom found out I'd known anything, I'd follow you to the grave in about a heartbeat."

I laughed out loud. "Help me fight demons?" I said. "When you can't even see them? How's that going to work?"

"Wick helps," he said, his tone surly. "I saw him last spring. And he's not a demon hunter either."

"No, he's not, but he *is* a guardian. They have their own powers, which includes seeing demons."

"Great. While he's training me to fight, he can teach me to be a guardian." Jamie smiled, certain he'd won that point. Unfortunately, he just couldn't shut up. "I can be *your* guardian. Take care of my little sister, like a big brother should."

That did it. The idiot had no idea what he was talking about, *and* he'd just dissed my fighting skills. Insinuating that I needed his protection. After I saved his worthless hide last spring. I snapped.

Leaping over the bridge's railing, I landed on the grass at the edge of the narrow neck of the lake, ran at Jamie, flipped him to his back on the soft lawn, and forced him to roll to his stomach by the simple expedient of twisting his arm. Kneeling against his back I leaned forward and whispered in his ear, "I don't need your protection. You'd just get in my way."

Standing up, I dusted my hands off and stalked back onto the bridge.

Jamie rose, his cheeks red and his blue plaid shirt grass stained and rumpled. "Fine." He spat the word like it tasted disgusting. "I'm not fit to help the super awesome demon hunting warrior woman. I still want Wick to teach me to fight. That's the price of my silence."

I glared at him, but his gaze didn't waver. Eventually, mine did. I looked down and shrugged. "Whatever. Drive me to Wick's and we'll let him decide."

Jamie had actually been pretty cool about the whole rescue thing. I mean, it couldn't have been easy to discover that a healthy, athletic guy needed his little sister to save him from a bunch of monsters. And then to find out that said baby sister was actually a hereditary demon hunter with natural fighting abilities, that she could probably wipe the ground with her big brother in several different humiliating ways…. Well, it had to have been a supreme shock to Jamie's system.

The fact that he was just now getting around to blackmailing me for fighting lessons — several months after the fact — spoke volumes as to how long it had taken him to truly wrap his brain around the issues.

"Great," he said. "Let's go."

I really needed to get my license. This dependency on Jamie for transportation sucked. Unfortunately, the magic sixteenth birthday was still nearly a year away. I'd almost be a junior before I could get my license. Of course, by that time Jamie would be off at college. This was his final year at Longmont High. My youngest older brother was a senior at last.

Who'd've thunk he'd make it this far? Certainly not me.

2

Warwick James, my guardian and mentor in all things demon, owned a martial arts dojo on Main Street, a block or so south of the fashionably renovated section of downtown. Not yet to the train tracks, but well beyond the well-groomed shopping district, his studio had been nothing more than a dilapidated, abandoned storefront before I came into my power.

Once my demon-hunting abilities surfaced, Wick and his partner Madame Simone quickly set up shop in Longmont. Wick as a martial arts instructor, Madame Simone as a psychic and tarot reader.

In reality, they were here for me. Wick made sure my inborn fighting skills were up to snuff, and Simone taught me all there was to know about demons. Their hierarchy, their relative powers, how they interact with normal humans, and how demon hunters like me came into existence.

You've probably heard the legends about seventh sons of seventh sons. Well, I'm here to tell you that there's a grain of truth in all that patriarchal, male chauvinist malarkey.

Seventh-sevenths do have power. We're the hereditary demon hunters, called into existence to defend humanity from an unseen, but very real, threat.

But we're not all guys.

Take me for example.

My dad is the seventh child in his family, but not the seventh son. That honor fell to Uncle Gus. My grandfather was a nut case about *seventh son of a seventh son* lore, and was evidently over the moon when Uncle Gus was born. Unfortunately, Grandpa's hopes were dashed before I was ever thought of. When Uncle Gus married, the family discovered to their sorrow that he and Aunt Ellen couldn't have children. The couple adopted and have a happy family, but the seventh son chain had been broken and Grandpa was in despair.

Until he noticed Mom and Dad.

They were happily married and making babies on a regular basis. Boy babies. When Jamie was born, Grandpa's dream was resurrected. Dad, with six sons in existence, was on track to start the legacy again. All they needed was one more boy.

When Mom was pregnant with me, Grandpa practically drove her nuts, making sure she ate well, got plenty of exercise, but took no unnecessary risks. He didn't want anything to happen to the baby he was sure would be the much anticipated seventh son.

And then Mom had the audacity to deliver me. A girl.

Grandpa was inconsolable.

But there was always next time!

Mom and Dad, having survived one pregnancy with Grandpa hovering, decided that seven children was sufficient. There would be no more babies in their household.

To this day, I'm a major disappointment to Grandpa.

Which is a shame, since I'm actually the seventh-seventh he dreamed of bringing into existence.

See, gender has nothing to do with it. It's not the seventh *son* of a seventh *son* who gains the power. It's the seventh child of a seventh child.

Maybe if he's really nice, someday I'll tell Grandpa the truth.

Nah. He was too old-school. He'd never believe me.

3

_____

The bell hanging over the door to Wick's dojo jingled merrily when I pushed over the threshold.

"Wick," I yelled into the empty studio. My voice reverberated off the polished oak floors and wide storefront windows. "It's me ... and I brought company."

My guardian, mentor, and friend, Warwick James appeared at the door to his office, a puzzled expression on his chiseled features. "Miss Erickson? Did we have an appointment that I've forgotten?"

Jamie stepped forward. "No sir," he said, walking confidently toward Wick. "Nothing like that. I asked Dani to come with me. I wanted to ask you a favor."

Wick inclined his head and gestured us into his office. "Of course, Mr. Erickson. Anything I can do to assist a member of Miss Erickson's family will be my honor."

I strode across the large open room, one wall lined with cubbies for students' belongings, the other stacked with red workout mats. "Hold on there, Wick," I said, the scowl on my face reflected in my voice. "Don't be making any promises before you've heard what he wants."

Wick nodded, his neatly trimmed beard bobbing. "As you wish, Miss Erickson. Please, both of you, come in and be seated. Would you like a beverage?"

Jamie swallowed and stammered a refusal, but I said, "Sure. I'll get them." I moved past Wick's desk to the small refrigerator, grabbed three bottles of cold water, and handed them around.

Plunking onto a folding chair across the desk from Wick and next to Jamie, I twisted off the bottle's lid and took a deep swig of cool, fresh water. Closing my eyes, I enjoyed the sensation as the liquid slid over my tongue and trickled down my throat, soothing tissues dried by anxiety. I'm not sure why I was so nervous about this meeting, not sure why I was so opposed to Jamie learning to fight. Maybe I was secretly afraid he'd steal my thunder.

Seriously?

Was I still afraid that Wick and Simone or ... well, Fate, would discover they'd made a mistake and chosen the wrong Erickson? Was I so conditioned by Grandpa's patriarchal views that I still doubted myself?

Hogwash!

I'd been a demon hunter for over a year. I'd defeated scores of the little, and not-so-little weasels. Heck, I'd even rescued Jamie from a trap they'd set for me using him as bait.

I had nothing to fear from Jamie asking Wick to teach him to fight. My big brother might learn some defense skills, but there was no way he could replace me as demon hunter extraordinaire! That was my gig ... and mine alone.

Breathing out my anxieties, I opened my eyes, more relaxed than I'd been since Jamie first broached the subject.

Wick glanced at me, then turned to Jamie. "How may I be of assistance, Mr. Erickson?"

Jamie's face reddened and his eyes darted to me, a pleading look in their depths.

I rolled my eyes and shook my head. I might be feeling more relaxed and self-confident, but I had no need to rescue my brother from this encounter. He wanted a favor; he could ask for it.

"I, uh, I wondered," he said, evidently more nervous than I would've guessed possible, "I, uh, well…" He paused, closed his eyes, swallowed and then blurted, "I want you to teach me to fight like Dani."

His eyes popped open and he glared at me. "You got anything to say about that?"

I smiled. I tried, I really did, to look as sweetly angelic as my demon hunting nature would allow. "Nope. Not a thing."

Jamie growled. Literally, he growled at me. Then he turned his attention to Wick.

"I see." Wick leaned back in his rolling office chair, steepled his fingers under his chin, and regarded each of us in turn. Solemnly. As if this were the most important moment in any of our lives.

"You do understand, Mr. Erickson, that I will not be able to teach you everything that your sister knows," he said, turning his attention to Jamie alone. "Miss Erickson has certain innate abilities, ones that I can help her perfect, but that I can in no way teach to another human being."

Jamie glanced from Wick to me, his gaze unsure, as if he were looking at someone he'd just met. Not the sister he'd been pestering his entire life.

It was unnerving to have my big brother look at me that way … as if he admired me.

"I understand," he said. "Well, no. I don't understand. I mean, she's my little sister. How can she be this ass-kicking demon hunter?"

Wick made no move to explain, simply sat silently, fingers steepled beneath his chin.

"Okay," Jamie continued. "I get the whole thing about my dad being the seventh child in his family and Dani being the seventh child in our family. I get it. Really. Grandpa's breeding program worked. Just not like he thought it would, but …"

He paused, glanced at me, then back to Wick. "I mean, who takes this crap seriously? We live in an age of science and technology. How can fairy tale stuff like demons and monsters and knights in shining armor exist?"

Wick sat forward, leaning his forearms on the desk, the golden amulet he always wore fell free of his shirt and dangled just above his clasped hands. "I cannot explain the mysteries of life to you, Mr. Erickson. You must choose to believe the evidence of your own experience. You will likely never see them again, but you pierced the veil. You saw the monsters your sister defeated in your defense last spring. You know the truth.

"Now, you have a choice. You can either bury that truth in your subconscious and continue to think of Dani as your little sister, a nuisance, though a beloved one, or you can acknowledge her as an extraordinary human being charged with protecting her race from a threat they don't even know exists."

Wick lowered his gaze to his folded hands, giving Jamie a little space. "I choose to assist her in this difficult position in which the Fates have placed her." He raised his eyes and skewered my brother with his stare. "Only you can decide how you will choose."

Without breaking eye contact, Jamie nodded. "I choose to help her too. Will you train me?"

"I will."

Both of them turned to me. "Will you accept your brother's aid, Miss Erickson?"

I glanced from Wick to Jamie, and saw the same intensity mirrored in both sets of eyes.

"I will."

4

After that, my life got a lot easier. I didn't have to pretend I was taking ballet lessons with my best friend Allie anymore. Jamie simply asked Mom and Dad if he and I could sign up for self defense lessons together.

Dad thought it was great idea. Mom agreed. Good wholesome exercise, a useful life skill, and something siblings could do together. What could be better?

Plus, he was now responsible for driving me to and from our training sessions ... and he became my sparring partner. I got to pound my big brother into the ground on a regular basis. Score!

Who knew having Jamie as an ally would have so many benefits?

"You know," Jamie said one afternoon as we walked into our favorite coffee shop, Kona Karafe, "you enjoy throwing me a little too much." He winced and stretched his right shoulder. "And you do it with way too much enthusiasm."

I grinned. "Hey, I didn't ask you to be my punching bag. You volunteered."

He scowled, but turned his attention to the line at the counter. "Hey, who's that guy Allie's talking to? I don't recognize him."

Alejandra Chavez was my best friend in all the world. Once upon a time, she was everything I wished I could be, but knew I'd never manage. Fortunately, that all changed when I discovered I was a demon hunter. Suddenly, being tall, lithe, and well-balanced became assets. I no longer needed to be Allie's brand of dainty, graceful and feminine to the core. I had my own version of graceful femininity … which included the ability to kick demon ass.

Allie and I were opposites, and that suited both of us just fine.

I glanced at my best friend, not at all surprised to see her smiling up at a good-looking guy. Only this particular guy wasn't what he appeared to be.

Grabbing Jamie's arm, I dragged him over to a table and pushed him into a chair.

"What?" he asked, frowning at me. "We haven't ordered yet."

"Never mind that, tell me what you see. What does the guy with Allie look like?"

"Are you feeling okay?" he asked. "That's a really stupid…" His words trailed off as his eyes widened and he glanced from me to the guy with Allie. He lowered his voice and asked in a gruff whisper, "He's not a normal guy?"

I shook my head. "My weird-o-meter is off the charts, plus I can see the demon behind the mask."

Jamie tensed. "Why can I see him? More importantly, what's he doing with Allie?"

I grimaced. "We've got to get her away from him," I said quietly. "I may be out of my league. If he can choose to be seen, can choose to use a glamour, then he's one of the big-wigs."

Jamie reached across the table and grabbed my hand. He stared into my eyes. "You're not out of your league," he said. "You don't have a league. Whatever happens, you can handle this."

I sucked in a deep breath and let it out slowly. "Thanks, Jamie. Listen, I'm going to step outside before that thing sees me. I want you to go up to Allie and make some excuse to get her to leave with you. We've got to separate them."

He nodded. "See you outside in a minute."

I ducked past a tangle of chatting teens and out the door, positioning myself where I could peek through the window to keep tabs on Jamie and Allie.

My big brother strolled up to Allie, tapped her on the shoulder and said something. She smiled and nodded. Turning to the demon, she motioned to Jamie. Looked like she was introducing them. A moment later, she followed Jamie toward the door.

I breathed a sigh of relief, and then sucked it right back in.

The demon left the counter and followed my brother and my friend. Worse than that, he glanced through the window directly into my eyes. He not only knew who Jamie and Allie were, he knew I was watching.

I ducked behind the brick façade of Kona Karafe and waited for my friends to emerge, my thoughts racing. Should I try to get Jamie and Allie to our car? Get them to drive away and leave me to deal with the demon?

No way that was going to work. Jamie wouldn't drive off and leave me, not even to save Allie.

Gawd! I wished Wick were here.

My thoughts settled and my pulse rate calmed. Wick. He would still be at the dojo and he didn't have any kids coming in for class this afternoon. Jamie and Allie and I would lead the demon to the dojo where Wick would provide back-up. He could protect my loved ones while I dealt with the demon.

Jamie and Allie came through the door and I shooed them down the sidewalk, ignoring Allie's questions.

She tried to stop, but Jamie and I each grabbed an arm and pulled her along.

"What are you doing, Dani?" she asked, her voice colored with annoyance. "What's so important that I had to leave without my chai latte?"

"Just keep walking, Allie," I said, glancing over my shoulder. "I'll explain in a minute."

"Where are we going?" Jamie asked.

"Back to the dojo," I said, picking up the pace. The demon was following. "We need back-up."

Jamie nodded. "Got it."

"You need back-up?" Allie asked. "You mean Wick, right?"

"Yep."

"That means," she stopped talking, looked over her shoulder, saw the guy following and tried to turn. "Demons," she hissed. "We have to warn, Collin."

Jamie and I propelled her forward.

"No," I said. "We don't. He knows. He is one."

Her eyes widened, but she stopped resisting and walked faster, nearly matching my much longer stride.

That's what I love about Allie. She trusts me. She didn't ask how I knew or why she could see him, just accepted that he was a demon and ran with it.

Literally.

We ran the last few yards to the dojo, yanked the door open and raced over the threshold.

"Wick," I yelled. "Arm yourself. Incoming!"

My guardian strode out of his office, a short sword in each hand, just as the front door opened and the demon paused on the threshold.

"Jamie, take Allie to my office and barricade the door," Wick said calmly, but with authority. "Don't come out until Dani or I tell you it's safe."

"Sir," Jamie began.

"No. This is not the time, Mr. Erickson. You will only distract your sister. Trust me. Trust both of us. Go!"

To my great relief, Jamie obeyed.

Wick came to my side, handed me both swords, then pulled two more from the behind his back. I raised an eyebrow, as I accepted the blades. "You didn't wear your gear to training today," he said with a shrug. "I assumed you were unarmed."

"You assumed correctly," I said quietly. "Why hasn't he attacked."

"Wards, Miss Erickson. He has to dismantle them before he can enter."

Other demons approached, whether the demon lord had summoned them or they'd simply been drawn to the impending conflict I didn't know, but we were badly outnumbered.

"In this case," I whispered, "I'm not sure wards were a good idea."

"Agreed," Wick said, assessing the numbers. "This will be no worse than when we rescued Jamie last spring."

I adjusted my stance and rolled my shoulders. "Are you sure about that? This demon was visible to humans and was wearing a glamour. Madame Simone said that only the demon lords can pull that off."

"I am aware, Miss Erickson. However, while we know what he is, he is unaware of your capabilities."

"And that's a good thing?"

He flashed a grin. "That's a very good thing, Miss Erickson. Trust your instincts."

The lesser demons poured through the door. Our wards were down and the time for chat was behind us.

Wick and I waded into battle. I stabbed and sliced, twirled and leapt, my blades flashing and promising death to the vaguely humanoid monsters who rushed to embrace the destruction I dealt.

Wick worked at my side with vicious efficiency. He couldn't kill … that skill belonged to me alone, but he could wound and maim. Many of his victims fled rather than face the killing strikes I wielded as my own battle allowed.

The polished oak floors were slick with gore before the demon lord approached.

"You fight well, little huntress," he said, not bothering to disguise the growl of his voice under human tones, "but you and your servant are no match for me."

He raised a hand, aimed his palm at Wick, and shot him with a beam of white hot light.

Wick was thrown backward into the cubbies, where he crumpled to the gore-stained floor.

"Wick!" I screamed, but stood my ground. Even if I died, I would not run from this demon again. This time I had no one to get to safety. *I* was the only safety Jamie and Allie had.

Gritting my teeth, I stepped forward, swords raised and ready.

The demon turned his palm to me, the light shot forth. I did the only thing I could … I sliced at the beam, a useless gesture, I knew.

To my complete amazement, the beam caught the broad side of the sword and bounced, burning a smoking hole in one of the exercise mats.

The demon's eyes widened, but he sent another blaze. I deflected that as well.

We danced around the room for what felt like an eternity, him shooting white hot beams in my direction, me countering not with a shield, but with the too slender edge of first one short sword and then the other.

At last, my sword reflected one of the blasts, not at the wall or a mat or even the floor, but squarely back onto the demon lord's chest. He wasn't tossed across the room as Wick had been. He absorbed the blaze and then expelled fiery light through eyes and ears and mouth. When the firestorm ended, the demon disintegrated.

I glanced at the door to ensure no enemies remained, then ran to Wick. He was still breathing, though I couldn't imagine how. Feeling gingerly through the tattered remnants of his shirt, I discovered the molten remains of a gold medallion seared into his chest. Using the tip of my sword, I pried the hot metal from his skin.

"Jamie!" I screamed. "If you can hear me, come out. Wick's wounded and I need help."

My brother – bless his cautious soul! – opened the door a crack, made sure the attack was over, and then ran to my side.

"What do you need?" he asked, staring down at where Wick sprawled on the floor.

Allie answered. She'd dashed from the office in his wake. "We need cool compresses," she said. "Find some towels, wring them out in cool water and put them on that burn."

"Right," said Jamie. "There's cold water in the fridge in his office I'll grab some bottles, you find the towels, Allie."

She grabbed his arm. "No. Cool water, not cold. Cold can cause tissue damage."

"Seriously?" he asked.

"Seriously," she said, solemn voiced.

"Right."

While Jamie and Allie found towels and wet them in the bathroom sink, I held Wick's head, willed him to hold on, and pulled my cell phone from my pocket. Madame Simone answered on the first ring.

"What has happened?" she asked. "Where do you need me?"

"At the dojo," I answered. "Wick is injured. We're treating the burn, but I'm not sure that's the only problem. He's breathing, but it's very shallow and wheezy. I'm scared, Simone."

"I'll be there soon."

Allie was awesome. She used her first aid knowledge to cool the burn while calming my fear with soothing words. Jamie moved back and forth between us and the sink, keeping Allie supplied with cool, damp towels.

After a few minutes, I pulled myself together enough to look around and make an assessment. I wasn't helping Wick by sitting on my butt holding his head, but I could clean up the mess in his usually spotless dojo. And, since I was the only person currently conscious who could see the demon corpses littering the room, I was the only one who could do the work.

Carefully easing out from under Wick's head, I grabbed a jacket from one of the cubbies, glad that some student had left it behind. Scrunching it up, I cushioned Wick's head on the soft polar fleece.

Trudging past the mess, I made my weary way to Wick's office, grabbed a bottle of holy water, and went to work dematerializing demonic detritus.

Each of us worked silently and diligently until Madame Simone arrived. She rushed into the room, the little bell over the door jingling merrily, and took in the situation at a glance. She met my gaze, nodded her approval of my clean-up, and then stepped quickly to Wick's side, eyes taking in every detail of his position and obvious wound.

Kneeling beside him, she praised Allie's quick thinking while her fingers assessed Wick's vital signs. When she was satisfied that he was stable, she turned to me.

"Tell me."

I moved to kneel beside her and gave a quick but accurate recap of the battle, choking back my fear when I described the demon's demise. "If the blaze was enough to disintegrate the demon lord, how is Wick still alive?" I cried, finally voicing my deepest fear.

"The burn Allie's been treating is the key," she said. "The protective amulet he wore melted and burned into his chest, but it deflected the main power of the blast." She laid a hand on mine. "You did extremely well, Dani. Wick will be so proud." She smiled, though her eyes brimmed with tears. "Yes, child, he will live to hear this tale."

My heart hammered and my vision darkened around the edges. A strangled moan escaped my lips, but my chest felt so tight that I couldn't seem to catch my breath. I closed my eyes, pulled my knees to my chest and wrapped my arms tightly around them. No way was I going to cry. Wick was going to live. It was stupid to cry now that Madame Simone was here and everything was going to be okay. But the tightness in my chest grew. I felt like my puny little human ribs were holding back a tiger. An untamed tiger full of the emotions that would consume me if I let gave in to those tears.

Then Jamie's arms were around me and he whispered into my ear, "It's okay, Dani. The danger is over. You don't have to be strong right now. Go ahead and cry." He kissed the top of my head and laid his cheek against my hair. "I won't even make fun of you or call you a little girl."

He squeezed my shoulders, and I succumbed to tears, sobbing my terror and relief against my knees while he held me tight and whispered soothing words I wouldn't remember.

The tension in my chest eased and, sniffling my way past the storm of emotions, I leaned against Jamie, too exhausted for words. Maybe having a big brother on my team wasn't such a bad thing after all.

V

DANGEROUS DAZE

DEB LOGAN

AUTHOR OF *FAERY UNEXPECTED*

DANGEROUS DAZE

SPUN YARNS
A *Dani Erickson* Short Story

1

My name is Dani Erickson and I'm a demon hunter.

Of course, I'm also a sixteen-year-old girl and a junior at Longmont High School, but that's just my age and place in normal society. Demon hunter is a much better description, because it not only tells you who I am, but what I was born to do.

See, I'm not just some delusional teen who likes to imagine that I'm a hero, or a girl who likes to indulge in cosplay. I'm an honest to goodness, born and bred, hereditary demon hunter. I'm the seventh child of a seventh child, and up until my fourteenth birthday, I was clueless about the existence of demons or how the accident of my birth order gave me a unique destiny.

Fortunately (but not accidentally), my guardians appeared just as my abilities manifested. Warwick James (Wick to his friends, of which I am one) and Madame Simone became my teachers, confidantes, and friends. Wick taught me to fight and provided me with weapons, while Madam Simone gave me the arcane knowledge necessary to defeat an enemy that normal people can't even see. They became like second parents to me.

And what about my real parents? The folks who brought me into this world and gave me this destiny? The totally normal, middle-class American couple who raised me with love and appropriate boundaries?

They're totally clueless about my demon hunting ways, and I work very hard to keep them that way, thank you very much!

Same goes for my siblings, my six older brothers … except for one. Jamie, my youngest older brother, discovered my secret when a demon lord kidnapped him and used him as bait to lure me into a trap. Unfortunately, the monster held Jamie prisoner near the portal he'd created to enter our world and bring his minions through. Proximity to a portal is necessary for a normal to see demons, so Jamie was exposed to the arcane world. He also saw me, his little sister, kick demon butt and destroy the creatures with sword and knives. Very skillfully, I might add.

Jamie was suitably impressed, and agreed to not only keep my secret, but to train with me so I didn't have to pretend to be taking ballet lessons with Allie in order to work with Wick.

Occasionally, older brothers can be useful. Sometimes even helpful. But now that the crisis has passed, Jamie can't see demons anymore than Allie can.

Who is Allie? Just the absolute BEST best friend a girl can have. Especially a girl who's also a demon hunter. Allie (Alejandra Chavez if you want to get all formal) is petite and pretty, graceful and popular. She's a true girly-girl, meaning she's everything I'm not … and everything my parents have always wished I could be. But even though we're complete opposites, she's also my very best friend. The only person besides Jamie who knows who I truly am, and who, even though she's a norm and can't see demons, believes me and trusts me and helps me in any way she can.

Allie totally rocks!

2

The front doorbell rang, and I glanced at the clock on the bedside table in my too-pink-and-prissy-to-be-believed bedroom. Allie was right on time, but I needed to get my butt in gear if we were going to avoid being late to school. I grabbed my favorite denim jacket (the one with a prowling lion embroidered on the back), the specially designed backpack Wick had given me, and raced down the stairs in my favorite knee-high boots — also specially designed for me by the artisans in Wick's clan of guardians.

"I've got it, Mom," I yelled as I skidded to a stop at the front door and yanked it open.

As expected, Allie stood on the porch playing with the end of her oh-so-chic French braid. Allie's hair looked great no matter how she wore it — long and straight and shining black, but that braid was eye-popping.

My own nut-brown hair had grown out and was now long enough to braid (which I did when I was training), but it never looked chic. More often than not, my not-quite-straight but not-really-curly locks frayed out of whatever I tried to do with them and just looked messy.

But I'd never been really concerned with my looks, so I could admire Allie's easy beauty with only a trace of female jealousy.

I joined Allie on the porch and was just pulling the door closed when Mom appeared. "And just where do you think you're going, young lady?" she asked.

"Uhm … to school," I replied with a sideways glance at Allie. "You know, it's that time of the morning."

Mom scowled at the flip remark. "I didn't see you in the kitchen," she said. "What did you have for breakfast?"

"Seriously, Mom? I'm sixteen years old and you're still monitoring my eating habits?"

"You may be a high school junior," she said with a prim purse to her mouth, "but I'm still your mother."

"Fine," I said. "I didn't eat yet, but I don't have time now. We're going to be late."

"It's okay, Mrs. Erickson," Allie said, jumping in before things got out of control, "I have a bagel in my backpack for her. I've learned to come prepared."

Mom smiled at Allie. "You are too sweet, Allie," she said, her voice suddenly soft and sugary (blech!), "but you shouldn't be responsible for feeding my daughter." She turned her attention back to me and her eyes narrowed. "From now on, you're to get up a few minutes earlier so you have time to eat a proper breakfast … in *our* kitchen."

"Yes, ma'am," I mumbled and escaped off the porch.

Allie kept quiet until we were across the street and on the path through Loomiller Park, then she burst out laughing.

"What's so funny?" I practically growled.

"You!" She ended her giggle with a most unladylike snort. "You should've seen your face! Dani Heleen Erickson, Demon Hunter

Extraordinaire, busted for not eating her breakfast … like a five-year-old!"

"Ha-ha," I snarled. "I'm *so* happy I could entertain you." I walked a few more steps, then held out my hand. "Hand it over."

"What?" she asked, her eyes going all wide and innocent.

"The bagel," I snapped.

She chortled, but swung her backpack around, opened a front pocket, and produced a cream cheese slathered bagel wrapped in a pretty pink cloth napkin. "Here you go, your highness."

I accepted my breakfast with as much dignity as I could muster, which wasn't much considering my mouth was actually watering. "Thanks," I said, and bit into the still warm treat. "You really are the best!"

By the time we'd crossed the park and made it onto school property, I'd finished eating. We waved to friends as they drove past on their way to the parking lot behind the school. You'd think Allie or I would be driving too—I mean, we're both sixteen, we have our licenses—but neither set of our parents thought we needed to drive to school when we lived so close. Besides, as both our mothers pointed out on a regular basis, walking is excellent exercise.

As we sauntered up the sidewalk to the main entrance, Brittney Dahl pushed past us, knocking Allie off balance. If I hadn't been right beside her, my BFF might have fallen. As it was, I caught her arm and steadied her while she got her feet back under her.

Once Allie was stable, I ran after Brittney, grabbed her elbow, and whirled her around. "Hey, Britt," I said, working to keep my anger under control. "You want to watch where you're going. You almost knocked Allie flat!"

Brittney glanced at Allie, then back at me. "So?" she said in her snottiest voice. "Isn't she supposed to be a dancer? She should have better balance."

My temper snapped. "Why you little…"

But Brittney didn't wait to hear my comment. She pulled away from me and hurried through the front door and out of sight.

"Never mind," said Allie, coming to stand beside me. "No real harm done. Just be glad we don't have to put up with her on a regular basis."

I nodded, and we entered the building.

Longmont High was a pretty laid back, easy going place. Most of the kids got along, and the place had a nice, relaxed feel … due in large part to my presence.

No. Really. I don't mean to brag, but LHS was a great place as high schools went because I kept the demon population to a minimum. When I first arrived, not too long after I'd come into my ability to see and fight demons, I'd discovered that most of my classmates (and many of my teachers) were demon-ridden. They had nasty little demons riding on their backs or shoulders sucking their life force and filling their minds with evil suggestions.

I put my training to work and dealt with enough of the vermin that most of them now avoided LHS. Hence the pleasant environment.

But not every human failure can be attributed to supernatural causes. Some people are just mean, and Brittney was one of them. She had never been a friend, not even to Allie, and Allie was one of those people who was universally loved. Well, almost. As I said, Britt didn't even get along with Allie.

I'd never understood what her problem was. She was a pretty blonde (when she wasn't scowling), her parents were wealthy (she always had the most fashionable clothes and the latest tech), and as far as anyone knew, her home life was great. So why did she feel the need to be such a complete and total grumpus?

Whatever. I had more than enough on my plate without worrying about Brittney. As long as she stayed in her corner, I'd stay in mine.

"See you at lunch," Allie said with a little wave.

I grinned and the two of us moved off to our respective classes.

Later, my weird-o-meter registered the presence of a dangerous, high level demon in my vicinity. I was in phys ed at the time, jogging around the track in my dorky blue shorts and white T with the rest of my classmates. I slowed to a walk and scanned the area, turning slowly to give myself a three-sixty view. He stood in the parking lot, beyond a chain link fence, at the south end of the track. To normal eyes, he looked like a distinguished older gentleman — steel gray hair, clean shaven, wearing a dark colored business suit with a red power tie—but I saw past the glamour. I saw a six-foot tall demon with deep red scales, back-curving horns, and a prehensile tail that ended in a blade-like triangular tip.

He met my gaze and smiled. At least, the glamour smiled; his actual expression was closer to a leer.

My heart raced and my breath became shallow. Adrenaline pumped through my system and it was all I could do not to sprint for the fence and tear my way through. I wanted to fight. I wanted to destroy this unnatural fiend who had dared venture onto my school grounds!

But that wouldn't be smart. I was dressed for phys ed, not for battle. I didn't have my weapons, and while after two and a half years of training I could take out the little personal demons without a weapon, a demon lord like this guy would require serious effort, and probably some planning.

No, the battle would have to wait. He was on my radar now. We'd meet again, and if possible, I'd have Wick by my side when that happened.

As if reading my decision, he gave me a little salute, and turned ... and my heart froze as he greeted someone. Brittney Dahl.

3

I grabbed Allie after school and practically dragged her across the park to my home. Demon imps danced just out of my reach for the entire trek, and even though I was armed and dangerous now, I ignored them. I had to get home, get the car, and get to Wick.

"What's the rush, Dani?" Allie panted as she trotted beside me. I'm a lot taller, so my stride is longer. Plus, when I'm in a hurry, I can *move*.

"I'll explain when we get to the dojo," I said, gritting my teeth and clamping down of the desire to play *whack-a-demon*.

When we reached the safety of my family's property (demons can't set foot on a demon hunter's land), I raced into the house, while Allie followed at a more sedate pace.

"Hey, Mom," I called, unloading school books from my backpack onto a long library table in the hallway.

"Hi, sweetheart," she answered, appearing at the other end of the hall. "You're home earlier than I expected."

"Hi, Mrs. Erickson," Allie said, following me down the hall.

"I'm sorry, Allie," Mom said with a smile. "I didn't see you."

"That happens a lot when I'm standing behind Dani," my best friend quipped.

I threw a scowl at her, but didn't respond. We stepped into our warm, sunny kitchen and I made a beeline for the row of hooks where the car keys were kept.

"What are you girls up to this afternoon?" Mom asked, narrowing her eyes as she watched me grab the keys to our older Subaru Outback. The old blue vehicle was manufactured before the turn of the century (the twenty-first century), but it was reliable, got great gas mileage, and the insurance was cheap, even for teenage drivers. Mom and Dad kept it as our "starter" car, and each of us kids had been given driving privileges to it as we earned our licenses.

Since Jamie was now in his freshman year at the University of Colorado, Boulder and lived on campus, the Subaru was my car exclusively.

"Allie and I are headed to the dojo," I said, keeping my voice casual even though I could see demon imps dancing in the neighbors yard where it abutted our property. "I have a couple of new moves I want to show off."

Mom's expression lightened. She and Dad had given me permission to take classes with Wick, all because Jamie had made a big deal of wanting to learn martial arts and had convinced them that I should join him. After all, a girl needed to learn self-defense in this day and age.

Even though Jamie was living in Boulder now, I continued to train ... with their blessing. Exercise was to be encouraged, and the parental units had been impressed both with the discipline of Wick's students and with Wick himself.

"That's very sweet of you, Allie," Mom said, "taking an interest in Dani's martial arts training."

"No biggie," Allie answered. "After all, Dani comes to my ballet recitals." She gave me an evil grin. "Plus, some of the guys she trains with are *hot*!"

I glared at her, but Mom just laughed and shook her head. "Only you would make a remark like that to me, Allie." She glanced at me and patted my cheek. "Don't be mortified, Dani. I know there are cute boys at the dojo. After all, Jamie used to be one of them!"

Allie blushed and I made a quick twirling motion with my finger so she'd turn around before Mom noticed.

"Thanks, Mom," I said and kissed her cheek. "We've gotta run." And I hustled Allie down the hall and out the front door.

"Drive carefully," Mom called after us.

Allie and I tossed our backpacks in the back seat and climbed into the car. Once we were safely inside, I said, "You should've seen your face! The mere mention of Jamie and you light up like a Christmas tree."

Jamie and Allie had been thrown together a lot in the past couple of years. Being my co-conspirators in the world of demon-hunting gave them a lot to think about, and no one they could discuss it with except me ... and each other.

After Jamie and Allie spent a terrifying half-hour barricaded in Wick's office while Wick and I battled a demon lord and his herd of minions last year, they'd realized they had more in common than just me. There was a strong physical attraction between them. They'd been dating steadily ever since.

And I couldn't be happier. My youngest older brother and my best friend in the whole world. What could be better? As long as Jamie didn't do anything stupid like hurt Allie, all was well.

If he ever did hurt her, well, let's just say that my Ninja skills could be used for more than fighting demons.

Allie sighed. "It's stupid, I know, but I miss him so much."

"He's just in Boulder," I reminded her. "Fifteen miles is nothing."

She rolled her eyes. "For you, maybe. You have a car. I don't, and neither does Jamie. At least, not this year."

I turned from Francis Street onto 9th Avenue and headed east toward Main Street. "Ugh. Don't remind me! If he gets a parking permit for CU next year, I may lose my car." I patted the dashboard affectionately. "And you like me better, don't you, Subie?"

Allie giggled. "You're a nut. You know that, don't you?"

"Pulled you out of your romantic funk, didn't I? Besides," I said with a quick sideways glance at my friend, "it's April. School will be out in early June. Jamie will be home before you know it."

I parked in front of Wick's dojo and glanced up and down the street. "No demons in sight. We're clear to go."

We jumped out of the car, locked the doors, and were across the sidewalk in mere moments. The bell over the door jingled as we stepped through the wards and into the safety of my guardian's martial arts academy. Wick emerged from his office at the rear of the large practice floor looking calm and unsurprised to see us.

Tall and trim, with great muscle tone, Wick was good looking, for a guy almost old enough to be my father. He sported short brown hair, a neatly trimmed mustache and beard, and his blue-green eyes were clear and honest. He'd trained me, fought beside me and been wounded in defense of those I loved.

I trusted Wick with my life. Literally.

"Miss Erickson. Miss Chavez. I'm pleased to see you, of course," he said as he crossed the room to meet us, "but as I wasn't expecting you, I must ask, what brings you here today?"

"I've been wondering the same thing," Allie said. "Dani's being very mysterious about this visit."

I ignored the jibe, and focused on my guardian. "We have a problem, Wick. I saw a demon lord in the school parking lot today. He wore a glamour," I paused, licked my lips, and blurted, "and he was talking to Brittney Dahl."

4

Allie gasped.

Wick frowned and glanced from me to Allie and back again. "And how is this Brittney Dahl significant?"

Allie answered before I could compose my thoughts.

"She's not a nice girl. A bully, really, and she dislikes both Dani and me."

I nodded. "To be honest, she dislikes everyone ... and pretty much everyone dislikes her right back."

"But she seems to *really* dislike us," Allie finished.

"I see," Wick said. He met my gaze. "And she's not demon ridden?"

I shook my head. "She had one, but I got rid of it. I expected that to make a difference, but it didn't. Not really."

Wick tapped his chin. "Interesting. Of course, demons aren't the only reason for human misbehavior. Some people are sociopaths, or even psychopaths, by nature, but there are fewer of them than popularly believed."

He paced back and forth across the practice floor, thinking, while Allie and I stuffed our backpacks into the cubbies that lined the wall for his students' use. Then we took our places on a mat, sitting tailor fashion while we waited for him to speak.

After another couple of passes, Wick dropped to the mat facing us.

"When did this take place? You said he was in the parking lot. Was it before school or after school?"

"Neither," I replied. "It was during my phys ed class, after lunch. We were running laps on the track. He was just on the other side of the fence from me."

"And did he take notice of you?"

I nodded. "He looked straight at me, and smiled."

Wick scowled. "I don't like this. He chose your most vulnerable time to reveal himself: you were unarmed and away from the safety of your home." He paused and shook his head. "He's too well informed for my comfort."

He stood and began pacing again. After a moment he stopped and pointed at me. "You need to be on high alert, Miss Erickson. Go nowhere unarmed. Find a way to stay out of phys ed until this is resolved. I will shadow you as closely as possible. If you feel his presence, go home. Don't ask for permission, just leave. We'll find a way to clear things up with the school later, but your priority must be personal safety."

Wick was scaring me, which given the seriousness of his expression was probably exactly what he intended. But I didn't like being scared. I also didn't like running away from a fight. I wasn't a green demon hunter anymore. I'd been fighting monsters for more than two years, and I'd even gone up against a couple of demon lords.

Of course, Wick had been badly wounded in our last encounter with one of the big-wigs of the demon world. Was it possible my guardian was afraid?

I studied Wick as he took a seat on the mat again. Yes, he looked grim, his face set in a deadly serious expression, but his eyes were calm and his voice hadn't shaken. His hands were steady as he folded them in his lap, and he met my gaze levelly.

No. Wick was cautious, but not frightened. The precautions he was suggesting weren't coming from a place of fear. He was, as he had said, safeguarding my continued existence.

But I had to ask, "Why are we avoiding the fight? Why don't we just drop Allie at home, hunt this demon down, and destroy him?"

"Because we don't know what he's up to," Wick answered promptly. He knew me well enough to expect the question. " He allowed you to see him on the school grounds, and he made sure you knew of his connection to Miss Dahl. He has a larger plan in mind, and we'll be better served to deal with the consequences if we know what it is." He skewered me with his gaze. "So for now, we wait and watch and maintain security."

He held my gaze until I nodded, and then turned to Allie.

"You must also be on guard, Miss Chavez." Allie's eyes widened and a pretty pink blush stained her cheeks. "You've been targeted before and would make an excellent hostage to use against Miss Erickson."

Allied nodded. "I'll be careful, and I'll stay away from strange men."

"Excellent," Wick said, clapping his hands together. "If you'll wait here while I pull my Jeep around front, we'll all leave together and I'll follow you home to make sure you arrive safely."

5

The next morning I dressed quickly, inspected my blades before sheathing them, and packed a supply of holy water in my backpack, then I ran down the stairs to the kitchen.

"Here I am," I said as I crossed the room and kissed Mom on the cheek. "Ready and willing to eat breakfast at the kitchen table."

Mom beamed. "See? That wasn't so hard, was it?"

"Nope," I said, reaching into one of the hickory cabinets and extracting my favorite cereal, a calorie laden combination of sugar coated wheat flakes and big fat raisins.

The kitchen was the heart of our home. Its terra cotta red walls, pale lemon curtains, and light hickory cabinets gave it a warm and welcoming feel. Just like Mom, who had designed the kitchen and was its main inhabitant, was the heart of our family. The one who held us all together with her warmth and love.

She might be a stern disciplinarian, and she definitely expected all of us to toe the line and obey the house rules, but all of us kids knew that she'd give her very life to protect any one of us. Yeah, I could make time to eat breakfast in the kitchen if it made Mom happy.

After I'd slurped down my cereal and milk, had my daily vitamin C in the form of a glass of orange juice, and loaded my dirty dishes into the dishwasher, I grabbed my backpack.

"I'm off to school, Mom," I said, heading toward the front door. If I hurried, I might make it onto the porch before Allie rang the doorbell.

"Have a good day," Mom called.

Allie was just turning the corner when I pulled the front door closed behind me. I waved and raced down the steps to join her on the sidewalk. Scanning the park across the street, I noted the complete absence of demons. I frowned. That wasn't normal. Usually there were a couple hanging out the trees, just watching our house. As long as they didn't bother anyone, I left them alone.

But this morning, even the sentries were gone.

"What's wrong, Dani?" Allie asked as we followed the path across the park.

"Nothing."

"Uh-huh," she said, giving me her *I-don't-think-so* expression. "Then why are you frowning."

"It's just that there isn't a single demon in the park," I explained. "There are usually at least a couple of the little guys around."

"And that's a bad thing?" she asked in a puzzled voice.

"No. Not a bad thing," I admitted. "Just out of the ordinary." I didn't add what I was thinking, that I didn't like out of the ordinary when there was a demon lord on the loose.

When we got to the school entrance, our path was blocked. Students milled around outside the doors, but no one was going in.

"What's happening?" Allie asked a guy near us.

He shrugged. "No idea. I just know the doors are still locked. No one can get into the building."

Allie and I shared a startled glance. Yet another out-of-the-ordinary occurrence.

Just then the students took a collective step back, and Allie and I hurried to conform. One of the doors opened and Principal Jerrold appeared holding a cordless microphone.

"Attention, students," he said, and the crowd quieted immediately. "We've had an incident on school grounds. The police are here and we'll be starting our day a little late due to security measures that the Longmont Police Department has put in place for your protection."

A buzz of conversation began and Allie took the opportunity to lean toward me and whisper, "Do you think this has anything to do with, you know, *him?*"

Principal Jerrold continued before I could answer. "Everyone will need to enter through this one door," he explained. "You'll be checked through into the school by a uniformed officer. Once you're inside, please proceed directly to your homeroom. Do not linger in the hallways."

He turned and glanced through the glass doors, nodded, and turned back to us. "We're ready to begin. Please form a single line and remain calm. Your teachers will brief you on the situation as soon as everyone is inside and in their assigned classrooms. Thank you for your cooperation."

More students had arrived while Principal Jerrold spoke, so Allie and I were now in the middle of the crowd. Everyone jostled around until we were in a line that stretched along the sidewalk and into the parking lot. A few teachers patrolled the line. They didn't answer questions, but their presence ensured our good behavior while we waited.

Finally, Allie and I reached the head of the line. A police officer stood just outside the door, watching the line. Two more were inside between the door and a table staffed by school personnel with laptop computers. A light flare on the glass kept me from seeing much beyond that point.

Allie entered first and I followed right behind her ... and immediately wished I was back outside.

I was in a chokepoint with no escape. No way to go except forward, and what waited in front of me would be my downfall.

Beyond the table with the computers and the staff with strained expressions on their faces stood a metal detector like the ones at the Denver airport. Manned by additional police officers.

And I was wearing stiletto blades in my boots and had a short sword concealed in my backpack.

I was toast.

I grabbed Allie's shoulder as the guy ahead of her approached the table and handed over his school ID. "Once you're clear," I whispered, "call Wick. I'm going to need him."

She gave me a startled look, but nodded. After the last demon lord had tried to lure Allie into danger in a coffee shop, we'd all agreed that she should have Wick's number. I'd programmed it into her cell phone myself.

Allie had half turned to ask me a question, when one of the staff called, "Next!" She approached the table and handed over her ID.

I sweated out the wait. I couldn't do anything else. No way out.

Once my ID had been checked, I licked my lips and walked to my doom. The young officer who held out his hand for my backpack didn't look much older than me. After a tiny hesitation, I handed it over. Another officer beckoned me forward and pointed through the metal detector.

"Step through, please."

I glanced at Allie, who waited on the other side. If only I could magically transport across the space to join her!

The young officer with my backpack yelled, "Sir!" just as I stepped into the detector. Alarms screamed. The officer at the door slammed it shut as all four of the other uniformed men rushed to surround me, guns drawn.

I met Allie's gaze, and she answered my silent plea with a nod. Wick would come. He had to!

6

My stilettos and short sword were confiscated. I was patted down for additional weapons, handcuffed, marched from the building, and stuffed into the back seat of a police cruiser. All in plain view of my classmates.

When we arrived at the police station, the cuffs were removed and I was locked in a gray-walled room with a huge mirror on one wall. I'd seen enough police shows on television to assume it was one-way glass. I sat alone in the sparsely furnished room (just a metal table and three metal chairs) and tried not to tremble.

Carrying deadly weapons was no laughing matter, not in this age of school shootings and mass murders. I'd missed the explanation of the incident that had caused the police response, but I was enlightened during the course of my arrest. The anniversary of the Columbine High School shootings was approaching and the police department had received evidence of what they believed was a credible threat against Longmont High. They took it seriously, and I was the one caught in the trap. Me. The one person who was actively working to protect the school.

I suppose it could've been worse; I could've been carrying a rifle.

Not that the type of weapon would make a difference. Heck, a grade-schooler had been expelled for taking a kitchen knife to school to cut his birthday cake. And my blades were far more deadly than a kitchen knife.

What were my parents going to think? They didn't have a clue about those weapons … or what I used them for. The only person other than Wick who'd ever seen me in action was Jamie, and he was in Boulder at CU.

Wick would help, of course, but I wasn't sure what he could do to protect me from law enforcement. I'd joked with him about getting expelled when he'd first given me the specially modified boots and backpack, but after two years of wearing them, I'd stopped worrying about that possibility. As Wick had said, "Better expelled than dead."

But now the worst had happened. I was about to be expelled, possibly imprisoned, and — even worse! — my secret identity was about to be exposed to my parents.

I repeat: I was toast.

The door opened and my parents were ushered in. Mom rushed to me and I stood for her hug. Dad glowered at the officer until the door swung closed, then he turned to me. I've seen Dad in a lot of moods, but I'd never seen such a jumbled mix of bewilderment, sadness, anger, and despair.

I wanted to disappear into the woodwork.

Mom still hugged me tightly. I hadn't realized she was crying until her tears soaked through my T-shirt. Gently, I extricated myself, feeling calmer than I had any right to. Now that the moment had come, my trembling ceased as my inner demon hunter took over. This was a different kind of danger, but I was always calm when the danger was deadliest.

"I don't understand, Dani," Dad said, stepping forward to give me a quick squeeze. "What were you doing with a sword?"

I nodded to the mirror and said quietly, "Not here."

Dad glanced at the mirror, clenched his jaw, and nodded. "Let's sit down. Our attorney should be here soon."

Since I was a minor with no prior record, I was released into my parents custody and a hearing date was set. As Mom and Dad herded me out of the building, I caught sight of Wick and Allie, and knew that they'd follow us home.

Good thing. I was going to need Wick's support when I tried to explain who and what I was to my parents.

We'd barely made it into the kitchen from the garage, when the doorbell rang. I started to answer when Mom laid a hand on my arm. "Let your father get it."

I stopped, nodded, and followed Mom to the scrubbed oak kitchen table. We sat as I strained to hear what was being said at the door. It was hopeless, all I could make out was a murmur of voices.

Footsteps echoed on the hardwood floor of the hall and Dad appeared followed by Wick and Allie. I jumped up and ran to my friends. Allie hugged me, while Wick stroked my back. I shivered with terror. Now that I was home and safe, my fear threatened to consume me.

Leaving me in Allie's arms, Wick stepped to my mother. "Mrs. Erickson, I don't know if you remember, but we met at Union Reservoir … on Dani's fourteenth birthday."

I looked up from Allie's shoulder in time to see comprehension dawn on Mom's face. "Yes, I do remember. Dani had an odd episode, a little seizure, and you were able to calm her."

He nodded and turned to Dad. "I'm not just Dani's martial arts instructor."

Dad's eyes narrowed. "Why didn't we know about this connection before? Have you been stalking our daughter? Are you the reason she's in trouble now?"

Wick gestured to the table. "Why don't we all take a seat," he said, his voice calm and soothing, yet firm. "We have much to discuss, and some of it has been put off too long."

Mom looked confused, but took her place at the table. Dad looked like he wanted to yell at Wick for ordering him around in his own home, but he glanced at Mom and then at me, and sat.

Allie and I took our places next to each other and Wick pulled out a chair across from Mom and Dad.

"All right," Wick said, "Now that we're all settled, let's begin. Miss Erickson, do you wish to explain or should I?"

Dad opened his mouth, but Mom touched his hand and he closed it again.

"I think you'll do a better job, Wick," I said quietly.

He nodded. "Mr. Erickson, I know you're familiar with your father's beliefs regarding the seventh son of a seventh son."

Dad sighed, his brow furrowed. "Of course. It's utter nonsense, but that's got nothing to do with this."

"On the contrary," Wick said. "It has everything to do with this. Your father was only mistaken in believing that gender was an issue." Dad looked like he was about to interrupt, but Wick held up his hand and Dad subsided. "The seventh child of a seventh child is a powerfully potent individual, a hereditary demon hunter, born with the ability to see what others cannot, and, when properly trained, to dispatch the unholy creatures who prey on unknowing humans."

He paused a beat and then announced, "Your daughter is such a person."

Dad jumped up and lunged across the table at Wick. "You're insane," he bellowed. "You've been filling Dani's head with nonsense and now you've caused her to be in trouble with the law!"

I jumped up too. "Dad! Sit down. Wick's not to blame. You and Grandpa are!"

Dad froze, then slowly turned his head to stare at me. "What did you say to me?"

My demon hunting calm had returned. My pulse no longer raced, but was slow and steady, my nerves were steel. I knew what needed to be done.

"I said, 'you and Grandpa are to blame.' Now stop yelling at Wick and listen to us. Wick's done nothing but help and protect me. You're just now hearing about this because I've forbidden him to speak to you."

I gave Wick an apologetic bow, and turned to Allie. "Allie's known about my abilities almost from the start. She's helped me hide them from you. We used ballet and singing lessons to cover my training with Wick and Madam Simone."

I glared at both my parents, daring them to interrupt. My expression must have been fierce, because they just stared at me in silence.

"But none of this would've been necessary if Grandpa hadn't decided he needed to produce a seventh-seventh. Sure he got the gender wrong, but his breeding program worked." I stabbed my finger at Dad. "You're the seventh child. You're the one who could pass on the inheritance, not Uncle Gus. And the two of you," I widened my glare to include Mom, "decided to have seven children. You're the reason I'm who and what I am. Not Wick. It's not Wick's fault that I'm a seventh-seventh. That's all on you and Grandpa."

I took a deep breath and sat down. "Not that I'm complaining about being born," I muttered. "I'm just stating facts."

Dad clutched Mom's hand and inhaled a trembling breath. "S-so y-you're saying you believe this crap?"

"Believe it?" I asked, my voice declaring my incredulity. "Of course I believe it! I'm living it!"

I closed my eyes and counted to ten. I had to remember, they couldn't see demons, they had no way to prove or disprove what Wick and I were telling them. I had to be patient. But at the same time, Allie was in the same boat, and she'd never doubted me.

Parents! They thought they knew everything.

I glanced at Wick, but he just raised an eyebrow and nodded for me to continue.

"Look," I said, schooling my voice to calm. "Do you remember when Jamie went missing? How I found him?"

Mom and Dad both nodded.

"Well, he wasn't exactly missing. I knew where he was instantly. I can tell where any member of my family is if I concentrate on them. I can also sense demons, where they are and what their relative strength is. It's one of the gifts Wick and Simone have been helping me master."

"Who is this Simone you keep talking about?" Mom asked.

Wick took that one for me. "Simone and I are part of an ancient clan of guardians. Our people monitor large families and watch for the advent of a hunter. We were both in Longmont for Dani's fourteenth birthday, which is when the power typically manifests, if it's going to."

"What do you mean, if it's going to?" I interrupted.

"There have been seventh-sevenths who have never manifested power. We don't understand why, but it happens occasionally. When it does, we leave the individual in ignorance."

"Lucky them," I muttered.

Wick stared at me until I met his gaze. "Would you really relinquish your gift, Miss Erickson?"

I continued to lock eyes with him while I considered the question. Would I give it up if I could? Would I return to being an unknowing victim of a race of unseen creatures? Would I be content to allow them to suck the life and joy from my family and friends?

"No," I said. Then with more strength, "I've come to terms with my destiny. I'm a powerful demon hunter and it's my job to protect those in my domain. I wouldn't go back even if I could."

Wick nodded. "Very good, Miss Erickson. Please, continue with your tale."

"Wait a minute," Mom said. "So it wasn't an accident that you were at the reservoir on her birthday?"

"No, Mrs. Erickson. It was no accident."

"And the incident, Dani's seizure…"

"Was not a medical condition," Wick answered. "It was the advent of her power. She began training with me the next day."

"And why would she trust you and not us?" Dad asked, anger evident in his voice.

I started to speak, but Wick silenced me with a glance.

"Even if she had told you, Mr. Erickson, you would've been unable to help her. You are not a seventh-seventh, nor are you genetically related to the guardian clan. She needed *us*. We can see demons. We can fight demons. But we can't destroy them, nor can we repair the rents in time and space that allow them to enter our world. Only a demon hunter possesses those abilities, and they are all too rare in this age of small families. Dani is a treasure that our world desperately needs."

"As to why she didn't tell you," Allie said, speaking for the first time, and with surprising ferocity, "I'd like to answer that." She stood and faced my parents. All five-two of her. "I really like you, Mr. and Mrs. Erickson, but I've watched you try to mold Dani into a girly-girl for as long as I've known her. 'Don't be a tom-boy, Dani. We have enough boys in this family, Dani.'" She mimicked my family's mantras rather cruelly, but very accurately. "I've thought for a long time that someone should smack you and make you realize that she's perfect just the way she is. She doesn't need to be a mini me. She's Dani, and she's awesome."

Allie sat quickly, looking suddenly embarrassed by her outburst.

Mom's cheeks flamed and Dad looked like an innocuous pet hamster had bitten him and drawn blood. They both glanced at me and then lowered their eyes.

"Look," I said quietly. "I love you both, and you're the best parents in the world, but you do try to put me in a box where I don't fit ... and when my power manifested, I finally understood that I'll never fit and why. I can't be a sweet little princess. I have to be an Amazon warrior. I'm a fighter; it's my heritage, my destiny." I took a deep breath and blurted, "And while we're being honest, can we please redecorate my bedroom? I hate pink!"

Mom looked ready to cry, but Dad burst out laughing. "That's the first thing you've said that I understand!" When he had himself under control, he wiped his eyes and asked, "What were you saying about Jamie?"

"Oh. Right." I took a deep breath and ripped off the Band-Aid. "Jamie was kidnapped by demons to bait a trap to take me out." Mom looked ready to deny what I was saying, so I raced on. "They held him close enough to their portal that he could see them. He knows they exist."

"What?" my parents yelped in unison.

"But he's okay because Wick and I went after him. Wick got Jamie out —or tried to, Wick was injured in the attempt—while I took out the demon horde. Call Jamie, have him come home. He'll tell you what he saw."

"I've never seen a demon," Allie said into the silence, "but Wick and Dani barricaded me and Jamie into Wick's office once last year to protect us while they battled a bunch of them." Allie shivered, and then continued quietly, "The things we heard … it was terrifying, and when Dani yelled that we could come out, Wick was unconscious and his chest was burned so badly we were really worried. I helped with some first aid until Madame Simone arrived. She has a special gift for healing supernatural wounds."

"Oh my God!" Mom exclaimed. "Dani! How could you have put yourself in such danger and not let us know?"

I sighed. "How could I tell you when I knew you wouldn't believe me?"

7

Dad called Jamie, and my brother dropped everything, caught a ride with a friend, and came home to support me. He arrived before dinner.

Jamie told Mom and Dad everything he knew. He wasn't a kid anymore, he was a college man, and while he apologized to my parents for not telling them, he stated simply that it wasn't his truth to tell and that he respected me too much to betray my confidence.

Color me amazed.

We had a good old fashioned family hug, and agreed to let bygones be bygones. What was needed now was a good strategy for moving forward.

Wick and Allie came back after dinner. Jamie met Allie with a hug, and then settled down next to her at the kitchen table, our designated war room.

Dad shook hands with Wick, thanked him for his service to the Erickson kids, and told Wick to consider himself part of our family.

Dad also asked if he could sit in on one of my training sessions. He wanted to see how his daughter handled herself.

Wick had an idea about how to deal with the weapons charges against me. Obviously, we couldn't tell the police the truth. They'd never believe my blades were used to defend my classmates and teachers from demons. Lets face it, Mom and Dad were having enough trouble with that information ... and they loved me.

"You may not realize that I've been teaching a self-defense class at the high school," Wick told my parents. "It was a way for me to be on campus and available in the early days when your daughter was first learning to handle things. At this point, there's not much need. Miss Erickson has pretty well cleared the school of personal demons. They now recognize it as being under her protection and steer clear."

"Seriously?" Dad asked.

"Definitely," Jamie answered. "Longmont High has a much nicer atmosphere since Dani arrived. Once I was introduced to the demon population, I understood why that was, but all my friends noticed the change. They just didn't attribute it to Dani's presence."

"Okay," said Dad, looking stunned, "but how does that help us now."

"Well," Wick continued, "I thought I might be able to go to the authorities and tell them that Miss Erickson is a gifted martial artist, and that I asked her to bring her blades to school so that we could give a demonstration to my self-defense classes, a kind of advertisement of the kind of advanced training they might aspire to learn."

He paused and looked around expectantly. "Well, what do you think?"

Mom and Dad exchanged glances. Finally, Dad said, "I don't know if that would excuse her carrying concealed weapons, especially since everyone has seen her with those boots and that backpack practically on a daily basis, but it's sure worth a try."

"Definitely," said Jamie. "Lots of people know she trains with you, and I can testify that she works with weapons. I do too."

"And," added Allie, "no one can prove that the blades have been in her boots and backpack any other time. I mean, I'm with her every day and I've never seen them at school."

"Excellent," said Wick. "I'll go to the police station first thing in the morning and make a statement."

A warm glow of contentment filled my soul. Mom and Dad knew my secret, and they still loved me. If anything, they felt bad that I hadn't felt safe enough to confide in them. Jamie loved me enough to cut classes and come home to defend me. Allie had told off my parents in my defense, and Wick had come up with a possible strategy to explain my apparent misconduct.

Maybe I wouldn't be expelled from high school and sent to prison after all. Maybe everything would work out.

The doorbell rang, and we all looked at each other. No one was expecting visitors.

Dad got up and strode down the hall. Jamie followed at a distance.

A moment later Jamie was back. "It's the police," he said. "They're here for Dani."

Everyone stood.

Dad returned to the kitchen, his expression grim, followed by two uniformed officers and two plain clothes types.

One of the plain clothes guys stepped forward and flipped open a badge case. "I'm Detective Schaffer and this is my partner, Detective Hobson. Homicide."

While he spoke, his partner circled the table to stand beside me. "Dani Heleen Erickson, you're under arrest for the murder of Brittney Dahl."

"What?" I yelled as he pulled my hands behind my back and cuffed them for the second time that day. "What do you mean? What happened to Britt?"

"Wait just a minute," Dad called. "You can't arrest her again. The judge released her into our custody!"

"That was for a weapons charge," Detective Schaffer said. "This is for murder. She's coming with us."

The uniformed officers ran interference while the detectives perp marched me out of my home and stuffed me into a police cruiser ... again.

So much for everything working out.

Y ou haven't lived until you've spent a night in jail.

Believe me, I don't want to live that way again. Ever.

By this time, I'd seen a lot of demons, but I'd never seen that many fat, sassy, self-assured demons attached to as many ugly, mean-spirited people. And me without my weapons.

Fortunately, because of my youth, I was placed in solitary, but I could still hear the cat calls and the demonic taunts. What a miserable experience, and unless I was very, very lucky, I might be getting a foretaste of my entire future.

Brittney Dahl was dead. I'd never liked the girl, but I hadn't wished her dead, just far away from me and mine.

Wick came to visit me the next morning and gave me the details he and Simone had ferreted out. Britt's throat had been cut with a sharp-edged instrument, just like one of my blades. Her body had been found stuffed in a shack behind the football stadium when the police were clearing the grounds at the high school. The coroner determined that she'd died sometime around midnight on the night before I was arrested the first time.

And the most damaging of all? The police found an entry in her diary stating that I'd called and asked her to meet me at that time and place.

"Why would she write that?" I asked Wick. "I've never called her, and I've certainly never asked her to meet me anywhere."

"Of course not," Wick said in that calm voice of his. "But you did see her with a demon lord. One who undoubtedly sent the police that credible threat that caused your blades to be discovered, and one who probably dictated exactly what she was to write. Poor girl had no idea she was sealing her own death with that entry."

My heart fluttered and my stomach roiled with nausea. Yeah, I was sorry Britt was dead, but I was a lot sorrier that she'd framed me. Of course, she hadn't known she was framing me for murder, but still, she'd disliked me enough to go along with whatever scheme the demon lord had sold to her.

"I'm going to prison aren't I?" I asked, feeling my options drying up.

"No," Wick said with such assurance that my mouth dropped open.

"Close your mouth, Miss Erickson," he said with a grim little smile. "You're far too valuable to waste away in prison. Yes, you could probably make life easier for the inmates and reduce their recidivism to almost nothing, but the non-criminal world needs your services too badly to limit the scope of your work to a single prison."

"Okay," I said. "I like the sound of that. I just don't know how you're going to get me released."

"My clan is working on it," he said, matter of factly. "Your parents have been apprised that a guardian will appear as your defense attorney and that they are to accept whoever steps forward, as long as I vouch for that person. You will do the same. Agreed?"

"Agreed."

"And if all else fails, know that you will be rescued from this place. No matter what the criminal justice system decides, you will not be incarcerated more than a few days. Understood?

I swallowed, thought about asking what he meant, but decided I didn't want to know. "Understood."

"Chin up, Miss Erickson. All will be well."

9

―――――――――

The next few weeks were the worst of my life.

Because of the seriousness of the crime, I wasn't allowed bail. I remained in jail, quarantined from the rest of the world.

The lawyer the clan provided was a wonderful woman, warm and caring when she spoke with me, fierce in my defense, and from the expressions I saw on the prosecutors' faces, she knew the law better than they had anticipated. She was well versed in obscure cases, ones that even the judge had to research.

And my family ... what can I say? The Ericksons, from Mom and Dad and all my brothers all the way up to Grandpa, know how to stand up for their own. Everyone was verbal in my defense, each of my brothers was willing to be interviewed at a moment's notice about how their little sister was not only innocent, she was incapable of murder.

I had to smile every time I saw Jamie do such an interview. He was always careful to qualify his statement, that I was absolutely incapable of taking a *human* life. If anyone else noticed his qualification, I never heard about it.

But despite their unwavering support and my lawyer's brilliance, when the moment came, I was convicted.

The courtroom exploded in a wave of angry outbursts from my family and friends … and then, absolute silence reigned.

Everyone froze in exactly the position they'd been in when the spell was activated.

I recognized the time spell. I'd used it often enough at Longmont High to battle demons while my classmates and teachers hung in suspended animation. I turned around looking for the caster, and found several people still animated, as well as a multitude of demons, from tiny personal ones that rode their human victims to bouncing imps, excited by seeing a hunter in trouble. But they were all low-level creatures and kept a wary distance from those of us who could not only see them, but could end their miserable existences.

Of the humans in the room, only four besides myself were mobile.

My lawyer.

Wick.

Simone.

And a young man I'd never seen before.

Of course. Members of the guardian clan would be as immune to the spell as I was. Simone had been the one who taught me to stop time.

The four of them gathered around me.

"What's going on?" I asked.

Wick smiled. "I told you we would not allow you to waste your life in prison, Miss Erickson," he said. "Allow me to introduce Gregorio Radovan. As I'm sure you've deduced, Greg is a member of the guardian clan. He will guide you to a safe haven."

"Hi," I said, feeling more than a little off-balance. Greg was only a couple of years older than me and seriously cute, with curly light brown hair and blue eyes that twinkled with mischief.

He held out his hand. "A pleasure, Miss Erickson. I look forward to working with you."

I accepted his hand, and he raised my knuckles to his lips and pressed a kiss to them. My heart raced and my cheeks blazed. He released my hand and stepped back beside Wick.

I wanted to fan myself, but managed to quash the impulse.

My attorney was speaking, and I forced my attention to her.

"We wanted to clear your name," she said, "so that you could remain here with your family, but that's no longer possible. Your life in this community, in this state, is over, Miss Erickson."

"I – What?" I said.

"You will have no further contact with any member of your family, Dani," Simone said gently. "If you ever return to this place, it will be many, many years from now. You are a citizen of the world now, Dani."

"But, I can't..." I closed my eyes and took a deep breath. When I opened them again, I'd called up my demon hunter calm. "I need to say good-bye. I can't just disappear."

"I'm afraid you must, Miss Erickson," Wick said. "Think about what you've been taught. If we release the time stop, we release it for everyone, and this will have been for nothing."

"We've brought Greg in to guide you because he is unknown," my lawyer said. "Wick and Simone and I will remain in place. We will be as astonished as everyone else by your disappearance. In a few days, I will go back to my practice in Washington, D.C."

"Simone and I will remain in Longmont for a time," Wick said. "In a year or two, I will close my dojo and move on."

"But I will remain here with your family," Simone said, picking up the tale. "To the outside world, it will appear that your mother has turned to new age spirituality after the unexplained disappearance of her youngest child. She will consult with me on a regular basis. Your father will seem to disapprove, but will not have the heart to deny her this source of comfort."

"In reality," she continued, "I will act as a conduit for you to communicate with your loved ones. You must never write or phone them, but the clan will relay messages to me and I will pass them along to your family. They will know that you are alive and well and fulfilling your destiny."

My eyes filled with tears, and I searched the faces of each member of my family. Not their best looks, frozen as they had been in the midst of crying, shouting, or shaking fists. But all those expressions spoke of their love for me. Their belief in my innocence. Their determination to have me free and happy and healthy and at home with them.

I memorized each of them, these people who had filled my life with love and joy and, occasionally aggravation — after all, SIX brothers! — and who I would miss every day for the rest of my life.

The clan offered me freedom and health, and probably even happiness, but I would never again know my first and best home. I was grieving already.

"I'm so sorry, Miss Erickson," Wick said. He folded me in his arms and held me close. "A hug from your father," he whispered, and I burst into tears.

EPILOGUE

A new chapter in my life has begun. I'm still Dani Erickson, still me, but I'm no longer a high school student or a citizen of Colorado. I'm not even sure I'm still a citizen of the United States. Simone spoke truly: I'm a citizen of the world now.

Greg and I are currently somewhere in the Carpathian Mountains of Romania traveling with a band of the guardian clan. I'm learning a new language and a new way of life.

I miss Allie terribly, but I miss Mom and Dad more. I even miss the aggravation of dealing with six older brothers and living in a pink and white bedroom. But I'm healthy and I'm free ... and I'm learning to be happy.

But best of all, I'm hunting demons! Greg fights beside me as Wick once did, and together we're making the world a safer place for all of mankind.

VI

RUSH!

Deb Logan

Author of *Faery Unexpected*

Rush!

A Very Short Story

1

I'd spent my life testing boundaries. My parents, well, adoptive parents — I had no idea who had given me life — worried about me constantly, too aware that I'd do anything for an adrenaline rush.

That particular concern had just ceased to exist.

Now I knew I had limits, but the lesson came too late.

When Andy shoved me against the railing of Amber's high-rise apartment patio, he didn't mean to kill me. He was just expressing the general view of Skyline High's ultra elite in-crowd: *You can come to our parties, but hands off our girls.*

Unfortunately, my rail-thin, freakishly tall body's center of gravity was higher than the norm. Instead of hitting the railing and crumpling, I tipped over the edge, my hip acting as the fulcrum of my doom.

My arms flailed wildly, hoping to catch hold of something. Anything. Adrenaline fired my veins and my heart banged like a bass drum on steroids. Out of the corner of one eye I saw Jason lunge forward. I jerked to a stop as he caught my foot, and relief washed across my soul. I wouldn't die today after all.

Thank God for Jason.

People screamed and fingers snatched at the leg of my jeans. Too bad I'd worn the skin-tight pair; they were having trouble finding purchase. Beneath the chaos, my heart-rate slowed and peace settled comfortably across my mind.

Until my shoe came off.

2

Gravity jerked me downward; a happy dog proud of the bone it had wrested from its opponent.

Too bad *I* was the bone.

Peace lasted for the space of several floors before reality smacked me. This was it. Unless Superman flew past and scooped me into his arms, I was about to be sauce on the sidewalk.

Realization triggered *The Voice*.

From the dark recesses of my mind the gong-like tones of a masculine voice commanded, *Forget what you know. Do what you must.*

Forgetting wasn't an issue; my brain was about to splatter across the pavement, but what was I supposed to *do*?

Again *The Voice* ordered, *Do it now!*

My body responded without my direction. Arms snapped together above my head like they were preparing to execute a perfect dive. Legs straightened, toes pointed, and a sudden tension sang through my arrow-straight body. I closed my eyes, not to block out the sight of the rapidly approaching sidewalk, but to visualize the star-studded velvet of the sky above me. My back arched and my trajectory altered. I executed a perfect U-turn in space and raced upward, an arrow shot from an invisible bow.

When I reached Amber's balcony, I landed lightly, pulled my shoe from Jason's limp fingers and gave him an appreciative nod. Without bothering to put it on, I limped over to Andy and stuck out my hand. "No hard feelings, man," I said with wry smile. "I know that was an accident."

Andy swallowed, his expression stunned. He took my hand without a word.

I mean, really? What could he say?

VII

LILAH'S GHOST

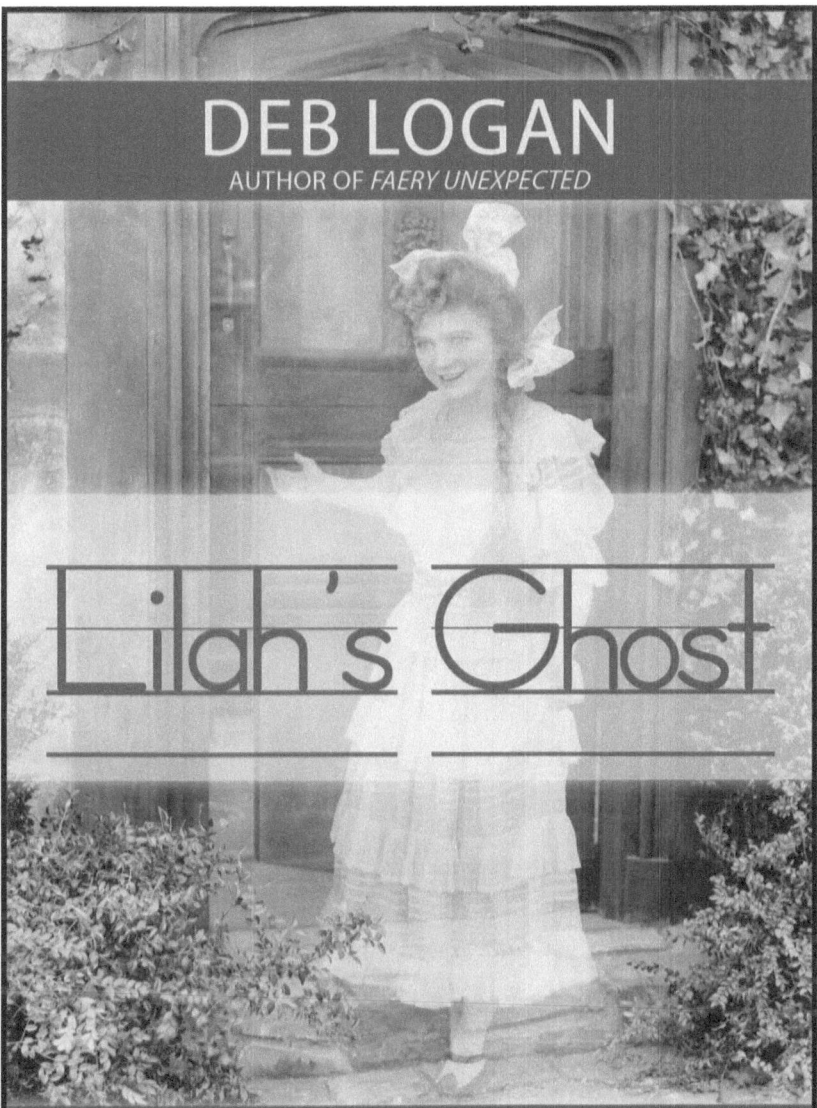

DEB LOGAN

AUTHOR OF *FAERY UNEXPECTED*

Lilah's Ghost

SPUN YARNS
A Middle Grade Short Story

1

My best friend is a ghost, but sometimes I forget she's dead.

I discovered Lilah at the end of June when my family moved into this old mansion on the remains of a Georgia cotton plantation. It's not as grand as it sounds. The house is practically falling down around us and the live oaks, lining the drive, drip with grey-green moss. Very creepy.

The owner, Bill Richardson, lives in Oklahoma. He hadn't been able to keep a tenant for more than a month in all the years he'd owned it. I bet that's because of Lilah.

I keep trying to guess when Lilah lived, but it's hard to tell. She looks like a pretty normal girl, except she's all silvery-white, so I have to guess at colors. Her hair is dark, like frosted coal, and she wears it in two long braids, the kind where each braid starts right at her forehead and ends in a little ribbon bow. She wears loose fitting jeans and a short-sleeve plaid shirt. My jeans aren't baggy and rolled up at the ankles, but I have a shirt that looks just like hers. Her shoes are the biggest clue. I described them to Mom who said they were called saddle shoes, because the darker piece of leather that runs across the middle looks like a saddle. I don't know anyone who wears shoes like that.

She's really a very nice girl, but most folks aren't too keen on chatting with the dead. Me, I'm used to it. Mom says I'm psychic and, since not every twelve-year-old talks to dead people, that I should keep this stuff to myself.

My name is Hannah Barnes and my family's been here in Fraser, Georgia about six weeks. Before that, we lived in Tulsa, Oklahoma. Dad met Mr. Richardson when he did some repairs on the guy's office. Richardson liked Dad's work and offered him this gig. A free place to live if Dad would make the needed repairs to keep the place standing. He forgot to mention the ghost.

Dad's making good progress restoring the mansion to its former glory while Mom works in town as a legal secretary. She tried helping Dad with the restoration, but the mansion makes her jumpy. She says the only way she can live here is to escape for forty hours each week.

Lilah and I try to help Dad as much as possible, but he gets jittery whenever Lilah hands him a tool. I guess it's 'cause he can't see her. Maybe flying nail guns would freak me, too. Anyway, he asked me to keep her away from his work area, said it wasn't safe for little girls to play with power tools. *Right.* He never had a problem with me helping him in Tulsa.

So, until school starts, I've got nothing to do but shoot the breeze with Lilah. Killing time with a ghost has its ups and downs. Lilah's shown me all the house's secrets from the priest hole behind the cellar wall to the loose floor board in the attic where an ancestor kept her diary. She's even shown me cool stuff on the grounds, like the secret spot under the roots of the huge, live oak by the river. The only thing she won't do is go beyond the big iron gate that separates the driveway from the road.

That's a real bummer, because the Sweet Pea Festival is next week and I really want to go. I know, just because Lilah can't go doesn't mean I have to stay home. But what fun is a Sweet Pea Festival if you can't share it with your best friend?

"Have you ever been to the Sweet Pea Festival?" I asked Lilah as we sat on the big porch that circles the house. Lilah calls it the verandah. I sat on the old-fashioned porch swing, pushing off every now and then with my left foot; Lilah sat suspended beside me. When I first sat down, it looked like she sat beside me until I started swinging. The swing kind of swooshed through her as it moved back and forth.

"Only once," she said. "I went with my parents and little brother when I was ten." She turned her silvery eyes toward me and I saw the sparkle of happy memory fade. "Something happened before the next one came around. Why are you asking about the Sweet Pea Festival?"

"Well, it's next week, and I was kind of hoping you'd break your rule about stopping at the gate and go with me."

The wooden slats of the swing pushed through her chest as Lilah shook her head. "Sorry, it doesn't work that way. I can't just decide to go somewhere new. I have, um, what's the word? Oh, yes, boundaries. I have boundaries."

Watching the swing move through Lilah started to make me queasy, so I anchored my foot and stopped swinging. "Who told you about the boundaries?"

She shrugged. "No one. It's like I'm on a leash from the main staircase. The farther I get from it, the harder it is to move." She pulled her legs up and sat tailor-fashion on the swing. "By the time I get to the gate, I'm so heavy, I can't move."

I nodded and put on my best sympathetic expression. I didn't under-stand, but I acted like I did. "Um ... when you ... you know ... died," I watched her face to see if the word bothered her. No reaction, "... why didn't you go to the Light? You did see the Light, didn't you?"

"Yes, I saw it." She closed her eyes and her face relaxed into a peaceful smile. "It was golden and warm and the most beautiful thing I'd ever seen." She opened them again, leaned forward, and said in a vibrant whisper, "I wanted to run right into it."

"Why didn't you?"

She leaned back, and her voice dulled. "I couldn't. My little brother needed me."

"I don't understand. Your little brother asked you to stay?"

Lilah jumped off the swing and paced between the house and the porch rail. "It wasn't his fault. He was only six. He didn't mean to push me down the stairs!"

She rushed to my side and grabbed my hands. I felt ice grip my fingers, but I didn't pull away.

"He cried so hard. He begged me not to leave." She dropped my hands and kind of wilted onto the rotting floor boards. "I love William. I couldn't leave him. Not alone and terrified."

"But he's not here anymore. He left you, didn't he?"

"Yes." She shook herself and straightened up again. "But now I have you," she said, "and you're the best friend ever. You'll like the Sweet Pea Festival," she said, and closed the subject of her death.

2

For a tiny little southern town, Fraser sure knows how to throw a party. The Sweet Pea Festival had country stuff like a petting zoo and hay rides, and all the regular fair rides like bumper cars and a Ferris Wheel. I'd seen a million carnivals in Tulsa, so I liked the local stuff best. The mayor sitting on a collapsible ledge, daring folks to dunk her for a dollar. The artists who set up booths and not only hawked their wares, but demonstrated their craft. After trying an "easy" project, most people could hardly wait to plunk down their hard-earned cash. The glass blower was the exception. He couldn't re-create the fires he needed to melt the glass ingredients into a gooey blob, so he settled for a video clip and invitations to drop by his studio.

My favorite part of the Festival turned out to be the corn maze. I'd heard of them when I lived in Tulsa and they sounded dorky to the max. But not this one. The folks in Fraser understood mazes.

Mom paid for my ticket and pointed to a huge maple a short distance from the exit. "I'll be sitting over there, in the shade," she said. "When you find your way out, I'll have lemonade waiting for you." She kissed my forehead and pushed me toward the opening. "Do you want me to time you?"

I grinned. Mom always liked to participate in my activities. She had no intention of slogging through a corn maze on a muggy summer afternoon, but she didn't mind sitting in the shade and timing my effort.

"No, thanks," I said. "This is my first maze. I'm taking my time."

I entered a green world. The corn stood an easy six feet, tall enough to tower over my not quite five-foot height. The stubble under my Adidas made me appreciate their thick rubber soles. The corridor, wide enough to allow adult shoulders easy passage, seemed to narrow down to nothing a few feet in front of me. I stood alone in a green-gold sea, and breathed in a musty, earthy scent seasoned with the bite of growing corn.

"Move along, little girl," said the ticket-taker at the entrance. "You've only got a five-minute lead before I let the next kid in."

Without looking back, I nodded and took my first steps into the maze. I didn't know green came in so many shades. Pale yellow-green tinged the stalks, while the leaves wore a deep, emerald gloss. It was the medium green of the shucks that drew my attention; it guarded the corn's budding kernels. Brown accents dotted the green; dusty tan stubble tripped my toes, while golden tassels crowned the growing ears.

It took me a minute, stumbling along the path, to pull my attention out of that green embrace and focus beyond the corn to the puzzle of the maze. The swaying stalks gave the impression of moving walls, making it harder than you might guess to see where the path branched and split. Several times, when I let my focus wander, I missed a quick turn and walked right into a wall of stalks.

I heard laughing voices ahead of me and tried to use sound as a guide. No good. Too many twists and dead-ends separated me from them.

Unhappy thrashing screamed behind me; the maze refused passage to someone. I heard the ticket-taker's soothing voice as he found the trapped participant and guided him back out. The laughter ahead faded as well, leaving me alone in a green-gold world of whispering breezes.

At least, I thought the wind made that whispery sound. When I reached the center of the maze and found the scarecrow, I learned differently.

"Welcome," he said. His voice tickled my ears like corn silks falling across bare legs. "I hoped you'd come. I want to talk to you."

The air pulsed with energy as I mopped sweat from my forehead with my shirttail. I decided I needed that lemonade Mom promised me. I'd heard dehydration could make you imagine things.

"I'm not a delusion," he said. "I have a message for you. About Lilah."

"What about her?" He had my attention now.

"You must release her from this bondage she's accepted. Find her brother. He must tell her she can move on."

"Her brother?" I asked. "Who's her brother? How do I find him?" I felt the energy flow away, leaving a lazy feel to the summer heat. "Wait! At least tell me if he's alive or dead!"

I sat down at the scarecrow's base and rested my head on my knees. It might be easier if this guy, William, was dead. I didn't have any trouble talking to ghosts. Real live humans were another matter. How was I supposed to find Lilah's brother when all I knew was that he was six when Lilah died? I didn't even know when she kicked off!

Voices drifted toward me from the incoming path. I stood, gave the scarecrow a final glower, and continued my search for the exit. A few minutes later, I joined Mom in the shade and gratefully accepted the promised lemonade. The ice cold cup, wet with condensation, reminded me of Lilah's cold grip. She needed the Light's warmth and

3

I spent the next two weeks badgering Lilah about her brother and her death. Every time I brought up either subject, her eyes brimmed with bewilderment. Lilah remembered the accident and William begging her to stay, but that was all. She couldn't tell me the year she died. She couldn't even tell me her last name! Now, I ask you, how can a girl forget her last name? Never mind. Ghosts are weird.

Finally, I dropped the subject. I enjoyed hanging out with Lilah and didn't want to annoy her into disappearing. To be honest, I didn't mind the lack of clues. I knew I should find another source of information, but hey, I tried. What did the scarecrow expect from a twelve-year-old?

"Hannah," Dad said after he clicked off from a long phone conversation, "I need you to help me straighten up the work area."

"Sure, Dad," I said, pulling a pitcher of tea out of the refrigerator. Mom and Dad had done a great job on the kitchen. After Dad made sure the room was structurally sound, Mom painted the walls a sunny yellow, stripped the hardwood floors and refinished them to a warm, glossy brown, and hung crisp, white curtains. I loved being in that kitchen. "Can Lilah help or do I have to ask her to stay away?"

Dad paled, took a swig of coffee, and said, "She can help you. Both of you should stay out of my way."

I loved that about Dad. He tried so hard to make it sound like both Lilah and I annoyed him, like he wasn't just weirded out by her.

"Why are we cleaning up? You haven't finished the dining room, have you?"

He shook his head. "Nah. Richardson just called. He's going to be in Fraser tomorrow and wants to stop by and see my progress. The walls and ceiling are done. If I pack up my tools, I ought to be able to slap a coat of paint on before he gets here."

"Cool," I said. "Can I help paint?"

Dad looked unsure.

"I won't let Lilah mess with it this time."

When we painted the kitchen, Lilah amused herself by dipping her fingers in the paint and drawing on the wall. Mom and Dad were fine as long as they thought it was me. But when we came back from a dinner of burger and fries at the local hamburger joint and found the wall covered in a sampler of the alphabet and the Pledge of Allegiance, they lost it.

"Please, Dad?" I wheedled. "She'll be good. I promise."

He sighed, wiped his face, and gave in. "Well, I could use the help." He glared at me. "Just make sure it's help I get, not hindrance."

"Yippee!" I squealed and ran to the dining room to get started cleaning up the mess.

4

It wasn't until Mr. Richardson rang the doorbell that I realized I could ask him about the house's former owners. Maybe he'd have a clue about Lilah's little brother.

The distinguished gray-haired man toured the downstairs rooms with Dad, nodding over Dad's special touches. I trailed along behind them waiting for an opening.

They stopped in the cheery kitchen while Dad poured three glasses of tea. Mr. Richardson pulled out one of the oak chairs and sat down at our round breakfast table. I took my usual seat by the window.

"Be honest with me, Barnes," he said. "Have you had any instances of, well, unexplained occurrences?"

My head shot up and I locked eyes with Dad. His lips thinned and he gave his head a slight shake. I took a glass from Dad and sipped the icy tea.

"My daughter has an imaginary friend," Dad's voice was an odd mixture of cheerful caution.

Mr. Richardson looked interested. He turned to me. "Really? Tell me about your friend." His voice sounded encouraging, but his eyes looked uneasy.

I glanced at Dad. He shrugged and nodded.

"Well," I started, "she's not imaginary. She's a ghost and her name is Lilah."

Mr. Richardson's glass slipped through his fingers and shattered on the polished wood floor. I jumped up, but Dad warned me away.

"Hannah! Stay away from the broken glass."

"I'm so sorry! Let me help clean this up." Mr. Richardson leapt to his feet, his face deathly pale.

Dad motioned him back to the chair. "Don't worry, Bill. Just let me get the big pieces. I can wipe the rest up with a rag."

Mr. Richardson sank back into his chair and turned his gaze to me.

"Why did you choose the name Lilah?" he asked.

"I didn't," I said. "It's her name; she told me. She died here when she was ten. Do you know anything about the people who used to own this house?"

Mr. Richardson kind of deflated in the chair. His shoulders slumped and he bowed his head.

"This land has been in my family since before the mansion was built." He raised his gaze and met mine. "Why do you ask?"

I sat still, frozen by an icy shaft around my heart. William. Bill. Bill Richardson. This gray-haired man could be, must be, Lilah's little brother. I bet the scarecrow sent him.

My heart hammered inside the ice. Even if Mr. Richardson was Lilah's brother, I didn't have to tell him what the scarecrow said. I could keep Lilah as my best friend. She'd waited this long to go to the Light, she could wait 'til I made friends at school. Mr. Richardson would come back to check on Dad's work another time. I didn't have to do anything right now.

My hand shook as I reached for my glass of tea. The clammy cold shocked my fingers. What was I thinking? Lilah was my best friend. She deserved better from me.

I took a deep breath and forced the question out before I could change my mind. "Did you have a sister named Lilah? Did she have an accident when you were six?"

"Hannah!" Dad glared at me. "That's enough, young lady. Go to your room. I'm terribly sorry, Bill. I don't know what's gotten into her."

I slouched to the sink, put my glass in, and turned to leave the room.

"Is Lilah here now?" Mr. Richardson's question stopped me.

Without looking at Dad, I turned to face Lilah's brother. "No. She disappeared when the doorbell rang." A flicker of grief crossed his face. "I can call her," I said, ignoring the ice in my veins. "Do you want to talk to her?"

"She must hate me," he said, his voice flat, eyes dull, "to have stayed to haunt me all these years."

"Oh, no, sir," I cried and ran across the room to grab his hand. "No, that's not it at all! She told me her death was an accident. She saw the Light. She wanted to go, but she couldn't because you begged her to stay. She loved you too much to leave you alone when you were frightened and crying."

Mr. Richardson's hand felt almost as cold as Lilah's. I heard Dad cross the room, felt his hands rest on my shoulders. "I think you should ask Lilah to join us," he said, his voice calm and deep.

I closed my eyes and thought of Lilah, sending my call through the many layers of the house's atmosphere. She answered quickly, as she always did. I watched her materialize behind Mr. Richardson.

"Hi, Lilah," I said. "William wants to talk to you."

"William?" she asked, coming to stand beside me so she could see his face.

"It's been a long time," I said. "William grew up."

She stared at him for a long moment, then turned and smiled at me. "Yes," she said, "but I can still see my little brother in his eyes."

"Is she really here?" Mr. Richardson asked.

"Yes," I replied. "She recognizes you."

A wary expression crossed his face. "Ask her our maternal grandmother's name."

"Ghosts have strange memories, sir," I said. "She might not remember."

"Matilda Owens," Lilah said, beaming.

My mouth dropped open. "You couldn't tell me your own last name, but you can remember your grandmother's whole one?"

"What did she say?" Mr. Richardson gripped my hand so hard it hurt.

"Ow!" I pulled my hand free and wiggled my fingers. "Matilda Owens. Is that right?"

"Lilah?" he said, scanning the room. "Lilah, I'm so sorry! I didn't mean to make you fall down the stairs."

I took on the role of interpreter.

"She knows that, William. She never blamed you."

"Why are you still here?" Anguish throbbed in his voice.

"Because she doesn't know how to leave. She only saw the Light once."

"But there must be a way."

"There is," I said, resisting the urge to keep the scarecrow's message to myself. "Dad, remember the corn maze at the festival?"

"Of course," he said. "What's that got to do with anything?"

"Something spoke to me in there. It told me to find Lilah's brother, to help Lilah move on." I turned to Mr. Richardson, ashamed I'd thought about not telling him. "She stayed because you begged her not to go. You have to release her. Give her permission to leave!"

His eyes widened and he glanced around the room. "Lilah, I'm sorry. I didn't mean to keep you here. I love you, Lilah. Go home. I'll see you on the other side."

I turned to look at Lilah. She smiled broadly, glowing around the edges with golden light.

"It's there," she said. "I see it. Thank you, William. I love you, too."

A warm breeze brushed my face, and Lilah disappeared.

"She's gone, sir," I said, grief pooling in my chest. "She thanked you and said she loved you, then she disappeared."

Mr. Richardson crossed his arms on the table and laid his head on them. "All these years I thought she haunted me because she hated me. I didn't know I'd trapped her."

Dad sat down across from Mr. Richardson and placed a hand on his arm. "You were just a child, Bill," he said, "and later, how could you possibly know?"

Mr. Richardson raised his head and met my eyes. "Thank you, Hannah," he said. "You've given me a priceless gift today."

"You're welcome, sir," I said, tears filling my eyes and overflowing into my voice, "and I'm happy for Lilah. I really am ... but I've lost my best friend."

Dad pulled me onto his lap and wrapped me in a warm hug. "I'm proud of you, Hannah," he whispered. "You did a great job being Lilah's best friend."

I sniffled and snuggled closer to Dad. I'd never forget Lilah, but I sure hoped my next best friend would be a real live human.

VIII

TERRORS

DEB LOGAN

AUTHOR OF *FAERY UNEXPECTED*

TERRORS

SPUN YARNS

A SEER CHRONICLES SHORT STORY

CHAPTER 1

A terror approached.

I cast my eyes down, fixing my gaze on the worn institutional tile beneath my feet, counting my heartbeats until it would be safe to look up again. The count was ingrained. A long practiced skill that no longer required my attention. Instead, my mind wandered, wondering what it would be like to unknow these denizens of the unseen world? To be a normal teen, with normal perceptions; a girl who walked this earth with no realization of what stalked her every step?

Unfortunately, that was not my life.

The count ended. I raised my eyes and glanced around quickly to reorient myself. High-ceilinged hallway, walls lined with lockers and classroom doors. Students milled around, chatted with friends, complained about their schedules. Everyone studiously avoided noticing me.

Yep. Same old invisible girl. The building might have changed, but the experience remained the same. I stepped away from the wall, pushed into the throng, and made my way to class without making eye contact with any of my peers.

I'd hoped high school would be different from middle school, that somehow, miraculously, the halls of McKinley High would be full of kids anxious to be my friends, and gloriously free of the beings that haunted my waking nightmares.

I'd been stupid of course. No such place existed.

Every single person I'd ever met considered me a freak. If truth be told, that even included my parents. And the others? The terrors? They ruled our world from the shadows, influencing our thoughts with whispered commands that were no more noticeable than the sigh of mosquito wings. Veiled suggestions of disease and despair, murmurs of treachery and disloyalty. Human souls rotted at the whim of foul creatures who fed from our life-force and lapped up our baser emotions like ice cream. No one knew of their existence, so no one guarded against their intrusions.

No one but me — and I'd learned early to hide my knowledge.

Mom and Dad had worried when my imaginary friends terrified me instead of entertaining. Other kids feared the boogieman in the closet or the monster under the bed, but were easily appeased by a nightlight or an extra bedtime story. Not me. Never me. I knew my monsters personally, recognized their reality with a sharp twist of terror in my gut.

Other kids embraced pacification, accepted that the monsters they perceived lived only in their imaginations. Not me. I learned to close my eyes, duck my head, and count the beats of my heart until the unholy creatures tired of watching me and moved on.

My parents noted my odd moments of seeming paralysis and sought psychological counseling. I developed yet another necessary life skill: I learned to lie. The doctor couldn't explain away my certain knowledge of monsters, but I could explain away my parents' concerns. Eventually, the adults in my life were appeased and I continued my uneasy existence, camouflaging myself from both my parents' concern and the notice of the creatures that stalk humanity.

I wished I understood why I could see my terrors and others couldn't. Why was I singled out to endure this curse? More than anything, I longed for a companion in this surreal world, someone to share my fears and woes ... but then, would I truly wish this ungodly knowledge on another human being? Especially a person I might learn to consider a friend? I don't know. Misery — at least mine, really would love some company.

And so I embarked on my first day of high school. Doomed to another four years of harassment at the hands of classmates who had no clue about the creatures that stalked them. Four more years of jokes about space cadets, morons, and total dweeb losers from kids who might have been my friends if only ... if only I could unknow the unseen, or my peers could have their blind eyes opened. Neither of which was going to happen.

I rolled my sturdy red and black backpack off my shoulders, claimed a seat at the back of my first class, and tried not to focus on the creature hovering just behind the teacher's left shoulder. Not an easy task; to give my attention to the solid little woman in her gray tweed skirt, pristine white blouse, and charcoal-gray cardigan, while pretending not to see the elongated, ethereal creature shrouded in a cloak that might have been made of wisps of fog. The real-as-the-desk-under-my-fingers entity with blue-tinged skin and flat black eyes who stood right behind the oblivious woman.

The noxious, evil creature that breathed terror into every day of my life bent nearly double to whisper instructions in my teacher's perfectly mundane ear. The contrast between the bright, cheerful red pepper earrings dangling from her earlobe and the scabrous three-fingered hand stroking her neck made me want to puke.

I shook my head, sucked in a deep breath, and reminded myself that giving them mind-space wasn't wise. The secret to anonymity was to control my reactions, to give no sign that I noticed when the creature moved or spoke. I'd become adept through years of practice, but only when I remained calm and uninvolved.

Controlling a shudder, I tightened my focus on my teacher as she read our morning's schedule. I couldn't afford to think about the slimy feel of their fingers as they stroked my cheek, or remember the horrible sibilant hiss of their voices as they whispered 'suggestions' in my ear. Giving brain-space to such thoughts made it so much harder to pretend they weren't there, to imagine that this was just another school day and I was just another terror-blind student.

I closed my eyes for an instant mimicking boredom, but giving myself a moment's rest from the stress of acting. If they gave out Academy Awards for avoiding terror detection, I'd be a shoo-in.

That's when it happened. The atmosphere in the class changed, became charged, and my eyes flew open. I skimmed the room looking for trouble — and found it immediately. A classmate, a boy I'd never seen before, stood paralyzed at the front of the class staring directly into the terror's dark gaze.

He looked so normal. White tee-shirt covered with an untucked blue plaid shirt; acid-washed jeans, the knees going white and nearly threadbare; scuffed black sneakers. His hair was dark and shaggy, with ragged bangs half-concealing his eyes. But those eyes weren't focused on the normal world. He was definitely studying the terror poised behind our teacher.

He inhaled deeply, pointed a trembling finger at the creature, licked his lips, and said in a shaky, yet fierce voice, "Begone, demon! I command you in the name of Michael the Hunter; leave this place and never return."

I sucked in a breath and barely kept myself from screaming a warning. Did he know what he risked? Calling its attention to his awareness? I bit my lip until I tasted blood, held my breath, and waited for his doom.

The rest of the class, teacher included, stared at him, mouths agape, and then titters of nervous giggles flared, but he took no notice. He stood his ground as the terror rushed him, stumbling back a step as the monster flowed through him and into oblivion.

The class erupted in hoots and catcalls while the teacher banged on her desk for order.

I breathed a sigh of relief as my heart rate regulated.

And then it happened.

The boy turned, pale as ice, and caught my gaze. Me. The only other person in the room who wasn't laughing, who probably looked even more drained and terrified than he did. He shrugged, nodded in acknowledgement, and turned to face his sentence: a trip to the principal's office for daring to come to school under the influence.

CHAPTER 2

I didn't see the guy again until lunch. I'd managed to keep my head down through my morning classes and had navigated the cafeteria crowd out into the late fall sunshine of the enclosed terrace. Other kids, popular kids, even not-so-popular-but-we-have-friends kids, sat around picnic tables in chattering clusters. I knew better than to join any of them. If I did, all talk would cease and an uneasy silence would descend until one-by-one the others drifted away to more congenial tables.

At least no one threw food at me anymore.

I shambled across the terrace, avoiding everyone, human and terror alike, until I came to a low retaining wall separating the flagstone patio from the landscaping. Huddled beneath a stunted aspen tree, I perched on the wall, unwrapped my sandwich and took a bite. The bread was a little soggy, but a burst of tart mustard shocked my taste buds and woke my appetite. I'd just stuffed the last bit of crust into my mouth and was reaching for my water bottle when a shadow fell across my space and two sneaker-clad feet entered my field of vision.

Glancing up, I shaded my eyes and found the new guy standing in front of me, tray in hand.

"Mind if I join you?"

I shrugged and swallowed, my throat suddenly tight. "Sure. Why not?"

"I saw you in first block," he said, settling beside me and dropping his tray on the grass beside a few scraggly primroses.

"Yeah. Well, I couldn't help but notice you." My gaze slid to his face, but skittered away before he could make eye contact. "First day at McKinley High?"

His turn to shrug. He tilted his head back and took a long swig of water. I watched the play of muscles in his neck as he swallowed, fascinated by the way his Adam's apple bobbed.

"My family just moved here. Hadn't planned on making an entrance, but, well, you know, shit happens."

I lowered my eyes again before he could catch me looking, and nodded. "Yeah. I know."

"You saw what happened, didn't you?"

Surprise knocked me into his trap. My eyes widened and I found myself staring right into his gray-eyed gaze. My pulse raced and heat suffused my face. "Well, sure. Everyone did."

He shook his head without releasing my gaze. "No they didn't, but you did. You saw it all. You saw the creature I banished."

Sweat beaded my upper lip and froze there. I didn't talk about the terrors. Not to anyone. My heart thudded harder than a bass drum and then slowed to a minimal blip. Darkness edged my vision as blood retreated to my core, leaving me dizzy and a little slow.

This wouldn't do! I needed my wits about me, clear and sharp. This guy was speaking openly about the creatures I'd been hiding from my entire life. Every cell in my being screamed, "Danger!"

I gulped a huge breath, grabbed my half empty water bottle and squeezed it like my life depended on holding tight. I don't know. Maybe it did. I wrenched my gaze from his steady gray eyes and leaned forward so that my long dark hair screened my face.

Fear screamed at me to jump and run. I should. I knew I should. He'd seen through my defenses, and my survival depended on staying invisible. I needed to get as far away from him as I could…

…but I didn't. I just sat there squeezing my water bottle and breathing like I'd run a marathon.

He sighed. Sadness embodied. Disappointment made audible.

I peeked past my hair. He stared across the terrace; an expression of melancholy loneliness etched his face. I knew that look. I wore it often myself.

Twisting off the cap of my poor, battered water bottle, I took a sip and whispered, "What's your name?"

He cocked his head and caught my gaze, a sparkle of hope lighting his eyes. "Jed Kendrick. What's yours?"

"Artie Woodward."

A slow smile curled the edges of his lips. "Nice to meet you, Artie Woodward. I've only known one other seer. What about you?"

He'd known someone else like us? Questions crowded my brain, but I just shook my head. I wanted to trust him, but it was too soon for confidences.

"Don't talk much, do you." It wasn't a question, but a statement of fact.

"No. Quiet is safer."

He nodded. "Understood. How many shrinks have they dragged you to?"

A defiant smile tipped my own lips and I sat a little straighter. "Only one. I'm a quick study."

His eyes widened and he laughed. The sound bubbled up from deep within and spilled past his lips. It winged around us, weaving a circle of camaraderie in its wake. When the outburst passed, he wiped moisture from his eyes and grinned at me. "Think you can teach me that trick? I've seen at least six shrinks and been institutionalized twice. Not that it's done anybody any good."

I reached out and touched his arm, an unprecedented familiarity. "I'm so sorry, Jed." The words were no sooner out than a terror glided toward us, undoubtedly attracted by Jed's laughter. I shrank back, pulled my hair down around my face, stared at the ground and thought invisible thoughts.

After the requisite number of heartbeats, I glanced up to find Jed staring at me. But the terror had moved on without stopping.

"How did you do that?"

I frowned, my heart still thundering from the near miss. "Do what?"

"It didn't see us. It moved right on past as if we weren't even here." He shook his head, eyes narrowed in concentration. "We need to talk, Artie. Compare notes."

My pulse spiked. I'd never had a friend. Never had anyone look at me with the mixture of awe and respect Jed was giving me. I straightened, pushed my hair behind my ears and smiled. Okay, it wasn't much of a smile, but then my smile muscles were highly under-developed.

"I'd like that."

CHAPTER 3

The rest of the day passed in a fog of contentment. I'd call it happiness, only I'd never really been happy before, so I wasn't sure what that felt like. But I was definitely more at ease, more content to be me, than I had ever been. The other kids in my classes even seemed kinder. No one spoke to me or smiled at me or gave any indication of being aware of my presence, but neither did they call me names, bump books out of my arms, or do any of the other myriad little annoyances that normally made my school days hell. All in all, it was an auspicious start to the school year.

I should have known it couldn't last.

The late afternoon sun blinded me as I stepped through the side door that led to the parking area where my bus would be waiting. Against my long-ingrained habit, my hair was tucked behind my ears and my posture erect. My day had given me a false sense of security, and I walked with a little bounce in my step. The air smelled of fresh cut grass, hot pavement, and car exhaust. White puffy clouds floated overhead, pushed along by a light, refreshing breeze. In short, it was a beautiful fall day and I gloried in it.

"Hey, freak!" A male voice called, yanking me from my pleasant reverie. "Where do you think you're going?"

I whirled, knowing the guy meant me. After all, I'd been the resident freak for as long as I could remember, but I was wrong. Someone else had stolen my limelight. Jed stood in a rough circle of athletic-looking boys. I hadn't paid much attention to his physique earlier, but he looked tall, gangly and under-fed compared to the jocks surrounding him.

As I stood rooted to the sidewalk, one of the boys pushed Jed, while another pulled his backpack from his arms and tossed it away.

"Who do you think you are, screw-up?" The speaker swaggered forward, ruffled Jed's hair before shoving him backward.

Jed stumbled and fell against two of the other guys, who pushed him back toward their leader.

The guy strutted around Jed, measuring his lack of reaction. "What's wrong, freak? No girls around to impress? I think you need a lesson in how things are done around here." He turned to his comrades. "What do you think? Should we teach this freak some manners?"

The other guys laughed, a dark growling sound, and shouted their agreement.

Things were about to get uglier than they knew. Several terrors drifted in their direction. My heart skipped a beat. I glanced at the bus; my escape route was filling up. The driver would close the doors and leave soon. But Jed was in trouble. My only friend in the world needed help. But what could I do? I mean, until his arrival, I'd been the butt of all the jokes. The one bullied by guys like those surrounding Jed. I had no power. No way to protect him.

Besides, I barely knew him.

And as for the terrors, he'd banished one this morning — something I'd never managed. He could do it again. Of course, that was assuming the jocks didn't beat him to a pulp for mouthing off while they were taunting him.

I chewed my lip, indecision eating at my gut. I had to choose. Now. The moment would pass and my chance would be lost forever. Which would it be? Safety, or the possibility of a friend?

No contest. I'd never had a friend before.

With a quick wave to the bus driver, I ran toward the group of guys, snagged Jed's backpack, and elbowed my way to his side. Grabbing his arm, I thrust the pack against his chest where he clutched it by instinct, then prodded him toward the bus.

"What are you doing? Our bus is leaving! You can mess around with your friends tomorrow. Right now we have to get home. Mom is waiting."

Surprise and inane chatter worked in my favor. The bullies fell back for a second, glancing at each other. I took advantage of their confusion to propel Jed to the bus. We leapt up the steps and inside, just as the driver closed the doors.

"Take a seat, you two," he said, shaking his head. "And be on time tomorrow."

I ducked my head, shielding myself from his view with my hair and mumbled, "Yes, sir." Then dragged Jed to the back of the bus where we settled in the very last row.

"Thanks," he whispered. He dropped his backpack between his feet and stared out the window at the gang of guys who were still watching the bus, shaking their heads. He ran his hands through his hair and slotted a sideways glance in my direction. "Do you have any idea where this bus is going?"

I tucked my hair behind my ears and grinned. "Yep. It'll drop us off about three blocks from my house. You got a problem with that?"

A wicked smile curved his mouth and lit his eyes. "Nope. I've never been rescued by a girl and then whisked away to her house before." He winked at me. "Kinda cool, ya know?"

I giggled and reached to tug my hair across my heated face, but Jed caught my fingers.

"Don't," he said quietly. "You don't need to hide from me." He pulled my hand to his lips and gazed into my eyes as he kissed my knuckles.

Shock widened my eyes while my heart pounded so loud I was surprised he didn't hear it. Totally speechless, I just sat there staring into his gray eyes.

He smirked, released my hand and held out his own. "Friends?"

My knuckles still tingling from the warmth of his lips, I placed my hand in his and shook. "Friends."

He relaxed and stared out the window for a few seconds, then glanced back at me. "Back there," he said, jerking his chin to indicate the direction of the school, "I didn't know you could string that many words together. What came over you?"

My cheeks flushed again, but I resisted the urge to duck behind my hair and shrugged instead. "Dunno. Looked like you were in trouble, and, well ... they were just guys."

To anyone else, that statement would've sounded stupid, maybe even moronic, but Jed understood. He nodded. "Yeah. I know. I wouldn't have enjoyed getting beat up, but they weren't ...well, you know."

I nodded. I did. We definitely needed to talk, but this wasn't the place. We were unguarded, exposed. I rarely spoke of the terrors — who would listen? — but I certainly didn't talk about them on a public school bus surrounded by dozens of kids who were clueless to their danger.

We settled into a companionable silence while the bus rumbled on, stopping every few blocks to disgorge students. Finally, when there were less than a dozen of us still seated, the big yellow vehicle rolled to a halt at my designated stop. I nudged Jed, stood, and shuffled down the narrow aisle following two other kids. When we hit the pavement, the other two waved to their friends who still sat on the bus and wandered off to the right. I pulled Jed left.

"Alone at last," he quipped as the bus pulled away from the corner.

I rolled my eyes. "Cute."

"Nice! She thinks I'm cute."

My face flamed again, but I couldn't help smiling. Jed had that effect on me.

"You're weird," I said after a few steps along the shaded sidewalk. We strolled through a quiet residential neighborhood. Freshly mown lawns, neatly tended flower beds with the last remaining blooms of summer nodding in a gentle breeze, tall trees lined the street guarding the sidewalk from the late afternoon sun. All in all, a pleasant day … especially since there wasn't a terror in sight. I breathed a sigh of relief and quirked a glance at Jed. "How come you're so friendly and, well, happy? Sounds like you've had it even tougher than me."

"Cool. She thinks I'm cute AND friendly." He rubbed his hands together and grinned. "This is going better than expected!"

I couldn't help it, my eyes rolled again and a groan escaped my lips. He really was too much.

His expression grew serious and the light left his eyes. A fierce determination hardened his face. "I act happy and friendly because how I feel is my choice. I refuse to let them control me, control my life." The ferocity faded and he smiled a little sadly. "I can't change what I see, but I can choose how I react. Just like you obviously chose what to say to the shrink to reassure your parents."

I nodded. "We can teach each other a lot."

"That's my game plan," he said, another grin lighting his features. "Plus, it's nice to finally have someone who understands."

"Tell me about it. Seeing them makes you lonely."

"Yeah. You can't talk about them or you end up in the loony bin."

"But it's hard to talk about normal stuff, 'cause it all seems so trivial and unimportant compared to, well, them."

He nodded. "That about sums it up."

We turned a corner and I pointed ahead. "That's my house. The yellow one with the white picket fence."

He stopped dead in his tracks, stared at my house, glanced sideways at me, and then laughed out loud. Laughed so hard he had to shuffle a few steps to lean against a maple tree while he caught his breath.

"What?" I asked, annoyance creeping into the word.

"I might have known," he said, wiping his eyes on the sleeve of his sweatshirt. "I meet the most un-normal girl in the world and she lives in a totally stereotypical suburban house, complete with white picket fence." He waved at the neighborhood in general and my house in particular. "I mean, really? Can you get any more Apple-Pie-American than this?"

I stared around me, absorbing the landscape, drinking down the scene I'd experienced every day of my life — and saw it with new eyes. Jed was right. This street, this neighborhood, my home; each was so normal, so stereotypically American upper-middle-class, and yet here I stood, as totally and completely *not* normal as it was possible to imagine. No wonder I'd never truly belonged here. A slow smile tugged at my lips. I hadn't realized how badly I'd needed someone like Jed in my life. Someone who could challenge my perceptions, make me take stock of my blind acceptance of other people's norm. Other people's. Never mine. Maybe Jed and I could define our own version of normality.

Slipping my hand into the crook of his arm, I drew him toward my house. "Come on. We've got things to discuss, notes to compare, and plans to make."

He grinned and performed a courtly bow. "Your wish is my command, milady."

CHAPTER 4

Mom met us at the front door. She tried to hide the look of shocked amazement that widened her eyes, rounded her mouth, and made her look even younger than me, but failed miserably. She was so surprised to see me with a boy at my side that she actually stammered.

Well. Really. Who could blame her? I'd never, ever brought a friend home. Not once.

"Er … uhm … I-I'm Estelle, Artie's mother," she finally managed to blurt, holding the screen door open, but blocking entry with her body.

"It's okay, Mom," I said, taking the door from her and nudging her to one side. No go. She was firmly planted and totally oblivious. I sighed. "This is Jed. He knows I don't have any friends, so you can relax."

Jed smiled his charming smile and stuck out his hand. "A pleasure to meet you, Mrs. Woodward. Artie and I met at school. My family just moved here, so she's showing me around."

"Er … uhm …N-nice to meet you, Jed." Mom gave me a sidelong look, but her color was returning to normal.

"Mom. Chill. Is it okay if we come inside?"

Finally the penny dropped. Mom's cheeks reddened and she backed away from the door into the front hall. "Of course! How silly of me. Standing here blocking the door. Come right in, Jed. What did you say your last name was?"

Jed stepped inside and I slipped past Mom to drop my backpack on a chair in the living room.

"Kendrick, Jed Kendrick. My folks just moved here from upstate New York. Dad's the new pastor at the Evangelical church."

I froze where I stood, jaw hanging open in shock. My new friend, the only other person I'd ever known who could see the terrors was a preacher's kid? I forced my mouth closed and stared into those guile-less gray eyes. Made sense in a way. Who else would have the authority to command the unholy?

"Well, how nice." Mom gave me a sidelong look, but her color was returning to normal. "I'll look forward to meeting your parents. Are you and Artie in the same grade?"

"Yes, ma'am," he said. "We met in first period and then found each other again at lunch time."

Okay. Enough chit-chat with the parental unit. Time to get down to work.

"I'm going to show Jed the park, Mom," I said, grabbing Jed's sleeve and dragging him down the hall toward the back door. "Would you mind driving him home before dinner? He got on the wrong bus by mistake."

"Of course. I'll be happy to drive you home. Do you need to call your parents and let them know where you are?"

He planted his feet to stop me from dragging him further from Mom and pulled a cell phone from his back pocket. "Already taken care of," he said with a grin. "If it's inconvenient for you, I'm sure Mom could use a break from unpacking, though it might take her a while to figure out how to get here."

Mom laughed. "It's no bother. Let's not add to your mother's stress. You two enjoy your walk to the park. I'll drive Jed home whenever he's ready."

I jerked my head toward the back of the house with a meaningful glance at Jed and waved over my shoulder to Mom. "See you later."

Jed followed me through the kitchen. I paused long enough to grab two apples and a couple of bottles of water from the fridge before leading him out the back door, across a brick patio, over the well-manicured back lawn, and through a thin spot in the evergreen hedge that bounded the rear of our yard. We emerged in an empty lot on the next street over.

"Come on," I said. "The park is just down this block."

Jed brushed a twig from his sleeve and gave me a quizzical look. "Why are we going to a park?"

I squinted both directions down the street and sprinted across to the sidewalk on the other side. "Best place I've found to think. I sit on the little kids' merry-go-round and spin slowly. Not fast enough to make me dizzy, but enough that I can keep a watch in all directions. They can't just appear out of the ground, so I have plenty of warning if one is coming."

I tossed him a bottle of water and an apple and then took a bite of my own. The flavor burst on my tongue, sweet and tart at the same time. Just the way I liked. I chewed and swallowed, twisted off the cap and took a swig of water, and then shrugged. "I figure what we need to discuss, we don't want overheard ... by anyone. The merry-go-round will give us plenty of privacy."

He nodded, following my example with the fruit, though I've got to say, the guy took huge bites. Looked like half the apple disappeared in his first mouthful. Once he'd tossed what little was left of the core, he continued the conversation as though we hadn't just taken a snack break. "Good thinking. Doors and walls might protect us from human ears, but you never know when one of them is going to glide right through brick or wood."

"I know," I agreed. "It's like the laws of physics don't apply. But I've never seen one rise out of the ground, have you?"

He considered that for a moment, took another swig of water, and said, "Nope. Can't say I have. Your merry-go-round sounds like as safe a place for a talk as we're likely to find."

I nodded and turned into a fenced walkway between houses, tugging Jed's sleeve to steer him along. We had a lot to discuss, important stuff, and I wouldn't feel at ease until we made it to the merry-go-round.

CHAPTER 5

We emerged in a small, rectangular, neighborhood park, bounded on all sides by houses, with two narrow walkways leading in and one street that dead-ended into a short side. The majority of the land was flat and grassy, perfect for a game of Frisbee or tossing a ball around. Play equipment nestled at the end nearest the street access, and a tall stand of pines shaded an area of picnic tables. Jed and I walked side-by-side to the merry-go-round. The park was deserted except for the two of us.

Frankly, it didn't see much use during the week. Even after school, most of the kids were still at day-care, waiting for their parents to evacuate their cubicle jungles and pick them up for the evening. I was luckier than most. Dad worked in the next city over — he was an architect and the prestigious firm that paid our bills required a better address than our little cow-town could provide, but Mom was self-employed and worked from home. So I'd never had to do the day-care thing.

Of course, Mom's career choice may have been influenced by the decidedly weird daughter she and Dad had spawned. I shuddered and veered away from that thought.

Jed and I settled on the circular piece of play equipment. We leaned against the handrails facing each other. What I couldn't see at any given moment, Jed could. Each of us dangled one foot over the edge, giving a gentle push every now and then to keep the thing gliding squeakily on its axis.

"So," Jed said, "where do you want to begin?"

I shrugged and traced the raised pattern of the steel under my fingers. "Dunno. Never really talked about them before."

"I hear ya. Let's start at the beginning. How long have you been seeing them?"

My head snapped up and I met his gray-eyed gaze with wide eyes. "Seriously? Can you remember a time when you couldn't see them?" He just stared at me, waiting for me to answer the question. I sighed and studied the lay of the land over his shoulder. "I've always seen them. At least, I think I have. I mean, who remembers what they saw as a baby?" Satisfied that the park remained empty, I met his gaze again. "What about you?"

"I started seeing them when I was eight. I remember, because it was right after my twin brother died."

A chill ran icy fingers down my back and I shivered involuntarily.

"Oh, wow. You had a twin. I'm so sorry." I wanted to ask what happened to his brother, but bit back the question. *Don't push.*

"Yeah. I thought the first one was Jerry's ghost, but even though he was a little ... odd, he was never mean. He'd never have wanted to scare me out of my wits."

I nodded, but kept still, hoping he'd tell me more.

"That first sighting added to Jerry's death sent me straight to a shrink. I'm sure you know what that's like." He shook his head, gulped some water, and looked at me slant-wise. "Now that I'm older and have had lots of time to think about it, I think Jerry was like you. I think he could see them from birth. I'm pretty sure he spent a lot of his short life protecting me and Mom and Dad."

He propped the nearly empty water bottle in the crook of his knee and stared at his hands, flexing his fingers as though getting ready to play a piano recital. I didn't say a word. I'd already done more talking today than I usually did in a month, but more importantly, I could feel Jed's stress. He was testing the ether; testing the bond between us, deciding how much weight it would hold. Deciding if I was trustworthy enough to hear what he hadn't said yet. What he still needed to say.

Silence stretched between us. I stared over his shoulder, remaining vigilant while he made his choices. A deep sigh pulled my attention back to his face. He continued to stare at his hands, splayed now against the faded blue of well-worn jeans.

"I was with him when he died," he said, his voice so quiet I strained to hear him over the slight squeaking of the merry-go-round. "We'd been playing in the backyard when he had one of his funny spells. He went all rigid, ducking his head and muttering a string of unintelligible words while he pushed me to the ground and held me there. He had one hand over my mouth and nose. I couldn't breathe, but I knew Jerry wouldn't hurt me, so I went completely limp and held my breath, waiting for his fit to pass. Only it didn't.

"Oh, he released me, but while I caught my breath, something picked him up and tossed him aside like a rag doll. He landed hard against a tree, cracked his skull. That's what did it. That's what killed him.

"I ran to him, right through something so cold it made my fingers cramp and my lungs seize, but I didn't care. I had to get to Jerry. I was screaming like a banshee and Mom and Dad came running to see what was wrong. Dad froze, staring at us like he'd seen a ghost, but Mom ran for the phone and called 9-1-1. It didn't matter. They were too late. Everyone was too late."

He fisted his hands and looked up into my eyes. Grief and anger and terror blazed in that gaze.

"I got to him first. I grabbed his hand and shouted his name over and over again. He opened his eyes once, squeezed my fingers, and said, 'You'll have to protect them now. You can do it. Michael will help.' And then he died. Just like that, my twin was gone. My best friend. My womb-mate. The person I loved more than any other left me crying in the backyard under a maple tree."

His eyes misted with tears, and he swiped them away with short, choppy strokes. "But that wasn't all. As he breathed his last, something happened. Something transferred from Jerry to me. I don't know if I inhaled it, or it passed skin-to-skin through our clasped hands, but suddenly I could see it. Could see the creature that had killed my brother, and something more. I saw Michael. The archangel. The hunter. The destroyer of those monsters.

"But just like everyone else that afternoon, Michael was too late to save Jerry. Was almost too late to save me. When I started yelling about angels and demons, Dad snapped out of it and grabbed me. I think he thought he'd lost both his sons."

"What about the terror?" I whispered.

He sighed, a weary, this-world-is-too-heavy-for-me exhalation. "I don't know. Dad was sobbing and praying and clutching me like he'd never let go. When I finally wriggled loose and looked around, the thing had vanished."

I leaned forward and caught his hand, noting the cool slickness of the not-quite-tears on his fingers. "Thank you for telling me," I said. "You're not alone anymore. Neither of us is. I can't replace Jerry." I swallowed a lump that threatened to cut off my words, and sucked in a deep breath. "Wouldn't want to if I could. But between us, we can figure this out."

He looked up from our clasped hands and frowned. "Figure what out?"

"This. Us. There's got to be a reason we can see them. Must be something we're supposed to do with our abilities." I scrambled off the merry-go-round and paced back and forth. "I've thought about this for a while now, but with no one to talk to, no one to bounce ideas off of, I've been stuck. Why me? Why can I see them when no one else can? What's the purpose? Did God just wake up one morning and think, 'Gee, I think I'll torture Artie. Make everyone think she's paranoid and delusional. It'll be a great laugh!'

"I don't think so. I think I'm supposed to fight them, but I haven't known how."

I stopped pacing, planted my hands on my hips and gave him a daring look. "But I'm not alone anymore." I nodded to him, purpose blazing in my heart. "Today I found a teammate."

He sat still as stone for another moment, staring deep into my eyes. Then he unfolded from the play equipment and held out his hand. "Woodward and Kendrick," he said when I placed my palm against his. "Partners."

We shook on it, and then sat down side by side.

"You're right. There's more to this than God torturing teens. I'll ask Michael about it."

I slanted him a look. "So who is this Michael guy? Is he really an archangel?"

Jed shrugged. "Couldn't prove it by me. I've only seen him the once with waking eyes. Most of the time, he visits my dreams and explains stuff to me."

"Uh-huh."

He laid back, his head toward the center of the circular play disc, feet planted firmly on the ground. "Hey, he's no weirder than any of the other stuff we see, and he's actually helped me. Whatever he is, he's definitely not one of them."

I nodded, my thoughts racing. "Cool. So this partnership may have divine assistance. I can live with that." I turned my next words over in my brain, examining them carefully before releasing them into the world. "Maybe his existence even proves my theory. I mean, if we're supposed to fight monsters, isn't it reasonable that God would provide a guide? A teacher of some kind? Otherwise, we'd end up like your brother — dead before we could even get started."

Jed covered his eyes with his forearm, but remained silent. I replayed my last words in my head and wanted to smack myself.

"I'm sorry, Jed," I whispered. "That was an incredibly insensitive thing to say." I shoved the ground with my foot, giving the merry-go-round another spurt of movement, and surveyed the perimeter. Anything was better than looking at the new friend I'd probably just alienated.

Jed sat up, his action adding to our momentum, and placed a finger on my cheek, turning my face in his direction. "Don't apologize for being right. Jerry didn't stand a chance. He was too young to take an active role. Michael shouldn't have let him; should have taught him to hide until he was older and stronger."

He dropped his hands and jumped to the ground. "Hell. I don't know, maybe he did. Maybe Jerry wouldn't listen. Maybe Jerry didn't have the knack for hiding. Whatever. He's gone and we're here. And we're going to need all the help we can get."

I released the breath I'd been holding since Jed started talking and nodded. We were still a team. I hadn't wrecked our fledgling alliance … yet.

"Who knows?" Jed continued, pacing around the merry-go-round. "Maybe now that we've found each other, Michael will join us when I'm awake."

He stopped, staring into space like he'd been paralyzed. The play equipment's momentum carried me away from him and I searched the area wildly. No terrors. What had happened to him?

I jumped off the platform and ran to him, grabbing a wrist to check his pulse. "Jed! What's wrong?"

A slow smile spread across his face as he focused his attention on me. I dropped his wrist and waited.

"Yes. It all fits," he said, grasping my upper arms. "You're the reason we're here. Dad didn't ask for this transfer. A letter simply arrived offering him the position. He was going to turn it down. Said he was happy where he was. Then he ... he had this dream ... and suddenly nothing would do but that we move across country to this unheard-of-place in Colorado."

He eased his grip on my arms, but didn't release me. I bent my elbows and clasped his arms as well, locking us together. Into a single unit.

"And who do I meet on my very first day of school," he continued, "in my very first class? You. The only other seer I've ever found." He nodded, his grin broadening. "You see? We were *meant* to find each other."

He stood still as stone for another moment, staring deep into my eyes.

A rushing sound, like wind through a canyon distracted us, bringing with it a noxious odor — bloody and sickly sweet and somehow oily. We released each other and stepped apart, glancing around in panic.

CHAPTER 6

Not one, but three terrors drifted out of the pines and came straight for us.

We'd lowered our guard, forgotten the danger, and now we would pay the price.

I stumbled back a step, grabbed Jed's hand for support, and ducked my head to fall into my trance. Nothing happened.

"Not this time, little girl," the tallest terror whispered, its voice harsh and raspy. "This time we see you."

They glided closer, gnarled, three-fingered, blue-tinged hands outstretched.

My pulse pounded in my ears. Horror clutched my heart. I couldn't concentrate, couldn't find my count. I was visible. They saw me. The terrors would destroy me.

Jed's fingers tightened around mine. He flung out his other hand and shouted, "Begone, foul demons! I command you in the name of Michael the Hunter; leave this place and never return."

The terrors laughed. Horrible scratching noises, like metal gears scraping without benefit of oil.

Jed and I stared at each other. Our powers were useless. We could see our enemy, and they could see us. Fear kindled in his gaze, while it pressed against my throat, strangling me. I grabbed Jed's free hand, stared deep into his eyes, Locked myself in his gaze. My partner. The only person who had ever understood me and accepted me as I was. The one who recognized me, who knew I wasn't crazy.

And suddenly, I understood: I could do anything with Jed by my side.

I ignored the terrors and their putrid smell. Instead, I breathed in the scents of the park, of my natural world, drying grass, pine resin, Jed's musky sweat, and expelled the deep-seated terror of the creatures' unnatural presence; exhaled the panic that had dogged my every breath for every other moment of my life.

Calm rolled across my soul, spreading a soothing balm through my body. My death-grip on Jed relaxed and I smiled. I'd been alone my whole life, but I wasn't alone now. Not when it counted. If death claimed me, I would meet it with a friend.

My new tranquility communicated itself to Jed. An answering light kindled in his eyes. He grinned, squeezed my hands gently, and leaning forward, kissed my forehead. We steadied each other for another heartbeat, and then turned to face the enemy.

"Leave," Jed said, his voice strong and firm. "You have no place in our world."

"Leave," I echoed. "You don't terrify me anymore. I unname you and unmake you. You are no longer terrors."

"Leave," we commanded, united in purpose, in heart, in our very souls.

The creatures stopped. Their arms dropped to their sides, their heads bowed, and then with a wail like the banshee of legend, they faded into oblivion.

Jed pulled me into his arms and squeezed until my ribs hurt, but I didn't complain. I did experience an instant of dizzy unreality — no one but Mom or Dad had ever hugged me before — but the weirdness passed. This wasn't just anyone; this was Jed. My friend.

I settled into his arms, rested my head against his chest, and listened to the steady beat of his heart. We'd done it. My friend and I had conquered terror, and the aftermath felt amazing. Exhilaration mixed with total exhaustion. Every muscle in my body trembled. If Jed hadn't been holding me up, I'd have been a puddle in the drying grass.

After a bit, we parted and, fingers still interlocked, moved to sit again on the merry-go-round.

"We've got work to do," Jed said, stroking the back of my hand with his thumb.

"Agreed." I studied Jed. What a difference a day made. This morning I'd been alone in a new school. A freak. Shunned by my world. Now I was … what?

Jed smiled at me, a slow lifting of the corners of his mouth coupled with a sparkle in his gray eyes.

I smiled back, and this time it was real, spontaneous. No longer a forced expression of an emotion I didn't understand. Happy. Content. I was both, for the first time in my life. Thanks to Jed, terrors no longer terrified me.

We'd been outcasts most of our lives, but we'd found each other and discovered our purpose. We were soul mates, but not in a mushy romantic way. Two halves of a single whole. Together, we could make a difference.

We would find a safe place to study — maybe the hallowed ground of Reverend Kendrick's church would offer us sanctuary — and we would learn all that Michael could teach.

And someday, when we were ready, we would banish terrors from the face of our good earth. Together.

IX

TO HAVE...AND TO HOLD

DEB LOGAN

AUTHOR OF *FAERY UNEXPECTED*

To Have...
And To Hold

SPUN YARNS
A *Seer Chronicles* Short Story

PROLOGUE

My name is Artie Woodward, and I'm the happiest girl alive.

Wow! I never thought that phrase would apply to me, especially when I was a kid. I mean, I'm a seer. I see things normal people don't, things they couldn't see, even if they wanted to, which no one in their right mind would. I mean, even I don't want to see the terrors, but I don't have a choice. I was born with this strange ability to see the unseen, to know the unknowable.

I thought I was alone. Thought I'd spend my whole life alone.

Sure, my mom and dad loved me, but even they thought I was weird. They worried about me constantly and dragged me to more shrinks than I care to remember. None of them helped. After all, they all thought I was imagining things. Except I wasn't. So I learned to hide.

I became adept at hiding. I hid my knowledge from my parents. I tried desperately to hide my weirdness from the kids at school. But most importantly, I hid the fact that I could see them, that I knew they existed, from the terrors themselves. And as long as I hid, I stayed safe.

Lonely, but safe.

So how did I grow up to be the happiest girl in the world? How did my life change from hidden and lonely to fulfilled and glowing with contentment?

Jed Kendrick found me.

We recognized each other, and our loneliness ended. We were both seers, and on our first day at McKinley High we became a team, but that's another story. Suffice it to say we've fought terrors together for nearly six years and have developed an unshakable bond.

And along the way, we fell in love.

And now, I'm the happiest girl in the world because in late September I'll become Jed Kendrick's wife, and he'll become Artie Woodward's husband. The Woodward-Kendrick team will be official in the eyes of the world.

But first, we had to make a pilgrimage to Ireland. Jed's grannie insisted.

1

On a beautiful summer day in mid-August, Grannie O'Toole met us at the Dublin airport. We emerged from a sea of people to find her waiting for us, an island of calm in the form of a small, lean woman with frizzy gray hair that Jed assured me had once been curly and deep red.

"Jedidiah Kendrick," she called, opening her arms and stepping toward us with lively impatience. "Come and give your grannie a hug!"

Jed obeyed without hesitation, wrapping the little woman in his long arms and lifting her right off the airport's tiled floor.

"It's so good to see you, Grannie," he said as he placed her gently back on her feet. He grinned like a loon as he released her and angled his body to include me in their conversation. "Grannie, this is Artie, the love of my life." His eyes twinkled as he reached for my hand. "Artie, this is Grannie O'Toole, the best Irish grannie a boy could ever dream of."

Grannie O'Toole reached for my other hand while still maintaining a firm grasp on my husband-to-be. As our fingers met, a circle of energy clicked into place. Suddenly, the three of us really were an island in a sea of people. The pervasive buzz of voices around us muffled, people flowed past us without seeming to notice our existence. We were a rock in the stream that they avoided without awareness.

Grannie nodded. "I wondered," she said, her voice calm and quiet. "I knew Jeremiah was a seer from the moment of his birth." She turned her faded hazel eyes on Jed. "You held the potential, but Jerry held the power. Even here in Ireland, I felt the change when he died and you accepted the mantle."

Jed startled. I felt the slight pull of his fingers on mine, saw his gaze tighten and focus as he stared at his grandmother. "You knew?" he asked. The question held a tinge of accusation, and I heard his unvoiced thought. *You knew what I was and you didn't bother to explain? Left me to discover everything for myself?*

"Aye, child. I knew."

Jed tried to withdraw, to pull away from this woman he thought he'd known, but she held him. She must've been stronger than she looked, for my big, strong man failed to break the continuity of our circle.

"Be at peace, my boy," she said in that calm, quiet voice. "It's part of the curse of our blood that we cannot acknowledge one another until our power is fully developed. I could no more help you to find your way than you'll be able to help the next seer in our line." She turned her attention to me. "But you," she said, "you're a surprise. I wondered about the young woman our Jed had fallen for, worried that she might be Fae. 'Tis why I insisted on meeting before the wedding. If you were less than human, I needed to ensure you revealed your true nature before my boy took vows that would bind him to you for eternity."

I was the one who startled now. Every instinct I owned urged me to hide, as I'd done so effectively before Jed and I found each other, but I willed myself to stillness and looked Grannie O'Toole straight in the eye. She met my gaze without flinching and I read nothing but sincerity and warmth.

"Fae?" I asked. "As in fairies? Are fairies real then?"

Her eyes widened. "Of course they are," she exclaimed. "Are you telling me you've attained the years necessary to contemplate marriage without ever encountering the Fae?"

My jaw dropped and I turned my gaze on Jed. "Is she saying that the terrors are really fairies?" I asked. "I always thought fairies were little winged creatures who danced in mushroom circles and slept on flower petals."

Grannie guffawed, there was no other word for the snort of laughter than emanated from her small body, pulling my attention back to her.

"Sorry," she said. "I can see we've a lot of catching up to do. Let's break this circle and speak of normal things until I get you home. My house is warded, strongly warded, against the Fae. We won't need physical contact there in order to have a private conversation."

And so saying, she broke our contact, as easily as if we'd both been toddlers. While she'd been able to hold me like a vise, I had no more luck clutching her fingers than I would've had capturing a moonbeam. I had the feeling Grannie O'Toole had a lot to teach me.

Thank all that is holy, I was absolutely correct.

2

G rannie O'Toole's house was a charming cottage in the Dublin suburb of Shankill. With its whitewashed walls, jewel-red front door, overhanging thatch roof, and blue window boxes filled to overflowing with red chrysanthemums and white baby's breath, the cottage was everything I'd ever imagined of finding in Ireland. The only thing missing from my perfect vision was its setting. Instead of being surrounded by acres of rolling hills in brilliant shades of emerald green, the little cottage was hemmed in on two sides by neighboring homes and in front by a heavily trafficked cobblestone street.

The three of us piled out of the cab Grannie had hired at the airport and soon stood with our meager baggage — a backpack and duffle for Jed and a carry-on size rolling case for me — in the street in front of Grannie's cottage. As we approached that red door, I felt a slight resistance, as if the house pushed me back to the street. An overwhelming urge to walk past swept over me. I stopped, glanced around, and noted a puzzled expression on Jed's face. He felt it too.

Grannie smiled, placed one hand on the door, then held her other out to us. "Touch my hand," she encouraged. "Just a finger will do."

When both of us complied, she nodded and said, "Jedidiah Kendrick and Artemis Woodward are welcome in my home. Please, come in."

The resistance vanished, as did my need to walk away.

Of course. Grannie had mentioned that her home was warded against the Fae. Evidently those wards worked against seer blood as well, and Jed and I had now been invited inside their protective shield. I shivered, but held my questions until we were safely inside those innocent looking whitewashed walls.

"I wasn't sure if you'd want to share a room," Grannie said breezily as she led us into a comfortable, lived-in front room. A well-worn sofa upholstered in a tweed fabric the green of budding leaves and heaped with throw pillows in bright jewel tones rested before an authentic fireplace complete with stone hearth and a planed log mantle. Two overstuffed chairs in matching upholstery provided additional seating. "But seeing as you're only handfast and not actually married, I've given you each your own space." She grinned. "That, and I didn't want to give up my own room!"

She led us through a cheery kitchen with white pine cabinets and pretty lace curtains, and up a narrow staircase. I hadn't expected a second floor and found myself on a compact landing between two doors leading to identical small rooms tucked under the cottage's eaves.

"These were originally children's quarters," she explained as Jed and I separated and stowed our luggage in the windowless cells. Each was furnished with a single twin bed covered with a colorful quilt, an old-fashioned washstand complete with basin and ewer, and a drawer unit cunningly built into space beneath the eaves. The sloping roof meant Jed could barely stand in his room, and only near the door. "They're tight, but you'll not be spending much time in them."

We trooped back down the stairs and Grannie completed the tour with a glimpse of her bedroom, spacious and sunny compared to the upstairs rooms, and a shared bath complete with old-fashioned claw-footed tub.

At her insistence, Jed and I settled in the front room while she bustled around the kitchen making tea. Once we were all possessed of steaming cups with a rose patterned plate of shortbread cookies resting on the pine coffee table, Grannie returned to the subject of seers and fairies.

"So," she said, settling into the depths of her overstuffed chair. "Tell me about your experience of the Fae. What did you call them? Terrors?"

I glanced at Jed, waited for him to take the lead.

"That's what Artie named them," he said with a nod in my direction. "She's seen them since birth. Like you said in the airport, I didn't see them until Jerry died. He was the seer, I was just his twin."

Grannie turned to me, her blue eyes seeming to pierce my very soul. "I know Jed's bloodline," she said, "know he inherited his ability from my line, but what about you, young woman? How do you come to see the Fae?"

Grannie's scrutiny unnerved me. Without thinking, I angled my head so that my long dark hair shadowed my face, closed my eyes, and concentrated on hiding, on being invisible. Stillness settled over the room and as I counted my heartbeats, I calmed.

Until Jed placed a hand on my arm.

"It's okay, Artie," he said, his tone soothing and soft. The kind of voice he'd use with a startled horse or a frightened child. "You're safe here. Grannie's no threat. She's family. No need to hide."

I opened my eyes and straightened, grasping Jed's hand and meeting his gaze. I nodded. "You're right," I said and turned my attention back to Grannie. "I'm sorry. You startled me and I reacted without thinking."

She stared at me a moment longer, then said with a sigh, "You've a powerful defense, Artie. Almost I lost sight of you ... and me a seer. I could feel the power coalescing around you, cloaking you, and even so I nearly lost the knowledge of you."

She glanced around the room, and following her gaze I glimpsed pale runes shimmering above windows and doors and centered on walls before they winked out of sight.

"If it weren't for my wards, I think you'd have succeeded in disappearing from my mind completely." She shuddered and took a sip of tea from the rose patterned cup she still held. After a moment, she continued. "Well, I think we've established you've seer blood. From a very potent bloodline. An ancient bloodline."

"More ancient than ours?" Jed asked.

She nodded. "I've never known a seer with that kind of power, but there are legends..." Another pause while she sipped more tea. I could almost see the thoughts tumbling through her mind as she considered.

"Legends?" Jed prompted when the pause grew lengthy.

"What?" Grannie startled, her eyes widening, as though she'd forgotten our presence. "Oh. Yes. Legends. Among the Fae, there's a legend of a pair who will defend the human race, who will banish the Fae to another realm. Make it impossible for them to feed off our fears and baser instincts. A pair who will free us from them for eternity."

She studied us over the rim of her cup. "I wonder..."

I frowned. "That can't be us. I mean, if we were destined for something, wouldn't someone know? Wouldn't *we* know? And how do you know about Fae legends anyway?"

"It's my family's," she gestured at Jed with the cookie she'd just plucked from the plate, "*our* family's business to know. We've spied on the Fae for years, kept journals of all we've learned. Journals I'll be handing on to you now, my boy. Now that I've seen for myself that you've the sight and your intended is the right sort as well."

Biting into the shortbread cookie, she chewed, swallowed, and took another sip of tea. "The best thing the Fae could do, if they felt the time of the legend approaching, would be to isolate the families. If your parents, and therefore you," she pointed at me with the half-eaten treat, "were isolated from those of us who know and understand what the Fae are, you'd come into your power without benefit of training. Without understanding our ancient enemy. You'd be weak, and easily destroyed."

"As Jerry was," said Jed, a stricken look marring his features.

"Exactly," Grannie said. "Except for an accident of birth, Artie's partner would've been destroyed and she would've gone to her grave without ever reaching her potential, discovering her destiny."

"But because Jed and Jerry were twins," I said, catching the direction of Grannie's thought, "Jed's potential awakened when Jerry died." I squeezed his hand tightly. "And fate brought us together."

Jed gripped my hand with both of his and gazed into my eyes. "Not fate," he said. "Divine intervention. Don't forget Michael. Don't discount Dad's dream that sent us to Colorado."

"Michael?" Grannie's voice was so sharp I felt like she'd pounced on the name with a tiger's unsheathed claws. "Who is Michael?"

Releasing my hand, Jed leaned forward, elbows on knees, and gazed directly into Grannie's eyes. "Michael, the hunter. The archangel. The commander of God's armies. At least, that's who I've always known him as."

Grannie's eyes narrowed. "And how exactly do you know this Michael?"

"I first saw him when Jerry lay dying. When my sight awoke. Every-thing changed, and when I looked around, I not only saw the thing that had killed Jerry, but I saw him … the angel … Michael, standing behind my father, his eyes full of sorrow and pity. That's actually the only time I've ever seen him when I was awake. Every other time he's come to me in dreams."

"In dreams?" Grannie prompted.

"Yeah. He's used dreams to teach me. To tell me how to fight the monsters, the terrors, as Artie calls them. He's given me strategy and curses or spells to defeat them. I'm pretty sure he's the one who visited Dad in the dream that caused him to move us across the country to Artie's hometown. He knew she needed me. That we needed each other."

She nodded, crossing herself quickly. "An angel. Well, imagine that. And here I thought I'd be the one training you." Dusting the shortbread crumbs from her fingers, she stood, collected our tea cups and turned toward the kitchen. "The pair of you really are special if an archangel has chosen to involve himself." She paused, and glanced back over her shoulder. "Since you've little formal knowledge of the Fae, we'll start your education bright and early in the morning."

3

The next few days were full of wonder. Who'd have guessed that I'd have to go all the way to Ireland to read fairy tales? Of course, these particular tales were true.

Grannie pulled out the family journals and we spent every evening studying the Fae. Jed and I learned about the various races of Fae, about their courts and their powers. We learned the places they were most likely to be found, the hills and rings and raths that covered the British Isles and much of Europe, places Grannie felt sure were portals to that other dimension where their true home lay.

We also learned about ley lines. Lines of power which connected those sites, running in straight lines from point to point and which the Fae traveled in processions ... invisible to all but those with seer blood. If an oblivious human had the misfortune to build a structure across one of those lines, death and destruction followed when the next procession occurred.

During the days, Grannie O'Toole took us to church yards and ruins and circles of standing stones, whatever we'd studied the night before. On one such outing we visited a construction site. All three of us could clearly see the blue ley line shimmering with energy in the morning sun … and running diagonally through the steel bones of what would someday be an upscale shopping mall on the outskirts of Dublin.

Grannie sighed and shook her head. "'Tis a shame it'll never be completed. The Fae travel this path every year at Samhain. Halloween," she added, correctly interpreting my confused expression. "I tried to warn the owner, but he laughed in my face. Fairy tales are for children, and the gullible, don't you know?"

I shivered, glad I'd be safely home in Colorado long before Halloween came around. The terrors I'd learned to battle at Jed's side were bad enough, but here, in the Old Country, the number and variety of Fae were daunting.

Everywhere we went, we saw Fae. Some were kindly, child-sized brownies caring for domestic animals or lending an unseen hand with household chores; some were tricksters, dwarves and goblins amusing themselves by moving keys or hiding reading glasses; but others rivaled the terrors in their malicious intent, feeding on their victims' positive emotions so that the individuals were left with only distrust and sociopathic thoughts.

Grannie O'Toole cautioned us to act as though we were oblivious to the presence of the Fae, no matter their type.

"Don't see them," she advised. "Whatever you do, never look directly at a Fae. If you must observe them, do so only with sidelong glances or have a reason to look past them. Focus on a bit of the landscape beyond where they stand."

Jed bristled at this advice. "Artie and I don't ignore them. We fight and banish them."

"Maybe at home you can afford to fight," she said with sad resignation. "Colorado must be a wonderful place if there are so few Fae that two young people can fight and win. But not here. Not in their stronghold. There are too many, Jed. You and Artie would be overrun and destroyed — or worse, taken as their playthings — in a heartbeat."

"If we are the legendary pair," Jed argued, "how are we supposed to defend the human race and banish the Fae by pretending we're not what we are?"

Grannie poked a finger in his chest, her expression fierce. "You'll defend our people by lying low until you know enough to fight. Remember Jerry. Remember what happens when a seer tries to do that which he's not yet strong enough to accomplish!"

"That's not fair," Jed said through clenched jaws. His voice was low and controlled, but I heard the anger simmering just beneath the words. "Jerry was a child. I'm an adult."

"Jerry was untrained," she retorted, "and you've only just discovered the existence of the Fae. You didn't even know enough to know what you were battling back home in Colorado."

I stepped between them, placing a hand on Jed's arm. "Enough. You're fighting over how and when to fight."

Grannie stepped back, and Jed turned his gaze on me.

"I don't like letting them get away with things," he said, quietly, but with a sullen edge. "They're hurting people."

"I know," I said, stroking my hand down his arm until I could entwine my fingers with his, "I don't like it much either, but I think Grannie's right. We need to hide our knowledge until we've learned all we can here … and then we need to plan."

He nodded, some of the fire leaving his eyes. "You're right. Whether or not we're the pair in their legend, we won't do anyone any good if we take on more than we can handle right now."

Grannie sighed loudly, but held her peace.

"Let's take a break," I suggested. "We've only got two more days in Ireland. Let's do something fun. Grannie," I said, turning to include her in the conversation again, "there must be something we can do that has a low probability of running into the Fae. What do you suggest?"

Grannie's brow furrowed slightly, then cleared as she nodded and smiled. "That's a grand idea, Artie, but I'm thinking we should take it a step further. Why don't we take a break from each other as well as the learning? I've some errands I've been avoiding, and I'll be surprised if the pair of you wouldn't like a bit of time together without me hanging on your every word."

I opened my mouth to protest, but the twinkle in her eye combined with the happy surprise on Jed's face kept me quiet.

She laughed with delight. "As to where you should go, you might enjoy the Dublin Zoo or the National Botanical Gardens. Both are tourist attractions and full of people, and therefore Fae, but if you wander the less traveled paths, you should be safe enough from their notice."

"That sounds lovely," I agreed.

Jed stepped to Grannie and drew her into a hug. "I'm sorry for picking a fight with you," he said, kissing the top of her frizzy head. "You're right, of course, and an afternoon of sight-seeing will give me a chance to clear my head."

She leaned back and reaching up, patted his cheek. "You're a good boy, Jedidiah Kendrick, and I'm pleased and proud to be your grannie."

Stepping out of his embrace, she swiped tears from her eyes with the back of a hand before using it to make shooing motions at us. "Be gone with you now. You can catch a bus to either the zoo or the gardens at the pub where we had dinner last night. Have a grand time and I'll see you this evening."

Unfortunately, we decided not to catch a bus from the pub in Shankill.

4

I'd just come downstairs from gathering my purse and a light jacket when Jed caught me in his arms.

"Alone at last," he whispered in my ear, and then his lips found mine.

My whole body responded to his kiss. My pulse skyrocketed while butterflies played tag in my belly; my toes even tingled. I was warm and happy and … home. It didn't matter that we were in Ireland, if Jed and I were together, I was home. They say that "home is where the heart is" … and Jed was, and always will be, my heart.

We broke the kiss, and I laid my cheek against his chest, listening to the steady beat of his heart. My arms encircled his waist, and his held me close, resting his chin on the top of my head.

"I've missed this," he said. "Time together, just the two of us."

I nodded, rubbing my cheek against the soft cotton of his favorite moss green shirt. "I've enjoyed meeting Grannie," I said quietly, "and I've learned so much, but I'm glad we're going home soon." I straightened, leaning back in his arms to smile up at him. "We've got a wedding to plan!"

He grinned back at me. "We certainly do." A slight crease in his brow signaled a change in subject. "Listen, do you mind if we don't go the tourist route? I'm not in the mood to be squashed on a bus and then mingle with hordes of people."

"Fine by me," I said, stepping out of his arms and catching his hand in mine. "We can see zoo animals and flowers back home."

"Good. Let's just take a walk instead. There's a really cool ruin just through the woods. Mom took Jerry and me there once. I think we were about six during that visit," he mused. "Every other time we saw Grannie, she came to us. Lots more affordable to fly one person across the Atlantic than four ... or even three."

A shiver skittered down my spine, but I associated it with the mention of Jed's dead twin, not with intuition. I wish I'd heeded my subconscious mind's subtle warning.

"That sounds perfect," I said instead. "It's a gorgeous day for a walk."

Jed led me down the street, around the corner, and into a children's play park. On the other side of the manicured lawn, an old growth forest brooded. Grabbing my hand, Jed strode quickly toward the trees. As we approached, an opening in the undergrowth appeared and I saw a path of dark earth strewn with moldering leaf duff.

We stepped under the trees and the village and all its modern sights and sounds faded away. A world of shadowy greens and browns enveloped us; no sound reached our ears but a low breeze moaning through the leafy canopy.

I squeezed Jed's hand, reassured by the warmth of his fingers. He grinned down at me.

"Don't worry," he said, pulling me forward into the forest, "this is nothing. The castle is even spookier."

"Wow," I said. "Way to reassure a girl." I rolled my eyes, but laughed at myself and picked up my pace. No need to make the man feel like he was dragging me to my doom.

The day was warm and the woods were still. I felt a bit like I was walking through a dream. To dispel that illusion, and just for the comfort of hearing his voice, I asked, "So where are we going?"

"There's this really frosty ruin in a meadow just the other side of these woods. It's called Puck's Castle. Jerry and I thought it was great when we were kids."

Sunlight glimmered through the canopy, and I realized we'd reached the edge of the woods. Just beyond the trees lay a paved road with the forest lining one side and a low rock wall on the other. We crossed to a metal gate and I had my first sight of the ruin.

Puck's castle looked like a giant's face, mouth open in horror, eyes slitted against a wind only it could feel. A cap of green hair trailed across one corner of its brow.

I shivered. "Why is it called Puck's Castle?"

Jed glanced from the stacked rock ruin to me. "You know, I hadn't thought about that, but I remember now," his brow creased in a frown. "It's supposed to be haunted by a pookah, a mischievous fairy who plays the pipes and hops around on the rocks."

That was when I noticed the muted glow of the ley line.

I grabbed Jed's hand, tugging him back toward the cover of the trees. "We have to go, Jed," I said, trying desperately to mask the hysteria rising in my chest. "Now. We have to go NOW!"

The glow of the ley line was no longer muted. The iridescent blue brightened as I watched, pulsing as though to a musical beat.

Jed ignored my panicked tug. He stared across the meadow to the forest on the far side of the castle.

"Jed," I cried. "Please!"

If he heard me, or felt me yanking on his hand, he gave no sign. My love, the man I intended to marry, stood as though turned to stone and stared as a troop of fairies left the shelter of the woods and marched along the ley line straight to Puck's Castle.

Too late, I thought. *Leaving now will only draw their attention to us.* So I did what I had always done, I hid in plain sight. And prayed that my gift would shield Jed as well.

I peered through the curtain of my dark hair, watching the approaching fairies through slitted eyes. One of their number peeled off and scampered up the rock tower, lithe as a mountain goat. When he reached the top, he danced from stone to stone, lightly skipping over the ivy that trailed in a glistening stream across one corner. His dance ended abruptly on our side of the castle, and I knew I'd been unsuccessful. The pookah saw us … or at least one of us.

His surprised cry caused the troop to halt, and me to close my eyes and redouble my effort to hide.

But my attempt was in vain.

Footsteps pattered across the green carpeted meadow, and I cracked my eyes open by the merest sliver to see the pookah and two tall, silver-haired companions standing on the other side of the gate from us.

Jed shook his hand loose from mine, as if I were no more than a bothersome fly, and stepped toward the fairies.

"Begone," he said. "You're not wanted here."

"How unusual," said the pookah. "This mortal has eyes that see."

"Unusual and unacceptable," said one of his silver-haired friends. The creature crooked a finger at Jed and said, "Come, mortal. You must meet our queen."

My Jed, my partner, the love of my life, placed a booted foot on the lowest rail of the gate and began to climb over, his eyes glazed, his expression vacant.

I couldn't stand still. I couldn't let them take my Jed!

Flinging my invisibility away, I grabbed Jed's arm. "Jedidiah Kendrick, hear me! Come away, Jed. Come away with me now!"

The three fairies startled, stepping back a pace.

"What's this?" cried the pookah. "From whence did this mortal appear?"

"She holds great power," said the second.

"No matter," said the third, the one who had held silent until now. He turned gleaming orange eyes on me and spoke directly to my soul. "Come. Your will is mine. Follow where I lead."

I barely had time to duck my chin and close my eyes before his words wove their spell. A nearly irresistible urge to climb the gate and follow Jed into the meadow flooded my heart and soul. But a sliver of my will had managed to hide, and that sliver fought the fairy's compulsion. If I fell under his spell, who would rescue Jed?

The thought of losing myself wasn't nearly as terrifying as the thought of losing Jed.

That sliver of self blazed with fear for my love, and the hot emotion broke the fairy's hold on my mind. I slipped into my own spell and the creatures forgot my existence. Jed was their one and only prey.

When the troop had passed, I sank to the ground and sobbed, grieving for the life we'd never share now. I'd been powerless to protect Jed, and my heart ached with loss.

5

Grannie was inconsolable. She paced the floor in front of the hearth and wailed her despair, while I held myself together, folded into one of the overstuffed chairs.

"He watched them cross the field? He stood there bold as brass and stared at a procession of fairies?" Her eyes were red with weeping and her voice scratched and cracked as though she'd inhaled a lifetime's cigarette smoke. "Did he learn nothing from me?"

She pulled her already frizzy hair, and then turned on me. "And you … how did you come home again, lassie? How are you here and not my Jedidiah?"

My own tears were gone, washed away in the flood I'd shed on the lane outside Puck's Castle. I had nothing left to give.

"I hid," I said. "I tried to shield him too, but they saw him anyway."

"You hid," she said, the words dripping scorn. "You claim to love my boy, but you did naught to save him. You hid."

"I tried," I answered, stung by the injustice of her accusation. "I cast away my protection and tried to call him back. He loves me. I love him." I sighed, futility washing over me yet again. "I thought my call would be stronger than theirs. I was wrong."

"Then how are you here?"

"I realized it wasn't working," I explained. "My sudden appearance startled them, gave me just enough time to slip back into my trance." I closed my eyes and rested my head in my hands. "Even so, I almost didn't make it. The only thing that saved me was the knowledge that Jed was lost if I gave in."

Her hand settled on my hair and stroked; the touch comforted me.

"I'm sorry, Artie," she whispered. "This is none of your doing and 'tis wrong of me to lay blame at your feet."

I rose and hugged her tightly. "I'm so sorry," I whispered. "I don't know what to do."

We separated, staring at each other through bleak eyes.

"How do we get him back?"

Grannie closed her eyes and sank onto the sofa, pulling me down beside her. "Oh, child," she said. "He's lost and there's nothing we can do about it."

I bristled, hot anger replacing despair. "I can't accept that," I said. "I won't accept that. I need him. We need each other. There has to be a way to steal him back."

She patted my arm. "I've never heard of the Fae releasing one of their toys," she said, but something in my expression made her change tack. "We'll search the old texts. Not just our family journals, but those in the clan library."

"Is yours the only seer clan?"

Grannie pursed her lips and thought. "I know a few other families. I'll ask them to search their journals as well."

I nodded, suddenly too weary to hold up my head. Research. It wasn't much, but it was hope, and I would cling to hope until I could cling to Jed again.

"Go to bed, Artie," Grannie said with a pat on my knee. "Neither of us is thinking clearly at the moment. We'll start our search in the morning."

I nodded and found my way to the second floor, where I was now the only occupant.

6

Our search was long and arduous, but Grannie O'Toole was a steadfast guide. We read every word of her family journals before moving to the headquarters of her ancestral clan, the O'Connors, and petitioning to search their library.

Fortunately, the O'Connor library was located in Dublin. Unfortunately, the older texts were indecipherable to me, and eventually proved beyond Grannie's skill at translation as well.

Days dragged by, followed by plodding weeks of reading ancient script until my eyes ached. Family and friends in Colorado called asking when Jed and I were coming home. I prevaricated, misled, and outright lied. I couldn't bear to tell anyone that he'd been stolen, kidnapped by supernatural creatures. No one would believe me anyway, so I hid behind a façade of a holiday too delightful to bring to a close.

August's myriad greens turned to the golds and reds of September with no solution in sight. Despair seized me by the throat as our anticipated wedding date approached ... and passed with me no nearer to rescuing Jed. I couldn't go on like this. I couldn't live without him, but I couldn't give up while he might be saved. Maybe the next document would hold the secret. I kept searching

By mid-October we had reached the limits of our ability to research, and I was desperately afraid I'd be forced to leave Ireland … to abandon the possibility of ever seeing my love again.

Just when our spirits had reached their lowest ebb, Laird Angus O'Connor sought us out. He found us in a dim library chamber where tattered scrolls and decaying journals lined shelves set against stone walls dark with age. An ancient oak table occupied the center of the room, its wood so stained and dark it seemed to absorb what little light filtered through the high, narrow windows. The most ancient scrolls dealing with the Fae resided in this room … scrolls filled with script that had defied even Grannie's ability to read.

The clan leader was an impressive man, with a broad chest, heavily muscled arms, a thick neck, and a full head of deep auburn hair. Though he was clean shaven and wearing a perfectly tailored suit, he looked like a warrior of legend.

"Maeve O'Toole," he called in a booming voice that filled the narrow chamber. "I've heard tales that you and your young assistant have fair taken up residence among the journals of our clan. Do you seek specific knowledge, or are you merely broadening your understanding of your heritage?"

Grannie scrambled to stand, so I followed suit, but when she gave the man a low bow, I merely inclined my head. He was not my laird, nor was he ever likely to become so, the way our search was going.

"Laird," said Grannie, standing as tall as her slight frame would allow. "We're looking for specific information … regarding the Fae."

"I see." He shot a piercing look at me, and I saw wariness and a shrewd intelligence in his gaze. "And who might your assistant be? If she's of our clan, I've no recollection of her."

Grannie folded her hands in front of her and lowered her gaze. "She is not of our clan ... yet. Laird Angus O'Connor, may I present Artemis Woodward. Artie, this is my clan leader, Angus O'Connor."

Laird Angus held out a massive hand, and I laid mine in it.

"'Tis pleased I am to make your acquaintance, Miss Woodward," he said, lifting my hand and brushing my knuckles with his lips. As he did so, a flash of recognition seared my mind. This man was not only a seer, he was far older than his looks suggested.

He smiled, a twinkle lighting his eyes. "Ah, I see your blood recognizes mine. Good. That will expedite matters." He released my hand, sat down at the long narrow table between the racks of books and scrolls, and gestured us to chairs as well. "What do you seek, and how may I assist you?"

Grannie raised an eyebrow in my direction, but remained silent. I sighed. I preferred to leave the explaining to her, but obviously she'd decided this was my tale to tell.

"Very well," I said, and gave my full attention to the laird of the O'Connors. "I'm engaged to Mrs. O'Toole's grandson, Jedidiah Kendrick. We came to Ireland so that Grannie could meet me before we married. Once here, we discovered that Grannie is a seer, like Jed and myself. However, we found Grannie to be much more knowledgeable, so we set out to learn what we could from her before we returned home to the United States, to our home in Colorado."

I told Laird Angus everything I could, every detail of how Jed had been taken and how I'd escaped. The telling was hard. During the weeks Grannie and I had searched for answers, I'd tried not to think about that day, tried not to remember exactly how I'd failed Jed. Instead, I'd concentrated on finding a solution. But it had all been in vain.

Grannie and I avoided speaking of the future. I lived in her house and we worked side by side searching the records for clues, but I knew in my heart I couldn't stay in Ireland forever. Yet, I couldn't imagine returning to Colorado without Jed. Frankly, I couldn't imagine living without Jed. If I left the Old Country without him, what point would there be for my existence?

And so I stayed, would continue to stay, until I found Jed or Grannie sent me away.

As I finished my tale, Laird Angus took my hands in his and stroked them with his thumbs. Compassion filled his gaze as he said, "Ah, lassie, 'tis sorry I am to hear of your woes, but the chances of you regaining your love are very slim."

Tears filled my eyes, but I blinked them back. "I know," I whispered. "Actually, they're about gone since even Grannie can't decipher these final journals."

"I can see you're a steadfast lass," he said, releasing my hands, "but have you courage as well as loyalty?"

I swiped at my eyes to clear the tears and met his gaze. "I've dealt with terror since my earliest memories, and did it on my own until Jed found me. We were in our teens by then. Together he and I fought the terrors, the Fae … and won. Until we came here." I lowered my eyes and studied the delicate opal ring Jed had given me when we agreed to marry. "There are so many more Fae here, and we had so very much to learn. I guess we failed."

Laird Angus lifted my chin with his index finger until my eyes met his. "I may know a way," he said, "but you'll have to act alone, and it will require more courage than most seers possess. I'll not fault you if you choose to leave this place with the tale untold."

My heart leaped. My pulse thundered so hard I could barely hear past its whooshing against my eardrums. "Y… you … you know how get Jed back? Tell me," I demanded. "Tell me now!"

"Oh, Laird!" Grannie said, and she looked so white I worried she might faint.

The big man laughed. "Call me Angus," he said. "We've no need for formalities between us. We're seers all, with much work to be done."

The plan was simple to tell, yet seemed impossible to execute.

As Angus explained, all I had to do was pull Jed out of line as the fairy troop processed along a ley line during a full moon ... and hold him until he recognized me.

"You can see them, so you can do it," Angus assured me.

"It sounds too easy," I said, frowning. "What's the catch?"

His eyes darted around the room as he looked for something to focus on that wasn't me. "The catch, as you say, is that you must hold him no matter what the fairies do. No matter what spell they throw at you." He sighed and met my gaze. "Their own laws dictate that they cannot harm you during the rescue attempt, but if you despair, if you lose hold of him for even an instant, both of you will be lost beyond recovery."

"Beyond recovery?" Grannie said, and I heard the fear and tension in her voice. "What does that even mean?"

"Exactly what it says, Maeve," Angus answered. "Only one attempt is permitted for Jed, and since Artie will be attempting to steal from the Fae, no attempts will be tolerated on her behalf. Either they both come home, or neither does."

I nodded, then made eye contact with each in turn. "That suits me fine. If I can't save Jed, I've no reason to go on."

Angus nodded, a fierce glare in his eyes. Grannie's eyes brimmed with tears, but she bit her lip and made no objection.

7

Halloween, or Samhain as the Celts called it, brought the next full moon.

Grannie and Angus prepared for the attempted rescue by creating a shield bracelet for me and embedding it with every protective sigil and ward they could discover. Angus also took my engagement ring and sealed it with a spell to enhance the love it represented.

"We can't go with you," he explained, "can't help you with this task, but we can see to it you carry as much positive energy with you as is physically possible."

I spent my preparation time writing down everything I could remember of the time Jed and I had spent together. From our first meeting in social studies on our first day of high school, through every battle with every terror we'd ever vanquished, right down to the way he'd kissed me before we walked to Puck's Castle on that fateful day. Those memories strengthened me. They reminded me of all we'd accomplished, of all we'd become to one another.

Jed was my life and I was his. No matter what, I would hold him. Nothing a fairy or a terror or any other foul thing that walked our earth could do would cause me to abandon my man. Jed was the other half of my soul and I refused to continue to be separated from him.

Halloween morning dawned clear and bright and biting with cold. The time had come. Tonight the moon would be full and the fairy troop that had stolen Jed would process right through the middle of an under-construction mall on the outskirts of Dublin … the one Grannie had shown us early in our visit.

"You're sure it's the same troop?" I asked, wiping damp palms on my well-worn denim jeans. "If he's not there, we'll have to wait for the next full moon."

"I'm certain, Artie," Angus said. "I've had spies out for the last few weeks. Experienced seers who know how to watch without being caught. Jed is with this troop, and except for being completely enthralled, he is whole and well."

I nodded, busying my fingers with binding my long dark hair in a single tight braid. I'd have no need to hide behind my hair this night. "Good. That's good."

"Come, Artie," Grannie called from the kitchen. "Let me fix you a nice dinner. You'll need your strength tonight."

I shook my head, remembered she couldn't see through walls, and called back, "No thank you, Grannie. I'm too nervous to eat. Besides, I'm stronger than I look. I'll be fine."

She hurried in to the front room a few minutes later carrying a tray of steaming mugs. "I thought that might be your attitude," she said with a wan smile. "Here, at least drink this broth. It'll fortify you without weighing you down."

"Good thinking, Maeve," Angus said with an approving nod, accepting his own mug. "Drink up, Artie. It'll be time to leave before you know it."

Angus and Grannie drove me to the construction site, timing it so we arrived just as the moon rose full and bright above the horizon. Grannie hugged me and wished me well, while Angus touched my ring and bracelet. "You're well warded, lassie, and ye've a stout heart. I've no doubt ye'll prevail."

I nodded and spoke past the lump in my throat. "We'll see you soon. Both of us." I licked lips that felt more like sandpaper than flesh. "But, if anything goes wrong, you have our story. Add it to your journal, please."

"There'll be no need, at least not until you've added another fifty years' worth of tales."

A quick grin and I left them to hide myself behind a pallet of bricks that was stacked beside the shining ley line. All that remained to be done was to wait for my love, my life, my Jed.

The moon floated just above the horizon, so round and full it seemed to fill the sky. A shining white orb starred with mars and craters against a velvet black sky studded with pinpricks of light. Surely such beauty boded well for Jed's rescue.

A soft jingle of bells wafted across the silent night. They were coming.

I hunkered low in a sprinter's crouch, one eye on the ley line, ready to spring the moment I saw him. My pulse raced, my vision wavered, my ears rang with nerves.

The first fairy appeared. An ageless female in a flowing green gown holding aloft a branch of silver leaves threaded with tiny golden bells. Behind her came a tall raven-haired male garbed all in deep blue carrying a purple banner trimmed in golden threads. Next came a throng of fair folk, easily thirty or forty individuals of all species, including a few Grannie hadn't described. Another bannerman and bell-bearer brought up the rear.

He wasn't there! Jed wasn't part of the procession!

How could we have been so wrong? What could I do now?

I closed my eyes against a suffocating wave of despair. And then I heard the clip-clop of horses' hooves on the moon-drenched ground.

My eyes flew open and I beheld a snow white unicorn following the final bell-bearer. The ethereal creature had appeared as if out of thin air, and sitting sideways upon his back was the most beautiful lady I could ever have imagined. The female was dressed in gossamer fabrics, like moonbeams on an icy lake, in shimmering shades of palest blue, rose-petal pink and tender green. Her face and form were perfectly proportioned, an alabaster complexion framed emerald green eyes and her hair had the shade and shine of molten gold.

Surely this must be the fairy queen the pookah had spoken of, I couldn't imagine her as anything else.

My heart leapt and my soul stilled almost before I realized what I had seen. Jed walked beside the queen's horse, his hand resting lightly on her slipper clad foot, his eyes glazed and unaware.

My moment had arrived.

I sprinted from my hiding place, knocking Jedidiah to the ground. Encircling his left wrist with my right hand, I threw my left arm around his neck and clung to him like a burr.

Jed spoke not a word, but lay like a mannequin on the ground beneath me. Could it be this easy? Could I have won already?

Almost I loosened my grip, but the ring on my left hand and bracelet on my right flared to life and I felt their protective sigils glow.

No, I hadn't won. I'd merely surprised my enemy. The battle had yet to be engaged.

The fairy queen called out in ringing tones more beautiful than I could describe. The troop stopped. All eyes focused on me … and Jed.

Unpronounceable, unknowable words tumbled from the queen's lips … and my reality transformed.

I no longer held Jed. Instead I clung to the head of a giant snake that raised itself … and me … into the sky. I closed my eyes and chanted a mantra to the man I knew I held though the evidence of my senses told me otherwise. "You are Jedidiah Kendrick and I am Artemis Woodward. I love you and you love me. Come back to me, Jed!"

The weaving head faltered, the massive jaw closed, and a huge forked tongue darted out, tasting my scent upon the air between us.

The fairy queen spoke again, commandment in every unknown syllable.

The snake shifted and I no longer clung to smooth scales. Now my left arm wrapped the coarsely furred neck of a Bengal tiger, while my right hand fought to hold its claws from my flesh. Golden eyes stared at the pulse in my naked throat and knife-sharp teeth gleamed in its open mouth.

I closed my eyes and held on still more tightly. No matter what form the fairy queen forced upon him, I refused to release my Jed. If she made him kill me, so be it. I'd rather die than fail him again.

Fear clogged my throat, but I opened my eyes, stared straight into his, and screamed, "You are Jedidiah Kendrick and I am Artemis Wood-ward. I love you and you love me. Come back to me, Jed!"

The tiger's claws relaxed and something flickered behind his eyes.

The fairy queen spoke again, her words strident and somehow desperate.

Jed writhed and bucked beneath my hands, but I refused to release him. When the transformation was complete, I found myself eye to eye with the biggest bird I'd ever seen. My left arm encircled his neck, pulling a razor sharp beak too close to my face, while my right hand held tight to the pinion of his left wing.

Intelligence flashed behind his eyes as he cocked his great head and blinked a nictitating membrane. I smiled, with more courage than I felt, and repeated, for the third time, "You are Jedidiah Kendrick and I am Artemis Woodward. I love you and you love me. Come back to me, Jed!"

He lowered his feathered head, touching my forehead with his own.

"I love you, Jed Kendrick," I whispered, "and I will never let you go."

The fairy queen spoke again, but this time her voice held defeat. The great bird that had been Jed deflated and morphed and became … Jedidiah Kendrick, a mortal man with his two feet planted firmly on the ground.

Jed stared into my eyes from where we stood, my right hand in his left, my left arm flung around his neck. He raised his right hand and caught the tear sliding down my cheek on his index finger. "I see you, Artemis Woodward. I know you. You are the love of my life."

Neither of us even glanced up when the fairy queen spoke. We had eyes only for each other.

"Congratulations, mortal female," she said, her voice distant and cool. "By the terms of our law you have won back my thrall. He is free from this troop, but I warn you, do not linger on these shores for all of my other troops will be anxious to avenge this slight. I now know both of your names and I do *not* wish you well."

Jed and I held each other without speaking until the troop had disappeared and Grannie and Angus ran to embrace us.

EPILOGUE

Thanksgiving is a uniquely American holiday and Jed and I celebrated it in Colorado with our families ... by pledging our lives to each other. Since our ordeal in Ireland had given us so much to be thankful for, we decided Thanksgiving was the perfect day for our wedding.

Grannie O'Toole arrived the day before, accompanied by Angus O'Connor. Jed was honored beyond words that the head of the O'Connor clan would come all the way to America just to attend our wedding.

I'd explained how Angus had been instrumental in Jed's rescue, but my love remained vague about the weeks of his captivity. Everything I told him of that time seemed to slip from his mind as soon as I said it, but I didn't mind. In fact, I envied him his forgetfulness. If I could erase the memory of my despair and grief, I'd do it gladly, except that it would also erase my knowledge of Grannie's steadfast support and how hard Angus had worked to help me bring Jed home.

The ceremony itself was a small affair. Jed and I exchanged our vows in the little neighborhood park where we'd first become a team. I wore a clean-lined white velvet dress, full length and long-sleeved in deference to the late November chill, and carried a small bouquet of gold asters and wine-red chrysanthemums. Jed looked regal in a black tux and a cummerbund, the latter in a deep gold shade that matched his aster boutonniere. Reverend Kendrick, Jed's father, officiated, and our vows were witnessed by Jed's mother, my parents, and Grannie and Angus.

Reverend Kendrick's face fairly glowed as he recited the age-old words, "Jedidiah Amos Kendrick, do you take Artemis Lucia Woodward to be your wedded wife, to love, protect, and cherish, to have and to hold from this day until the end of time?"

A slow smile spread across Jed's face, lighting his eyes and making him even more handsome than usual. He squeezed my hands. "I certainly do."

His father turned his gaze on me. "And do you, Artemis Lucia Woodward, take Jedidiah Amos Kendrick to be your wedded husband, to love, protect, and cherish, to have and to hold from this day until the end of time?"

The memory of those moments when the fairy queen had transformed my love from one deadly form to the next flitted through my mind. I had held him then, I would hold him forever.

"I do," I said without a single doubt.

Jed pulled me into his embrace and our lips met in a kiss that caused everything around us to fade into the background. I'm sure his father intoned the final words of the ceremony, but I didn't hear them. I didn't need to.

I was Jed's and he was mine ... and there wasn't a terror or a fairy in sight.

What could be more perfect?

X

SELKIES IN PARADISE

DEB LOGAN
AUTHOR OF *FAERY UNEXPECTED*

Selkies
in Paradise

SPUN YARNS
A *Seer Chronicles* Short Story

PROLOGUE

My name is Artie Woodward-Kendrick, and I'm the luckiest woman in the world. I'm married to my very best friend, Jed Kendrick.

Who could've guessed I'd ever find someone to love; that I would ever marry? Certainly not me!

You see, I'm a seer. I see things normal people don't, things they couldn't see, even if they wanted to … which no one in their right mind would. I mean let's get real; even I don't want to see the Fae. But I don't have a choice. I was born with this strange ability to see the unseen, to know the unknowable.

I thought I was alone. Thought I'd be alone my entire life. I knew I'd never find love.

Sure, my mom and dad loved me, but even they thought I was weird. They worried about me constantly when I was a kid, dragged me to more shrinks than I care to remember. None of them helped. After all, everyone assumed I was imagining things.

Only I wasn't.

So I learned to hide.

By the time I made it to high school, I was adept at hiding. I hid my knowledge from my parents. I tried desperately to hide my weirdness from the kids at school. But most importantly, I hid the fact that I could see what I'd named *the terrors*, that I knew they existed, from the terrors themselves. And as long as I hid, I was safe.

Lonely ... but safe.

So how did I manage to find a man who not only befriended me, but who grew to love me? How did my life change from hidden and lonely to fulfilled and glowing with contentment?

Jed Kendrick moved to my hometown in Colorado.

We recognized each other, and our loneliness ended. We were both seers, and on our first day at McKinley High we became a team, but that's another story. Suffice it to say that over the last six and a half years we've fought terrors and other forms of Fae from Colorado to Ireland.

And somewhere along the way, we fell in love.

Now, I'm glowing with happiness because just a few days ago, on a glorious late November day — Thanksgiving Day to be exact — I became Jed Kendrick's wife, and he became Artie Woodward's husband. The Woodward-Kendrick team became official in the eyes of the world.

What's next, you ask? Who knows! But whatever it is, we'll face it together.

Right after we get home from the awesome honeymoon our family and friends arranged for us ... in Hawaii!

1

On a crystal clear day in late November, our plane landed in paradise. Aside from a fateful trip to Ireland to meet Jed's Grannie O'Toole, I'd never been beyond the borders of Colorado, so when I stepped from the plane into the open-air terminal at Lihui Airport on the Hawaiian island of Kauai, I was overwhelmed. I stopped in the midst of a throng of people, clinging to Jed's arm, and inhaled the exotic mixture of sea salt, tropical flowers, and lushly green growing things.

Jed squeezed my hand and smiled down at me. "We're here," he said, his voice tinged with amazement. "We're actually married and on our honeymoon."

I nodded, momentarily lost in the love and wonder shining in his eyes. There had been moments in Ireland when I'd despaired of ever seeing Jed's handsome face again, and now here we were … married and on the island of Kauai.

Before I could answer, a pretty young woman with a waterfall of shining black hair and sun-kissed skin stepped up to us. She wore a sleeveless red dress patterned with huge white flowers, and her arms dripped with brightly colored flower leis.

"Aloha," she said as she placed a lei around each of our necks. "Welcome to Kauai. We hope you'll enjoy your stay."

I smiled my thanks, but my attention was caught by the beauty of the flowers that made up my lei. I'd never seen, or smelled, anything like them. I recognized white carnations in the necklace of flowers, but the other varieties were a mystery.

I glanced up and met her gaze. "Thank you. These are beautiful, but what kind of flowers are they?"

She held up another of the leis she carried and indicated a white, star-like flower edged in delicate pink. "This is plumeria. Most of the fragrance of your lei comes from it. You'll see them often here in the islands. Sometimes in pink, often in yellow." Pointing to other flowers in turn she said, "We also use tuberoses, carnations, orchids, and jasmine, but you'll see many other types of leis during your stay." She smiled again, and with a little wave, turned to greet another couple.

Jed fingered the lei around his neck — his was made up of darker, more bold colors than mine and featured quite a bit of greenery — and said, "Wow. I didn't expect to be given flowers just for walking off a plane."

"They look good on you," I said, grinning up at my tall, lanky husband. I'd nearly lost Jed in Ireland. He'd been ensorcelled and held thrall by the Fae, and I'd almost given up hope of finding a way to rescue him. But Grannie O'Toole and Laird Angus had helped me and … well, that was a tale I didn't want to think about right now.

It was enough to have him here with me, to be able to watch him examine his lei while I admired his more-than-six-foot frame, his tousled black hair, and his gentle gray eyes rimmed by long and lovely dark lashes. His full lips twitched as he noticed my stare.

"Like what you see?" he asked, his eye color darkening to a smoldering, smoky gray.

"Always," I replied, my heart beating faster as memories of our wedding night crowded my mind. "Let's find our luggage."

"Yes," he agreed, licking his lips. "I think we need to check out our accommodations." He swallowed, his Adam's apple bobbing. "Soon."

2

Our hotel suite was stunning. The laird had gone all out for us after our Irish misadventure. He'd booked us into a luxury resort on Kauai's north shore and made sure we had all the amenities. I wandered through the sitting room and stepped through the sliding glass door onto the ocean-view lanai, while Jed tipped the young man who'd brought our luggage up.

A soft murmur of voices, the muffled thump of a closing door, and a moment later Jed was beside me, his arms sliding around my waist. We gazed at the picture postcard view of palm trees, white sand and impossibly blue water and then turned to each other.

"Welcome to paradise," Jed murmured as he drew me close and bent to kiss me.

His lips were soft and warm, and I melted into his embrace. Jed loved me. He understood me. He was my partner in life, my equal. And now ... right now, he was my lover.

Our kiss deepened, became more passionate, and when the spark it kindled grew to a flame, he pulled away. The light in his eyes echoed the smoldering heat growing in my core. In one quick movement, he bent and, moving one strong arm behind my knees, swept me off my feet and into his arms. Without a word, my lover carried me across the sitting room and into the bedroom ... to the perfectly arranged and very enticing king-size bed.

"You're wearing too many clothes," he whispered as he placed me gently on the pillow-soft mattress.

"So are you," I answered in voice so husky I barely recognized it as my own.

We remedied that little problem and spent the next few hours doing what newlyweds have done since time immemorial: exploring each other's bodies and discovering new depths of our love.

———

OUR FIRST DAY on Kauai was drawing to a close when we emerged from our hotel suite in search of food. We opted for dinner on the terrace overlooking Hanalei Bay. I watched the sun sink into the darkening water, marveling at the vivid shades of red and gold as I savored firm, sweet flakes of mahi mahi flavored with mango sauce and delicious coconut rice.

Jed caught my free hand in his, stroking my fingers with his thumb. We didn't speak. No words were needed. We simply drank in the moment, appreciating the tranquility and peace of this beautiful place.

After dinner, we wandered through the open air hotel lobby and down a stone-paved path to a pristine white sand beach. The rolling waves of the bay beckoned us with their froth of white lace.

We strolled hand-in-hand in the moonlight, serenaded by the susurrus of water on sand, cooled by a light sea breeze that lifted my long dark hair and ruffled Jed's black locks. As we rounded the curve of the bay, I noticed a woman in a long white dress sitting in the sand at the edge of the water. Her knees were pulled up so that her chin rested on them, the gentle waves kissing her feet with each inward flow. We walked a few steps closer, and she raised her head and glanced at us. Moonlight shimmered on her face, and I saw that it was glazed with tears.

I laid my free hand on Jed's arm to stop him, disentangled my fingers from his, and stepped nearer to the woman. Closer now, I saw that she was young, not much older than me, with lovely dark slanting eyes. But the moonlight played tricks with her hair, making the nearly waist-length sable waves appear to have a silvery sheen.

"Are you hurt?" I asked, just loudly enough to be heard over the waves. "Can we help you?"

And then Jed was beside me, pulling me back toward the resort. "Come away from her, Artie," he whispered urgently in my ear. "Can't you see what she is?"

I looked again, and saw what my love had seen.

The young woman had risen. She stood with her feet in a froth of water, her long white dress wet to the knees, one hand held out to us in a gesture of supplication. An unearthly glow surrounded her, one not detectable by normal human eyes ... but neither Jed nor I were normal humans. We were seers. And right now our sight showed us a woman of the Fae.

"Please," she said, making no move to approach us. "Please, can you help me?"

Jed pushed me behind him, but made no move to flee. "What could a mortal do to help a Fae woman?"

She gasped and stumbled back a step. "Y-you know what I am?"

I stepped to Jed's side, despite his annoyed glance. "Not precisely," I said. "Only that you aren't human."

Nodding, she moved closer, hesitantly, like a wild animal. Curious, but cautious. And always with her feet in the waves.

"I'm a selkie," she said, her dark eyes wide and full of pain, "but I can't return home to the sea. Someone has stolen my skin. I'm marooned here, with no one to tell my kin what has become of me. Can you help me? Can you at least carry a message to my colony?"

A selkie. One of that ancient race of shape-shifters who live in the oceans of the world, appearing to human eyes as seals in the water, and transforming into human form on land. But the transformation required a catalyst. To become human, a selkie had to shed its skin, which was then carefully hidden. Very carefully, because without its skin, the creature was powerless to shift into its true form and return to the water.

"We've learned to distrust the Fae," Jed said, his voice low and menacing. "My wife may be sympathetic, but I won't risk her on what could be a trick."

Tears streamed across her cheeks as she shook her head. "It's no trick. I'm desperate, and you're the only ones who can possibly understand my plight. Please, help me." She wiped her cheeks with trembling hands, took a deep breath, and continued. "If you won't seek out my kin, at least tell Maris where I am and what has happened."

"Who?" Jed and I asked simultaneously.

"Maris Grainger," said the selkie woman. "She lives on Maui. I have no money and I can no longer swim, so I can't reach her. Go to Maui, to Maalaea Harbor. Look for Captain Bill's Island Cruises. Her father works there. He'll tell you how to find Maris. Tell her Serena needs her help. She'll go to my family. Maris will know what to do."

I frowned. "Is she a seer?" I asked, confused. "How can this Maris Grainger help you?"

"Maris is special," she said. "Different. Neither Fae nor human, but she's kind and cares for all who inhabit the sea. She'll help. She'll know what to do. Please, tell Maris Serena needs her."

Jed and I exchanged a glance. We'd planned to do some sight-seeing on Maui anyway, and an island cruise sounded lovely. I quirked an eyebrow at him and he shrugged his shoulders in a *might as well* kind of way. I grinned and stood on tiptoe to kiss his cheek.

"We'll see if we can find Maris tomorrow," I said.

The selkie nodded. "Thank you."

Jed and I turned and practically ran back to the resort.

"Well, that's a first," Jed said quietly when we were safely back in the open air lobby. "A member of the Fae asking for our help."

I nodded. Every other encounter we'd ever had with that race of supernatural creatures had been hostile. As we took the elevator to our suite, I wondered what manner of being this Maris Grainger might be. Not Fae. Not human. Then what exactly was she?

Evidently a being who was kind and cared for sea creatures.

How intriguing!

3

The next morning we caught an island hopper flight to Kapalua Airport on Maui, rented a red Jeep Wrangler, and drove to Maalaea Harbor. What a wonderfully adventurous start to our day! Flying over the emerald jewel of Kauai and the diamond-tipped sapphire of the Pacific before landing on Maui's northwest coast. We drove south along Highway 30, the open-topped Wrangler giving us clear views of the ocean to the west and the stunning West Maui Mountains to the east.

We arrived in Maalaea Town a little before noon and went in search of Captain Bill's Island Cruises. The young woman manning the ticket booth told us that the Graingers sailed on the Sea Princess, which was currently on a whale watching run, but that we could book seats on the Sea Princess for its 2:00 p.m. snorkeling cruise.

Jed pulled out the credit card Laird Angus had provided and paid for our afternoon adventure. The young woman advised us to be back by 1:30 to board the Sea Princess and grab choice seats.

Pushing his wallet back into his pocket, Jed turned to me. "Shall we find some lunch? We've got a little over an hour to kill."

As if on cue, my stomach growled, loudly.

"I'll take that as a 'yes,'" Jed said with a laugh, and we turned and strolled across the street and down a block to King Kamehameha's Crab Shack. Snagging a table on the patio overlooking the bay, we studied the menu, a large chalk board hung above the serving window.

"I think I'll try the crab cakes," I said, mouth watering in anticipation.

"Yeah, those look good," Jed answered, eyeing another patron's plate briefly before looking back to the menu, "but I'm going for the coconut shrimp." He glanced at me, smiled, and said, "You sit still and enjoy the view. I'll go order."

The view was certainly worth savoring. The deep blue waters of Maalaea Bay; the dark outline of hills around the curve of beach; the neat masts of ships in their slips along the dock, as well as the full-bellied sails of those returning from their errands on the ocean's deep water. All covered by a sky so clear and blue it felt unreal. I'd always thought my little corner of Colorado enjoyed clear skies, but that was before I came to Hawaii.

Jed came back carrying plates loaded with delicious smelling food.

"Wow," I said, accepting my lunch. "That was fast."

He nodded, sat down, grabbed a piece of breaded shrimp and dragged it through a deep red sauce. "I didn't expect to be handed our plates as soon as I paid." He popped the shrimp into this mouth, chewed, swallowed, and grabbed another. "This is really good!"

I cut into my first crab cake with my fork, lifted it to my lips and sighed with contentment as the moist, flavorful tidbit hit my tongue. "Oh, yeah," I murmured between bites. "If we were staying on Maui, I could eat here every day."

We finished our meal, but lingered at the crab shack's table, sipping POG, a refreshing passion fruit-orange-guava juice drink, and alternately watching the bay and our fellow tourists. The number of people walking around in skimpy swimsuits and flip-flops made me feel positively overdressed in my khaki shorts and bright pink T-shirt. Of course, Jed and I both wore swimsuits too; we just wore regular clothes over them.

A little after 1:00 we saw the Sea Princess slip into place at Captain Bill's dock. Happy tourists disembarked, their necks slung with cameras, the afternoon sun glinting off sunglasses and binoculars.

Jed stood and held out a hand to me. "Shall we?"

"We shall," I answered with a grin. "I'm really anxious to meet this Maris person. I wonder how Serena expects the girl to help?"

"No clue. I just hope she's actually on the boat with her dad and not off having a picnic with friends or something."

I nodded. We'd made this trip to meet Maris Grainger, and one way or another, we would do so. If she wasn't aboard the Sea Princess, we'd just have to keep an eye on her father, Richard, until he led us to her.

We needn't have worried. When we boarded the Sea Princess, we were greeted by a teenage girl with short, curly red hair, dozens of freckles across her nose ... and a faint other-worldly glow outlining her trim young body. She was dressed much as I was, in neatly pressed khaki shorts and a T-shirt, but her T was emblazoned with Captain Bill's name and logo.

"Welcome aboard the Sea Princess," she said, taking our tickets and checking our names off on a clipboard. "Please find a seat. The mate will explain what we're about in a few minutes."

We walked on. No point it trying to talk to her now; she needed to get the rest of the passengers aboard.

Moving forward, we claimed seats along the bow rail of the little ship. A few minutes later a tall man wearing khaki trousers, a short-sleeved white shirt, and wrap-around sunglasses unhooked a microphone and called for our attention.

"Welcome aboard the Sea Princess," he announced. "I'm Richard Grainger, and I'll be your guide today. We'll be setting sail in a minute or two for Molokini Crater where you'll enjoy some of the best snorkeling in the islands. Our sailing time will be about an hour, so please pay attention while I give you some necessary safety information."

I listened to the man's speech, at least enough to take note of where the life preservers were stowed, but most of my attention was focused on Maris. True, we hadn't asked the teen's name, but normal human girls didn't have a glowing aura.

Frowning, I watched the girl as she moved quietly and confidently across the deck. Something was off. She definitely had a nimbus, but it wasn't as bright and clearly defined as that of most Fae. Hers was somehow softer, more misty than I'd come to expect.

Neither did I see the image of her true form upon her human body. When the Fae choose to be seen by mortal men, they wrap themselves in a glamour. They appear human, no matter what their true forms may be.

Because of our unique heritage, Jed and I see the Fae for what they really are. Our *sight* allows us to see past the image they project to their true selves. We see their human disguise superimposed upon their other-worldly forms.

Maris presented a soft Fae nimbus, but I saw no trace of another form.

"What is she?" I wondered quietly to Jed.

He shook his head and adjusted his sunglasses on his nose. "I don't know," he answered, just as quietly, "but her father is pure human." He nodded toward our guide. "I wonder if he's really her father, or just some poor schmuck she's ensorcelled into believing they're related?"

"No telling, but we've got an hour to find out what's going on."

Richard Grainger had ended his spiel by inviting the passengers to explore the ship, enjoy non-alcoholic beverages and snacks in the lounge off the galley, and watch for passing humpback whales, which he promised to point out if any were spotted by the crew.

With forty or so passengers moving freely around the decks, we'd be able to approach Maris easily.

"Let me talk to her first," I said, laying a hand on Jed's arm. "We don't want to scare her by ganging up on her."

He nodded. "Okay, but stay in plain sight. We don't know what she's capable of."

I patted his arm. "Don't worry. I won't underestimate her."

Maris stood against the wall in the lounge, presumably keeping an eye on the platters of food in order to restock as needed. I picked up plate, arranged a slice of pineapple, some bits of cheese, and a couple of crackers on it, and then moved to stand beside her while I nibbled.

"This is a nice boat," I said, trying to sound casual. "Is it a yacht?"

The girl smiled and her nimbus glowed a bit brighter. "The Sea Princess is a double-hulled catamaran, a very stable yacht."

I wiped my fingers on a napkin and held out my hand. "I'm Artie," I said, and nodding toward Jed, added, "that's my husband, Jed. We're on our honeymoon." I grinned, blushing slightly.

Maris took my hand. Hers was warm, her handshake firm. This close, I could see the ghostly image of long, slim fingers, webbed almost to the tips.

"I'm Maris Grainger," she said. "Congratulations."

"Thanks." I released her hand and, picking up a piece of cheese, nibbled a bite. "Grainger," I said, as though considering. "Are you related to the mate who's our guide?"

She dimpled. "He's my dad. We moved out here from Kansas about a year ago."

"Kansas? Really? And you're both working on a sailing ship? That seems a bit odd."

She shrugged. "Dad was a sailor before he met my mom. They lived in Hawaii for a while, but moved inland when I was a baby."

"How interesting!" I glanced around for more people in Captain Bill T's. "Is your mom on board too?"

Her smile disappeared, a deep sadness filling her eyes. "No. Mom died in a car accident in Kansas.

"Oh," I said quickly. "I'm so sorry."

We stood in silence for a few moments. I glanced at Jed, who met my gaze with solemn reassurance. He couldn't hear what Maris and I had said, but stood ready to assist if needed.

I took a deep breath and decided to take the plunge. The lounge held only a few people, no one near enough to hear what I said to her next.

"Maris," I said quietly, "Jed and I, well, we're what's known as *Seers*. We see things other people can't." She stiffened, and I placed a hand on her arm. "We can see that you're not, well, you're not exactly human."

She startled, tried to pull away. I tightened my grip on her arm.

"Please don't leave," I said, putting as much compassion in my voice as I could. "We mean you no harm, but we have a message for you."

She stilled. I knew she was ready to flee, but stood her ground, quietly wary. I dropped my restraining hand.

"What kind of message?"

"Do you mind if Jed joins us?" I asked. "We didn't want to scare you by both approaching you at once."

She glanced in his direction, moved a little to her left, giving herself a clear path to the door, and nodded. "All right. He can come over, and I'll listen, but if you try to hurt me, I'm screaming for Dad."

I beckoned to Jed as I said, "We're not interested in causing you any trouble, Maris. We just need to talk to you."

Jed strode across the room and stopped beside me. "You must be Maris," he said, holding out his hand and giving her his most charming smile. "I'm Jed Kendrick and I'm very glad to meet you.

She put her hand in his, a bit timidly, but managed a smile when he released her after a brief shake.

"I was just about to tell Maris about our encounter last night," I said.

"Great," he said. "Why don't we sit down at that table. We might as well be comfortable while we talk."

Once we were all seated, I told Maris our tale. "We're honeymooning on the north shore of Kauai, and last night while we were strolling along the beach, we met a young woman. Only she wasn't … a woman, I mean. She was a selkie in human form." I paused and studied Maris's face. "Her name is Serena." Maris's eyes widened. She knew Serena.

"Someone stole her skin," I continued, "and she's stranded in human form. She told us about you. Asked us to find you and tell you that she needs help." I paused again, a frown tightening my brow. "The thing is, neither Jed nor I can imagine how you, a teenage girl, can possibly help her."

Maris exhaled the breath she'd been holding and said, "Oh! That's terrible. I may not be able to help, but I can let her colony know where she is and what's happened to her. They may be able to figure out how to get her home. At least she'll be with her family again, even if she is cut off from the sea."

"Her colony?" I asked blankly.

The girl nodded. "She's a member of a colony of selkies that lives on Ni'ihau."

"The Forbidden Island?" Jed asked.

"That's right," Maris said, nodding. "It's a private island and most of it is uninhabited. It's a haven for Hawaiian Monk seals, and the selkies decided to make it their home as well. They're related to the Monk seals, after all."

"They are?" Jed and I said together.

"Sure. The Hawaiian selkies are descended from a few Scottish selkies who decided to try their luck with human sailing. When their ship was destroyed in a storm, they managed to grab their skins, transform, and swim to safety. They joined a herd of Hawaiian Monk seals and eventually interbred and became the selkies of Ni'ihau."

"Wow," I said. "I had no idea."

"And how do you fit into all of this?" Jed asked. "What exactly are you?"

Maris glanced around the lounge, but we were the only occupants at the moment. The loudspeaker had announced a whale sighting a few moments before and everyone but us had raced to the port rail to see.

"I'm a siren," she said. "Well, technically, I'm only half siren. My dad, as you probably noticed, is completely normal. Evidently my mom was a real siren."

She shrugged. "I'm a little fuzzy on the details 'cause I didn't know anything about it until last year. Mom kept me away from salt water because she didn't know if my blood would be strong enough to allow me to transform, but she knew I'd be drawn to the sea. So I grew up in Kansas."

"And she never told you?" Jed asked, a little callously in my opinion, but then he hadn't been there to see the look in Maris's eyes when she spoke of her mother's death.

"She died before she got around to explaining," Maris said.

Jed had the grace to look uncomfortable. "Sorry," he said quietly.

"But now I know," Maris continued, her tone brightening, "and Dad and I live here now and I get to swim in the ocean with my friends every day."

"So, do you snorkel with the tourists?" I asked.

"No. I stay on the Sea Princess while everyone snorkels." She grinned. "Wouldn't want to scare away the tourists."

"Of course," Jed said with a nod. "You wouldn't need any equipment, and you probably change shape."

She nodded. "Not as much as a selkie, but it's noticeable. I can swim with my dad, but no one else. At least not in salt water. In fresh water, I stay human."

"Fascinating." I said, and Jed nodded his agreement.

———

SNORKELING at Molokini Crater was wonderful. The turquoise waters were crystal clear, with no sediment to impede our vision. We marveled at the many types of colorful tropical fish as they darted around us, and thrilled to the stately sea turtles that swam so close we could almost touch them. I was truly disappointed when it was time to board the Sea Princess and return to port. But Maris met us with towels and promised to introduce us to a pod of dolphins before we left, so I was content to act the compliant tourist.

As we drove the Jeep back to Kapalua Airport, Jed and I agreed we'd had a very successful day. We'd done the tourist thing, had a taste of snorkeling in paradise, and had fulfilled our promise to Serena. Best of all, Maris had promised to meet us the next afternoon at Hanalei Bay, where we hoped to give the selkie good news.

It was nice to know that not all Fae were evil creatures. Far from needing to protect humanity from selkies, it seemed that, in Hawaii at least, selkies needed protection from humans!

4

The next afternoon we strolled the white sand of Hanalei Bay again, only this time we had to thread our way past beach umbrellas and relaxed people resting on towels soaking up the bright Hawaiian sunshine. Swimsuit clad humans frolicked in the gentle waves, while the more adventurous could be seen adjusting their masks and fins before plunging beneath the surface of the salt water.

Jed and I meandered around the curve of the bay to a rocky outcropping where a lone figure sat staring out to sea, her dark hair billowing in the breeze.

"May we join you?" I asked Serena when we were close enough to speak comfortably above the susurrus of waves and wind.

She glanced up and nodded, a small, sad smile gracing her lovely features. "Of course. It's good to see you again."

I settled on a flattish rock beside her while Jed squatted at my other side. "We found Maris," he said, shading his eyes and glancing out to sea.

Serena sat a little straighter and stared at him, hope shining in her eyes. "What did she say? Will she help?"

I nodded, answering before Jed had the chance. "She said she'd meet us here this afternoon. I don't know when exactly, but…"

"There!" cried Jed, pointing at the water. "I think she's coming. That swimmer is too far out to be a tourist."

Serena and I both gazed in the direction he pointed, and after a moment's searching, I saw something bobbing in the water. Something that came closer and became more distinct as I watched.

"It's her," Serena said, excitement ringing in her voice, "and look! She's not alone. She's brought one of my colony."

A few moments later — faster than I would've thought possible — Maris emerged from the sea, like a red-haired, bikini-clad goddess. She was followed by a seal, who dipped beneath the surface and emerged again as a man with dark hair graying at the temples.

If I hadn't been watching closely, I wouldn't have noticed the unnatural elongation of Maris' hands and feet, or the webbing between her fingers and toes. Her transformation back to human-appearing teen was nearly instantaneous.

The man who followed her onto the rocky outcrop carried what looked like a wet ball of fur, held strategically since he wore no clothes. He didn't seem at all embarrassed by his state of undress. In fact, I had the impression that he held what was undoubtedly his seal skin in that precise location for my benefit alone.

Jed and I rose to our feet as Maris and the selkie approached. Serena jumped to her feet and ran to the man. He dropped his skin and enveloped her in a hug.

"Serena," he said. "We've been so worried. I'm relieved to find you whole and well."

"Father," she said with a sob. "I'm stranded. I can't come home!"

I glanced away from the selkies, feeling that I intruded on their reunion. I turned my attention to Maris instead, and saw that she too carried a wet ball of fur. Puzzled, I glanced back at the father and daughter. No, the man's skin lay at his feet, where he had dropped it to embrace his daughter.

Turning back to Maris, I quirked an eyebrow and nodded to the skin in her hands. But before she could answer my unspoken question, the seal-man cleared his throat.

"The Selkies of Ni'ihau are in your debt, Seers," he said with a formality that rang with Fae magic. The Fae rarely acknowledged obligation to humans, but when they did, it carried a binding geas. Jed reached for my hand, and we held tight to each other.

"We thought our daughter lost forever, but the message you carried has restored her to us." He inclined his head to us, his dark eyes shining with sincerity. "We acknowledge our debt. Word will be sent from dolphin to whale to seal until every one of our kind in the world knows of your deed. If ever you are in need and a selkie is near, we will render what assistance we can." He paused to stare directly into Jed's eyes and then my own. "Selkies do not forget. Never would we have expected such a kindness from a seer. You are unique ... and we will remember."

Chills ran down my spine despite the sun's heat. I knew I should respond, but no words came. My mind felt frozen by the selkie's words.

Fortunately, my husband has always been the socially adept member of our team.

"We acknowledge your gift," he said solemnly, "though we don't feel its need. What we did was a small thing. Carrying your daughter's message cost us little and gained us knowledge, not only of your kind, but of Maris as well. We value such knowledge. Let us part as friends ... with no debt between us."

I squeezed Jed's fingers in appreciation of his words.

The selkie studied us for a long moment. "You are gracious, Seer. We release the obligation of indebtedness in favor of friendship. May the Selkies of Ni'ihau and the members of your bloodline remember this day to eternity. Let there be friendship between our people."

He inclined his head to us, and Jed and I responded in kind.

"And now," he said, turning to his daughter, "we must get you home."

Serena sobbed and tears streamed down her cheeks. "But how? My skin is lost!"

Maris stepped forward, speaking for the first time. "Your mother sent you her skin," she said, holding out the dripping fur. "Wear it for your journey home."

Serena's eyes widened as she accepted the skin, stroking it wistfully. "Is this possible, Father?"

He nodded. "Only from a close relative can such a sacrifice be made, and only in extremis, but yes, you may wear your mother's skin for this journey."

He turned back to me and Jed. "We will take our leave now, Seers. Know that our offer of future assistance holds." He held up a hand when Jed started to object. "Not out of debt or obligation, but out of friendship. Farewell, Seers-Who-Are-Friends-of-Selkies. May your lives be rich and fruitful."

"Farewell, Selkies of Ni'ihau," Jed responded. "May that which is lost be found."

And with that, Serena and her father slipped into the water, donned their skins, and swam swiftly into the depths of the blue Pacific.

EPILOGUE

J ed and I had been home from our Hawaiian honeymoon for less than a month when we received a letter from Maris. I opened it quickly and read aloud.

I just wanted to let you know that Dad and I contacted the police about what was stolen from Serena. Of course, we didn't mention exactly what was taken, only that thieves were preying on tourists on both Kauai and Maui, and that thefts had even happened on our cruises.

The thieves were caught and when the arrest was made, a seal pelt was discovered among the loot. The thieves claimed it was a magical artifact taken from a selkie, but no one believed them. The police saw it as evidence of the slaughter of Hawaiian Monk seals, an endangered species.

Dad says the judge will throw the book at them for that!

Now that Serena's family knows where her lost item is, they'll be able to get it back ... but not until after the trial. The family is anxious for those men to be imprisoned.

Hope everything in Colorado is great!

Your friend,

Maris

I folded the letter and smiled at Jed. "We're friends with a siren."

He nodded. "Not to mention a whole colony of selkies." He grinned and pulled me into his arms. "Who'd've ever guessed we'd be friends with any species of Fae?"

"Certainly not me," I said. "Life is full of surprises."

"Definitely," he said, hugging me even more tightly, "and I can't wait to discover the next one!"

XI

THE JOURNAL

DEB LOGAN

AUTHOR OF *FAERY UNEXPECTED*

THE JOURNAL

SPUN YARNS
A *SEER CHRONICLES* SHORT STORY

CHAPTER ONE

A rtie Woodward-Kendrick pulled down the collapsible staircase to the attic in her childhood home. She'd always hated the attic, had found any and every excuse to avoid going up there. But then, Artie's childhood had been filled with terrors.

Literally.

Creatures no one else could see.

Creatures that fed from the life energy of the people around her. She'd learned to hide from their sight, had learned to keep herself safe. But until she met her husband when they were both teens, she'd had no idea that it was possible to fight them. Her life had changed irrevocably when she met Jed Kendrick, and she'd never been happier.

Time to face yet another of her childhood fears.

Wiping sweaty palms on her well-worn jeans, Artie pushed up the sleeves of her red flannel shirt, grasped the rails of the collapsible stairs and climbed into the dim and dusty attic. She thought she heard something scurry away as she landed on the wooden floorboards, leaving dusty imprints of her sneakers with every step, but her heart was pounding so hard she couldn't be sure.

Where was Jed? He'd agreed to help her with this.

Her parents were selling the house and moving into a condominium and while they sorted and packed the contents of the main floors, she'd been given the task of inspecting the attic and determining what was worth keeping and what should simply be lobbed into the trash bin. She'd wanted to refuse, but her parents were so proud of what they saw as her recovery from her childhood instability ... well, she didn't want to disappoint them. And she *was* strong now. But she was so much stronger with Jed by her side.

She found the slender pull chain that controlled the single light bulb attached to one of the rafters and yanked it on. Light flooded the center of the room, but left the edges and the spaces behind boxes and old wardrobes in shadow. She shivered, but forced herself to walk deeper into the room.

It's just old stuff, she told herself sternly. *There's nothing here that can harm me. It's only creepy because there's not enough light and everything is covered in dust and cobwebs. There's nothing dangerous living in my parents' attic.*

She'd reached the grimy, round window at the far end of the room when a noise on the staircase started her heart pounding again. Turning to face the hole in the floor, she saw a dark head appear. Her racing heartbeat and jittery stomach urged her to scream, but she stifled the impulse. A moment later, she smiled as the man of her dreams stepped into the attic's dim light.

"Hey, sweetheart," Jed said in a cheerful voice as he surveyed the boxes and dilapidated furniture. "Sorry I'm late. How do you want to tackle this?"

Artie released the breath she hadn't realized she'd been holding and gestured around the room. "Pick a box, any box, and evaluate the contents. Let's make three piles: one to keep, one to trash, and one to donate."

"Sounds like a plan," he said, clapping his hands. "Let's get started."

Artie had moved three boxes to the trash heap and one box of out-of-fashion, but serviceable clothes to the donation pile, when Jed gave a low whistle.

"Come take a look at this, Artie."

He stood before an ancient piece of furniture, a secretary her mother would call it. The slanted lid opened to become a flat writing surface and the back portion was filled with little drawers and cubbies for holding who knew what.

"Look what I found," Jed said, his voice loud in the still room. "A kind of secret compartment."

She walked over to stand beside him. What looked like a carved, columnar divider between two of the cubbies was actually a hidden vertical drawer. Jed had accidentally loosened it, and taking a chance, had pulled. It slid out revealing a book with a cracked leather binding and yellowing pages.

But even more unexpected than its hiding place was the book itself. The volume glowed to Artie and Jed's special sight. For Artie Woodward and Jed Kendrick weren't normal humans. They were *Sidhe Seers*. Both were descendants of an ancient Irish clan which had been given the ability to see the Sidhe, the ancient Celtic name for what the mundane world called fairies.

Jed could trace his lineage directly to the ancient O'Connors, but Artie had no idea where her connection originated. She only knew that she could see what she'd always termed *Terrors*, but now knew were a particular race of Fae.

"What do you think it is?" she asked, her earlier nervousness slamming back into action. "Do you think it's safe to touch?"

Jed shrugged. "Only one way to find out," and he pulled the book from its hiding space, opened the cover, and began to read aloud.

January 30, 1919

My name is Maeve O'Connor Woodward and this is my journal.

I'm a newly married woman and a Sidhe Seer. My husband, Michael Woodward, is an English groom. He accompanied his lord from his home in Somerset to the lord's newly purchased manor in the Dublin countryside last year. Michael and I met when he was sent to my family's farm to buy hay and oats for the lord's stables.

I fell in love with him at first sight. Tall and well-built, with golden hair and gray-blue eyes, so unlike the local lads. I longed to run my fingers through that hair, thick and wavy, it was, and the strands that had come loose from the black ribbon with which he'd tied it back enticed me. His hair didn't spring into unruly curls like my own auburn locks, and I wondered what it would feel like between my fingers. Smooth as silk, I imagined. Not the knotted mess mine so often became.

I'm not sure Michael even noticed me that day, but as I would soon come to know, our fates had been bound by the Sidhe, or as some have come to call them, the Fair Folk. 'Tis my belief that they're so called in order not to offend, for the Sidhe I've seen are far from fair. To be sure, ungifted mortals who've been granted a glimpse of the Sidhe are always astounded by their beauty, but that is because they see only the glamour the Sidhe choose to allow.

I'm a Sidhe Seer, from a long line of seers. I see past their glamours to their true countenances, whether they wish to be seen or not. 'Tis a blessing and a curse. I'm not likely to fall prey to their tricks, but if they realize I see them when they believe themselves hidden ... well, 'tis a fine line I walk in order to secure the safety of me and mine.

But I digress.

I was telling you that this is my book. I am keeping this journal to secure a record of my gifts for future generations. If you are reading this, you are my

CHAPTER TWO

Jed paused in his reading and glanced at Artie. "Well, now we know where your seer blood comes from."

She nodded. "Too bad I didn't find this years ago. It would've spared me a lot of grief to know who and what I am. Do you think we should tell my folks?"

Jed frowned. "You get it from your Dad's bloodline according to Maeve's name ... has he ever shown any sign that he has *The Sight?*"

"No, and he never tried to talk to me, to tell me I wasn't alone." She shrugged. "They both acted like they thought I was nuts and carted me off to a psychiatrist before I learned to hide. I think *The Sight* skipped him."

Jed nodded. "According to Granny O'Toole, that's common." He paused, frowning at the book. "Plus, there's something weird about this book."

"Other than the fact it glows?" she asked.

He grinned. "Yeah, other than that. It's the way she assumes that if you're reading it, you have *The Sight*. I wonder...."

He wiped his dusty fingers on his jeans, grabbed Artie's hand and pulled her to the stairs. "Let's test a theory."

They clambered down the collapsible stairs and wound their way around boxes and packing supplies to the kitchen where Artie's mother, Estelle Woodward, was carefully wrapping dishes in newsprint and wedging them into a cardboard box.

"Hey, Estelle," Jed said, leaning against a counter a few feet from where his mother-in-law worked. "How's it going?"

Estelle looked up at the two young people, wiped a strand of hair out of her face with the back of her hand, and smiled. "Getting there." She leaned against the counter as well, happy to take a break from the repetitive work of reaching, wrapping, and bending. "How's the attic coming along."

"We're making progress," Artie said, finding an open bit of floor space and dropping to sit cross-legged.

"Actually," said Jed, "we just found a hidden compartment in an old secretary. This was stashed inside." He held the book out to Estelle. "Thought you might like to see it."

"How odd," she said, accepting the book and examining the cover. "A hidden compartment ... that sounds very intriguing."

The back door opened before she could say more and Richard Woodward stepped into the kitchen carrying a drill and a small blue tool box. He glanced around in surprise.

"What's this?" Richard asked. "Break time?"

"Jed and Artie discovered a secret compartment in an old piece of furniture in the attic," Estelle explained. She held up the book. "This was inside. Any idea what it is?"

Richard placed the drill and tool box on the counter and took the book from his wife. "No idea," he said, opening the cover and flipping through the pages. "Why would anyone hide a blank book?"

Jed laughed, a bit too heartily to Artie's ears, and took the book back from Richard. "It's a mystery. Probably something someone put away to give as a gift and forgot where they hid it. Interesting old secretary though. Do you want to keep it, or should I mark it for charity?"

Estelle grimaced. "Charity, definitely. If it's been tucked in the attic, we haven't needed it, and we already have too much furniture in the main house for our new condo."

"Right," said Artie, scrambling to her feet. "Well, come on, Jed. It's back to work for us."

"Thanks, kids," said Richard. "We really appreciate your help."

"I'm going to order a pizza for lunch," Estelle said. "We'll call you down when it gets here."

"Sweet!" Jed grabbed Artie's hand and gave her a quick tug. "Race you to the attic."

CHAPTER THREE

Once back in the attic's dim light, Artie turned to her husband. "Well, we learned a couple of things."

Jed nodded. "Your dad's definitely not a seer."

"And Maeve had mad skills," added Artie. "I wonder how she managed to write words that only another seer can read?"

"Dunno. Maybe that'll be one of the lessons she'll cover later in the book." He opened the journal and flipped through the pages, each one crammed with small, precise penmanship. Every page was filled, even the back cover bookplate.

Artie took the book from him, walked to the end of the room and propped it against the grimy round window. "I'm anxious to learn more from my great-great-grandmother," she said, "but right now, we need to earn our pizza."

Jed moved to stand beside her. Placing an arm around her shoulders, he reached out with his free hand and stroked the journal's cover. "We're looking forward to learning what you have to teach, Maeve."

Artie rested her head on his shoulder for a moment, then drilled a finger playfully into his side. "Come on, you. There's sorting to be done!"

As they moved to tackle yet more forgotten boxes, Artie surveyed the attic and sighed with contentment. Yet another childhood fear banished. Too bad she hadn't conquered it years ago. If she'd found that book when she was young, her life might have been very different.

Her gaze fell on Jed, earnestly rifling through a box of long disused household items.

No, she wouldn't waste time worrying about what might have been. The events of her life had led her to Jed, and he was worth every awkward or unpleasant moment she'd ever endured. Knowledge was good, and she didn't doubt that they'd learn a lot from Maeve's journal, but she'd learned from experience that knowledge came when the time was right ... and this book had come to her now.

She smiled and opened another box. Now, when she and Jed could study the journal together.

The timing was perfect!

XII

PALADIN SHIELD

DEB LOGAN

AUTHOR OF *FAERY UNEXPECTED*

Paladin
Shield

SPUN YARNS

A *Seer Chronicles* Short Story

1

My name is Artemis Lucia Woodward-Kendrick. My husband, Jedidiah Amos Woodward-Kendrick, and I recently purchased our first home.

I stared at the words I'd just written in the journal that Jed and I had decided would hold the record of our lives together in this house, our first home.

Our home.

Not my parents' home, or my in-laws, or even Grannie O'Toole's quaint cottage in Dublin. No, this sweet little house on the outskirts of McIntosh, Colorado was *our* home. Jed's and mine. Since we were newly married and as yet unemployed, we'd been able to afford this investment in our future thanks to the generosity of our friend and benefactor, Laird Angus O'Connor.

Life had been a whirlwind since I'd rescued Jed from enthrallment to the fairy queen in Ireland last Halloween. But that horrendous ordeal was behind us now. We were safely married, had enjoyed a fabulous honeymoon in Hawaii— again, thanks to Laird Angus— and had celebrated Christmas with friends and family here in Colorado.

We'd been home from our honeymoon for a scant three months, but already the new year had brought even more change. My parents had decided to downsize, moving from the home I'd grown up in to an upscale condominium on the shore of Lake McIntosh. Of course Jed and I helped with packing and their move, but since we'd been staying with Mom and Dad, that event had also necessitated a search for a home of our own. Jed's parents had offered us a room in their home, but we'd decided it was time to find our own place in the world.

And now, thanks to Laird Angus, we're the proud owners of this lovely little cottage situated on the very edge of national forest land. The cottage sits on an acre and a half of land, shaded by old growth pines and firs. Though it was only mid-March, crocuses and daffodils were already shooting up in the front garden and buds were showing on the apple tree in the backyard.

Inside, the cottage was snug and cozy, reminding me of Jed's grand-mother's home in Dublin. The main floor boasted a comfortable living room which Jed and I had furnished with second-hand items, including a few pieces my parents didn't have room for in their new condominium. Like the well-worn brown leather sofa that used to live in the great room of my childhood home and the antique mahogany secretary Jed and I discovered when we were cleaning out the attic.

I smiled, well pleased with the look of the room. From the hardwood floors with their braided rag rugs to the mismatched sofa and over-stuffed chairs to the secretary, lovingly cleaned and polished, the room spoke of comfort and contentment. Which was exactly what I wanted.

Opening my *sight*, I studied the room again, this time nodding with satisfaction at the warding runes glimmering on the walls and surrounding the windows and doors. Jed and I would be safe within these walls. No wandering Fae would break through those wards.

Moving into the kitchen, I sighed with happiness. From the cheery yellow walls and white pine cabinets to the farmer's sink, brushed steel appliances, and terra cotta floor tiles, the room suited me perfectly. I glanced across the half-wall with its serving counter to the dining area. Jed and I had found a wonderful pine trestle table and six matching chairs at an estate sale. We intended to share many meals at that table, enjoying the view from the wide windows that overlooked the tame carpet of our back lawn as well as the wild beauty of the old growth forest beyond.

Finally, I turned my attention to the bedroom... and shivered as a tingle of delight ran down my spine. The room was dominated by a king-size rustic aspen log bed topped with an heirloom log cabin quilt done in blues and reds and golds. The quilt was a gift from Jed's parents, but the bed itself was our gift to each other. We'd seen an example of the craftsman's work on a trip to Estes Park and had known instantly we had to have one. The bed was our one splurge. Everything else in our new home might be second-hand, but our bed would be our own. We'd special ordered it that very day, and now here it stood, in our own bedroom, in our own home.

Anticipating the night to come, my heart raced. I was almost as excited as I'd been on our honeymoon! Forcing my thoughts back to the here and now, I continued my examination of the house, moving to the narrow staircase.

Much like Grannie O'Toole's home, our cottage also included a second story—two small bedrooms tucked beneath the eaves with a shared bath. At the moment they both served as storage for the crates and boxes we'd yet to unpack, but we intended to set at least one up as an office.

Of course, an office suggested we had a clue about our future careers. Which neither of us did... at least not yet.

Sighing, I returned to the kitchen. Opening the refrigerator, I removed a pitcher of orange juice, grabbed a tumbler from the cabinet beside the sink, and poured myself a glass. Carrying the orange juice to the trestle table, I sat and sipped the tart liquid while staring at the huge trees beyond the yard and pondering our future. Life had finally settled down. Mom and Dad were happy in their condominium. Jed and I had a place to call our own. It was time to establish a routine, and that meant finding a way to support ourselves. We were adults now. Time to make our own way in the world. No more dependence on either set of parents, or even Laird Angus, the head of Clan O'Connor, and my friend and mentor during those dark days in Ireland.

We needed jobs, but what kind?

Sure, we had skills. Unique skills that had been passed through our bloodlines for generations, but those skills weren't exactly marketable.

Jed and I were hereditary *Sidhe Seers*. We could see what other mortals could not. We saw the Fae— in all their beauty and horror. And more than that, now that we'd found the journal left by my *Seer* ancestress, we were learning that we had the ability to banish the Fae from the mortal world.

But since regular folks had no idea the Fae existed, except in children's tales, our skills weren't exactly a hot commodity. Sure, we'd gone to college. Jed had decent IT skills and I was an excellent researcher, but information technology and library science were unlikely to support us; not when we might have to drop everything on a moment's notice in order to fight an incursion of Fae!

I had no idea how we were going to solve this puzzle, but knew we'd figure it out. I shook my head, remembering what was important: Jed and I were together. When he'd been enthralled by the fairy queen in Ireland, I'd been terrified that he was lost to me forever, that I'd never find a way to rescue him. Yet here we were, married with our own home in Colorado. Finding jobs would be a snap compared to breaking the fairy queen's hold on my best friend... and the love of my life!

Before I could do more than take another sip of orange juice, I heard the front door open and footsteps pound across the hardwood floor.

"Artie!" Jed's voice called. "Where are you? I've got news!"

2

"**I**'m in the kitchen," I called, placing my glass on the table and standing to meet the man I loved.

Jed burst into the room, strode to my side and swept me into his arms, hugging me tightly. "You'll never guess," he said, twirling in a circle before setting me on my feet and holding me at arms' length.

"What?" I cried, laughing and working to find my balance after his enthusiastic greeting. "What are you so excited about?"

"Angus!" he said, his grin so wide it was a wonder he could speak. "Laird Angus is coming. I just got off the phone with him. He's at the airport now."

"In Dublin? When will his flight land in Denver?"

"No," he said, his eyes alight with merriment. "He called from Denver! He's renting a car and will be here within the hour."

My happy surprise turned to horror. "Here? Now? Jed! We don't have a spare bedroom set up yet." Not that we'd really planned to have a guest bedroom. We intended for those small bedrooms upstairs to be storage and an office. At the moment, both were disaster areas! I glanced toward our bedroom with its beautiful king-size bed and sighed. Our first night in our new bed would have to wait. The laird would have our room and we'd make do with sleeping bags among the boxes upstairs.

Jed laughed and pulled me into his arms. "Don't worry about it, sweetheart. Angus can afford a suite at the Hilton, though I expect he'll make do with a less fancy hotel here in McIntosh."

I sighed, more relieved than I wanted to admit, and nodded. "Okay. Did he say why he was here?" I asked, and then hurried to add, "Not that I'm not delighted, of course, but Colorado is a long way from Ireland."

Jed released me and moved to the cabinet beside the sink. Grabbing a tumbler, he poured himself a glass of orange juice and we settled at the table.

"Not really," he said after chugging half of his juice. "He just said he needed to talk to us and he'd be on his way as soon as he had keys to a car."

I nodded and sipped my juice. I wasn't worried about him getting lost on the way; he'd made the drive from Denver to McIntosh last fall when he'd accompanied Grannie O'Toole to our wedding. But why was he here at all? What could the clan chief of the O'Connors need to talk to us about? I suspected there was more to the man than most people knew— when I first met Laird Angus my *sight* had hinted he was far more powerful, and far older, than he seemed— but I'd kept my suspicions to myself.

Perhaps we were about to discover more about our benefactor.

A little over an hour later, Jed and I stood on our front porch as Laird Angus O'Connor parked a dark blue Subaru Outback in our driveway. I reached for Jed's hand as Angus stepped from the car and made his way to us.

"Mr. and Mrs. Woodward-Kendrick," he said with a gallant bow. "It's pleased I am to see ye in your new home."

"Welcome, Laird Angus," Jed said, letting go of my hand and stepping forward to shake the Laird's. "We're always glad to see you."

Laird Angus turned to me, mischief sparkling in his eyes. "And ye, Artie? Are ye glad to see me?" He cocked his head and raised an eyebrow.

I laughed and threw myself at him, startling him so that I nearly knocked him to the ground, but he caught me in his arms and we hugged each other tightly. "I owe you my life and my happiness, Angus," I whispered, tears gathering in my eyes. "You will *always* be welcome in my home."

Jed cleared his throat and I stepped away from the Laird, wiping my eyes and smiling. "Well, don't just stand there," Jed said. "Come in and see the place you helped us buy!"

Jed and I proudly escorted Laird Angus through our home, even leading him through the mess of the upstairs bedrooms and detailing our plans for them once we'd finished unpacking and could find the floor. We finished by standing on the back deck, pointing out where our land ended and the national forest land began.

"Ah, 'tis a bonny place ye've chosen," he said as Jed opened the patio door and led us into the dining area. "I'm sure ye will be verra happy here." He glanced above the door, his eyes losing their focus, and I knew he was examining our wards. When satisfied, he nodded and smiled at me. "Ye've done verra well. 'Tis proud I am to have ye in my clan."

I grinned. "About that..."

"Aye, yer Grannie Maeve told me. The mystery of yer lineage has been solved," he said, his eyes twinkling. "I'd like to have a peek at that wee journal while I'm here."

"Of course," said Jed, "but before we start talking business, why don't we sit down? Maybe have a cup of coffee or tea?" He cocked his head and continued, "Here or the living room? Your choice, Angus."

The Laird clapped, rubbed his hands together, and nodded. "A cuppa wouldna go amiss," he said with a smile. "Tea, if it's no trouble, and let's settle in that pretty living room."

"No trouble at all," I said, moving around the counter to put the kettle on. "Jed, why don't you show Angus the journal while I make the tea."

Jed nodded and the men left the kitchen.

A few minutes later I carried a tray into the living room to find Angus standing by the window studying the journal Jed and I had discovered in the antique secretary in the attic of the home where I'd grown up; the same secretary that now stood in the corner of this room in all its newly refurbished glory.

"Well," I said, setting the tray laden with mugs of tea and a plate of oatmeal cookies on the oak coffee table, "I'm glad to see you haven't been wasting time."

Angus looked up and grinned. Closing the book he strode across the room and settled in one of the overstuffed chairs. Jed joined me on the sofa and handed out napkins and cookies while I arranged the mugs of tea within everyone's easy reach.

I took a sip of my tea before gazing directly at Angus and asking, "So, Laird Angus, what brings you to Colorado?"

He held up the small book he'd been studying. "This journal for one thing," he said solemnly, and then gestured to me, "and to welcome a long-lost daughter into the clan."

I frowned. "That can't be all. Regardless of that journal, I became part of your clan when I married Jed."

"True enough," he agreed, "but this journal clears up your bloodline. 'Tis good to know which line of my descendants you belong to." He laid the journal on his knee and patted it. "I lost track of this lassie when she came to America. I'm glad to know her line continued and her blood ran true."

Whether he'd intended to or not, Angus had just confirmed my long-held belief that he was far older than he looked. I glanced at Jed and saw with amusement that he'd had no idea. His eyes were fairly popping out of his head and his jaw hung slack.

I took the mug from Jed's hand and placed it on the coffee table, nudging him with my elbow as I did so. "Close your mouth, my love," I said quietly. "You look like he hit you with a two-by-four."

Angus laughed as Jed composed himself. "You're not surprised, Artie?" Angus asked in an amused rumble.

"My insight suggested as much when I first met you in the O'Connor archives," I said.

"But you never said anything!" Jed protested.

I shrugged. "I didn't know for sure. Besides, it wasn't my secret to tell."

"Ye are wise beyond yer years, lass," the Laird said. Turning to Jed, he continued, "I am not only the laird of the O'Connor clan, Jedidiah Amos Kendrick. I am *THE* O'Connor. The first and original *Sidhe Seer*. My longevity is due to the fact that I am half *sidhe*. My father is a *sidhe* prince; my mother was a mortal woman." He shrugged and took a swallow of tea. "And I? I am as you see me... and have been so since before the Romans invaded the British Isles."

"B...but...but," Jed stammered. "But the *sidhe* are FAE!"

Angus nodded. "Indeed they are. *Sidhe* is the old name, the Gaelic name. They've been known as the *fair folk*, which devolved into *fairy*, for centuries now. I prefer to name them *Fae*, myself."

Jed shook his head. "But if you're part Fae, aren't you, aren't *we* hunting your own family?"

Angus nodded. "I despised the way the Fae treated mortals, my mother included, and vowed to protect humans from the *sidhe*." He cocked his head and gazed intently at Jed. "I heard about your interactions with the selkies and that part-siren girl in Hawaii. You didn't banish them. In fact, you helped them."

"They weren't hurting anyone," I said quickly, my cheeks heating and my pulse quickening at the implied criticism.

He held up his hand. "Peace, Artie. I wasn't questioning your decision, merely making a point. If the *sidhe*, the Fae, leave mortals in peace, I'm content to instruct my clan to leave them be. 'Tis only when the Fae prey on mortals that me and mine intervene."

We were all quiet for a few moments, each considering the ramifications of the Laird's remarks. I bit into an oatmeal cookie, savoring the rich flavors of creamed butter and sugar, oats and raisins as I considered the man's long life. Not to mention the fact that I wouldn't exist if he hadn't married in the far distant past and sired children. I wondered exactly how many people alive today could trace their lineage back to Angus O'Connor? Certainly both Jed and I could.

My eyes widened and I inhaled so sharply I almost choked on a bit of cookie. Didn't that mean that Jed and I were related? Should we have married? Would the Laird's revelations end my relationship to the man I loved more than life itself?

My thoughts must have shown on my face, for Angus reached across the coffee table and patted my knee. "Relax, Artie. I checked. Yer line and Jed's parted company before America was even discovered. Ye are nowhere near being closely related, despite the fact that ye both descend from me."

My cheeks heated and I lowered my head, allowing my hair to fall forward, shielding me from his gaze. Before more than a heartbeat or two had passed, Jed touched my arm.

"Don't, Artie," he said quietly. "You're safe with me, and Angus means us no harm. You don't need to hide."

I straightened, pushed my hair behind my ears, and leaned into Jed's arm. "Thanks," I told him. Turning to Angus, I said, "Forgive me, laird. It's an old instinct."

Angus studied me. "Yer defense is formidable, Artie. I almost lost sight o' ye, and I'm fully aware ye are here." He cocked his head, his eyes narrowing. "I don't think I've ever seen that ability before, though yer grannie did mention she'd seen it once."

Knowing I'd be embarrassed, Jed rubbed his hands together and said, "All right!" before grabbing a cookie, stuffing the whole thing in his mouth and chewing rapidly. He washed it down with a swig of tea, and said, "So, the facts as we know them." He held up a finger. "One: Angus is ancient." A second finger joined the first. "We're all related." His ring finger rose. "If the Fae don't bother us, we don't bother them."

He glanced around. "Is that all there is? You came all the way from Ireland to tell us not to bother any Fae that doesn't threaten us or the community around us? When you already had proof we'd do that anyway?" He narrowed his eyes and pointed at Angus. "I don't think so. I also don't think you came to confess your age. I'm guessing most of the O'Connor clan has no idea you're the original O'Connor. So what really brought you to Colorado?"

Angus smiled and nodded. "Verra astute, Jedidiah. Ye're correct on all counts." He picked up a cookie, took a bite, and chewed. Slowly and deliberately. As if he had all the time in the world. Which, of course, he did. Quite literally.

Jed bounced up and paced around the room, coming to a stop behind the sofa. Resting his hands on the back, he leaned forward and glared at Angus. "Come on, man! Spit it out!"

Angus's eyebrows rose almost to his hairline and he glanced at the last bite of cookie in his hand.

Jed scowled. "Not the cookie," he almost shouted. "The reason for your visit."

Angus finished his cookie, took a swallow of tea, and said, "Oh. That." He glanced at me. "This is verra good tea, Artie."

I tried not to smile as I said, "Thank you, Laird, but I think you need to answer Jed's question before he explodes. He's not as patient as I am."

Jed threw up his hands, muttering in disgust, and strode around the sofa to plop down beside me again.

"Fine," Angus said cheerfully. "If ye must know, I came to offer ye jobs. Both of ye."

3

_____

"What?" Jed and I exclaimed together, though to be fair, Jed almost roared ,while I definitely squeaked.

"Jobs," Angus repeated. "Employment. Ye know, a way to earn money to pay for yer home and food."

"I know what a job is," Jed growled. "I just don't know how you expect to employ us when you're in Ireland and we're in Colorado." His eyes narrowed and he leaned forward. "We're not moving to Ireland, if that's what you're thinking."

Angus leaned back, comfortable in the overstuffed chair. "And why would ye be thinking I want ye in Ireland when 'twas I who ensured ye had the wherewithal to buy this house? Don't be daft, boy. A man who's lived as long as I have has varied business holdings and more capital at his fingertips than ye can imagine." He stopped talking, seemingly engrossed in examining said fingers.

"And?" I prompted before my husband could growl again.

Angus glanced at me and smiled. "I'm opening a Denver branch of one of my IT companies, Paladin Shield. I want the two o' ye on my payroll as consultants."

Jed sat back, his expression neutral. "What kind of IT company and how would we consult?"

"'Tis designed for computer security. Keeping systems up to date and impervious to hacking. I know ye studied information technology at university, Jed, so no one will question yer credentials, but I'm no interested in yer computer skills. I have experts on staff for that. Purely mortal men and women who have no knowledge o' the Fae."

He paused and studied our faces. "Nay, I want the two of ye to be my paladins. My knights— though ye willna be wearing shining armor— to defend humanity from malicious Fae. Ye'll be on the payroll of Paladin Shield, but ye'll have no need to set foot in the building; ye'll report directly to me. The only folk in the Denver office who'll know aught about ye will be the head of HR, who will have employment files that I'll create, and the financial director, who will authorize yer pay."

I frowned. "Why paladins?"

Angus shrugged. "A nod to my longevity. I knew Charlemagne's paladins. Rode with them on a few quests. A more noble group of knights never existed. They were honorable men who fought to protect the people given into their care."

He stopped, his eyes glazed with memories of the distant past. After a moment, he shook himself and met our gazes. "So? What do ye say? Want to become modern day paladins, roaming the earth to protect mortals from dangers they canna even see?"

"Of course," we answered together, then grinned at each other.

"Seriously, Angus," Jed said. "That sounds perfect."

I nodded. "Exactly what I dreamed of, but couldn't figure out how to achieve."

Angus slapped his hands on his knees. "Excellent! Ye'll have access to a private jet hangered at the Denver airport. I'll give ye each a dedicated cell phone just for this purpose and will let ye know where ye need to be when trouble arises."

"Wow," Jed said. "A private jet? Dedicated phones? This is starting to sound like James Bond."

Angus laughed. "Not quite. Ye'll have no 'Q' building fancy weapons and gadgets, but the O'Connor clan does provide me with an enviable intelligence network. Not all of my descendants have the *sight*, but enough do to keep me informed about conditions around the world, and fewer still have the means to fight the Fae. Most can only observe, and that only with great discretion. The two o' ye are unique. Which is why I want ye to be the paladins of the O'Connor clan."

Jed and I nodded, too overwhelmed to speak.

"When you're not on quest," Angus continued, "ye'll live and train here in McIntosh. I'll arrange for a mixed martial arts master to work with ye when ye are in residence." He turned his gaze on Jed. "I'd also like for ye to appeal to yer guardian angel. See if he will join ye in the physical world and train both of ye to fight the supernatural more effectively."

"How did you…" Jed began, then closed his eyes and answered his own question. "Grannie O'Toole."

Angus nodded. "Maeve O'Toole is an invaluable part of my intelligence network. Will ye make the request?"

"I will, but Michael visits when he sees fit, and then only in my dreams."

"I understand," Laird Angus said, "but perhaps a prayer would not be amiss?"

Jed nodded. After all, his father was the pastor of one of the local evangelical churches. "I'll visit my dad's church and pray for intercession."

"Excellent," Angus exclaimed again. He rose and clapped his hands. "Now that our business is concluded, may I take my favorite paladins out for a steak dinner?"

Jed and I agreed readily, and I moved around the coffee table to hug our ancestor, benefactor, and... employer!

4

Spring blossomed into summer before Jed and I were called upon to act as Laird Angus's paladins.

The months between the Laird's visit and our first assignment were busy ones. Angus arranged for a small dojo to be built at the back of our land once Master Kenji approved its placement.

"The trees enfold this space like the arms of the dragon," our sensei told us when we met for our first lesson in our private training space. "You will learn safely here." The sensei worked us hard, meeting with us three days a week and insisting we practice *tai chi* every morning before breakfast.

But mixed martial arts weren't the total extent of our training. We also trained with Michael three days a week. Not the same days, thankfully, but between the sensei and the archangel, Jed and I had only a single day without scheduled training sessions.

True to his word, Jed had gone to his father's church the day after Angus's visit and spent an hour in prayer, asking for Michael's help in defending the human race from malicious Fae. The archangel had replied swiftly. He visited Jed's dreams that very night and listened attentively to Jed's description of the Laird's plan.

"When your training space is complete," the warrior angel had said, "I will come. But you and Artemis will be the only witnesses. I will be invisible to anyone else who happens upon our training."

While Master Kenji taught us to fight, he also taught us to meditate. To clear our minds of all distractions and to act with focused deliberation. We learned calmness in the face of danger, and practiced until our bodies could react without conscious thought.

Archangel Michael also taught us to fight deliberately and without fear, but his teaching concentrated on more arcane methods. From Michael we learned the uses of holy water, of specific prayers for the sanctification of weapons, places, and people. He taught us how to call upon the forces of light and life to aid us in the protection of innocent lives. Michael taught us faith. Not in church or creed, but in the god who created us and the forces of good he had set in motion in our world. Michael agreed wholeheartedly with Laird Angus (and us) that as long as the Fae were not in opposition to that good, they were not to be harmed.

It was an intense three months, but when the call came from Angus in early July, we felt ready.

Jed answered our dedicated phone and engaged the speaker function so neither of us would miss a word.

"And how are ye progressing, my paladins?" Laird Angus asked.

"Michael and Master Kenji are satisfied with our progress," Jed said. "Of course we won't know for sure until we're tested, but I'm confident in our abilities."

"And ye, Artemis?" Angus asked. "Are ye confident as well?"

I nodded, though the Laird couldn't see me. "I am. Jed and I fought well together before our training. We have a lot more techniques to put into action now."

"Verra well," Angus said, and I could almost see him nodding. "'Tis time for my paladins to take the field. Ye are needed in Glasgow. A particularly mean-spirited clan o' Fae have moved into the city. They're terrorizing the citizenry, though the locals are attributing the violence to gang wars and the like."

Jed and I glanced at each other, our expressions grave.

"How do you want us to proceed?" Jed asked.

"Get ye to the airport. I've already alerted the pilot. He'll have the jet fueled up and the flight plan logged by the time ye arrive."

I grabbed a pad of paper and a pen and wrote down the details as Laird Angus fired them off: which hangar to approach; where to park; the pilot's name. All the information we'd need not only for this mission, but for future ones as well.

When all the details had been passed along, Laird Angus said, "One o' my O'Connor lads will meet ye when ye land in Glasgow. He'll take ye to the clan keep. The other *Sidhe Seers* there will fill you in on the specifics. They won't be able to help ye fight, but they'll support ye in any way they can, so don't be afraid to tell them what ye need."

Jed and I nodded. "We understand," I said.

"We'll keep you posted," Jed said.

"Dinna worry about that, lad," Angus said. "The Glasgow clan members will give me regular reports. Ye'll be there to protect the city, not to be doing paper work and chatting with me."

"We won't let you down, sir," Jed said. I nodded my agreement.

"I've every confidence in ye both," the Laird said. A moment later he added, "After all, I've seen young Artie at work first hand."

Jed turned to me and grinned; my cheeks heated with a flush. "She's pretty amazing," he said. "I'm a lucky man."

"That ye are, lad. That ye are."

The flight to Glasgow was amazing. I'd never set foot on a private jet before and was overwhelmed by the luxury. Comfortable white leather seats seemed to mold to your body and swiveled for ease of conversation or reclined for relaxation. Deeply cushioned chocolate brown carpeting. Cherry wood tables and architectural accents were polished to a velvety glow. Curved white walls with strategically placed windows for viewing the world as we skimmed above it.

Having only flown commercial flights before, and those only rarely, I was overcome with nerves. I closed my eyes and concentrated on the meditation exercises Master Kenji had taught me. I couldn't afford to allow the butterflies fluttering in my belly to get the best of me. If I gave in to nerves now— over the transportation the Laird had provided!— how would I ever manage to control myself when it came time to battle the Fae?

Jed didn't seem nearly as nervous as I felt. No, my tall, handsome husband acted like a ten-year-old boy turned loose in a candy shop! He sat in every seat but the one I'd chosen, checked out all the cubbyholes, chatted with the pilot, and asked if he could join him in the cockpit and check out the controls. The pilot laughed good naturedly and said not today, but he'd check with the Laird about a future flight.

At last the pilot retreated to the cockpit and Jed settled in the seat across from me. Buckling our seatbelts, we prepared for take-off, which was so smooth as to be practically unnoticeable. The minute we levelled off and the *fasten seat belts* warning clicked off, Jed jumped up and said, "This is awesome! Want a snack?"

I laughed, my nerves dissolving immediately. My Jed was irrepressible!

"Sure. Why not?" I unbuckled my seatbelt and joined him in exploring the compact, but well-stocked galley. We opted for fresh-baked chocolate chip cookies and bottles of spring water. I'd eyed the selection of fresh fruit— apples, oranges, bananas, and a medley of berries — but decided I could be health conscious another day. This first flight was all about luxury!

A little over nine hours after leaving Denver, we landed in Glasgow. While it was only early evening for me and Jed, it was past midnight in Scotland. We disembarked from the jet and were met by a sleepy-eyed man with auburn hair and beard in a rumpled dark blue suit.

"Jed Kendrick and Artemis Woodward?" he asked, stifling a yawn.

We nodded and Jed held out his hand. "It's actually Woodward-Kendrick for both of us," he said, shaking the man's hand. "We decided to combine our surnames when we married."

"O' course," the man said, extending his hand to me. "I'm Gareth O'Connor. Laird Angus asked me ta help ye get settled and act as yer guide." He motioned toward a waiting car. "If ye'll come this way…"

We followed the man across the tarmac, but as he opened the door of the car, I placed a hand on his arm.

"I know it's late here," I said, urgency buzzing beneath my words, "but I feel a need to confront the Fae now. Before they're alerted to our presence."

Jed nodded. "She's right. It's not even time for dinner yet as far as we're concerned. Take us straight to the area most effected by the Fae's malice."

Gareth studied our faces, his expression revealing his skepticism. Then he shrugged and his face cleared. "Fine. Th' Laird ga' me no specific instructions about yer mission, only that I should gi' ye what aid I could. I ken where th' Fae are most active and if ye wish to go straight there, I'll take ye."

When we were settled in the car and underway, he added, "Ye do understand that I'll no be going wi' ye? If th' Fae know I'm a *Seer*, my usefulness to th' clan will be at an end."

Jed, who sat beside Gareth on what would have been the driver's side if we were in the States, nodded. "We understand."

"We expect to fight alone." I reached forward from the back seat and laid a hand on Gareth's shoulder. "It's what we've been training to do."

"Where are we going?" Jed asked. "And what types of Fae have you seen there?"

We'd left the airport behind and now drove through quiet streets. In the distance, across what I knew must be the River Clyde, lights shone in what was undoubtedly the vibrant heart of the city. But Gareth guided the car away from those lights.

"I'm taking ye to Easterhouse." Gareth's knuckles whitened with the strength of his grip on the steering wheel. "The Fae ha' been riling up those who're disaffected anyway, and the pubs o' th' area ha' been dealin' wi' even more violence than usual lately." He glanced over his shoulder at me. "Two men ha' died in th' last week alone."

Jed and I digested that information as Gareth guided the car across a bridge over the River Clyde. After a few moments, he spoke again.

"As to the type o' Fae, I've seen goblins and redcaps, and…"— he grimaced and swallowed— "and sluagh."

Jed whistled softly, and I shivered.

Sluagh. The Host of the Unforgiven Dead.

Jed turned in his seat and met my gaze. I nodded, knowing he was thinking as I was that it was a good thing we'd been training with Michael.

"Right," Jed said, directing his words to Gareth. "You'll want to stop a few blocks from where you expect the trouble to be. Artie and I will need to gear up."

We'd entered a part of the city that seemed less well kept. The houses, apartment buildings, and even the businesses had a disillusioned, unkempt air about them. Almost as if the structures themselves despaired of hope and happiness. Gareth pulled the car to the curb and Jed and I stepped out.

My spirit sank as I set foot on the pavement. The very air seemed to urge me to return to the car and escape. I straightened my shoulders and joined Jed as he pawed through the cases we'd brought with us.

"Let's see," he mumbled, almost to himself. "We'll want holy water and the swords Michael blessed." He handed me items as he spoke.

As I buckled on my sword and stowed the holy water in pockets of my calf-length black leather duster, I rehearsed the prayers of sanctification and protection Michael had taught us.

Jed also donned a black leather duster, though he cut a much more impressive figure than my five-foot-two physique could command. Tall and lanky, my warrior husband towered over me. His normally gentle gray eyes flashed with deadly fire as we prepared to battle supernatural forces for the souls of the people of Glasgow.

We moved away from the car as Gareth pointed us in the direction we should go. "I'll shadow ye," he said. When Jed cocked his head and lifted a brow, Gareth shrugged. "I'm ta report on yer success ta th' Laird." He grinned. "And if ye are no successful, I'll be there ta drag yer carcasses out o' danger."

I smiled, but Jed laughed out loud. "Good to know you've got our backs."

Finding the trouble wasn't hard. We heard the ruckus before we turned the corner toward the pub. When we came within sight, we saw a large gang of men slugging it out. Glass from the pub's broken front window glittered in the light spilling from the open door. Men and women stood just inside the door and others leaned carefully over the frame of the shattered window. Those who weren't fighting yelled catcalls, egging their favorite fighters on.

But this wasn't a friendly scuffle between mates. The atmosphere felt dark and malicious. Many of the catcalls were vicious, as if the bystanders thirsted for spilled blood.

I engaged my *sight* and saw the supernatural elements that orchestrated the brawl. Redcaps ensured that falls resulted in cuts from broken glass. Goblins pushed and shoved, making sure no combatants retired from the fight, while the sluagh flitted among the mortals, filling their minds with battle rage and lust for others' pain.

Jed and I glanced at each other, pulled our swords, and strode into the fray reciting prayers for protection of the mortals as we met the supernatural enemy.

Gareth told us later that it looked like a dance—a deadly dance. We slashed and cut, twirled and leapt, separating the Fae from the mortals they sought to harm. The skirts of our dusters flared as we moved from goblin to sluagh to redcap.

Lunge. Thrust. Parry. Feint.

We moved as a unit, always aware of where the other fought as we dodged and blocked, and swept our enemy from the street.

The mortal men and women stepped back as our prayers took effect. They shook their heads and stared at each other as if wondering why they were bloody and bruised.

But they all turned to watch us fight, and since none could see the enemy, they told themselves they were watching a display of antique skills, for no one fought with blades in this modern world.

When the last redcap fled, Jed and I sheathed our swords amid cheers from the watching crowd. Gareth appeared at our sides, and the barman called everyone inside for a round of drinks... on the house!

6

"They are a sight ta behold, Laird." Gareth spoke into his cell phone while Jed and I packed the last of our belongings. "Th' locals won't be forgettin' the late night *exhibitions* the master swordsmen ha' been puttin' on this seven-day." He paused, listening. "Aye, I'll be tellin' 'em."

Gareth ended the call and turned to us. "He's right pleased, is the Laird. Says ye are ta rest up and be ready for his next call."

Jed and I glanced at each other and grinned. Rest up indeed! Our battles in Glasgow had shown us where our weaknesses were. When we got back to Colorado, we intended to train even harder. We had specific scenarios to describe to both Michael and Master Kenji, and we expected our mentors to help us work out new, more effective strategies.

As he drove us back to the airport, Gareth provided a running commentary on the effects of our work. "Even the locals, those wi' not a whit o' the *sight*, can feel th' change in Easterhouse. Friendlier, they say. There's hope in th' air and folk are cleaning up th' neighborhoods.

Men as were fightin' and growlin' at each other a week ago are workin' together ta rebuild and refurbish."

He shook his head. "If I hadna seen it with me own two eyes, I'd ne'er ha' believed it possible." He parked the car near the private jet and helped Jed and I with our luggage.

When we were ready to board, he shook hands with each of us. "'Tis proud I am ta know ye and claim clanship wi' ye. Go wi' grace and know ye'll always ha' friends in Glasgow."

"Thanks," I said, "and the same is true of you. If you ever come to Colorado, we'll be glad of your company."

We boarded the jet, sank gratefully into white leather comfort, and smiled. Happy, but exhausted. We'd survived our first mission. More than survived! We were now full-fledged paladins. Battle-tested and ready to go wherever the clan needed us. We would fight to shield mortals from the wrath and spite of the supernatural enemies they couldn't even see.

Laird Angus had named his IT company well. *Paladin Shield*. We, Jed and I, were the true paladin shield... and we were proud to carry that responsibility. Blessed to be able to protect those given into our care.

EIGHT STORIES BY DEBBIE MUMFORD

I

THE WEDDING CAKE

UNCOLLECTED ANTHOLOGY

MAGICAL ARTS

ISSUE 26 · UA · DECEMBER 2021

THE WEDDING CAKE

DEBBIE MUMFORD

1

Sally Ann Grainger admired the spectacular cake she'd just finished decorating for her best friend's wedding. Sally had baked the three tier cake from scratch using only the freshest ingredients and imbuing the batter with her finest spells for health, happiness, and enduring love—though she'd been careful to limit the love spell to Amy and her soon-to-be husband Aaron. No need to include all the guests who would enjoy a slice of cake in that particular incantation!

And now the glorious confection was complete. Three tiers of rich, layered spice cake, iced smooth in almond buttercream frosting and decorated with sprays of fresh and fondant flowers cascading from the top tier. In deference to the fall season, Sally had tinted the frosting a pale peach and chosen fall blooms in vibrant reds, yellows, and oranges. Her fondant rosebuds were perfect and the marzipan leaves added an elegant finishing touch. Truly, Amy's wedding cake was a testament to Sally's skills, both as a baker and as a kitchen witch.

Sally Ann's magic was homey and comforting. She was a wizard in the kitchen. Her soufflés never fell. Her pies always had perfect, flaky crusts. Her bread rose consistently and the crust browned beautifully. And her soups and stews? Nourishing and healthful. Perfectly spiced and able to drive out the common cold with a single bowl.

Her pickles and preserves would have astounded judges at the county fair. If Sally Ann canned it, the jars sparkled and the contents glowed with color. Why, her pickled beets practically begged to be tasted! Not that Sally Ann would ever enter a cooking contest of any sort. It wouldn't be fair to the non-magical participants.

But Amy's wedding cake was another matter; it would be seen and appreciated by guests young and old. And all that was left for her to do was to deliver her masterpiece safely to the church, a mere six blocks away.

She was in the middle of casting a temporary protective spell over her creation, to ensure its safe transportation, when her doorbell rang. Momentarily distracted, she completed her incantation, wiped her hands on her apron and hurried to answer the door.

Pausing just a moment to catch her breath, Sally Ann swung the heavy, carved oak door wide and grinned at her visitors.

"I might have known," she said with a laugh, then hugged her mother and younger sister as they stepped across her threshold.

Ellen Grainger studied Sally Ann. "I had a feeling I should be here. Nothing is amiss, I hope?"

All of the women in the Grainger family were witches, but each had unique talents. While Sally Ann was a gifted kitchen witch, her sister Carol Lee's talent was gardening. To say she had a green thumb was a gross understatement. Carol Lee could grow *anything*. And their mother Ellen's specialty? Timeliness. Ellen Grainger always knew when she was needed and made sure she arrived to do what was required. She wasn't prescient, not precisely. Ellen never knew what was going to happen in advance, but she always knew when her assistance was needed... and she was never late.

"Not a thing," Sally Ann said, leading her mother and sister down the hall and into her kitchen. Stepping to the side, she gestured to Amy's wedding cake. "What do you think?"

Her sister's jaw dropped and her eyes widened. Then Carol Lee let out a whoop and clapped her hands. "Oh, Sal! You've outdone yourself this time. Amy's going to flip when she sees this."

"Well, let's hope she's still wearing jeans then and not her wedding dress," Sally Ann said drily, though she was thrilled with Carol Lee's reaction.

Ellen moved to her elder daughter's side and placed an arm around her shoulders. "It's truly a work of art, my dear. And now I know why we're here."

Sally Ann glanced at her mother and cocked an eyebrow.

"You're going to need help getting that beautiful cake to the church."

An hour later the Grainger women had successfully transferred Amy's wedding cake from Sally Ann's kitchen to the reception hall at the church where the wedding would take place that evening. The frosted masterpiece now stood in pride of place on a table dressed in pristine white linen and dripping with fall flowers. Other smaller tables littered the reception hall, each with a white tablecloth and boasting a centerpiece of fragrant red and gold flowers.

Sally Ann had just stepped back to study her cake's final effect when she heard a quick indrawn breath and a sob. Turning, she saw Amy, the bride-to-be... and her best friend in all the world.

Amy stood frozen in the doorway to the reception hall, still dressed in worn blue jeans and a red and black plaid shirt. Her blonde hair was pulled back in a pony tail and her hands covered her mouth while her eyes glittered with tears. Sally Ann's heart plummeted; Amy was disappointed. The cake wasn't what she'd hoped for. And now it was too late to start again.

Moving quickly to her friend's side, Sally Ann gathered Amy into a hug and whispered, "I'm so sorry, Amy," while her own tears thickened her voice.

Amy stiffened, pushed Sally Ann back, and stared at her. "Sorry? Whatever for?" A little frown creased her brow. "What do you know that I don't?"

Sally Ann cocked her head and studied her friend's confused expression. "Nothing," she said finally. "Except that you're disappointed in the cake and I don't have time to start over."

Amy's mouth fell open, but no sound came out. She glanced from Sally Ann to the cake and back again. "Disappointed?" she finally managed to say. "You think I'm disappointed by that amazing cake? Are you crazy? That cake is stunning! It's more than I could've possibly dreamed of."

"Then why are you crying?"

Amy managed to laugh and scowl at the same time, then hugged her friend tightly. "Because it's my wedding day," she said, her voice a bit wobbly, "and my emotions are off the charts." She pushed Sally Ann to arm's length and gripped her shoulders. "They're tears of joy, you goose. Now show me my wedding cake. I want to see every square inch of that amazing work of art!"

3

At seven-thirty that evening, Amy Elizabeth Jenkins and Aaron David Matthews were married in a candlelight service. Their vows were witnessed by two hundred of their closest friends and family and presided over by a pastor who had known each of them since birth. The bride was radiant in a full length white velvet gown with a fingertip length veil atop a riot of golden curls. The groom appeared both dazzled and proud in his white tuxedo jacket with black trim and matching black pants.

Sally Ann observed from the back of the sanctuary. Amy had asked her to be maid of honor, but the two had decided that adding those duties to that of creating the wedding cake was a bit too much responsibility for one woman and both knew that Sally Ann was the *only* person who could create the cake of Amy's dreams. So Sally Ann, dressed in a gown of autumn gold velvet, waited at the rear of the church to escort the bridal couple to the reception hall where she could be the first to give her best friend a congratulatory hug... and then help arrange the newly married couple and their parents into a receiving line.

While Amy and Aaron greeted their guests, Sally Ann checked in with the caterer. Amy and Aaron had opted not to host a full sit-down dinner, but instead to serve hors d'oeuvres and other finger foods along with punch and, of course, cake. Satisfied that the caterer had the food service under control. Sally Ann moved quietly among the guests enjoying their comments regarding her cake.

"I've never seen anything like it," one woman exclaimed. "Not in the real world. In bridal magazines or online, of course, but in person? It's absolutely enchanting."

"I heard that Grainger girl made it," another observed. "What's her name? Oh yes. Sally, I think it is. Sally Grainger."

Close enough, Sally Ann thought with a smile.

"Why the decorating alone must have taken forever," yet another matron added. "I wonder what flavor they decided on?"

"We'll find out soon enough," said a distinguished-looking gentleman. "It looks like the receiving line is about to finish. They'll be cutting the cake soon."

Taking that last comment as her cue, Sally Ann glided past the wedding cake one last time, making sure the cake knife and server were in place along with dessert plates, forks, and plenty of napkins. Once Amy and Aaron had enjoyed their first taste—and the photographer had memorialized the moment, the caterer would step in and make quick work of slicing the tiered layers into servings for the guests.

As Amy and Aaron took their places beside the magnificent cake, Ellen Grainger stepped to Sally Ann's side. "Is there a problem?" she asked quietly.

Sally Ann gave her mother a quizzical look. "Not that I know of. Why?"

Ellen shrugged. "No idea. I just know I need to stay close to you... and close to that cake."

"Huh." Before Sally Ann could think of anything else to say, Amy picked up the cake knife, and with Aaron's fingers resting lightly on hers, attempted to make the first cut on the lowest tier of the cake.

A little frown appeared on Amy's face while Aaron's expression turned puzzled. The cake knife hung a fraction of an inch from the pale peach frosting. Sally Ann watched in confusion as the bridal couple exerted downward pressure, but the knife refused to budge.

Ellen grasped her daughter's hand. "Did you put a protective spell on the cake before we moved it?"

Sally Ann gasped. Of course! She'd intended the spell to be temporary, but the doorbell had interrupted the flow of her thoughts. She must have missed the final phrase that would ensure the spell's disintegration!

What to do? She could remove the spell in an instant, but not with Amy and Aaron exerting that much downward force... they were likely to topple the whole table. She needed them to relax, to try again once the spell had been removed.

"Mother," she whispered to Ellen, "I need you to distract the guests while I have a quick word with Amy and Aaron... and the cake."

Ellen nodded, stepped in front of the cake table, and clapping her hands turned to the assembled guests. "It looks like our beautiful young bride is having trouble deciding to cut into the masterpiece my daughter created for her wedding. Let's give the girls a moment more to admire the cake while we all have another cup of punch. I'm sure Sally Ann will call us back when she and Amy have had a last moment to be girls together."

While the guests moved away, laughing and chattering, Sally Ann stepped to Amy and Aaron.

"What's wrong, Sally Ann?" Amy asked, her eyes filling with frustrated tears. "Why can't we cut the cake?"

"I'm not a superstitious man, Sal," Aaron said, a frown furrowing his brow, "but this feels like a bad omen. Isn't sharing the wedding cake supposed to symbolize our future happiness? Does this mean our union is doomed?"

"Aaron," Amy cried, "how could you say such a thing?"

"Easy now," Sally Ann said, taking the cake knife from their hands. "Relax. Both of you. This is just a minor bobble in what will be a long and happy life together. Blame it on me! Just think of me as your lovable local witch who forgot a minor bit of magic in a thoroughly magical day."

That earned a smile from both of them. "You're such a goose, Sally Ann! Imagine calling yourself a witch on my wedding day. How silly."

"Right. What's a friend for if not to be silly when there's a minor crisis? Now, you two take a second to compose yourselves while I check this one little item."

When the happy couple stepped back to gaze into each other's eyes and sigh, Sally Ann recited a few words under her breath, traced a sigil over the cake, and then touched the tip of the cake knife to the frosting. It sliced through a fondant rosebud like, well, like a knife was supposed to do.

Turning back to Amy and Aaron, she handed them the cake knife. "Everything will be fine now." Catching her mother's gaze, she nodded and smiled, and Ellen clapped her hands and regathered the guests.

When the photographer nodded, Amy and Aaron sliced into the almond buttercream frosting, straight through the luscious layers of the lowest tier of spice cake and served each other a delicious sliver of Sally Ann's enchanting wedding cake!

4

When the happy couple had changed into traveling clothes and driven off in a car decorated with paper flowers and trailing streamers of white satin ribbon and rattling tin cans, Sally Ann sank into a chair at one of the guest tables. The remainder of the reception had gone off without a hitch, and most of the guests were now gathering their wraps and moving toward their cars.

"What a lovely wedding," Ellen said as she settled into a chair beside her daughter. "And that cake! Not only was it a work of art, but delicious as well."

Stifling a yawn, Sally Ann smiled. "And your timing was perfect as always. No one would've had a clue what the cake tasted like if you hadn't been here to help distract people while I removed that protective spell."

A small frown wrinkled Ellen's brow. "On the other hand, if our earlier arrival hadn't interrupted your concentration, the spell would've disintegrated as you'd intended." She tapped a finger to her chin thoughtfully. "Maybe I need a tune-up. It seems I was a bit *too* timely this morning."

Sally Ann laughed. "Whatever. Everything worked out." She patted her mother's hand and smirked. "I even told Amy and Aaron I was a witch." At her mother's shocked expression she hurried to add, "Of course, I phrased it in such a way that they thought I was joking."

"Thank the Goddess!"

"Nothing to worry about," she continued with a wave of her hand. "Amy even called me a *silly goose* afterward."

No. There was nothing to be concerned about. Amy and Aaron were safely married, the wedding cake had been a success, and the top tier had been removed, packaged, and sent home with Amy's mother to be frozen. The happy couple would receive another dose of Sally Ann's best spells for health, happiness, and enduring love when they enjoyed the last of her cake on their first anniversary.

With a contented sigh, Sally Ann Grainger stood, and bending down, kissed her mother's cheek. "Thanks again for all of your help," she said, "but it's time to call it a day. I've had enough excitement to last for quite a while."

EPILOGUE

In the bridal suite of a luxury hotel many miles from the church where they'd been married, Amy nestled into her husband's embrace and drifted to the edge of sleep. Suddenly, unexpectedly, her eyes popped open and she tapped Aaron's chest.

"Are you still awake?"

"Barely," he murmured drowsily.

"What did Sally Ann do to that cake? How did she fix it? We couldn't cut it, and then she said something, and we could! What did she do?"

Aaron cracked an eyelid and peered at his very warm, very lovely wife. "I don't know. Does it matter?"

She thought a moment, then shrugged and curled more closely into his arms. "I suppose not." But she didn't sleep. At least, not right away. Her mind was busy remembering her best friend's words... *Just think of me as your lovable local witch who forgot a minor bit of magic in a thoroughly magical day.*

Amy and Sally Ann were going to have a very frank, very heart-felt conversation when Amy and Aaron returned from their honeymoon. Witch indeed. What had Sally Ann been thinking to say such a thing?

Silly goose, Amy thought as she drifted into a deep and peaceful sleep.

II

BENEATH AND BEYOND

DEBBIE MUMFORD

BESTSELLING AUTHOR OF *SORCHA'S HEART*

BENEATH AND BEYOND

SPUN YARNS
A Short Story

1

D r. Erin Carstedter stepped out of the harness and away from the access shaft. She tried not to think about the weight of the glacier pressing down on this tiny bubble of air. The cavern glowed with an eerie blue-white light, cast by a battery-powered lantern suspended from a piton driven high into the wall. The ice's ability to simultaneously reflect and absorb the light fascinated her.

A haphazard pile of boxes and tools occupied the space just below the lantern. On the opposite wall stood the object of her team's efforts — a magnificently carved door enthroned in an ancient wall. Technicians had already thawed its hinges, leaving heated gel packs plastered to the surface to keep the door movable until the techs could pull out and the team's archaeologists move in. She busied herself checking equipment while waiting for her friend and colleague to finish his descent into the blue-tinged bubble.

Sensitive new sonar imaging had detected a land mass and its ruined city buried under hundreds of feet of arctic ice some fifty miles north of Alert, Canada's northernmost settlement. The more romantic among the team's members whispered "Atlantis!" But not Erin. Her thoughts revolved around solid, observable, measurable data. Though she longed to know when and how a human settlement had prospered this far north, she scoffed at the notion of the mythic lost continent. Hadn't people ever heard of fiction? Did they suppose the tendency to imagine idealized, fairy-tale societies a new wrinkle in humanity's collective unconscious?

She reached out to stroke the frost-whitened marble door. The climate had to have undergone drastic change to support a civilization on the scale disclosed by remote sensing. Their access shaft, and this cavern, revealed only a minute portion of the long-buried city.

The decision-makers, after weeks of careful study of the sonar map, had finally decided to sink the access shaft at this location. Archaeologists had vied to guess which buildings might house what artifacts from the safety of wind-scoured Quonset huts staked to the surface of the glacier. Yet, even in the heated interior of insulated shelters, men and women worked bundled in sweaters, scarves, and fingerless gloves. All to allow Erin to stand in admiration of a door carved from marble who knew how long ago.

"Ready to step into the past, Dr. Carstedter?"

Erin turned toward the voice. She knew the figure hunched in the little cavern to be her friend, Matt Davidson, the team's archaeometry specialist, but his voice and the name on the duty roster were her only clues. The shapeless mass of arctic parka, complete with fur-edged hood and oversized snow pants, effectively hid his identity. Goggles and huge outer mittens completed his disguise. Still, the lilt in his voice flashed an image of her friend's mischievous blue eyes to Erin's mind.

She grinned, though her own protective clothing undoubtedly prevented him from noticing. "I thought we already had." She gestured to the ice-white ground beneath their feet. "How long do you suppose it's been since this bit of earth saw the light of day?"

"I wouldn't want to guess," he said. "Someone else's department. What I want is to get through that door." He moved closer to the ancient threshold. "Shall we?"

"After you, Dr. Davidson." She gave him a courtly bow, or tried to. Arctic gear didn't lend itself to bending.

Matt removed his cumbersome outer mittens and ran gloved fingers over the frosted marble. He pulled the thermal packs free and swung the door wide.

Erin edged out of his way, moved back, dragged a post driver into position, and staked the door open. The machine's boom reverberated through the cavern and her flesh alike. She winced, reminded again of the fragility of their airy bubble.

"Are you sure your name's not Alice?" Matt's voice cracked, and a nervous chuckle ricocheted off the ice.

Erin straightened, glanced at Matt's goggled silhouette, and then allowed her gaze to follow his flashlight's beam into the ruin's interior. Only it wasn't a ruin. A wave of vertigo washed through her system; she grabbed Matt's arm for support.

"Do you see it too?" Erin whispered.

Matt's echoing laughter died away, and he answered in a gruff whisper. "It's a helluva cold rabbit hole, Alice, but at least we've fallen through together."

Erin teetered on the threshold a moment longer and then stepped through the looking glass onto soft, green grass beneath a cloudless, sapphire sky. An enormous monarch butterfly danced across her field of vision, and she glanced back at Matt and the entrance to the ice cavern. Matt stood a few paces behind her, looking ridiculous in his arctic gear, but the opening into their world no longer existed. Erin pivoted slowly on the spot. An unbroken horizon of meadowland, forest, and mountain greeted her vision. However they'd arrived in this unexpected place, they wouldn't be returning by the same route.

"This has to be a hallucination," she muttered. Panic-stricken, she sank to the ground, squeezed her eyes shut, and recounted the facts of her situation. "I'm in a centuries-old ruin, buried under tons of ice. It's too cold to support life."

Keeping her eyes firmly closed, she removed her mittens and pulled off her left glove. With deliberate care, she lowered her hand to the ground beside her. She encountered what could only be grass; soft, resilient blades of grass. Approximately six inches high, the leaves bent easily beneath her questing fingers and gave way as she sought the soil below. Warm, damp earth. She lifted her fingers to her muffler-wrapped nose and breathed in the slightly musty scent of dirt spiked with the tang of freshly bruised grass.

She'd expected a cold so bitter it burned her exposed flesh. Instead, her senses screamed Summer! Sweat trickled down her neck to pool at the base of her spine. She needed to shed several layers of clothing, but her intellect refused to accept her body's testimony, insisting she'd freeze to death if she unwrapped.

"This is absolutely impossible," said Matt. "But it's a helluva lot more comfortable than the ice shaft."

Eyes still squeezed closed, Erin listened to his movements, felt his warm, calloused fingers pull her hand away from her face.

"Snap out of it, Erin. We've got a whole new world to explore." His words penetrated the fugue in her brain, and she opened her eyes to focus on his handsome face. Matt's tousled blond hair needed a trim, and his chin sparkled with golden stubble, but she could see his face!

"Matt," she cried. "Are you insane? I don't care what kind of mental aberration we're suffering; you'll die of exposure dressed like that!"

He knelt beside her in nothing more than a pair of sweat pants, tee-shirt, and his fur-lined boots. A grin lit his good-looking face. Erin shook her head, glancing in disbelief between him and the nearby pile of discarded protective gear.

"If this is an illusion, it's a good one. My outer layer of dermis should be dead by now, my lungs seizing." He stroked her bare hand. "Your skin seems fine too."

He stood and pulled her up with him. "Come on, Erin. Lose the parka or you're going to roast."

Struggling against his grasp, she twisted away, yanked on her glove and mittens, and turned to glower at him.

"Listen," she said, working hard to keep the rising hysteria out of her voice, "you may be suicidal, but I'm not. Obviously something in the atmosphere of this ruin is causing us to hallucinate. We need to sit tight until the rest of the team gets nervous and comes to check on us. The door is open now, so the fumes, or...whatever ... will have a chance to dissipate."

She dropped to the ground again and glared up at him, though her gear hid her expression. "We've got to stick tight. If we wander away ...." She swallowed, the lump in her throat threatening to choke her. "If we wander away, they might not be able to find us!"

Matt stared at her, eyes narrow and jaw tight. When he spoke, his voice carried the condescension of an adult speaking to a wayward child.

"Will you listen to yourself? Sit tight? Wait for rescue? Erin, look around! I don't know where we are, or how we got here, but we're sure as hell not in a ruin at the bottom of an ice shaft."

He spun away from her, paced a few steps, kicked a large rock out of his path, and strode back to tower over her, hands jammed into his pockets.

"Get up, Erin," he said. "We can't just sit here doing nothing."

He reached for her again, but she twisted away and scuttled a few feet sideways.

"If you want to get lost in this maze," she said, "go for it. I'm staying right here until my head clears."

"I'm sorry, Erin, but I can't walk away. You're just stubborn enough to sit here in the blazing sun, bundled to the teeth, until your core temperature pushes you into a stroke."

He launched himself at her, wrestled her onto the grass, and straddled her hips while he freed her upper torso from its protective gear.

Erin sputtered and fought, angry as a wet cat. He wrenched the parka free, exposing her sweat-drenched tee-shirt and hair to the warm breeze. A violent shiver convulsed her body.

Matt dodged away, and she sprang to a sitting position, chafing her arms and running shaky fingers through her short mop of curly hair. She glared at Matt, lips sealed in a thin, tense line. No way would she admit he'd been right.

"Get up," he ordered. "Lose the parka pants. We're going to hike to the tree line, and I don't want you overheating."

"I can't," she snapped. "I'm not wearing sweats." Defiance sizzled in her blood, but she forced herself to remain calm and gazed toward the distant trees. "Why that direction? Why not back toward the door?"

He offered his hand. She hesitated briefly, rolled sideways — away from him — and pushed herself upright.

"Because those trees look like they could be growing along a stream," he said, dropping his hand to his side. "We're not going back, because there's nothing to go back to. Look for yourself." He pointed to the heap of thinsulite and fur — his arctic gear. "I'd barely stepped through the door when it disappeared. If it existed, it'd be right there."

She nodded curtly and strode off across the sun-drenched meadow toward the line of trees Matt had indicated. She shelved the problem of where they were. Evidence would present itself, if she kept her eyes open. In the meantime, she catalogued the world around her.

"This feels like a setting from 'Little House on the Prairie,'" Matt said, gesturing to the terrain around them, "except they were in Kansas, and Kansas doesn't have mountains."

"True," she said. Analyzing data would keep her mind occupied and hysteria in check. "I see no evidence of civilization as we know it and definitely nothing of the ruin we expected to find. There aren't any power lines or roads, paved or otherwise." She stopped, listened intently, and shook her head. "No traffic noise, either. But I do hear a stream." She glanced at Matt, irritation dwindling as her bewilderment increased. If they weren't suffering from a fume-induced hallucination, where the hell were they, and how had they gotten here?

"Okay, we're not under an arctic glacier and we're not in Kansas." He grimaced and wiped his forehead on the tail of his tee-shirt. "It's not much, but it's a start."

She shook her head, wishing she could shed her thermal pants and heavy boots. "I'm still not convinced I haven't suffered a complete mental breakdown. I can't get past the impossibility of us being anywhere other than that Arctic ruin."

He eyed her with skepticism. "I thought you were a stickler for empirical evidence. Where do you see ice or artifacts?"

Erin scowled. "Let's just say I'm not convinced either of us is a reliable witness right now."

They reached the line of trees and stepped gratefully into its shadow. Matt leaned against a sturdy, young oak and said, "You're right, it's a physical impossibility, but I have to believe I'm sane. Otherwise, what's the point of doing anything? I'm going to keep trying to figure out where we are. If we can solve the puzzle, we might have a chance of getting home."

"Fine. We can't go back the way we came, and obsessing over my sanity won't help." She bit her lip and glanced away. "But I hate losing the reference point of the door."

Matt shook his head. "The door disappeared. We couldn't just sit and wait. We had to act."

Erin raised her hands and moved toward the sound of running water. "You want action," she muttered, "I'm acting. Though I can't see what tramping through the woods is going to accom—"

She stopped so suddenly Matt walked into her. "What are you ...?"

They stood at the edge of the woods where a small clearing ran down to the water's edge. There, on the bank of the stream, reclined a living being. The creature relaxed in a patch of sunlight. Its torso resembled an adult lion with the addition of sleek, leathery wings folded close to its flanks. Tawny gold fur covered the powerfully muscled body, but instead of a feline face, a man's bearded head sat atop the sinewy shoulders. Dark eyes shone from behind a tangled mass of honey-colored hair and beard.

Great, thought Erin, one more reason to doubt my sanity. She fought to stay calm, to think of rational explanations, as she gazed into the dark eyes of a living, breathing sphinx.

Erin waved him to silence and peered forward, so focused on what lay ahead she barely noticed when he moved to her side ... and froze.

3

"Do you see a sphinx?" Erin whispered, not daring to look away from the incredible creature.

"Yeah," breathed Matt. "Maybe you were right. Maybe we have lost our marbles."

"No." She gave her head a tiny shake and breathed her whispered response. "Illusions should be individual, unique to our own fears and desires. Besides, this creature doesn't conform to any single mythology. It's like a conglomerate. You were right. This is real."

Matt gave a quiet grunt, half satisfied, half exasperated.

"What do you remember about sphinxes?"

"I don't know," he said. "They ask riddles and kill folks who answer wrong?"

"That's one possibility." Erin darted a look at Matt's face. "Are you any good with riddles?"

He stared into her eyes for a moment and then shifted his gaze back to the sphinx. "Lousy."

The sphinx, whose tail had thumped in a rhythmic beat during their quiet conversation, rose in a fluid motion and padded toward them. He stopped a few paces away, sat on his haunches, and curled his tail around his front paws.

"You may leave the shelter of the trees," he said. "I have eaten today, and neither of you smells particularly enticing."

At the sound of his growling, gravelly voice, Erin's blood rushed to her core, leaving her light-headed and a little unsteady. Perhaps she wobbled on her feet. She didn't know but she appreciated the unasked-for support of Matt's hand on her elbow. His grip tightened, and she welcomed the sudden jolt of pain. It shattered the haze of panic and allowed her to move forward of her own volition.

"Can you tell us where we are?" asked Matt.

Erin admired his calm voice, though she detected a tremor in the hand on her elbow. She doubted she could have found her voice at all right then. Her mouth felt dry as the Sahara that should have been this creature's home.

"I can," the sphinx said, "but I will not. My answer would be meaning-less to you. Suffice it to say you stepped through a portal into my waiting room." He smiled, showing teeth more suited to a leonine body than a human face. "Whether you return to your world, remain here, or advance is at my discretion." He stood, paced back to his orig-inal spot by the water's edge, circled once and lowered himself regally onto the sunlit grass.

"Advance?" Erin forced the single word past uncooperative lips.

"Waiting room for what?" Matt continued to grip her elbow as if worried she would disappear, but his voice remained calm.

"This is the anteroom of the gods, and I, Enki, am the keeper of the gate."

Erin's knees buckled, and she slid to the ground. Matt's grip had gone slack; he made no effort to keep her upright.

"Gods?"

Erin managed a trembling smile. The sphinx had reduced Matt to single syllables, as well.

"Your earliest ancestors understood us to be gods," said Enki. "Your species has now evolved far enough to posit the existence of other intelligent life in the universe. These days you would recognize us as visitors from other star systems. In a word, aliens."

Matt lowered his tall frame to sit beside Erin in the lush grass. "Are you suggesting that beings from our various cultural myths exist? That our myths are actually first contact stories?"

"Yes," he said. "You've summed it up nicely. I believe you would call us 'tourists.'" He smiled a toothy grin. "Why do you struggle with the concept? The evidence — me — is available for inspection."

"Why did your species stop coming?" Erin asked. "Why haven't we seen any of you in recorded history?"

The sphinx turned his dark-eyes upon her and studied her face. His gaze unnerved her, but she refused to look away.

"When a species develops enough cognition to form tribes, we restrict tourism. The Intergalactic Union has strict rules about interfering in the natural development of primitive societies."

"But we remember your visits," Matt blurted. "Your fingerprints are all over our early mythologies."

"Yes. You made an unprecedented leap in cognition. You caught us unprepared. We have had to watch your species rather more carefully than is the norm."

Erin made a cognitive leap of her own as she sat in the cool grass beside the rushing stream. "The ruin under the ice," she said, her voice quiet, meditative, "it's not a ruin, is it? It's a functional city — a blind from which to observe our planet."

"Exactly," Enki said, inclining his head and closing his eyes for a moment. "It is a transfer station and a center of anthropological study. A university, if you will."

"And that's why we're here," said Matt, gesturing around the clearing, "you couldn't allow us to just walk into your observation booth."

The sphinx bowed his head and blinked again.

"What now?" asked Erin, panic receding in the wake of understanding. She could deal with intelligent alien species, even if they did resemble mythological monsters.

"Now," said Enki, "I must determine what to do with you and your colleagues. You two will be tested. You will represent humanity. Your actions will determine whether your race will be accepted into the Intergalactic Union with apprentice status, or whether you two will be returned to your glacier with your memories modified and all records of the transfer point wiped from your instrumentation. The key to humanity's immediate future is in your hands."

"So, the sphinx will ask a riddle, after all," said Matt.

"In a manner of speaking, though you need not worry about being torn limb from limb. The only rending I will do is of your memories."

He stood, paced forward a few feet, and looked back along his long, lean body. "Follow me. You will be allowed rest and refreshment before your trial begins." He padded away without bothering to see if Erin and Matt followed.

4

Erin pushed tidbits of fruit around her plate, trying to make it look like the food tempted her. A queasy stomach prevented her from enjoying the meal. Here she sat, on a Persian carpet unrolled on emerald grass beside a large, slow-moving river, holding a golden plate while a green-haired nymph fed grapes to Enki ... and her only concern was a queasy stomach? She needed a therapist to help her discover the serious psychic disconnect that allowed her to accept these bizarre circumstances with such aplomb.

Matt didn't appear concerned about their surroundings. He ate like a horse, ogled the flimsily clad nymph assigned to keep him satisfied — Erin thought his eyes would pop when Enki uttered that particular phrase. She imagined, in vivid detail, how she'd kill Matt if he so much as touched the nymph's curvaceous body — and talked animatedly to the sphinx. Heaven forbid he should chew his food and swallow before starting the next sentence.

"What about you, Dr. Carstedter?" asked Enki, dismissing his nymph with a swipe of his mighty paw. "Are you ready to continue?"

Erin jolted from her reverie, wondering what she'd missed.

"Yes," she lied, attempting to cover her distraction with a weak smile. "I'm ready. Where do we go from here?"

The sphinx grinned, a feral grimace, making Erin wonder why he'd been willing to settle for a meal of fruit. "From here," he said, "you quest."

"Quest?" asked Matt. "You mean a literal search for an object?"

"I do, within specific parameters. You will have twenty-four hours ... measured by this timepiece," he nodded toward the green-haired nymph who displayed what looked like an old-fashioned pocket watch, "to gain possession of a barb from the tail of the eldest dragon."

Matt choked on a bite of melon, turning an interesting shade of fuchsia as he coughed and pummeled his chest.

"Let me get this straight," said Erin when she was satisfied Matt would live, "you want us to slay a dragon and bring you his tail-barb in twenty-four hours? Why not just kill us now and save us the trouble?" Her head throbbed, her stomach roiled, and now this alien monster from her mythic past wanted her to kill a dragon? This day just got better and better.

Enki chuckled, a gravelly little growl that left chills running down Erin's spine.

"No, Dr. Carstedter," he said, "you are not required to slay a dragon—such a quaint phrase. Gormleigh will give you his tail-barb, for a price. No, my dear child, your quest is merely to find Gormleigh and meet his requirements." He smiled again, and sunlight glinted from pointed incisors. "Think of it as a rite of initiation. There will be no need for violence."

"Well, then," said Matt, pushing to stand and rubbing his hands on his pants, "point us in the right direction."

The sphinx's laughter roared across the soft, summer breeze. "You humans," he said, "you never cease to amaze me. This is your quest,

Dr. Davidson. I have given you all the aid I am allowed." He nodded to the nymph, who handed the watch to Matt. "Your time begins ... now!"

The aliens vanished.

5

Erin jumped to her feet and spun around. She turned to face Matt and recognized an echo of her own bewilderment etched on his angular face.

"How did they do that?" she asked. "I haven't seen any trace of mechanical equipment. I wish he'd stayed around long enough to answer a few questions."

"Me, too, but we're on a countdown," he said, the expression in his blue eyes reminding Erin of a confused child, "and they've left us without a clue about what to do next."

"We'll just have to follow our instincts." She gave him a grin, or tried to — the knot in her stomach might have twisted it into a grimace. "Actually, we should probably follow your instincts. If we'd followed mine, we'd still be sitting in the grass in full arctic gear."

Matt smiled. A genuine smile that pushed the bewilderment out of his eyes. "You're okay, Erin," he said. "We may not be ready for this but we'll give these aliens our best shot." He scanned the riverbank and then surveyed the forest. "Want to flip a coin? Heads we follow the river, tails we move into the forest?"

"Fine with me," she said with a shrug. "My instincts still think I'm in a cavern under tons of ice."

"Tell your instincts to stand down so that logical mind of yours can attack this puzzle." He shook his head and dug a quarter out of his pocket. "I can't believe I'm supposed to find a dragon named Gormleigh and talk him into giving me a barb off his tail."

Erin laughed. "I can't believe you had a quarter in your pocket when you were dressed to explore a ruin buried under tons of ice. Were you expecting to feed a parking meter?"

"Hey! You should be glad the Boy Scouts trained me to be prepared." He flipped the quarter in the air, caught it, and slapped it onto his left forearm where it remained covered by his right hand. "Otherwise, we'd never know we're supposed to go ...," he lifted his hand to display Washington's profile, "along the river."

"Lead on, Dr. Davidson."

He glanced at the watch again, pocketed it, and moved into the scrub brush lining the edge of the river. They scrambled over rocks and skirted fallen trees for close to an hour before finding another clearing.

Erin longed to collapse on the uneven ground but stayed upright through sheer determination. Matt looked a little the worse for wear too. Tired as she was, it took a moment for Erin's brain to register the fact that Matt had frozen in the act of wiping sweat from his brow with the hem of his tee-shirt.

"Erin," he said, his words little more than a breath, "don't make any sudden moves. We're not alone."

Moving as little as possible, she turned to follow the direction of his gaze. A column of smokeless fire shimmered at the edge of the glen. At least, she thought it was fire. She saw no evidence of wood at its base, nothing to account for its cylindrical nature, and though a heat-shimmer surrounded it, the nearby trees and the grass beneath appeared undisturbed. It moved, and Erin gasped. The motion revealed the outline of a torso within the heart of red-orange flames.

"I am of the Djinn."

The voice licked through her mind, firing nerve-endings and lifting the tiny hairs on her arms. Matt must have heard the words too; he dropped his shirt and clenched his fists.

"We wish to assist," said the electrifying voice. "Come into my embrace. I will transport you to Gormleigh."

Erin shivered but took a step forward.

Matt grabbed her arm and hauled her back. "No," he said. "We prefer not to touch you. Fire harms our bodies."

The Djinn moved closer. "You will not be burned; your quest will be accomplished. I offer you an easy solution."

"I believe him." Erin tugged at her arm.

"Yeah, well, you wanted to sit and suffocate." His grip remained firm, his gaze never left the Djinn. "Thanks, but no thanks."

"As you wish." The upper portion of the Djinn's body inclined toward them. He straightened and disappeared in a flash of white-hot incandescence.

Matt's grip relaxed, and Erin wrenched her arm free.

"I can't believe you didn't even try to —"

"To what?" he yelled. "To immolate ourselves? Erin, wake up! This isn't a dream. This is real. We can't just step into the arms of fire and expect to live."

"You're right," she said, her voice as icy as the arctic where they'd begun. "This is real, and we've got a real time limit. You can't afford to reject help without at least checking to see if it's viable."

"That creature was a living flame!"

"That creature offered to help us," she spat back, "and in case you didn't notice, there's not so much as a charred blade of grass where it stood."

Matt opened his mouth, closed it again, and strode to examine the grass where they'd seen the Djinn.

"Okay," he said after a close inspection, "maybe I overreacted." He looked grim but not regretful. "I'll try to keep an open mind if we meet anyone else."

Erin sighed. "Yeah, well, you might've been right. We just don't know." She ran her fingers through her sweat-dampened hair and shrugged. "Let's keep moving."

She trudged on, staying close to Matt as they continued to follow the riverbank. They discovered a stretch of sandy shore and sighed in relief. The tightly packed sand provided a firm path, a welcome reprieve for their tired feet. A little further ahead, an overhanging tree marked the end of the easy road. A flock of birds burst from its branches. Erin paused, wondering what had spooked them.

Matt stopped beside her, shaded his eyes with his hand, and peered toward the tree.

"There's someone there," he said.

"Where?"

"See the huge branch swooping down toward the water? The one that looks like it's begging for kids to run out on it and jump into the pool? Someone's looking into the water right under it."

Erin's gaze followed his direction. There, in the tree's shadow, she spied a figure hunched over the water. She'd looked right past it earlier, mistaking it for a moss covered boulder. As she watched, the figure moved. A head lifted, and the curve of the boulder resolved into the creature's rounded back.

She clutched Matt's arm and tried to ease her trembling with several deep breaths before she spoke. "Look at the hair .... It's moving. The air is still, but the hair is moving."

Erin looked away from the alien beneath the tree and into Matt's familiar, blue eyes. "It's a gorgon," she said. "Whatever happens, don't look at its face."

He paled, but determination glittered in his eyes. "Okay. This time we're forewarned. We'll treat this creature like an intelligent being, find out what it knows about Gormleigh."

"Agreed." She released his arm and lowered her head to keep her gaze away from the gorgon's face. Breathing deeply, Erin followed Matt toward the tree.

"Hello." Matt stopped beside the gorgon's quiet pool.

"Ah, the humans," she said. "The sphinx said you might find your way to me."

Erin stared at the gorgon's reflection in the water. Her green-tinged complexion echoed the deeper green-black of the snakes writhing from her scalp. Each snake possessed jet-black eyes and a forked tongue of muddy scarlet. The gorgon's eyes were also black, making Erin wonder if her tongue was forked as well.

"We wondered if you could direct us to the dragon, Gormleigh?" asked Erin, keeping her eyes on the reflection in the pool. The gorgon met her gaze in the quiet water.

"If you want my help," she said, "the least you can do is show me the courtesy of looking at me when you speak."

"No disrespect intended," said Matt, "but legend says we'll die if we look at you."

Erin's gaze flicked from the gorgon's reflection to Matt's. He stood beside Erin, and, following her example, gazed at the gorgon in the water's mirror. Her attention returned to the gorgon at the sound of the creature's laughter.

"A legend, indeed," cackled the snake-haired female. "Looking at me won't kill you. I don't find you very attractive, but the sight of you hasn't hurt me!"

A sheepish grin spread across Matt's features.

"Matt, no!"

6

Erin's warning came too late. Matt met the gorgon's stare, and the silly smile froze as his features hardened to stone.

"You lied!" Erin wanted to launch herself at the smug alien, but forced herself to remain still.

"I did not," the gorgon replied. "Your man isn't dead, merely petrified. If you succeed in gaining Gormleigh's tail-barb, you'll be able to restore him. If not, he'll remain on this riverbank for eternity. I hope you fail; I rather fancy him like this. His expression is so ... cute."

Before Erin could gather her thoughts into a coherent question, the gorgon rolled into the water and swam away.

"Oh, Matt!" Erin sank to the grass at her friend's feet and sobbed out her frustration and fear. She didn't know if she could do this alone. Hell, they hadn't had much chance as a team! But if she didn't find the dragon and get the blasted tail-barb, Matt would be a statue forever. She might not have to live with the memory of failing, not if Enki had told the truth and failure simply meant a lost opportunity and no memory of the experience, but Matt would pay a terrible price.

She cried until she had no more tears, until her sobs subsided into chest-deep gasps for oxygen. She lay there, at the stone feet of her friend and colleague, waiting for her breathing to calm and for sleep to claim her exhausted body.

The night sky sparkled with a thousand stars when she awoke. She stretched and wondered how long she'd slept? How much time remained for her quest to save Matt and open the stars to humanity?

She glanced at the overhanging tree, the midnight-black water, and rested her gaze on the moon-bright alabaster of Matt's face. Tentatively, she touched his leg. The flesh beneath was stone-cold and rigid, but his clothes remained supple. Perhaps she hadn't lost the timepiece after all. She stood, wiped her sweaty palms on her own heavy snow pants, and slipped her hand delicately into Matt's pocket. An odd sense of guilt swamped her emotions, but she disregarded it, forcing her fingers to search for the watch. Matt's life depended on her ability to complete the quest; they both needed her to retrieve the timepiece.

Her fingers encountered cold, hard metal, and the breath she hadn't realized she was holding exploded from her lungs. She glanced apologetically at Matt's frozen features, took a firm grasp on the watch, and yanked it from his pocket. The force of movement pitched her back a few steps, but she maintained her balance. Tears brimmed her eyes, preventing her from reading the countdown. She blinked them away, annoyed at her emotional reaction, and glared at the stop-watch. The read-out ticked mechanically away. Twelve hours, fourteen minutes remained.

Twelve hours? She thought back over their journey but couldn't account for more than six hours. She frowned at the crushed grass at Matt's feet. How could she have allowed herself to sleep?

She paced back and forth in front of her friend's statue. Twelve hours gone, and she was no closer to their goal than when the sphinx announced it.

She stopped, touched Matt's alabaster cheek, and said, "I'll be back. I'll release you, or die trying."

Stuffing the watch in her pocket, she ducked under the overhanging branch and continued her trek along the bank of the ever-widening river.

In an attempt to distract herself from Matt's plight, she catalogued details while she scrambled over rocks, wove through trees and bushes, and trudged across shifting sand. The terrain remained remarkably earth-like; no alien plant- life or rock formations made her list, and a single moon brightened the pre-dawn sky. The only sounds she noted were the steady gurgle of the slow-moving river and the soft sighing of the breeze through the leafy deciduous canopy. No plops of jumping fish, or rustles of small animals scurrying out of her path.

A sudden, overpowering stench of rotting fish surprised her, and she gagged. Eyes watering, she covered her mouth and nose with the hem of her shirt and glanced around for the source of the foul odor.

Another creature of legend rose from the dark surface of the water a few yards from the bank. Water streamed from yellowish-brown, seaweedy hair surrounding a stern, masculine face. His features resembled a sea turtle more than a man, but the chest, shoulders and arms shining golden brown in the moonlight were decidedly human, albeit scaly.

"I am of the Merfolk," he said, his words a rush of surf against the early morning stillness. "We wish to assist you in your quest."

Erin lowered her makeshift mask and tried to breathe through her mouth while she contemplated her reply. She'd been drawn to the Djinn but felt repelled by this slimy creature. Her knowledge of mythology had saved her from the gorgon but provided no clue to this being's nature. Still, she'd chided Matt for losing an opportunity with the Djinn; she couldn't afford another delay.

"Thank you," she said, struggling to maintain a calm, rational tone. "Can you tell me where to find Gormleigh?"

"I can and I will, but you must trust me."

She hesitated, searching for neutral words. "My friend trusted the gorgon. Now he's a statue."

The merman inclined his head before meeting her gaze with a firm, level stare. "I am not a gorgon. Merfolk do not play childish games with words. If I say it, it is so."

He disappeared beneath the surface of the water, and Erin's heart sank. She'd insulted him, lost another possibility of aid.

A sudden splash signaled the return of hope. The merman rose again, water streaming from face and hair.

"Forgive me," he said. "I can breathe your air but I require the rush of water past my gills every few minutes."

Erin thought of her pledge to Matt and made her decision. "What must I do?" If she died, she'd die trying.

The merman nodded. "Shed those layers of cloth you wear. Join me in the water."

She hesitated and then sat down to remove her heavy arctic boots. "You understand I can't breathe underwater, don't you?"

"I do," he said. "I shall breathe for us both. Come quickly, there are other species who will not appreciate me giving you assistance."

Erin peeled down to her underwear, stuffed the ticking watch inside her bra beneath her left breast, and waded into the murky water. The moon had set while she spoke to the merman, and now the sky showed promise of the coming day. She prayed she'd live to see the next twenty-four hours unfold.

The merman grasped her wrists and pulled her beneath the surface of the river. Holding her in a lover's embrace, he propelled them forward with swift, sure movements of his powerful tail. Erin squeezed her eyes shut, held her nose, and tried to relax; to imagine her lungs weren't screaming for oxygen. Just when the instinct to gasp for air became too strong to resist, the merman parted her lips with his beaky mouth and forced a bubble of air past them. Blessed relief eased her burning lungs.

This process repeated itself again and again. Erin felt like she'd strapped herself to a torpedo. She ceased to worry about drowning and began to wonder about their destination. Once or twice she opened her eyes, curious about her underwater adventure. But seaweed hair and scaly neck filled her range of vision, so she closed them again in favor of imagining the wonders zipping past.

At last, their motion slowed, and they angled upward. They broke the surface together, and she gasped her first unaided breath in hours. The sun shone well above the horizon, and water stretched in every direction, save one.

"Gormleigh's island," said her savior. "You could not have reached it without the aid of another species." His eyes, deep green pools of sincerity, gazed into hers. "You accepted my aid with dignity, though you had no way of judging my worthiness. I wish you well, human."

"Erin," she said, "my name is Erin, and I am forever in your debt."

"I am Trocar," he said. "Be well, Erin. Seek Gormleigh in the mountain's heart." He flipped and vanished beneath the waves.

7

Erin swam to shore but allowed the surf to push her onto the beach. She crawled out of the foam, stood, and raked her hair out of her eyes. Retrieving the watch from its place above her heart, she prayed it still worked. The countdown continued; five hours remained. She surveyed the landscape. Five hours to reach the island's heart, find Gormleigh, and convince him to relinquish a barb from his tail. Five hours to save Matt's life.

Pushing herself upright, she wished for Matt's quarter. Which way? His voice sounded in her mind, *You're dithering, Erin.* Her cheeks flamed. She wasn't dithering, she was analyzing.

Gazing upward, she studied the prominent peak of the island's central mountain. Undoubtedly volcanic, probably the origin of this little mound of arable land and ... its heart!

That's what Trocar meant. Gormleigh will be in a cave as close to the island's core as he can get.

A nervous giggle escaped as she imagined finding the dragon asleep on a horde of gold.

Erin set off toward the mountain, intending to circle it until she found a cave large enough to shelter a dragon. The stubbly undergrowth tore at her tender feet, but she pushed on, placing her steps as carefully as possible. Vegetation slapped her bare skin, and swarms of insects feasted on her sweaty body, but she focused on the goal. Thoughts of Matt's invulnerability to such discomfort gave her an odd appreciation for the irritants.

A single hour, sixty short minutes, remained on the timer when the entrance to the cave came in sight. Weak with exhaustion and fear, but elated by the discovery, Erin stepped inside. A good-sized boulder provided a resting spot. She sat and caught her breath, praying her assumptions were correct. Time and options had run out. Facing a dragon with nothing but her wits ... what kind of a plan was that? Her brain had always been her strongest asset, but that was before she stepped out of her reality into a place where she didn't know the rules. The ticking clock forced her to her feet. Squaring her shoulders, Erin marched into what she hoped was a dragon's lair.

Before she reached the back wall of the outer cave, an unusual odor convinced her she'd found the right place. An acrid mixture of sulfur and copper coated her nose and clung to her tongue as she rounded a corner into a dark passageway. She crept forward. The rock wall scraped against her soft fingers while she felt for each step with her bare feet. The absolute blackness terrified her. She stifled an urge to bolt. Only the thought of Matt, captive in a stone body, forced her forward.

A rasping, sibilant sound hissed along the cave wall. Her pounding heart skipped a beat. Scales, slipping and sliding over rock, slithering who knew where. The sound echoed against the rock walls, impossible to locate. Erin hoped it originated in front of her, not behind.

She pushed on, pulse hammering, blind and helpless, prey to her own active imagination. A dim, red light appeared, but she doubted its reality, certain her desperate mind had conjured it.

But the glow strengthened with each step, illuminating a wide curve in the tunnel. She stepped around the bend and found Gormleigh in his lair.

Knees trembling, she leaned against the rock. *Great. I found the dragon. Now what?*

Red light emanated from a steaming fissure running the length of the cavern, bathing the sleeping dragon in a fiery glow. His head, longer than she was tall, rested on his front paws, and faint puffs of smoke accompanied each exhalation. The massive body rose and fell with every breath, an elegant mass of shining, red scales. Leathery wings furled close to his sides, and a long tail curled around to caress his cheek with gemstone barbs.

Just one of those barbs, the tiniest, least faceted, most imperfect of those barbs would save Matt's life. If Gormleigh had been on her side of the rift, Erin would've been tempted to snatch one and run. But fate, or the dragon's cunning, prevented the attempt.

She checked the timepiece. Thirty minutes remained. How did one wake a sleeping dragon? More importantly, how did one wake a sleeping dragon and live to win a tail-barb?

"One thinks loud, obnoxious questions," said a deep, resonant voice. "Go away. Come back when you've learned to think more quietly. You're disturbing my rest."

A great eye blinked once and met her gaze. She dropped to her knees, lifting her hands in supplication.

"Excuse me, sir," she said, her voice a high-pitched squeak. "I've been sent to ask you for a tail-barb."

Gormleigh raised his head, a glint of curiosity in his eye. "Human, aren't you? Who sent you? How did you find this place?"

She cleared her throat and sought her normal voice. "Yes, sir. I'm human. My friend and I stumbled into the observation post under our polar ice cap. We were transported here. The sphinx, Enki, sent us to you."

"I see only one. Where is your companion?"

"The gorgon petrified him."

"But you escaped?"

"I remembered our legends and didn't trust her."

"And how did you reach my island?"

"A merman named Trocar brought me."

"I see. You escaped the gorgon by not trusting her, yet you stepped into the water with Trocar?" He rose to sit on his haunches, towering over Erin.

She didn't know whether to bend over backwards to retain his gaze or lean forward and grovel before him. Frankly, groveling sounded tempting. Instead, she sat back, folded her legs tailor-fashion, and held his gaze.

"The gorgon said Matt could be saved if I gained your tail-barb. Trocar was a calculated risk."

Gormleigh chuckled, filling the cavern with a landslide of sound. "You're either very brave, or too stupid to live. I think I'll credit you with courage for the moment."

"Sir," said Erin, glancing at the timer, "I don't mean to be rude, but my time is running out. Will you give me a tail-barb?"

"I'm sure it is," he said. "I doubt Enki expected you to get this far." He glanced around the cavern and stretched, cat-like. "We will negotiate quickly. What are you prepared to give me in exchange?"

Erin's heart leapt to her throat. "Give you? In exchange?"

Gormleigh smiled a fearsome grin. "Come, come, little human," he said. "Surely you didn't think my barb would be free?"

"I, uh, well, frankly, I'd hoped you'd ask me a question, a riddle or something."

"A riddle?" roared the dragon. "You confuse me with the sphinx! No, I prefer profit in my dealings. What will you offer me, little one?"

"Forgive me, sir, I forgot your nature. But, I don't have anything to barter with. I left everything behind when I let Trocar bring me here." She held up empty hands. "See? Nothing but my wits."

"Then use them to your profit ... and mine," he said, his eyes glittering with greed. "What will you offer me?"

He'd asked the question three times now. Erin glanced at the watch. Ten minutes remained. What could a nearly naked human offer a dragon? She sighed. It looked like she'd be returning to the ice cavern in her undies. Unless Enki took pity on her and returned her to the encampment on the surface, she'd die of exposure before the sphinx had a chance to wipe her memory. And Matt ... he'd be gathering moss on the riverbank for eternity.

Just thinking of the ice cavern made her shiver. She rubbed her hands over her arms in remembered cold, and a preposterous idea lit her soul.

"Gormleigh, when was the last time you felt cool?"

"What did you say?"

"Well, it's just that it's very warm here in the heart of your volcano. I wondered if you wouldn't enjoy a change, maybe a trip to a land of cold, soothing ice. A place where your scales could slide on silky, smooth surfaces? Where your eyes could savor the stark glacial white?"

He licked his lips, and an avaricious sparkle lit his eye.

Bingo.

"You know of such a place?" he asked. "I saw nothing like that when I visited your planet."

"My world has changed since your last visit. Will you trade a tail-barb for my knowledge of an icy retreat?"

Gormleigh bent his head low, inspecting her through the rift's curtain of rising steam. "I will give you a tail-barb when you accompany me to this fictional place."

"Will that satisfy the sphinx?"

"It will," growled a voice behind her.

Erin whipped her head around. The lion/man amalgam stood just inside the final bend of the tunnel.

"You've done well, Dr. Carstedter," he said. "Complete your transaction with Gormleigh. I will ensure the gorgon releases Dr. Davidson. He will be returned to your encampment unharmed. Once Gormleigh is satisfied, we will make arrangements for humanity's new apprentice status." He smiled, his teeth glinting red in the cavern's fiery light. "Earth has entered a new epoch. Your leaders will be proud. Instead of uncovering history, you and Dr. Davidson have made it."

EPILOGUE

Matt glanced at her and winked. Erin's heart launched into a rapid staccato rhythm, but she maintained her composure. The alien assembly already considered humans immature. She didn't want to supply further evidence.

She and Matt had been home for six months, but the experience on Orion III still gave her nightmares. What if she'd failed?

Relax, she scolded herself. *You didn't fail. You satisfied Gormleigh's demand for payment and met the deadline Enki established. Matt isn't a statue. Earth is about to join the Intergalactic Union. Breathe ... and pay attention.*

An unusual group gathered in the General Assembly Hall of the United Nations. Despite its seating capacity of nearly two thousand, the hall was crowded. Aliens from dozens of worlds mingled with humans of every nationality. Enki and Faruq, the Djinn who had offered assistance to Erin and Matt, sat on the dais with the President of the United States, Great Britain's Prime Minister, and the Secretary General of the United Nations. Matt and Erin sat between Enki and

Faruq. They'd become international celebrities since their return with an invitation to join the Intergalactic Union.

The Secretary General was speaking, and Erin understood every word despite his lack of English. Alien technology had eliminated all language barriers. So much had changed in such a short time. The dignitary finished his speech, closing yet another day of successful negotiation. Everyone stood. Applause rang through the hall.

"That went well." Matt leaned close to be heard above the cascading applause. "Want to grab something to eat?"

She concealed a smile. "We're not dating, remember?"

"Only because you keep refusing my offers."

Enki joined them. "I must get back to my nymphs. I've spent too much time away since arriving on your planet."

"I'll take you now," Erin said, shrugging her shoulders at Matt in implied regret. The government had retained an entire floor of the Hilton for Enki and his entourage.

"That would be excellent," the sphinx said with a wry smile. "And then I think you should put this young man out of his misery."

"What?" Erin and Matt spoke in simultaneous horror.

Enki stared at them in bland amusement. "I seem to have misspoken. I merely meant that you should spend more time with him ... since he so obviously desires it."

Matt laughed, and Erin sighed.

"Oh," she said. "Your word choice implied that I should kill Matt."

Enki growled and padded toward the door. Erin followed with Matt beside her.

"My apologies. No violence was intended. However, have you never heard that heroes deserve reward? Matt desires you. You desire Matt. Stop procrastinating and begin to live."

Erin rolled her eyes. Relationship advice from an alien, and a sphinx at that.

"I knew I liked this guy," said Matt, slapping Enki on the withers. "I'll come with you. We'll deliver Enki to the Hilton then we'll grab some food."

"You're moving awfully fast," she said. "I haven't agreed to anything yet."

They reached the lobby, and Matt held the door for his companions. "Erin, you saved my life. Quit stalling; let's figure out what's between us."

"Yes, Erin," agreed Enki. "Quit stalling. Your aura of indecision fogs my thoughts during negotiation."

Face flaming, Erin stepped into the late afternoon sunshine. New York City awaited. "Well, I certainly don't want to throw the meetings off. You win," she said, gazing into Matt's blue eyes. "I've been through the looking glass with you; I guess dinner in New York is safe enough."

"Safe?" Matt quipped. "Who's looking for safe? We're intrepid adventurers, remember?" He grinned and handed her into the chauffeur driven limousine.

"Thanks, buddy," he whispered to Enki as he assisted the lion/man into the car.

"Anything for a friend," said the alien. "Anything for a friend."

III

WAKINYAN'S VALLEY

DEBBIE MUMFORD

BESTSELLING AUTHOR OF *SORCHA'S HEART*

WAKINYAN'S VALLEY

SPUN YARNS
A Short Story

1

Footsore and grimy our little bank slogged along a pot-holed, mountain road, hauling the remains of our former lives in bicycle trailers designed for Yuppie toddlers. A week's worth of dust clung to our clothes, and we reeked of sweat and dirt and desperation. Hot showers. Laundromats. Hope for the future. Hard to imagine I'd once taken all of them for granted.

A spark of hope remained, one we nurtured diligently. We would find a place of our own — a safe haven where we could raise our kids in peace.

The late spring sun beat down on my head, while a sparkling mountain stream danced parallel to the road. I paused for a short breather. Leaning the bicycle-trailer combo against a tree, I yanked my ball cap off, wiped sweat from my brow, and listened as the stream caroled a mocking song: why should I be hot when it was cool? Why did I strain to push a load uphill when it tumbled joyfully along its rocky path?

Jake and Phil trudged past, each pushing a bike-and-trailer of their own.

"You okay?" Jake asked without breaking stride.

I didn't blame him for not stopping. The slope would make it tough to regain my momentum. Should've waited for a level spot.

"Yeah," I said. "Just needed a breather."

He nodded and kept pushing.

"See you at the top," Phil said with a grunt.

I replaced my ball cap, grabbed the bike's handlebars, and shoved forward.

"Kevin! Mark! Everyone! You've got to see what I found!" Maggie darted past Jake and Phil and skidded to a halt beside me. Pebbles skittered away from her worn hiking boots. "I wanted some watercress, so I followed this stream...."

She paused to catch her breath, and the rest of our group crowded around to hear what had her so excited.

"The stream disappears into a canyon. It's barely visible, just a pleat in the cliff face covered in scrub oak and sage brush." Maggie's dark eyes danced, and her deep cocoa complexion glowed with excitement. "You've got to see it, Mark. It could be just what we've been searching for."

Her husband, who'd been at the rear of our little band, chivvying children, joined us. "What's up?" he asked, taking off his ball cap and swiping his sleeve across his forehead.

Maggie threw herself into his arms and said, "Oh, Kevin! I think I've found a hidden valley. One with running water and everything!"

Kevin and I followed Maggie back along the stream. Phil Brooks volunteered to stay behind and guard our belongings while the rest of our troop trailed along after us. The thought of a casual drifter running across our burly ex-mechanic brought a smile to my lips. No one would bother our stuff with Phil on guard.

Our small band of survivors had lucked out in the talent department. Before The Fall, Maggie Harris had been a nurse with a special affinity for herbal remedies. We'd already had cause to thank our lucky stars for her medical knowledge.

Maggie's husband, Kevin, had been a lawyer; the Davidsons, Jake and Tina, had been teachers; Phil's wife, Beth, had owned a bakery — and man could that woman cook. My own wife, Janet, had owned a small gift shop. Me, I'd been a ski-instructor and an Olympic-class biathlete, not exactly great skills in our present situation. Sure, I could put a bullet through a squirrel's eye in the top of the tallest pine, but only as long as our meager supply of ammunition held out.

Maggie's description of the canyon opening had been accurate. From a distance, the stream appeared to rise from an underground spring; the cliff face appeared solid. Scrub oak and sage brush crowded the bank on each side, so the only way to examine the opening was to wade in. Not many people would make that effort. Only Maggie's desire for watercress had allowed her discovery.

Jake Davidson and I exchanged hiking boots for sandals and waded upstream to see what hid behind that pleated stone. The five remaining adults planted themselves on the creek's grassy bank and watched the kids splash and play. The unexpected release from travel drudgery demanded celebration.

We must've waded a good quarter-mile up that canyon. The rock on either side rose to dizzying heights, and most places we could've touched both sides by stretching out our arms. I slogged along, thoughts of our kids chasing through my brain. I really wanted this canyon to lead to a safe haven. Somewhere our kids could grow in peace.

They were resilient little buggers. Their splashing laughter echoed behind me, making me smile. Amazing how little crap they gave us about the hardships of this new life, how easily they found joy in their surroundings. Like now; give them a break from hiking, a mountain stream, and they made instant merriment.

Hell, I bitched and moaned inwardly about ninety-percent of the time, but our kids? They held up like troopers. Kevin and Maggie's twin girls, Evelyn and Elaine, were the oldest at nine. They helped a lot with the little ones. Next came the boys, Jason Brooks, a feisty seven-year-old, and Tim Davidson, the most active six-year-old I'd ever seen. Four-year-old Amy Brooks was our youngest member. She beat my own daughter, Ellie, out of that honor by an entire year. Hard to believe that Tim, Ellie, and little Amy would never set foot in a school. Public education had gone the way of the dinosaur in the new world order.

"I'm gonna be glad to get out of this water," Jake said. The narrow rock canyon opened before us, only to be replaced with scrub oak and sage brush again. "My feet are frozen."

Grunting my agreement, I followed him past the undergrowth. He stopped so suddenly, I planted my face squarely in the middle of his backpack."

"What do you think you're dong?" I snapped. "Don't just stand there, move it!"

"Mark," he whispered, his voice tight with awe, "you're not going to believe this. It's perfect."

"I sure as hell won't believe it if you don't move your fat ass out of my way."

That got his attention.

"Oh, yeah, right," he said and stepped forward past the bushes and out of the stream.

Jake cleared my line of sight, and my jaw dropped. The mountain valley described a perfect bowl — meadow in the center surrounded by a wide fringe of aspen and tall pine. Beyond the forest, the mountains soared to the sky. The stream we'd followed in ran around to the right and then disappeared. My gaze followed its estimated course and, at the back of the valley, a long ribbon of white cascaded from a sheer cliff. A waterfall! Phil would have a heyday with that. Visions of hydroelectric power danced through my brain.

"Man! When you're right, you're right." I clapped Jake on the shoulder and stepped out of the water. "This is perfect. Running water, trees for lumber and fuel, open ground for fields, and...." I stopped and looked straight into Jake's grinning face.

He nodded and finished for me. "It's hidden. Thugs would have to be beating the bushes to find that opening."

Excitement sizzled through my veins. This secluded valley promised security for our families. "Let's get the others. We'll explore tomorrow."

It took all our strength to get the bikes, trailers full of gear, and kids through that waterlogged canyon. But when the rest of the group saw the valley, they agreed it had been worth the effort. Too tired to move further, we set up camp just inside the opening. Morning would be soon enough to scout out a permanent campsite.

With everyone settled in for the night, I reclined against a tree with Janet in my arms.

"I hope this isn't a dream," my wife said and leaned back, shoulders sagging as she snuggled against my side. "It's too perfect; someone must live here."

I kissed her forehead and closed my eyes. "We'll take turns on guard, like always. If anyone's here, we'll find out."

Janet and I gazed across the valley, at peace for the first time since we'd fled Willow Springs, the Rocky Mountain ski community that had been our home.

Home. Man, that sounded good. I bowed my head and prayed this valley would be a new home for our small tribe. We'd been through a lot together already.

The night the virus took out the computers, our four families had been having a party at Kevin and Maggie Harris's house. The adults had talked and laughed around the kitchen table while the kids played in the great room. Evelyn and Elaine had been unwitting harbingers of doom with their complaint that the TV had gone on the fritz.

Once we understood what had happened, we banded together — a "safety in numbers with people you can trust" decision. Our group held fast through the devastation of an east coast nuclear attack, grateful to be living in the Colorado Rockies. Willow Springs sheltered us while the world's great nations collapsed, but after the final communication links blanked out, mob violence raged. We made the decision to flee the remnants of "civilization" after the first riot.

God! We needed this valley, needed a safe haven and a defensible island of sanity where our kids could grow to adulthood.

2

The creature appeared on my watch, just before dawn. The sky glowed with burgeoning color. Not enough light to see properly, but a hint to promise the sun's reappearance. I must've been out on my feet, because I'd swear I heard the rush of air past gigantic wings. I scanned the brightening sky but couldn't pick anything out. Glancing back toward the center of the valley, I saw it — a vast, indistinct darkness rising from the ground about a hundred yards in front of me.

I raised my rifle, the last remnant of my hoped-for Olympic glory, and aimed at the center of the hulking darkness. "Identify yourself," I yelled. "I'm armed and I'm a crack shot."

The mass stopped, and the sky lightened. My friends stirred behind me, and I strained my eyes, trying to force the darkness to resolve into a distinguishable shape.

Time stretched, an elastic bubble doomed to burst. Jake took his place beside me, baseball bat gripped firmly in locked fists.

The darkness loomed larger for a moment before the strengthening light revealed a blanket being thrown back from the head and shoulders of a stately woman.

"My name is Winona," she said, her voice clear and strong in the early morning silence, "and you are on my land. Will you shoot an unarmed woman?"

I lowered the rifle and rubbed my eyes. The woman and her blanket couldn't possibly account for the massive darkness that had filled the predawn glow.

"Sorry, ma'am. We didn't realize the valley was occupied." I handed the rifle to Janet — my tall, auburn-haired wife was an excellent shot — and opened my arms. "Please, join us. We'll make a pot of wintergreen tea."

Jake let the baseball bat drop to his side and walked over to stand beside Tina. Maggie stirred the coals, while Beth poured water into our battered kettle.

I stepped toward Winona, arms still widespread. "I'm Mark Whitehorse. This is my wife, Janet, and these are our friends. We have several children in our party. We mean you no harm."

Winona walked calmly into our camp and listened while I introduced the other adults. She carried herself with a grace that belied the years her white braids proclaimed. Her copper skin, long straight nose, and high cheekbones declared her Native American heritage. A leather tunic covered worn jeans, and her feet were clad in moccasins.

The kids slept on, blissfully unaware of their parents' distress, but all eight adults greeted Winona with solemn disappointment. The valley was taken; we'd have to push on.

Winona made eye contact with each of us in turn, an essayer determining our worth. Weighing our souls like so much gold dust.

"You are four," she said, "the sacred number. You are complete: red, yellow, black, white." She dropped to the ground, sat cross-legged before our fire, and chanted in a rhythmic monotone.

We exchanged glances and paired into couples, taking comfort from our committed bonds. I didn't understand how fourteen people translated into four but couldn't argue with the woman's color sense. Our party covered the spectrum of human skin pigmentation. Red for me, Lakota Sioux. Tina Davidson, a petite second-generation Chinese-American woman, represented yellow. Kevin, Maggie and the twins claimed black. Everyone else fell in, or near, the white category.

Beth broke the spell. "I don't know about the rest of you but I'm hungry. Let's fix breakfast."

Energized, we resumed our morning routine. By the time Winona stopped chanting and opened her eyes, we had hot tea, oatmeal with dried berries, and six bleary-eyed children sitting around her.

"The spirit guides have spoken," Winona said, as if the conversation hadn't lagged. "You may stay in the valley. You are complete."

Maggie handed her a bowl of oatmeal. "Thank you. But I don't understand. How are we complete?"

Winona accepted the bowl with a gracious nod. "Four is a sacred number. There are four seasons, four cardinal directions, and you are four families." She paused to take a bite of oatmeal and sip the tea Jake handed her. "And there are four colors of man; you contain them all." She smiled, showing strong, white teeth.

Winona finished her breakfast, wiped her mouth on a threadbare handkerchief, and proclaimed, "The spirits accept you. The Rainbow Tribe is welcome in this valley."

3

The next few weeks passed quickly. Kevin and I completed a survey of the valley while the rest of the group set up a semi-permanent camp near Winona's cabin. One evening after dinner, the discussion turned to our plans for the future. The adults sat around Winona's fireplace, with Kevin's sketchy map stretched on the floor before the hearth. Our kids read or worked on a puzzle at the table across the room.

"The wheat fields belong over here," Kevin said, pointing to the north-east section of the map. "That's closest to the stream for irrigation and should get the most sunlight."

"Good point," Jake grunted.

"Wheat fields?" Winona skewered me with her gaze. "You intend to plow the earth?"

"Well, sure," I said, heat rising in my cheeks as my defenses engaged. "We're going to need a dependable food supply."

"I've survived by hunting and gathering, following the traditional ways of our people."

She expected me to understand because of my Lakota blood. And I did, but I couldn't let outdated beliefs endanger our survival.

"I honor your traditions, Winona, but our people were nomads when they relied on hunting and gathering to sustain the tribe." I paused, aware of the others' silence as they strained to decipher the palpable tension. "One person can live by gathering what's available in this valley and just outside the cliffs. Fifteen can't."

Winona stared at me, face immobile. Then she gave a quick nod. "Make your plans; I will consult Wakinyan. You must not scar Maka's breast without his permission." She stood and strode from the room.

As soon as the door closed behind her, the others burst into questions.

"What was that all about?" asked Maggie.

"What's a Walkin, uhh, whatever she said?" asked Phil.

I raised my hands and cleared my throat.

Everyone quieted.

"We've got a culture clash happening," I said. "Winona follows the old ways. Maka, the earth, is one of the primary gods. She can't be owned and isn't to be harmed. Our people don't even dig graves. Maka doesn't like man-made tools ripping her flesh."

Tina sighed. "I can see why planting wheat fields would be a problem. What'll we do?"

"Don't underestimate Winona; she's a smart woman. She knows we can't follow nomadic ways in the current world." I met each gaze around the circle. "She also knows we'll strip this valley of edible plants in the first season. She'll come around."

"You didn't answer my question," said Phil. "What's a Walky-whatsit?"

"Wakinyan," I said. "The name translates as 'Winged One.' Tradition-ally, he's known as the Thunderbird. Inyan, the rock-god, the frame-

444

work of the world, created Wakinyan to be his agent. Wakinyan interacts with the shaman, and the shaman guides the tribe.

"My mom's dad was a shaman. He told me all the old stories." I stood and stretched. "I'm surprised to find anyone who remembers the old gods, let alone believes in them. Don't worry. Winona will accept the necessity of planting."

Our discussion returned to optimal locations for fields, cabins, and the community kitchen. The others, engrossed in happy dreams of a prosperous future didn't notice, but a rush of wind, like the beating of giant wings, sounded just outside the cabin.

"Did you hear that?" I sprang to the window but couldn't see anything in the inky blackness.

They all stared at me blankly, all except Ellie. My daughter gazed at me, dark eyes wide with wonder.

"I heard it, Daddy," she cried. "Was it the dragon?"

4

The next morning, Winona announced that Wakinyan accepted our need to plant and build in his valley. We heaved a collective sigh of relief and began work on the community kitchen complete with stone ovens designed by Beth, our baking expert. The next task would be to plant the kitchen gardens and wheat fields. Family cabins would come last. The tents would have to suffice for sleeping quarters until the crops were safely in the ground.

Our first major problem came after we'd picked the rocks from our future wheat field. Time to plow. Jake had scrounged a plow and harness from a deserted farm outside the valley, and the men had wrestled the heavy iron implement in through the canyon with the aid of a bike trailer, but our commune didn't include a horse. So, the men harnessed up in pairs and pulled the plow while the women took turns guiding our efforts and sowing the seeds.

Winona watched the slow torture the first afternoon. That evening, as we lay aching and exhausted by the hearth, she asked, "Wouldn't this be faster with a horse?"

I bit my tongue to hold back an obnoxious retort. Thankfully, Kevin answered her in reasonable tones.

"A horse would be a godsend." He raised his head and looked at Winona. "You don't know where we can get one, do you?"

Winona shook her head. "No, but Wakinyan could bring one."

Kevin sighed and rested his head on his folded arms. "Right. Wakinyan."

"Winona," I said, savoring exquisite pain as Janet massaged my over-worked shoulders, "you tell your spirit-guide that if he can provide a horse, we'll be eternally grateful." After that, the conversation kind of faded into the background, and I dozed off.

Two days later, a horse stumbled out of the canyon and ran wild-eyed straight to our log kitchen. He blew and snorted like a demon but calmed as soon as he reached the building. I swear, he acted like something was chasing him and he recognized humans as a source of protection.

"Well, what do you make of that?" Phil stood in the kitchen's shade, gazing at the heaving horse. He waited a beat, and then approached the skittish animal with an outstretched hand. The horse, a bay with four white feet, took a deep whiff, whuffled, and allowed Phil to grab his mane and stroke his neck.

"It's okay, pretty boy," Phil murmured. "Whatever spooked you didn't follow you in."

Jake appeared in the kitchen doorway, wiping his blond mustache on his sleeve. He spotted the horse and stopped short. "Guess we'll have to work out that eternal gratitude thing with Wakinyan," he said with a grin. "What say we take a day off plowing and put together a corral and shelter for this guy?"

"Yeah," I agreed, remembering Winona's words. "Think we should put an order in for a milk cow, a couple of pigs, and a few chickens while we're at it?"

Everyone laughed, but deep down, the coincidence spooked us all.

5

Once the seed we'd smuggled out of Willow Springs was safely in the soil, we turned our attention to building individual homes...and learning to hunt. Setting my rifle and sparse ammunition aside for emergencies, we concentrated on renewable weapons. Winona became our teacher. She taught us to craft bows and arrows and promised that Wakinyan would call the game.

"Damn," said Kevin as another bow cracked under the stress of his pull. "I sure wish Dave was here." David Parks had been Kevin's law partner. He died last spring in a flash flood — one of those freak accidents that can happen when a dry climate is inundated with an unusually hard rain.

"He was a pro with a bow and arrow." Kevin wiped his hands on his jeans and gazed at the broken pieces of bow. "I used to tease him about being born in the wrong century." He shrugged and unwound the string from the splintered wood. "Who knew?"

Winona also introduced us to the atlatl. Easier to construct than a bow and arrow, it looked deceptively simple. We soon discovered the technique required consistent practice. Releasing the dart at just the right point in the arc proved surprisingly difficult.

Beth and Tina became our food preservation experts. Both women had grown up on remote farms and knew non-electricity-dependent methods. Winona added tribal lore to the mix. The three enjoyed rousing debates on the merits and drawbacks of individual ingredients for the pemmican they planned to make after our hunt.

Maggie and Winona made a game of teaching the children to forage. The women traded herbal remedies while training the little ones to recognize useful plants and avoid harmful ones.

"Wakinyan knows you miss eggs," Winona announced one evening as she ladled soup into mugs. "He told me where to find a flock of chickens."

"This Wakinyan guy is handy to have around." Phil smiled as he picked up his mug and spoon. "First a horse, then a few head of cattle, now chickens. He's turning this into a proper farm."

Tina nodded. "He's forgotten the pigs, though." She glanced at Jake. "Remember my mother's pork fried rice?"

Jake groaned. "Stop! That's torture; no pork and no rice." He raised his mug to Winona. "But damn fine soup!"

I laughed and turned to Winona. "So, where are these chickens, and how do you suggest catching them?"

"What? They're not going to just appear in our coop?" Phil asked, his face contorting in a mask of horror.

"You should show more respect, Rainbow Tribe," Winona scolded. "Wakinyan has been merciful."

"You're right, of course," I soothed. "We're very grateful that you and Wakinyan took us in." I scowled around the table. Heads dropped, hiding suspiciously penitent faces.

Ellie ran up and hugged Winona's knees. "I love Wakinyan!" She turned to me, chestnut eyes sparkling. "He's a dragon, all black and shiny, with big red eyes. He's my friend."

Winona placed her right hand on my daughter's dark brown curls. "You have a shaman's vision, Ellie." She closed her eyes and chanted for a moment. When she opened them, she turned to face me.

"You should listen to your daughter ... and your shaman blood. Wakinyan deserves your reverence."

6

Janet and Beth danced around the kitchen like kids at Christmas. The prospect of chickens and eggs delighted them.

"Oh, omelets!" Beth inhaled deeply, as if she could already smell the eggs sizzling in the pan.

"And fried chicken," said Janet, stuffing my pack with supplies. She zipped the backpack closed and handed it to me. "Go get us that flock," she said and punctuated the command with a kiss.

I grinned, hugged her and saluted Winona, and then Phil, Jake, and I embarked on the Great Chicken Roundup.

A few hours later, we found the flock exactly where Winona had said it would be.

"How's she do that?" Phil asked, looking expectantly at me.

"Haven't got a clue," I said with a shrug. "I know for a fact she hasn't been out of the valley since we arrived."

Jake laughed, a hearty sound that caused our quarry to scatter under nearby bushes. "You two know Wakinyan told her."

I scowled. "Don't tell me you're falling for her tribal demi-god gobbledy-gook."

"Hey, I don't know what your problem is," he said. "She's telling the same stories your grandpa told."

"Yeah, but you didn't believe them then, and I'm not falling for them now."

Jake raised an eyebrow and studied my face. "What about the horse?" he asked.

"And the cattle," added Phil. "What about them?"

"Coincidence," I said through gritted teeth. "Quit giving me grief, and let's round up those birds."

Before either of them could resume the debate, I grabbed the windbreaker I'd brought to use as a chicken net and moved stealthily away from the bike trailer. The birds had settled into a clearing on the far side of a clump of trees. I counted at least a dozen hens and one big rooster. A couple more birds might have been adolescent males; I couldn't tell. The only chicken I'd ever touched was either wrapped in plastic at the grocery store or cooked on my plate.

I skulked behind a tree, targeted a nice plump hen, and readied my nylon jacket. Timing my moves precisely, I stepped away from the tree, tossed the jacket at the bird, and dove for the resulting lump. Unfortunately, my quarry turned out to be a rock.

"Shit," I exploded, and the flock whirled away from me in a flurry of squawks and feathers. Muffled laughter caused me to turn and glare at Jake and Phil.

"Thanks for the demonstration," said Jake, smothering a snicker.

"Yeah — how not to catch a chicken in one easy lesson." Phil looked like he was about to bust a gut, his fair face beet red.

"I'd like to see either of you do better," I snapped and grasped Jake's outstretched hand, letting him pull me upright.

"Okay," Jake said, "we don't need the whole flock...couldn't stuff 'em all in the bike trailer even if we managed to catch 'em."

"Right," Phil agreed. "Let's concentrate on the rooster and then see how many hens we can snag."

After a moment's consultation, we surrounded the big male. At Jake's whistle, all of us threw our jackets over the bird. Mine landed squarely, and Phil grabbed the snared bird before he could escape.

I ran to unzip the mesh door of Ellie's bright yellow bike trailer, while Phil triumphantly carried our prize. Once the rooster had been secured in his makeshift coop, we traded high-fives and went to work rounding up his harem.

Two hours later, a rooster and six hens nestled in the trailer. Sweaty and scratched, we headed for home. Chicken dinners would have to wait until nature saw fit to increase our flock, but we laughed and traded insults as we walked, recounting the morning's exploits in graphic detail. I guided the bike and trailer while Phil and Jake poked at each other in imitation chicken wrangling. We hadn't seen a soul on the entire journey, so we relaxed and followed the old highway. The sleek ribbon of asphalt made travel fast and easy.

It also made us sitting ducks.

7

The motorcycles roared up behind us before the unfamiliar sound's significance registered.

"Well, well," said a filthy man on a beat-up, red Harley. The other three bikers circled us. "What've we got here?"

Jake and Phil moved back to flank me as I reached for my rifle, strapped to the bicycle frame. I prayed these guys intimidated easily; I'd used the last of my ammunition hunting elk the week before. Except for the motorcycles, we were evenly matched. Three against four, but the three of us were well-fed and healthy.

"Just caught a few chickens," I said, stating the obvious in a friendly fashion. "If you're interested, there are a few more in a stand of aspen down a dirt road about two miles north of here."

The filthy biker leaned sideways and spat on the pavement. "Thanks, but we'll take what you've got there." He grinned and motioned his cohorts into a tighter circle. "Along with whatever else looks good."

Jake whipped his baseball bat out of the trailer's side pocket while Phil grabbed a tire iron from the opposite one. I raised my rifle and aimed at the leader's forehead.

"You don't want to die over a flock of birds, now do you?" I asked, pulling the safety off. "Your gang might be able to take them, but I guarantee you won't live to eat them."

The leader turned green under the layer of dirt and grease that grimed his face. "Easy, man," he said, "we was just funnin' you. No harm done." He motioned to his men, and they turned their bikes and moved slowly north along the highway. "See? We'll be movin' along now."

"You do that," I said, keeping him square in my sights until they rounded the bend and the roar of their bikes died in the distance.

"Let's get the hell off this highway," said Jake. "Any ideas how to keep these chickens quiet?"

"Man," said Phil, stowing the tire iron before wiping sweaty hands on his pants. "I knew we shouldn't have risked the highway."

"Too late for regrets," I said, stowing my rifle but keeping the straps loose. "Let's get home fast, but carefully. We don't want to lead them in."

8

Not leaving a trail was easier said than done. The three of us possessed enough trail lore to make our tracks hard to follow, but a bike trailer full of chickens left its mark on the terrain. As we neared the canyon, I lagged behind and covered our tracks. Maybe the bikers would be too lazy to follow us. But maybe they wouldn't. The possibility of gang-hardened bikers finding our families spurred us to move as quickly and carefully as possible.

Once we had those damned birds through the canyon, Phil scrambled to the top of the ridge to keep watch. Jake and I raced to the compound to alert the others.

Jake spotted Jason Brooks before we reached the communal kitchen.

"Hey, Jason," Jake called, "your dad's at the top of the ridge. Why don't you climb up there and keep him company?"

The boy trotted off, and I turned a quizzical expression on Jake. He shrugged. "Now Phil can send word if he sees anything."

I nodded. "Good thinking."

The rest of the community was in the kitchen cleaning up after dinner. One look at my face, and Kevin instructed the twins to take the birds to the newly constructed coop. The rest of the kids danced along behind, anxious to admire their new critters. Jake moved the adults to the table where we delivered the bad news and discussed defense strategies.

Jason burst through the door. His dad needed reinforcements on the heights.

"Winona! Get the kids and head to the waterfall. Keep them out of sight. The rest of you, grab your weapons and follow me," I said, taking my atlatl from above the mantle.

Reaching the plateau at the top of the quarter-mile canyon, I scrambled over to where Phil rested belly-down in the dirt.

"What's up?"

He pointed to the scrub oak that guarded the fold in the rock. "They've found the canyon's entrance." He looked at me with despair in his eyes. "And they've brought reinforcements. There're ten now...and several have rifles."

My gut writhed and knotted. I swallowed hard. "Okay. Here's the plan. As soon as they get to that first narrow spot, we're going to brain them with rocks."

"That's it?" he said, gaping at me. "That's the whole plan?"

I flushed. "What did you expect? There aren't a lot of options. I mean, we brought the weapons, but atlatls aren't good in close quarters, and none of us can hit squat with an arrow yet."

He dropped his head on his arms. "Yeah," he murmured, "I know." He raised his head, tears glistening in his blue eyes. "Well, it was nice while it lasted."

The eight of us cached a supply of rocks and crouched atop the first narrow. The ten bikers slogged single file through the creek. We waited, straining to be still, not wanting to give ourselves away with a dislodged pebble. They reached the designated point, and we hurled rocks with all our strength. The canyon exploded in noise — shouting voices, the crack of rock hitting rock, thuds when rock hit flesh — and finally, the repeated staccato of rifle fire.

The bikers backed out of the canyon, but our victory cost us. Beth took a bullet. The slug lodged in the fleshy part of her right shoulder. Not life- threatening, thank all that was holy, but she was out of commission. Phil's fear and rage confounded us. He jumped up and rushed the edge of the cliff. I don't know what he intended to do; I only know Kevin took a bullet throwing his friend to the ground.

Things looked grim. The wound in Kevin's side bled profusely, Beth was white with pain, and the bikers had moved back out of throwing range. The stand-off couldn't last, but it gave us a chance to tear shirts into strips and bind up wounds.

We debated how to get Kevin and Beth back to the compound while Janet kept an eye on the bikers. She raised her head to check on their position. Ka- ping! The bullet skimmed her temple before rebounding off a rock and lodging in Jake's thigh. My heart stopped. First Janet, now Jake; I couldn't take any more.

"Janet," I screamed and launched myself to her side.

Blood cascaded over her face and covered my hands and wrists as I cradled her in my arms. Maggie tried to examine the wound, but I snarled. My love opened her eyes and gave me a wan smile.

"I'm okay," she whispered before her eyes fluttered shut. I eased off and let Maggie check her out. "It's just a graze, Mark," Maggie said. "Facial wounds bleed like the devil, but it's just a scratch. Really."

My world narrowed with my options. This rivaled The Fall for me. That had been worldwide, a catastrophe beyond my ability to prevent. This was personal — the death of our hopes and dreams as well as literal death for the eight of us perched precariously on that plateau.

I prayed the children would survive, prayed Winona could keep them safe. Lowering my head, I wept silent tears of despair while Maggie bandaged Janet's head.

9

A sudden breeze kicked dust into the air, and the whoosh of wind against giant wings assaulted my ears. How many times had I heard that sound since our arrival in this valley? Now I witnessed the reality as a small mountain of dragon flesh landed silently before me. Not feathered wings like a bird's, but leathery, with well-oiled suppleness. Shielding my eyes, mind paralyzed with disbelief, I stared wordlessly at the massive creature and sniffed the air, expecting the acrid tang of sulfur, but didn't find it. The dragon — Thunderbird? — smelled more like horse than fire.

"Do you wish to survive, Rainbow Tribe?"

The dragon gleamed, so black it shone iridescent in the afternoon sun. His red eyes whirled in a dizzying pattern. I averted my gaze to preserve my sanity.

"What...who are you?" I asked, knowing the answer, but needing to hear it spoken aloud.

He bared his teeth in a grisly grin. "You know me, Mark. You've known me since your grandfather first told you my story."

I hugged Janet tightly and bowed my head. "Forgive me, Wakinyan."

The roar that echoed from the cliffs forced me to look up. Wakinyan stood on his hind legs, snout raised to the heavens. He dropped his forefeet to the earth and gazed around at his valley's meager defenders.

"Ask for my assistance, Rainbow Tribe." He didn't suggest, he commanded.

Transferring Janet to Maggie, I fell to my knees, and my hands lifted in supplication. I swear I didn't raise them; they lifted of their own accord. "Help us, Wakinyan. We're out of options."

"Will you pay the price for my protection?"

Jake answered for me. "What price is that?"

The lava-redness of Wakinyan's eyes paled to bloody-spittle pink. "I require a sacrifice...of shaman blood."

My friends gasped, but my mind closed in on itself. Wakinyan existed. He offered my family and friends protection. I'd gladly sacrifice myself to save Janet and Ellie.

"I'll do it," I said, grateful for Janet's unconscious state.

Wakinyan studied my face. "No," he growled. "You are not the shaman blood I desire. Give me the girl-child."

My heart leapt to my throat. I gagged, tasting bile. Unable to breathe, unable to force words past paralyzed lips, terror suffocated me.

Kevin roused himself and swore, "Go to hell! We're not giving you our children to save ourselves."

Wakinyan flapped his wings and stared at us. "They'll be mine when you're dead."

The quiet assurance of his words silenced us.

My mind engaged, and I gasped air into oxygen-starved lungs. "Why offer to save us?" I rasped. "If it's the kids you want?"

"I want all of you. Worship me, Rainbow Tribe. Sacrifice to me, and I will protect you from all danger." He peered over the ledge and then glanced at each of us in turn. "Your enemy approaches. I ask again, do you wish to survive?"

"I'd rather die, and Ellie with me, than teach her to worship a demon. I won't give you my child. None of us will." I glared at the demi-god my grandfather had loved. "I won't bargain with Ellie's life."

Wakinyan gazed at the sky.

"Agreed. Your children will choose for themselves." He paused, red eyes whirling. "Will none of you worship me?"

He searched the eyes of each conscious adult. My friends flinched away from his scrutiny, but each denied him. He nodded his massive head and exposed rows of razor sharp teeth.

"So be it. Accept me as part of your tribe. I will provide you with security; you will provide me with companionship."

My heart dropped from my throat to my stomach. This wasn't possible! Tribal demi-gods didn't bargain for favors. I glanced around the circle. Huge eyes stared from blanched faces, but heads nodded hesitantly. I focused on Kevin.

"Kevin, as our contract lawyer, will you speak for Rainbow Tribe?"

Kevin's usual coffee-and-cream complexion turned a sickly ash grey, but he nodded.

"On the condition that you harm none of us," he said, his voice calm despite sweat beading his forehead, "we accept your offer. Let this be a straightforward contract, service for service. Rainbow tribe accepts your protection. In return, we offer our companionship. However, no form of worship or sacrifice is offered or implied."

"Let it be so." Wakinyan sniffed Kevin's wound and then exhaled steaming breath over the bandage-covered hole. The rest of us watched in fascination as the bandages dissolved, the bullet popped out, and the flesh healed. "The bargain is sealed in your flesh. See that it is kept."

Color returned to Kevin's face, and the underlying strain of pain disappeared. He fingered his side, nodded, and mumbled his thanks.

Wakinyan turned his attention to Beth, Janet, and Jake. Their wounds disappeared, and he commanded, "Return to your compound. The tribe's enemies are mine to destroy."

The bloodstained red leached from his eyes, replaced by a cool silver-white. His gleaming black body dulled to a lackluster gray as he stood on his hind legs, lifted his snout to the sun, and beat his wings in the clear mountain air. The eight of us clung together to avoid being blown off the cliff by the force of the gale Wakinyan created.

Air thickened and swirled around him. Clouds formed, echoing the silver-white of his eyes. A scent of water mingled with the dust-filled air, and lightning sparked around Wakinyan's awesome head.

I broke from the group, scrambled to the edge of the cliff, and peered over. The bikers stood squarely in the middle of the narrow defile, staring at the windswept sky. Bile rose in my throat and burned my flesh. Wakinyan's plan crystallized in my mind. I crawled back to my friends.

"Let's get out of here," I shouted above the howl of the storm-laden wind.

Jake tore his gaze from the lightning-wreathed dragon. "Ab-so-lutely!"

We scrabbled down from the cliff and scurried through pelting rain to the shelter of the communal kitchen where Winona and all six kids huddled by the hearth.

"I'm sorry, Mark," she said once everyone was inside and the door secured against the storm. "Wakinyan insisted we stay here." She wiped tears from Amy's eyes and helped the child blow her nose on a scrap of cloth. "He guaranteed our safety."

Ellie ran into my arms, and I hugged her tightly. "I'm the one who should be sorry. I didn't believe Wakinyan existed." I shivered, but not from the soaking. "I still can't believe he's real, but I saw him with my own eyes."

Wakinyan. The mighty Thunderbird, the dragon demi-god, commanded the skies and hurled a flash flood through our canyon. I shivered again and pictured the bikers, arms and legs flailing, drowning in those raging waters. They would've killed us without a moment's hesitation. Still, they were men, humans like ourselves.

I drew Janet into my arms, hugged Ellie tighter, and considered the fate we'd just avoided. There had been no choice; we'd made our bargain. Safety. Health. No sacrifice from our tribe. But a price yet to be paid. Only time would tell if the bargain had been a wise one.

Time — and experience coexisting with a dragon.

IV

SEVENTH

DEBBIE MUMFORD

BESTSELLING AUTHOR OF *SORCHA'S HEART*

SEVENTH

SPUN YARNS
A *Gus & Ghost* Short Story

1

The crime scene investigation I worked today turned sour when the victim spoke to me.

My partner, Jack Barnes, and I had been called to a dimly lit alley in downtown Portland. The early morning mist had burned off, leaving the pavement damp. The multi-story brick and mortar buildings on either side huddled close as if protecting the small figure centered in their midst, though she was far beyond anyone's help.

The air at the mouth of the alley smelled of freshly baked bread and cinnamon, but the odor turned fetid as I neared the corpse.

Jack joined the uniform who'd called it in, but I kept walking, accompanied by a steady drip of water from an overhanging eave.

I knelt beside the body, taking in her position on the damp gray pavement, the congealing blood pool, and the utter destruction of the back of her head.

That's when it happened.

Blue eyes popped open and short, well-manicured nails dug into my wrist. "Help me," she whispered, her voice parched and cracking. "Don't let him do this again."

I yelled, fell backwards into a shallow puddle, and scrambled to get to my feet and as far away from her as possible.

Her eyes snapped closed.

My partner glanced my direction over the bowed head of our lone witness and raised his eyebrows. "What's up, Gus?"

I wiped my hands on my pants, backed another two steps from the corpse and asked, "Who called her death?"

Jack's brows pulled together as he strode to my side. "The uniform. He was first on the scene. Didn't take any brains."

"Get the medics in here. She's still alive."

He grabbed my arm and squeezed. "Get a grip on yourself," he whispered, his gaze darting around to see who else might be listening. No one paid us any attention. "What's wrong with you?"

I looked down at the young woman who had just spoken to me and acknowledged the obvious. She was an undeniable corpse. Blue-tinged skin, stiff limbs, a neat little hole in her forehead and a crater the size of Texas where the back of her skull had been.

But she'd spoken to me. My wrist still tingled from the bite of her nails.

I wiped sweat from my forehead with the back of my sleeve. I needed a break. The dead had never spoken to me before, and I'd been working homicide since I earned my release from a patrol car last year. I'd seen a lot of stiffs in my work, but never on my birthday. My twenty-eighth birthday.

Seven quadrupled.

I hated the number seven … with good reason. I was the seventh son of a seventh son, and I'd spent my whole life explaining that yes, the birth order thing is true, but no, I'm not psychic, and no, I sure as hell don't know what the blonde at the next table thinks of you.

People can be such idiots.

But now a dead woman had spoken to me. Shit. What if all the seventh-seventh crap had a basis in fact?

I couldn't bring myself to approach the body again, so I dusted off my hands and forced myself to look Jack square in the eyes.

"Why don't I finish the interview and you check out the corpse?" I worked at sounding nonchalant, but my hands shook and Jack's wary expression told me my face must be white as my grandmother's sheets.

"What?" Jack asked. "Is our resident seventh-seventh feeling a little woozy?"

I scowled at him and marched over to the kid he'd been interviewing. I had no intention of discussing my own personal mythological hell. Ever. But especially not when I was spooked.

The kid's story checked with what the uniforms had learned. A bunch of high school boys had been playing skateboard tag on the street, generally raising a ruckus and terrorizing pedestrians when our witness had veered down this alley and run smack into a crime scene. He'd hightailed it back to the street and gone looking for the nearest cop. It hadn't taken long. The solid citizens had complained about the havoc the boys had been wreaking.

The patrol officer who answered their call had gotten significantly more than he'd bargained for. His perpetrators had morphed into witnesses and his quiet lecture on respecting others' rights had given way to a full-scale murder investigation.

I closed my notebook and rubbed my temple. Dead end. No one saw anything suspicious, other than the corpse, and no one heard the shot that destroyed the victim's skull.

But she'd spoken to me.

Hell's bells. How was I supposed to work *that* into my report?

———

"THE VICTIM'S name was Dr. Sarah Allen, a twenty-seven-year-old resident at Sisters of Mercy Hospital. She was in excellent physical condition prior to death and there were no indications of sexual molestation."

The medical examiner paused in his recitation and glanced up at me and Jack. "In short, she died of a gunshot wound to the head. I'm guessing a .45, possibly a magnum, to cause this much damage. Did you guys find the slug?"

Jack shook his head while I avoided looking at the victim's remains. Light bounced off flat white walls, chrome covered counters and instrument trays. Antiseptic assaulted my nasal passages and made my eyes water. At least I hoped it was the antiseptic. I didn't like being this close to the dead woman's corpse.

"Too bad," Jack said. "Her being a doctor and all ... she could've saved a lot of lives."

The M.E. nodded. "Yeah. A real shame."

"Well," I said, moving toward the door, "let us know if anything useful shows up in the lab results. We've got to get back to the precinct."

We pushed through the swinging doors and walked to the elevator in silence. I breathed a sigh of relief. She hadn't spoken. I'd been in close proximity to the corpse, but nothing weird had happened.

"So," said Jack in a too-casual voice, "how are you feeling? Still a little psychotic?"

"The word is *psychic,* Jack. And we've been over this before; I'm just a normal cop."

He smirked. "Yeah. It's perfectly normal for a murder cop to think an obvious stiff is still kickin.'"

I groaned and punched the elevator button several times in rapid succession. I'd rather have been punching Jack, but you take your physical release where you find it.

The lights above the elevator doors counted down and the gleaming chrome slid aside with a soft whoosh. Jack stepped inside, but I balked. An attractive young woman shimmered at the back of the car.

Yep, shimmered ... and not just any woman. Sarah Allen. Whole and unblemished, dressed in pale blue scrubs and soft-soled white shoes, with her long blonde hair tied back in a pony tail.

"Gus," Jack said, holding the door open, "snap out of it, buddy. Look, I'm sorry about the psychotic crack. Just get in the elevator. I promise I'll behave."

Yes, Gus, said a quiet contralto. *Get in the elevator. We have a lot to discuss.*

The hairs on the back of my neck tried to yank me to the opposite wall, but I took a deep breath and stepped into the car. The doors slid closed sealing me in a metal coffin with my oblivious partner and a dead girl's ghost. Could this birthday get any worse?

2

I ditched Jack the moment we got back to the precinct, lied to the captain — told him I had a family emergency, and drove like a maniac to my downtown studio apartment. Trust me. A ghost in the passenger seat doesn't make for a relaxed commute.

I didn't speak to her. I didn't want to believe she existed. Thought if I ignored her, maybe she'd disappear. Hey, it could happen! Hell's bells, if the seventh-seventh crap was real, what had triggered it today?

It's your twenty-eighth birthday, she said. *Seven quadrupled, remember? You were thinking about the seventh-seventh legend when we met in the alley.* Her voice sounded calm, resigned. *I didn't make it to mine — twenty-eighth birthday, that is. Consider yourself lucky.*

Great. Just what I needed … to be haunted by a ghost with a dry wit.

I bit my lip and refused to legitimize my delusion by responding that kneeling next to a corpse hardly qualified as *meeting.*

Look, Gus, she said, *I won't go away just because you ignore me.* She sighed, too loudly for a being who could no longer draw breath. *Who else am I going to talk to? You're it. Lucky me.*

I reached my building and turned into the underground parking facility. After locking the car, I sprinted to the elevator and jabbed the up button. The doors slid open to reveal Sarah, arms crossed, leaning against the back wall.

Can we stop playing hide-and-seek? she asked. *You know, I'm not any happier about this than you are. In case you've forgotten, I had my brains blown out last night!*

"I know," I mumbled, "and I'm sorry about that. Truly. I am. But I'm not interested in being haunted and I don't want to be psychic."

The doors opened on my floor and I moved quickly to my apartment door, unlocked it and stepped inside. With the door firmly bolted, I pulled off my jacket, dropped it next to the hall closet, shrugged out of the shoulder holster, placed it and my service revolver carefully on the end of the kitchen counter and collapsed on the hide-a-bed. That's the great thing about a studio apartment ... everything within reach.

My eyelids closed and I relaxed for the first time since arriving at the crime scene.

You need to grow up, Gus.

I groaned and pulled a throw pillow over my head.

You can't change what you are. No one cares if you want *to be psychic. You* are *psychic.*

I sat up and glared at the ghost in my apartment. "What do you want from me?"

I want you to quit whining and get to work!

"And just what work is that?"

What do you think? she asked, hands on what had been very attractive hips. *You're a detective. So ... detect. Figure out who did this to me.*

I jumped up from the sofa and prowled around my compact apartment — past the picture window framing a view of the Willamette

River, past the built-in bookshelves and television, past the bathroom door and entry hall, past the kitchen nook and back to stand in front of the wide window. "Okay, great. Let's solve your case. Who killed you?"

She opened her mouth, but no sound emerged. Frowning, she cleared her throat and tried again. Still nothing. Her gaze met mine and I read a mixture of surprise, irritation and fear. She shrugged and drifted over to perch on the end of the sofa. *I don't seem to be able to say his name.*

"But you know who did it?"

She nodded.

"Great. I'm being haunted by a murder victim who has all the answers, but can't cough them up." I loaded my words with sarcasm. "Were you this useless when you were alive?"

Sarah shot off the sofa and slapped my face with all the force she could muster. Nothing happened. Her hand whooshed through my jaw, leaving a slight chill in its wake. The expression on her face morphed from anger to shock to despair.

"You missed," I spat. Good thing, too. I had the feeling if that swing had connected, I'd've been feeling the imprint of her hand for hours.

Grow up, Gus, she repeated, gliding back to the sofa, dejection in the slant of her shimmery shoulders. *I can't hit you and I can't give you a name. Neither one makes me happy.*

"Okay," I said, resuming my laid back position on the folded up hide-a-bed. "You can't give me a name. I couldn't have gotten a warrant on your say-so anyhow. Can you tell me anything?"

Look, she said through gritted teeth. *I'm new to this dead stuff. I'm still adjusting, so back off and give me a chance.* She rose gracefully from her perch on the sofa and kind of paced the room. I mean, it's hard to pace when you can't even make contact with the carpet, but she wasn't exactly floating either.

I wonder, she said, recalling my attention to the case rather than the fact that my only witness was a ghost.

"What?"

Are you up for an experiment?

My heart skipped a beat and my mouth went dry. "What kind of experiment?"

Well, since I can't say the words, I wonder if I could show you my death?

"What?" I asked. "Like some kind of Vulcan mind-meld?"

She stopped moving and stared at me blankly. *What?*

I rolled my eyes. "Seriously? Didn't you ever watch *Star Trek?*" A little frown creased her forehead, and my heart rate steadied. She was kind of cute, really. Too bad she was dead. "Never mind. Sure. Let's try your experiment."

She moved to stand in front of me. *Close your eyes.*

The last thing I saw before my eyes drifted shut was Sarah bending over me, hands stretching for my temples. Damn those hospital scrubs. Not even a glimmer of cleavage.

Soothing coolness enveloped my agitated mind. I relaxed.

Weird, huh? I mean, an alien presence penetrated my thoughts, the very core of my being, and I relaxed, but Sarah's touch felt so good, so cool, so … right. A deep inhalation and exhalation and I sank deeper into the sofa cushions. A guy could get used to this kind of relief…

…and the vision began.

I stood just outside the wide automatic doors of the emergency room at Sisters of Mercy. A car pulled up and I lifted my hand to wave.

Note to self: meticulously clean 2015 Lexus LS 460, white, license plate 728-PHL.

The driver lowered the passenger window with a flick of his finger and leaned over to look up at me.

"Well, this is an unexpected pleasure, Sarah," he said. "Need a lift?"

"That would be great," I said, my limbs trembling with exhaustion. The door locks disengaged with a muffled click. I lifted the car's door handle and slid gratefully onto the gray leather seat. "I've been on shift for twenty-four hours and barely had time for a cat-nap. Thanks."

The driver chuckled, swinging the Lexus out of the driveway and into traffic. "I remember my own residency," he said. "It can be grueling."

I nodded and closed my eyes, relishing the support of the firm leather seat. We rode in silence for a few moments.

He's had medical training and knows her well enough he doesn't have to ask for an address or directions.

"Tell me, Sarah," he said, his voice low in the Lexus' ultra-quiet interior, "are you experiencing any unusual symptoms? Any unexplained headaches or visual aberrations?"

What the fuck kind of question is that?

"Nothing," I said, eyes closed, drifting perilously near the edge of sleep. "Other than sleep deprivation, I'm perfectly healthy."

"Good," he murmured. "That's very good."

An odd disappointment colored his voice. Unusual enough that I opened my eyes and rolled my head left to watch him. An attractive older man, his silver hair gleamed in the passing street lights, revealing remnants of the strawberry blond it had once been. Firm jaw, no facial hair; no glasses either. He wore an expensive dark gray suit with a conservative white shirt and royal blue tie. A pillar of respectability.

"Would you be willing to help me with a little experiment?" he asked, flashing a serene smile my direction. "If you're not too tired, that is."

"Tonight?" I yawned, a jaw-cracker, and belatedly covered my mouth. "I don't know, I'm really beat."

"Trust me, Sarah," he said, eyes straight ahead, guiding the car through traffic. "This won't take a minute. You'll be able to rest soon."

I nodded and closed my eyes again. The car purred around me, racing me to who knew where. A seed of doubt sprouted in the back of my mind. Why the unscheduled experiment? Why in the dead of night? I wasn't his research assistant anymore. Didn't he have a new student to help him with this stuff?

Years of trust smothered the seedling and exhaustion claimed me.

"Sarah?"

His voice sounded muffled, as if he called from a great distance.

"Wake up, Sarah. We've arrived."

I struggled to orient myself. Who was I? Gus, or Sarah?

Get a grip, man! You're Gus, dreaming Sarah's murder. Just because she relaxed enough to fall asleep doesn't mean you needed to. Hell's bells, man. The woman's about to be murdered! Pay attention.

I opened my eyes and stared around the moonlit night. He'd parked the Lexus in an alley between multi-storied buildings. The streetlights were out, but the full moon shone from the zenith.

"Where are we?"

"I told you," he said with gentle patience, "I want to try an experiment. Step out of the car."

The seedling struggled to lift its head above my ingrained trust. "Aren't we going to the university?"

"Trust me, Sarah. The sooner you get out of the car, the sooner you can rest."

Obviously the alley led somewhere important to his work. Delay only robbed me of much-needed sleep. I unbuckled my seatbelt, opened the door and stepped out into the narrow alley.

He beckoned me forward. "This way. Come stand right over here. That's right. Center yourself in that patch of moonlight. Do you know what day this is?"

I frowned. Residents kept bizarre hours. I often lost track of the days of the week, let alone the date.

"It's, ah, June twentieth, no, twenty-first."

"Actually, you're right on both counts. We're on the cusp of the summer solstice. Midnight at the beginning of the longest day of the year. The perfect time for my experiment, and you're the perfect subject."

He pulled a gun from beneath his suit coat and aimed it at my head. The seedling engorged to a full-size oak. Why hadn't I paid attention to my instincts?

"What are you doing?" I gasped, desperate to delay his trigger finger.

"I'm sorry, Sarah, but you're the only one who can answer my question."

He pulled the trigger and …

… Sarah pulled her hands away from my face.

My eyes popped open and I sat bolt upright. Adrenaline coursed through my veins and I jumped to my feet and paced the small apartment.

"Shit! You knew the guy? You trusted that madman, and he…" I gulped and wiped clammy hands on the seat of my pants, "he blew your brains out."

Yes, I know.

"Okay. I know who the bad guy is. Give me his name and I'll figure out a way to get a search warrant."

I can't. At least the memory transfer worked.

"Who made these stupid rules?" I asked. "And what question did that bastard think he could answer by killing you in the middle of the night?"

Sarah shrugged, but remained silent.

"Never mind. I've got enough to go on. Good old fashioned detective work will find his name." I stomped to the hall where I'd dropped my jacket and yanked a small spiral notebook from an inside pocket. I needed to jot down the Lexus' license number before I forgot it. My only clues to Sarah's murderer: some kind of doctor; a license plate number; and a face I felt certain wouldn't show up in any mug shots. Hell's bells, why couldn't the woman simply tell me the bastard's name?

A shiver ran down my spine. Forget that. Why in the name of all that's holy could I communicate with a dead woman at all? What a great birthday present ... my own personal ghost.

Not.

J ack glared at me when I reached my desk at the precinct.

"Where the hell have you been?"

He didn't so much ask the question as he chewed up the words and spat them at me. Not a good sign.

"I've been following a tip," I said, deftly avoiding his gaze.

"What tip? Nobody gave us any tips."

"An anonymous tip. It came to me at home." Not the whole truth, but not a bad lie.

Jack tapped a pen against his chin and then threw the slender cylinder on his desk. Like all the partners in the precinct, our desks butted against each other, so that when we were seated we could see each other, discuss our findings.

Right now, I wished my computer monitor occupied the center of my desk instead of sitting to one side. I wouldn't have minded hiding behind its 17-inch screen.

"Well," he growled, "you gonna fill me in, or you just gonna sit there like a lump?"

I pulled the notebook from my pocket, copied the license number onto a scratch pad and pushed it across the desk to him. "That's what I've got. The tip said it was attached to a white Lexus LS, probably a 460 model. Have we got anything else?"

"Nada. Do you think your informant is reliable?"

I shrugged. "Who knows with these anonymous types. Could be solid, could be totally bogus, but at least it's a lead."

Jack nodded and turned to his keyboard. "I'll run it now."

"Great," I said, edging around the desk. "I want to check out the board."

The whiteboard was mounted to the wall across from our desks. So far the only information was Sarah's name and age, the address of the alley where her body was found, and the estimated cause and time of death. The last item was what interested me—between 11:30 p.m. (June 20th) and 12:30 a.m. (June 21st). I had to give the medical examiner credit, he'd nailed the time according to Sarah's memory. The perp had pulled the trigger just as one day ended and the next began.

"Got it," called Jack. "That plate is registered to a Jason Morgan."

I sprinted to Jack's desk, flipped my notebook open and jotted down the name and address. "Great. Let's see what Mr. Morgan has to say."

"Yeah, and we should check out the vic's friends and co-workers at the hospital while we're out. Might be one of them will give us something useful."

Half an hour later, I stood face to face with the man who had gunned Sarah down in cold blood. A full professor of sociology at Portland State University, Dr. Jason Morgan was a well-respected academic. He didn't look like a murderer, but in my experience they never did.

"Good afternoon, Detectives," he said, ushering us into a bookshelf-lined office filled with dark wood and heavy upholstery. "How can I be of assistance to Portland's finest?"

Jack flipped his notebook open, glanced at the notes scrawled inside and said, "Dr. Morgan, do you own a white Lexus LS 460, license number 728-PHL?"

"I'd have to check on the license number," he said, a slight frown furrowing his brow, "but, yes, I do own a white Lexus. What's this all about?"

"Your car was seen leaving the scene of a homicide early this morning," I said, watching his eyes for any flicker of fear.

His gaze moved from Jack to me. Cool, steady as glass. His face gave nothing away.

"I'm afraid you've been misinformed, Detective," he said, studying my face with those cool blue eyes. "I was home all night. My car was parked in my garage and the door was locked."

He paused and his gaze flicked back to Jack. "Someone has been murdered?" he asked, eyebrows raised in academic interest.

"A young woman," said Jack, "a doctor. A resident at Sisters of Mercy."

Morgan shook his head. "How very sad. A healer ... her talents lost." He clicked his tongue in a *tsk-tsk*-ing sound.

You murdering bastard. Why me?

My heart thumped wildly and I glanced sideways at Sarah. I hadn't noticed her standing beside me.

"Did you know Sarah Allen?"

His eyebrows shot skyward and then drew together in concern as bits of information fitted together. "Sarah? Why yes, she was my research assistant a few years back. You're not suggesting..."

Jack nodded, a sympathetic expression on his grizzled face. "Dr. Allen is the victim in this case."

Morgan's face blanched. He fumbled for the arm of his desk chair and lowered himself into it. "Sarah? Dead?" he whispered, and then with more vitality, "There must be some mistake. Sarah can't be dead. I saw her at the hospital just last week."

You bloody hypocrite, Sarah seethed.

Jack flipped his notebook shut, stowed it in his breast pocket and edged toward Dr. Morgan's desk. "Well," he said, "I think that about wraps things up for now. If you think of anything that might help our investigation, please call the precinct." He dropped a business card on the smooth oak surface and turned towards the door.

That's it? Sarah cried in outrage. *You're not going to arrest him? Not even taking him in for questioning?*

Morgan glanced in my direction, a slight frown pulling his brows together.

"That's it for now," I said, apparently to Morgan, but really for Sarah's benefit.

Jack and I showed ourselves out, Morgan still glancing around the room, a puzzled expression on his face.

We strolled across the park that fronted the administration building and back to our car, Sarah trailing sullenly behind. Jack rattled the keys in his pocket creating a counterpoint to our muffled footsteps. The afternoon was clear, but muggy. We reached the car in silence. Jack unlocked the doors and I slid into the passenger seat. Sarah settled in the back, arms crossed, foot tapping. I faced forward and tried to ignore her irritation.

"Well," Jack said as he inserted the key into the ignition, "I guess your informant was wrong. I've never seen a guy more surprised. He's a college professor, not an actor ... that was genuine shock."

"Yeah. I agree, but I don't get it. He's the one, I'm sure of it. So why was he so shocked?"

Because he didn't expect you to connect him with my murder, Sarah answered. *He was shocked that you showed up and he had to act surprised or you would've been suspicious.*

Jack snorted and pulled the car away from the curb. "That must have been one convincing snitch," he said. "We've got nothing on that guy and I say he knew nothing about the murder until we told him. Your informant was wrong. Get over it."

Idiot, she seethed. *You have an eye-witness account. Go arrest him!*

"Maybe," I said. Listening to Sarah while talking to Jack took a lot of concentration. "But I'm still going to dig into that guy's background."

"Knock yourself out," Jack said with an exasperated sigh. "But for now, let's go interview her colleagues at the hospital."

———

THE HOSPITAL INTERVIEWS proved to be a royal pain. I had to endure shocked and grieving medical personnel while ignoring an agitated and highly vocal ghost.

What are you doing? Sarah shouted in my left ear. *These people don't know anything. You know perfectly well who killed me. Leave my friends alone and go get the guilty guy!*

Standing in a hospital corridor beside my partner and a boatload of doctors and nurses was not the place to carry on a detailed conversation with a ghost. I was forced to ignore her, which only steamed her clams.

You're wasting your time! If you're going to be this thick, I'm not sure I want to work with you.

And so it went. I interviewed the other residents Sarah trained with, the doctor in charge of her work this quarter, and the nurses she came into contact with on a daily basis. Jack made the rounds of her patients—the ones capable of answering questions, and hospital administrative staff who'd dealt with her directly.

The composite we came up with was of a hard-working, dedicated young doctor. Her superiors all agreed Sarah was gifted. Her fellow residents admired her and admitted to being jealous of her obvious talents ... but Sarah had been too sweet to resent. Not only was she gifted in dealing with her patients, she was generous in assisting her co-workers without stealing their thunder. In short, everyone was going to miss Sarah Allen.

Everyone but me, that is.

I had a raging headache by the time I excused myself and made my way to the men's room. Predictably, Sarah followed.

After assuring myself that the stalls were empty, I rounded on the relentless ghost.

"Look," I said, "you've got to back off and give me some breathing room. I know Morgan's guilty, but I don't have any proof. If I don't do my job — and interviewing everyone who knew the victim, sorry, everyone who knew *you*, is a major piece — if I don't do my job thoroughly and effectively, I'll get canned, and then where will we be? So shut up and give me some time to think."

I don't know if ghosts can cry — I mean where would they get the tears? — but Sarah looked like she was about to spring a major leak.

I'm sorry, Gus. You're right, of course.

She gulped and kind of shivered all over. If she'd been solid, I would've put my arms around her and hugged her. Hell's bells, if she'd had a real body I'd have been tempted to do a lot more than that ... but she didn't, so I couldn't.

"I'm not trying to be mean," I said and my voice sounded rough and gravelly even to my own ears, "but you can't talk to me when we're not alone."

But what if I've got information that you need? What if it can't wait?

"Fine. If you've got something pertinent, tell me," I held up one finger and tried to look stern. "But it's got to be information only. You can't be asking me questions. I can't talk to you when there's anyone else around. Agreed?"

She sniffled, but her eyes weren't full of unshed tears anymore. *Agreed.*

"Okay. Let's get out of here and get back to work."

I pulled the bathroom door open and held it while my ghostly partner sailed through. Yeah, I know. She could've sailed through the wall, but old habits die hard.

4

Late that night, I sat on my sofa staring out the wide picture window at the lights reflecting on the Willamette River and nursing a cold beer. Sarah floated near the counter in the kitchenette, chin resting on one fist, pretty little lips flattened into a grim slash. I'd been trying to distract myself with the dancing lights on the river's black surface, but it was no use. Sarah's unhappiness permeated my apartment.

"Look," I said, giving up the pretense of not noticing her, "I can't do anything tonight. Hell, I probably won't be able to do anything tomorrow either. We don't have any evidence against him. No probable cause."

She opened her mouth, probably to lambast me, but my cell phone rang. I grabbed it like a life preserver and tapped it on. "Collier."

"Detective Collier," said a man's voice, "this is Jason Morgan. We met this afternoon."

"I remember," I said, glancing meaningfully at Sarah. "What can I do for you Dr. Morgan?"

"I wondered if you might meet me at the fountain at Waterfront Park. I have some thoughts about Sarah Allen that might be helpful to your investigation."

"It's a bit late," I said, though my curiosity was piqued. "Wouldn't tomorrow morning be better."

He hesitated, his breath whispering through the phone. "Of course," he said finally, "if you're too busy tonight … I just thought you'd want to hear my information right away."

"Sure. Sure. I can meet you at the park. Give me twenty minutes."

"Fine," he said, relief evident in the word. "I'll see you in twenty minutes."

I disconnected the call and met Sarah's sober-eyed gaze. *Be careful, Gus,* she said. *He's a murderer.*

"I remember."

Twenty minutes later, Sarah and I stood between the fountain's dancing water and the shining blackness of the Willamette River. The night air smelled of fish, chlorine, and the heavy sweetness of new mown grass. My usual cop's calm eluded me as I peered into the shadows the streetlights couldn't penetrate, unusually aware of the weight of my service revolver in the shoulder holster under my leather jacket.

I should've called Jack. I knew better than to meet a suspect alone, especially late at night in a deserted park. I knew better, but I wasn't alone and this wasn't a normal case. Sarah shimmered just behind my right shoulder and while she couldn't physically effect this meeting, her presence helped relax the tension spasms in my gut.

"You're a seventh-seventh, aren't you Detective Collier."

I whirled around, amazed that Morgan had been able to get so close to me unnoticed.

"What?" I said, totally caught off-guard.

"Don't act like you don't understand," he said. Light glimmered from his silver hair, white shirt, pale skin, almost like he glowed from within. "It's the only reason she'd be with you." He turned his gaze on Sarah. He looked directly at Sarah.

She floated forward, stopping just short of his nose. *Why?* she asked. *Why did you murder me? What did I ever do to you?*

"I'm so sorry, Sarah," he said, as if she were alive and I was the unseen ghost. "I had nothing against you, but I had to know. Had to discover if the power of a seventh-seventh could be co-opted." He turned to me and smiled. "As you can see, it can.

"And you, Detective. You're newly come into your powers, aren't you? Still adjusting to your new reality?" His smile widened. "I could see it in your reactions to Sarah earlier today in my office. Today is your twenty-eighth birthday, isn't it?"

I nodded. Wary, but not yet alarmed.

"How fortuitous for me," he said, extending his hand from behind his back. He held a matte black magnum revolver, "and how unfortunate for you."

I reached for my weapon, knowing I'd waited too long, that I didn't have a chance in hell of getting off a shot before he blew my brains out.

But I hadn't reckoned on Sarah. Neither had he.

My annoying ghost flew screeching into his face. *No! You will NOT kill again. You will NOT harm Gus.*

Morgan flinched away from her, giving me the instant I needed. Deeply ingrained reflexes came to my aid; I dropped to one knee, aimed my service revolver and fired, hitting him in his gun arm. He dropped the weapon, fell to the ground howling and cursing the dead woman who continued to scream at him in rage.

5

J ack stared at me, disbelief etching his unshaven face. "You mean to tell me that lunatic killed a woman over the seventh-seventh crap?"

"Yep. No clue why, but he dug into Sarah's family history when she was working as his assistant and discovered that, including a set of still-born triplets, Sarah was a seventh-seventh. I'm betting Sarah had no idea and had never even heard of the legends. Morgan seemed to think if he killed one of us on a solstice or equinox just before a twenty-eighth birthday, he'd get our 'power,' whatever that's supposed to be."

I shook my head for Jack's benefit, but glanced over his shoulder to where Sarah smiled with satisfaction. She'd seen the light after Morgan's arrest, but had opted to stay with me. We'd come to appreciate our newfound partnership.

"Shit, Gus," Jack said, grabbing my shoulder and squeezing. "If there are nut-jobs out there who would kill you over it, I'll never tease you about being a seventh-seventh again."

I smiled. His new-found sensitivity would evaporate like the morning mist, but I appreciated the sentiment while it lasted.

V

SEVENTH: FIRST FRUITS

DEBBIE MUMFORD

BESTSELLING AUTHOR OF *SORCHA'S HEART*

SEVENTH:
FIRST FRUITS

SPUN YARNS
A *Gus & Ghost* Short Story

1

I'm a homicide detective. Portland, Oregon is my beat. It's also my hometown. Not a hotbed of crime, but not exactly peaceful either, and today was starting off with a bang. Barely zero-seven-thirty and we already had a murder to investigate.

My partner, Jack Barnes, parked our department issued dark blue sedan across the street from a marijuana dispensary on Northeast Sandy Boulevard. The uniforms had already cordoned off the area with yellow crime scene tape, but even this early in the morning civilians were piling up on the sidewalk to either side, trying to get a look. I'd been a murder cop long enough to know that regular, law-abiding citizens got a thrill out of being near the scene of a crime... as long as the police were already present and said citizens knew everything was safe.

Jack figured it was a result of too many cop shows on television. I thought their fascination with death was part of human nature and had existed long before TV crime shows found their way into our shared world view.

Whatever.

The civilians were there, and we ignored them as we exited our car and ducked under the crime scene tape. Occasionally the perpetrator would join that crowd, curious about how his work was perceived, but not often. A quick glance confirmed that one of the uniforms was scanning the civilians with a cell phone camera. Good. All the bases were covered.

Jack took the lead as we flashed our badges to the uniform in charge.

"I'm Detective Jack Barnes and this is my partner, Detective Gus Collier," Jack said, pulling a small spiral-bound notebook from his pocket and clicking his pen open. Glancing at the man's name badge, he continued, "What can you tell us, Officer Reynolds?"

The uniform nodded. He stood at ease, relaxed but ready, feet solidly planted, thumbs hooked in his belt. "I was walking my beat this morning and noticed the lights on inside. That's unusual at zero-seven hundred when they don't open until ten hundred hours. So I looked in, saw the body, and forced the door." He glanced at the building and shook his head. "Guy was already dead. I called it in and secured the scene."

"The door was locked?" I asked.

Reynolds nodded. "The back too. I checked when I cleared the building. No sign of a break-in. Everything seemed secure, except for the body… and it looked like he had help getting dead."

Jack grunted his thanks and strode into the building accompanied by Officer Reynolds. I hung back, surveying the scene. A normal, well-kept Portland sidewalk beside a busy four-lane street. The marijuana dispensary was a single story, stand-alone building— flat roofed, its exterior walls painted dark green with deep gold trim. The display windows were clean, the shop well-lit. In short, it appeared to be a solid small business operation.

Time to get moving and see what Jack had found inside.

Wait, Gus. Don't go in yet. Sarah appeared beside me, floating a few inches above the sidewalk and shimmering in the morning sunlight. My ghostly partner had been with me for close to six weeks now— ever since I'd investigated her murder at the summer solstice— but her unexpected appearance still caused an adrenaline rush that made my heart hammer.

I glanced around. The uniforms were all occupied and no one was close enough to notice, so I answered her. "Why not?"

Look at the threshold.

I knelt down and examined the space between the sidewalk and the doorframe. A fine line of some type of powdered crystal ran from one side of the opening to the other.

"What is it?" I murmured.

Part of a ward, Sarah answered. *Use your* sight. *Examine the doorframe.*

Six weeks wasn't really long enough to change the habits of a lifetime. I'd always considered myself a regular guy. Sure, I'd been teased my whole life about being the seventh son of a seventh son, but I never put any stock in the legends. After all, I'd never had any special abilities. At least, not until six weeks ago; not until Sarah's ghost turned my understanding of reality upside down.

My twenty-eighth birthday just happened to fall on the summer solstice this year, giving me a double whammy of weirdness. Twenty-eight is seven quadrupled, which makes it a very auspicious time for a seventh-seventh to come into his power. Plus, the summer solstice is one of the *Old Ones'* eight holy days.

The universe chose to celebrate my awakening by allowing a corpse— Sarah's as it turned out— to speak to me at the murder scene I'd been called to investigate. And while I've grown fond of Sarah, I've got to tell you, I've had better birthday presents.

I discovered that Sarah Allen was another seventh-seventh, and that she'd been murdered in a blood magic ritual in order to steal her nascent powers. My partner Jack Barnes and I solved the case... with Sarah's supernatural help. But by the time it was all over, Sarah and I had bonded. She chose to stay in this realm instead of moving on, and I was happy to have her help.

But she still freaked me out when she just appeared out of thin air.

Now, I know what you're thinking: "This seventh-seventh nonsense is just that... nonsense. Supernatural hooey dreamed up by superstitious people with too much time on their hands and overactive imaginations."

Trust me. I wish you were right, but you're not. Sarah is a real ghost, and I'm not delusional.

And yes, she's female, so how can she be a seventh-seventh? Well, it turns out that even though I fit the traditional profile— the seventh son of a seventh son— gender isn't really an issue. Birth order is the determining factor. Sarah is the seventh child of a seventh child. If she'd made it to her twenty-eighth birthday, she would've come into her power. Unfortunately Jason Morgan murdered her on the cusp of the summer solstice in order to co-opt her abilities before they had a chance to blossom.

Abilities I now possessed, but still needed to be reminded to use.

I sighed, ran a hand across my eyes, and allowed my *second sight* to slip into place. When I looked at the doorframe again I saw that the deep gold trim paint was covered in glowing glyphs and runes. The lowest ones actually touched the powdered crystal. The entire opening shimmered with power.

"But people have been moving in and out through that door all morning," I whispered. "Hell's bells! Jack went in just a couple of minutes ago."

It's not a ward against normal humans, Sarah said. *I'm not exactly sure what it protects against, but I'm betting I won't be able to cross it. I can feel the power from here.*

"What about me?"

She shrugged. *No clue. Try it and see.*

I scowled at her. "Thanks for your concern." I said, trying to keep my sarcasm in check.

Really. I tried. Scout's honor.

Sarah grinned, and I stuck a finger into the open doorway. A buzz of power stung me and I jerked my hand back. If a finger caused that much of a jolt, I didn't want to consider crossing that void with my whole body.

Jack appeared on the other side, a frown creasing his forehead. "What?" he asked. "You waiting for an engraved invitation or something?"

Jack's not the best looking guy in the world— his hair is thinning and going gray, his cheeks are constantly stubbled, and he's got a definite spare tire around his middle— but he's a solid detective and a good friend. He used to give me a lot of grief about the seventh-seventh thing, but after discovering it was the motive for Sarah's murder, he'd stopped teasing me. He decided if some loony took it seriously enough to kill for, it wasn't a laughing matter.

He doesn't know that I came into my power during that investigation, or anything about Sarah other than as a murder victim, but his decision has made my life easier, so I'm grateful.

"Look at this," I said and knelt down to examine the powder again. Jack mimicked me from the other side. "What do you make of it?"

"No clue," he said. "Might be important; might not. Better grab a sample just in case." He pulled an evidence bag out of his pocket and scooped a bit of the powder into it, breaking the seal.

The wards winked out of existence, allowing Sarah and me to follow Jack into the shop's interior. The corpse, a young man, sprawled face down in front of a softly illuminated, and very bloody, glass-front display counter. Blood pooled on the floor around his upper body.

"Someone slit his throat?" I asked Jack, glancing at the pattern of arterial spray that coated the front of the glass display.

He nodded. "The medical examiner will say for sure, but it looks like he was kneeling in front of the counter when someone grabbed him from behind and...." He didn't finish the sentence, but pantomimed slicing a throat.

I swallowed and nodded toward the counter. "Yeah. If he'd been standing, the spray pattern would be higher. On the top of the counter and the wall behind, not just on the front." I paused before asking, "Identification?"

"David Howe, according to his driver's license." Jack nodded to a wallet encased in a plastic evidence bag and resting on top of the display case. "That was in his pocket. Cash and credit cards are still there."

"So, not a robbery," I said. "Or at least, not of him. Any idea if anything was taken from the store?"

"Place looks pretty neat," he said, and I had to agree. Except for the blood, the display case appeared untouched and the shelves behind the counter boasted neat rows of various types of cannabis products.

Officer Reynolds approached. "Excuse me, detective. I've got the information you asked for."

Jack turned to confer with him, while I stepped aside to examine the scene... and talk to Sarah.

"Where's the ghost?" I asked quietly.

He's already moved on, she said. *I saw the light while we were still outside.*

I nodded and breathed a sigh of relief. I didn't really want to have to deal with another ghost. I'd learned with Sarah that even though the victim might know who killed them, they were incapable of providing the information. A fact that was frustrating to both the living and the dead.

"Reynolds is contacting the owner," Jack said, turning to join me again. "Nothing looks out of place, but there could've been a lot of cash on hand."

I nodded. Marijuana dispensaries were in limbo as far as finances went. They were legal in many states, including Oregon, but credit card companies wouldn't deal with them since they weren't recognized nationally. Most banks refused to do business with them as well. This meant that dispensaries tended to deal in cash, and often had to store that cash on the premises. A risky enterprise in more ways than one.

Hell of a coincidence, Sarah said, gazing at the sign proclaiming the name of the business.

I quirked an eyebrow at her to encourage her to elaborate. Jack was too close to risk asking her directly.

This place is called "First Fruits", she said.

I shot her an annoyed glare. I could read after all.

She glared right back. *I thought you were reading up on the ancient holy days,* she said, shifting her position so her cute little fists rested on her nicely curved hips. She'd been a very attractive young woman, blonde and blue-eyed with a lithe, athletic body. Too bad she was forever doomed to wear the blue hospital scrubs she'd been murdered in. Sarah had been a doctor, a resident in her last year of training at Sisters of Mercy Hospital.

Today is Lammas or Lughnasadh, she explained. *It's also known as the Celebration of First Fruits.*

My eyes widened and my jaw dropped. She was absolutely right. Today was August 1st, the traditional day to celebrate the early harvest. I was standing in a marijuana dispensary named *First Fruits* on an *Old Ones'* holiday of the same name... and I had needed Jack's help to pass through a powerfully warded door.

A shiver ran down my spine. I was very much afraid this investigation was going to involve the supernatural.

Good thing I had a ghost on my team.

2

Back at the precinct, Jack set up our murder board— a whiteboard mounted on the wall directly across from our desks — while I pulled David Howe's information up on the computer. Nada. Howe seemed to be a solid citizen. No rap sheet. No arrests, no charges (false or otherwise), not even a list of shady associates. Just a single white male residing at the address we'd already determined from his driver's license. The one thing the background search did reveal was his employment record.

Since he'd been found in *First Fruits*, I'd assumed he was an employee. Not true. Howe was a certified public accountant and owned his own firm.

"Interesting," I said to Jack's back as he scrawled data on the murder board. "Our vic was a CPA. What do you suppose he was doing in the dispensary before opening?"

Jack's dry erase marker stopped moving, and he turned to face me. "A CPA?" he asked, a frown creasing his forehead. "What would an accountant be doing alone in a marijuana dispensary?"

I shrugged. "Well, not alone. He didn't slit his own throat. At least, it didn't look self-inflicted to me. The M.E. will say for sure."

"True, but Reynolds said the doors were still locked when he arrived on scene." He paused, capping the marker and flipping it in his hand while he thought. "If Howe was murdered, how did the perp leave?"

"Maybe he had a key," I suggested. "We don't have a time of death yet, so we don't know when this all went down. Do we have the owner's name and contact information? Maybe he can shed some light."

"Yeah. Reynolds pulled it from the dispensary license. Place is owned by a Gerald Adamson. I've got the address in here somewhere." He riffled through his notebook. "Got it." He turned, wrote a West Hills address on the board, and said, "Let's go see what Adamson has to say."

I pulled my dark tweed sport jacket from the back of my chair and shrugged into it as I strode to the elevator. I wasn't surprised to see Sarah appear in the elevator car when Jack and I stepped on.

I've been thinking, she said as I turned to face forward, appearing not to notice her. *The killer has to have been a normal human, otherwise he or she couldn't have crossed the wards.*

I cleared my throat, our signal that I'd heard and understood her comment.

But someone must've been worried about supernatural interference, or there wouldn't have been any wards.

I gave another little cough.

Jack glanced sideways at me. "You coming down with something?"

I grimaced and motioned to my throat. "Nah. Just a little tickle. I'm fine now."

Sarah snorted behind me.

Her comments were true, but there was another possibility, which I couldn't share in our present circumstances. Whoever cast those wards could undoubtedly cross them. I'd have to watch Adamson very closely. I didn't have a clue what kind of an aura a witch would present, but that was the only mortal I could think of who would be able to cast the wards we'd seen. I might have paranormal abilities, but rune work and wards weren't among them.

If Adamson hadn't cast the wards, who had? And had that person done so at Adamson's request? And how was I supposed to ask those questions with Jack beside me?

Life had certainly gotten more complicated since my powers had manifested.

Jack guided our dark blue sedan out of downtown and up into the hills. Barely ten minutes later we were winding through Arlington Heights, a well-to-do neighborhood of classic homes owned by lawyers, doctors, and business owners. The inhabitants of this area appreciated being perched above the city, while staying only a few minutes from their downtown offices.

Adamson's home was a grand specimen of a Prairie style home, with clean horizontal lines that would've made Frank Lloyd Wright proud. I thought about voicing this opinion to Jack, but stifled the impulse. The style of the home wasn't germane to our investigation, and even though I'd taken a few architectural design classes in college and still found the subject interesting, Jack would think I was nuts to bring it up.

So I kept my thoughts to myself as we followed a walkway across an immaculately landscaped yard to the front door.

Jack readied his badge and rang the doorbell.

Sarah appeared beside me. *Nice place.* I gave her a tiny nod and readied my own badge.

The door opened and I had my first sight of Gerald Adamson. A tall, thin man in his late forties or early fifties, Adamson had silvery blond hair that allowed his pink scalp to show through. His eyebrows were similarly colored and his complexion such a pasty white that if his eyes, a light, watery blue, had appeared red or bloodshot I would have suspected albinism.

"Can I help you?" he asked, looking us over with suspicion.

Jack and I help up our badges. "Portland PD," Jack said. "I'm Detective Jack Barnes and this is my partner, Detective Gus Collier. We have a few questions regarding the murder in your marijuana dispensary this morning. May we come in?"

Adamson stepped back, opening the door wide and gesturing us inside. "Of course. I've been expecting someone to come by. Terrible business." He shuddered, shaking his head. "Poor David!"

We stepped into a spacious entry hall, well-lit with white paneling and polished oak floors. Adamson led us to the back of the house and into a lavishly decorated living room with floor-to-ceiling windows providing a panoramic view of the city below, as well as the mighty Columbia River.

Adamson gestured us to a silvery green couch while he seated himself in a pale brown leather armchair. "I was so distraught when the officer contacted me this morning," he said. "I wanted to rush right down to the shop, but the officer— Reynolds, I believe?— discouraged that, saying the building was an active crime scene and that someone would contact me."

He glanced back and forth between me and Jack. "I assume that's you. How can I be of help?"

Jack pulled out his notebook and flipped it open. I studied Adamson. That was our habit. Jack jotted down information; I kept my eyes open. We compared notes later.

"Do you have any idea what Mr. Howe was doing in your dispensary after hours?" Jack asked.

"I'm afraid I don't," Adamson answered. His eyes widened for a beat and then his brows drew together in a little frown of perplexity. "David was our accountant, of course, but I didn't have any meetings scheduled with him until the end of the quarter." He glanced from Jack to me before adding, "The end of September, when we'd finalize our quarterly report."

"Did any of your staff have dealings with him?" I asked.

"Well, I think everyone had met him, but no, I was the only one who met with him. For business at least."

Jack glanced up from his notebook, interested. "Did any of them have a personal relationship with him?" he asked.

Adamson lowered his gaze, leaned forward and adjusted a floral display on the white oak coffee table that separated us. "I don't like to say," he mumbled. "We're a small business, and I can't help but notice, but it's not my place..."

"Mr. Adamson," I said, "we're conducting a murder investigation, not writing a gossip column. Now what do you know... or suspect?"

He sighed, sat back, and met my gaze. "Of course. My apologies. As I said, I don't *know* anything, but I believe one of my clerks, Tammy Wilcox, was rather taken with David. As they're both unmarried and she doesn't deal with my bookkeeping, I noticed, but wasn't concerned. I've no idea whether or not either of them acted on the... attraction."

I nodded and exchanged a significant look with Jack before he scribbled down the name. "Thank you, Mr. Adamson. We'll look into it." I hesitated, glanced at Sarah who hovered near the picture window. "By the way," I said, trying for casual, "we noticed some kind of powdered crystal lining the threshold of your store's front entrance. Can you tell us anything about that?"

His brow furrowed and he glanced between us again. "Powdered crystal? At the threshold? I have no idea what you're talking about. Is it important?"

I've been a cop long enough to read most people, and he came across as genuinely surprised and baffled. I shrugged. "Probably not. I just thought I'd ask since it seemed odd."

I paused a moment, and then said, "We'd appreciate it if you could meet one of our officers at *First Fruits* and go through the place. See if anything is missing. Do you know if there was much cash on hand last night?"

"Now that I can answer for certain," he said. "No. There was no significant cash on hand, only the petty cash in the register that would be necessary to open this morning. I took the deposit to our bank myself just after closing last night."

I frowned. "I thought banks were wary of dealing with marijuana dispensaries."

He smiled wryly. "They are, but they're happy to rent me a good-sized safe deposit box. I don't feel comfortable keeping too much cash on the premises, even in a safe, so I store it at the bank until it's needed."

"I see," I said, nodding. Watching his face for micro expressions that might call his words into question, I asked, "Do you know if Howe had any enemies? Anyone who disliked him enough to do him harm?"

Adamson shrugged and shook his head. "I'm afraid I can't help you there. He would've had no reason to mention anything like that to me. David and I had a business relationship; nothing more, nothing less."

Jack nodded, then flipped his notebook closed, pushed his pen into his breast pocket, and rose. "Thanks for your time, Mr. Adamson. That'll do it for now."

I stood and handed Adamson one of my cards. "If you think of anything that might be helpful, please call."

He accompanied us to the door and watched as we drove away.

"What did you think?" Jack asked. "Victimized business owner or murder suspect?"

I frowned and tapped my fingers against my leg. "His reactions seemed genuine," I said, "but it's too soon to take him off the list. What about you?"

"Same, though he did have his answers pretty handy," he said, keeping his eyes on the winding residential street. "Almost seemed rehearsed."

Agreed, Sarah added from her perch behind my left shoulder. *Something was off with him, but I'm not sure what.*

3

I opened the tablet computer mounted to the car dashboard and accessed Tammy Wilcox's information. Her driver's license was current and listed an address near Laurelhurst Park. A few minutes later Jack guided the car onto a narrow, tree-lined street of older homes.

"Nice neighborhood," he said, "but a real come-down from the boss's digs." He parked in front of the house, and we crossed the sidewalk and followed a neatly edged concrete path to the front door. The house was a blue two story bungalow with white shutters and several wind chimes dangling from the eaves. They jangled in the light summer breeze, serenading us while we waited.

A young woman opened the door and stared at us with open curiosity. From her license, I knew Tammy Wilcox was in her late twenties, but she looked like a high school girl. Her dark hair was pulled back in a high pony tail with stray bits curling around her face. She wore a sleeveless gold top and a billowy, ankle-length skirt; her feet were bare.

"Can I help you?"

We flashed our badges and repeated the standard police detective introduction.

"Oh," she said. "What's this about? I mean, I don't have any criminal tendencies." She smiled, displaying a cute little dimple. "Unless you count believing in the sanctity of Mother Earth."

Jack glanced at me, rolled his eyes, and then turned his attention back to Tammy. "I take it no one has contacted you regarding the incident at your place of employment?"

"*First Fruits?*" she asked, her eyes widening and her grip on the door-frame tightening to almost white-knuckle status. "No, I'm not sched-uled to work today, so no one has contacted me. What happened?"

I answered before Jack could blurt out the news. "If we could step inside," I said, "we'll fill you in… and then we have a few questions." Her face paled and her breathing quickened. Time to calm the situa-tion. "Nothing to worry about," I added. "Just routine police work."

She nodded, her lips pressed into a thin line, and opened the door wide. We followed her into a small living room with worn green shag carpeting and a drab brown couch whose cushions looked sprung. A black cat with white tips to its front paws watched us from a well-worn overstuffed armchair done up in a floral slipcover.

Tammy scooped the cat into her arms and dropped into the vacated chair. Jack and I perched on the couch. Sarah floated into the room and settled near a fireplace that looked like it hadn't been used in years.

A slight frown creased Tammy's brow as she followed Sarah's progress with her gaze.

This was going to be interesting.

"I'm sorry to have to deliver bad news, Ms. Wilcox," I said, reclaiming her attention, "but there was a murder at *First Fruits*."

She gasped, and squeezed the cat so hard it yowled and wriggled out of her grasp. "Oh! I'm so sorry Prissy." She reached to pet the cat, but it hissed and ran from the room.

Closing her eyes, she inhaled deeply, exhaled fully, and then did so again twice more. When she was calm again, she opened her eyes, met my gaze, and asked. "Who died and when?"

I glanced at Jack, startled. The first question was expected, the second part, not so much.

"A man named David Howe," I said. "I understand that you knew him."

Her face paled and then flushed. "Yes," she said quietly, clasping her hands together and lowering her gaze to stare at them. "We'd been seeing each other for about a month. H-how did he die... and when?"

Jack took that one. "We aren't at liberty to discuss the manner of his death— it's an ongoing investigation— and we won't be sure of the timing until the autopsy is complete." He paused to let that sink in before continuing. "Is the time important?"

She sat back, closed her eyes again, and massaged her temples. When she opened them, she looked wan, but in control. "I doubt you'll believe me, but I'm a witch. I practice the old faith and observe the *Old Ones'* holy days."

"What's that got to do with the time of the murder?" Jack asked.

"Today is August 1st, the Feast of Lughnasadh or First Fruits. There should have been a celebration last night between sundown and midnight. A libation of oil and grain should have been offered. I told Mr. Adamson about it. I told him that especially in our business, the old rites should be observed."

"Why especially in your business?" I asked, ignoring Jack's squirms beside me.

She shook her head and sighed. "Our society has lost touch with the old ways. Our food comes from grocery stores, packaged and promoted. But *First Fruits*, the business, deals with products of nature. Marijuana is a plant with natural healing properties, and Lughnasadh recognizes the *Old Ones'* bounty." She stopped, gazed over our heads toward the window, then glanced at Sarah and quickly away again. "But what has been given can be taken away. A harvest can be lost."

"You warded the entrance to the store," I said quietly.

She glanced up startled, but Jack said, "What?" before she could respond.

I quelled Jack with a glance. "The powdered crystal," I said. "It was part of a ward against supernatural evil."

Tammy drew a sharp breath, glanced toward Sarah again, then met my gaze. "You know she's here?" she asked quietly.

I nodded.

"Know who's here?" Jack asked, irritation evident in his growling tone.

She shuddered, but didn't drop her gaze from mine. "Yes. I warded the entrance, both of them. The windows too."

"But Howe died anyway."

"If he died before midnight...." She swallowed, shuddered, and tried again. "If he died before midnight, he was a sacrificial offering."

"And if after?" I asked.

"It was the *Old Ones'* retribution."

4

On the way back to the precinct Jack grumbled about our interview with Tammy Wilcox.

"What was all that crap about wards and witches and what the hell are *Old Ones*?" he asked as he guided the sedan along the shortest route to the precinct. "You don't believe all that hooey, do you? And what was that about another female being in the room?" He glanced my direction with an expression of betrayal.

I shrugged. "I was just playing along with her fantasies. Seeing where the discussion led us."

"Right," he said, returning his gaze to the road. "And where, exactly, did it lead?"

"Well, we know that she thinks she's a witch and she was concerned enough about this supposed holy day to try to protect the windows and doors in a very non-standard manner." I stopped. I didn't like making light of Tammy's actions, because I knew her concerns were real... as were her powers as evidenced by the fact that she was aware of Sarah and that I'd been stopped by her wards. But Jack didn't, and I didn't have any way to explain what I knew. Not in a way he could accept.

I sighed and continued, "But I don't think she had anything to do with Howe's death. My take is that she was genuinely fond of him, and, given enough time, that fondness might have turned into love."

Jack grunted. "Yeah. She might be a sandwich or two short of a picnic, but I don't see her as a killer." He pulled the car into our assigned parking space, and we made our way back to our desks in silence, each thinking about what we'd learned and what was still a mystery.

I left Jack to notify Howe's next of kin by phone— his parents lived in Florida— while I wandered to the breakroom to think and hopefully confer with Sarah.

I poured myself a cup of coffee and settled at a table near the room's only window. I'd barely tasted the bitter, but hot brew when Sarah manifested and appeared to perch on the chair opposite me. Fortunately, we were alone.

"So," I said, setting the insulated paper cup on the table, "Howe's girlfriend is a witch."

Sarah nodded. *And she definitely has power, otherwise she wouldn't have been able to see me.*

"What do you think about her theory? Could Howe have been murdered in a ritual sacrifice?"

Possibly. If he really was kneeling, and if the killer stood behind him and used the knife as Jack suggested, it would fit.

"But if we're talking an offering of first fruits, why kill a man? Wouldn't the grain and oil Tammy mentioned make more sense?" I swirled the dark liquid in my cup while I thought. "A blood sacrifice seems like overkill."

Sarah grimaced. *Poor choice of words, but I agree.*

"And what about her other assertion? Do the *Old Ones* take retribution? In this day and age when practically no one has even heard of them, let alone believes in them?"

Sarah shrugged, floated to the window, and stared out. *I've never heard of them doing so, but I'm still very new to the supernatural world.* She turned to face me. *We need more information.*

"Agreed," I said, taking another swig of the swill the precinct called coffee. "Is there anyone you can ask about the *Old Ones?*"

A cute little frown creased her forehead as she thought. *Maybe. What are you going to do?*

"Time to check in with the medical examiner," I said, standing and pitching the remains of my so-called coffee in the trash. "If she's not finished with Howe, I'll see if I can hurry her along."

Great. You don't need me for that, she said with a delicate shudder, *and I don't want to ever visit that place again.*

If I could've, I would've given her a hug. Watching her own corpse being autopsied had been traumatic, even for a doctor who'd nearly completed her training. Instead, I gave her a sad smile and said, "Let's meet at my place after shift and compare notes."

Sarah faded out of sight just as two patrol officers entered the break-room. Timing is everything, and except for her being dead when we met, ours has been pretty good.

———

JACK ACCOMPANIED me to the morgue, having finished his notification of Howe's parents.

"They're pretty broken up," he said as we strode down the long, spot-lessly white hallway that led to the M.E.'s office. "He was their only child, and they never expected to outlive him."

"Are they flying out?"

Jack nodded. "They want to arrange for burial here, where he had friends. He never lived in Florida. They retired there a few years ago, and he'd only visited over the holidays."

The M.E., Dr. Sandra Rayden, led us into the autopsy room and gave us a full run-down on her findings. David Howe's corpse rested on a stainless steel table under bright white lights. A thin sheet covered his privates, but everything else was laid bare, including the neatly stitched Y-incision... evidence of Dr. Rayden's recent work.

Death doesn't leave a man much dignity.

"Your victim was a very healthy thirty-five year old male. His organs were in excellent condition and his muscle tone was exemplary. I found no evidence of drug use, legal or otherwise. His lungs were healthy and showed no indication of nicotine use; his liver showed him to be a non-drinker. In short, if he hadn't been murdered, he would've lived a long life."

Jack cleared his throat and swiped away a bead of sweat that was making a trail down the side of his face. My partner was an excellent detective, but visits to the morgue unnerved him. "So you're ruling this a homicide?" he asked. "He definitely didn't slice his own throat?"

Dr. Rayden glanced up, startled. "That's correct, Detective. This was no suicide. The angle and depth of the cut show that another hand, a very steady hand, inflicted the fatal wound."

She pointed to the angry red line across Howe's throat as she spoke. "The cut was made from left to right, beginning there, very close to his left ear, and ending here, just below the right jaw. In addition to the blood spatter evidence shown in the crime scene photos, subtle blood pooling around his knee joints indicate that he was kneeling at the time of his death. His head was jerked back with enough force that some of his hair was pulled out, his throat sliced, and his body allowed to fall forward into the position in which it was found."

"The cut was from the vic's left to his right, and the perp was behind him," I summarized. "So we're looking for a right-handed person?"

She nodded. "That's correct."

"Any indication as to whether the perp is male or female?"

"There's no way to assign gender based on the evidence I've seen. A woman would've been able to pull his head back and make that slice just as easily as a man, especially since there was no indication of a struggle."

Jack's eyebrows rose and he cocked his head. "So our vic just knelt down and allowed someone to slit his throat?"

Dr. Rayden shrugged. "That's what the evidence suggests."

"Was he drugged?" I asked, silently agreeing with Jack.

"Tox screen isn't back yet," she said. "I should be able to answer that question in the morning."

I nodded, waited a beat, then took a deep breath and, avoiding Jack's gaze, asked, "And the time of death?"

Dr. Rayden turned to a clipboard, flipped a page, and said, "Between 10:00 and 11:00 p.m."

"You're sure he died before midnight?" I asked, maybe a little too sharply since Jack scowled at me.

"Definitely," Dr. Rayden said. "His body temp and other factors are irrefutable." She turned to a tray, extracted a plastic evidence bag, and held it up. "Plus, his watch broke when he fell. It stopped at 10:38."

5

By the time I got to my apartment, all I wanted to do was grab a beer, put my feet up, and chow down on the pepperoni pizza I'd picked up on the way home. I was ready to put the murder on the back burner and unwind with a little mindless TV.

Unfortunately, Sarah had other ideas. She materialized in the kitchen before I even had a chance to put the pizza box on the counter.

So? she asked, perching on the counter right next to where I wanted to set the pizza down. *What did the medical examiner say? Did Howe die before or after midnight?*

"Hold your horses," I growled. "Let me get settled before you start the interrogation." Dropping the pizza box on the counter, I pulled off my jacket, tossed it on a chair, shrugged out of my shoulder holster and placed it and my service revolver carefully on the end of the kitchen counter. Yanking a plate from the cupboard, I slapped a couple slices of pizza on it, then turned to the refrigerator to grab a cold beer. Carrying my dinner to the living room, I toed off my shoes, sank onto the couch and put my feet up on the coffee table before biting into the warm, gooey bliss of a thick crust pepperoni pizza, heavy on the cheese.

Sarah floated over and hovered beside the coffee table, arms folded across her nicely padded chest. *Are we all comfy now? Ready to get down to business?*

I sighed and filled her in on Dr. Rayden's report between bites of warm pizza and swigs of cold beer. Sarah might not need to recharge, but I definitely did.

"So it looks like he was sacrificed," I finished, "by person or persons unknown."

Sarah, who had been pacing— if you can call it that since her feet had no need to touch the floor— while I talked and ate, stopped across from me and said, *Good.*

I frowned, a bite of crust suspended in midair. "Exactly what part of a guy having his throat sliced while he's kneeling in a marijuana dispensary do you consider *good?*" I asked, the day's stress revealing itself in my tone of voice, which was decidedly peevish.

Sarah waved away my comment. *He was murdered by another human. No ancient gods were involved.*

I nodded and popped the crust in my mouth. After chewing and swallowing— I wasn't raised in a barn— I asked, "What did you find out about the *Old Ones* and the possibility of retribution?"

She settled onto the brown leather recliner that sat beside my couch. *Not much. From what I can tell, they still exist, but have removed to another plane of existence. There simply aren't enough believers anymore to keep them fed.*

"Wait a minute," I said, pulling my feet off the coffee table, planting them solidly on the floor, and sitting up straight. "What does 'to keep them fed' mean?"

Just what it sounds like. They're like... I don't know... energy vampires. They feed off the emotions of communities that believe in and worship them.

"Yuck! And here I was thinking they were the good guys."

Well, they are. Sort of. At least, in comparison to the dark forces. They don't harm humans. Evidently we don't even notice the energy they draw from our worship. But that's what the rituals and ceremonies are for... they intensify the emotions of the worshippers, and thereby increase the amount of energy available to the Old Ones.

"Okay," I said, leaning forward, elbows on knees, chin on fists. "But don't people live a lot longer now than they did when the *Old Ones* were being worshipped? Modern science attributes that change to better diet, hygiene, and medical care. What if it's because we aren't having our energy siphoned off anymore?"

Sarah shrugged. *I suppose that's a possibility, but there's no way to prove or disprove it. Besides, what's that got to do with David Howe's murder?"*

"Probably nothing. Unless..." I stood and carried my plate and empty beer can to the kitchen while I allowed the thought coalescing at the surface of my mind to gel. After tossing the can in the recycling bin and putting the plate in the dishwasher, I turned to face her. "Jason Morgan murdered you to co-opt your power, right?"

Sarah eyed me warily, but nodded.

"What if this perp murdered Howe in a ritual sacrifice, at a very specific time and place, in order to feed on his life source, his energy?"

But the Old Ones have moved on, Sarah objected. *They've left this plane of existence.*

"All of them?"

I... I don't know.

"Let's review what we know," I said, pacing from the kitchen to the picture window framing a darkened view of the Willamette River, over to the built-in bookshelves and television, past the bathroom door and entry hall, and back to the kitchen. Doesn't take long to make a complete circuit of my studio apartment.

"One, Tammy Wilcox, a witch with demonstrable power and a believer in the *Old Ones*, was employed at *First Fruits*. Two, Tammy not only believes in the old rites, she told her employer they should be observed. Three, Tammy was twitchy enough to feel the need to ward the doors and windows of the shop. Four, someone... or something... was able to pass through her wards and lure its sacrificial victim to the shop at the appropriate time."

So, you're suggesting that an Old One *killed Howe in order to feed? Why David Howe? Why not Tammy? She's already a believer. She'd be easy prey.*

I shook my head. "Whatever it is, it couldn't sacrifice Tammy. She's its ongoing meal ticket. She provides a constant source of belief, and if left alone, is likely to add others. If she hasn't already, she's likely to develop a coven, and the more people she influences, the more energy the being gains for food."

But Tammy was dating David. Wouldn't killing him take away a potential believer?

I warmed to my subject, excitement buzzing through my veins. I was right. I could feel it.

"Not if Howe was eroding Tammy's faith. What if instead of Tammy influencing David, he was pulling her back toward the mainstream of modern thought? Our *Old One* can't afford to lose Tammy. She's its lifeline."

Sarah floated over to me and stared directly into my eyes. *If you're right, and I think you are, how do we bring a demi-god to justice?*

"We read up on exorcism," I said, without blinking, "and then we convince Tammy to help us free her boss from a dangerous, perhaps even demented, *Old One*."

Adamson, she said, nodding. *Of course, it explains why his responses felt so off and yet neither of us could detect anything unnatural about him. He's human, but possessed.*

"I'm betting the *Old One* can bury himself deep enough in Adamson's psyche that the wards Tammy cast didn't affect it."

Which is why the purely human part of Adamson wasn't aware of my presence. She clapped her hands, though the action produced no sound. *Let's get to work.*

6

Two days later we had everything we needed to attempt to free Gerald Adamson from his *Old One* possessor.

Sarah and I left Jack out of the loop. We were dealing with forces he didn't understand and wouldn't believe even if we explained. So he and I did our due diligence, searching for incriminating evidence against Adamson—the only suspect who made sense from a purely human perspective. The tox screen came back clear, which bugged the hell out of Jack, but made perfect sense to me. An *Old One* would have no need to drug its sacrifice into compliance; it would have supernatural powers that would come into play.

When I wasn't working with Jack, Sarah and I studied exorcism and, when we'd learned what we needed to know, had a long, hard talk with Tammy Wilcox.

We sat in Tammy's living room again. Tammy and her black cat, Prissy, sat in the chair with the floral slipcover, while Sarah and I perched on the drab brown couch with the sprung cushions.

"So you're saying this is all my fault," Tammy said, tears shimmering in her eyes. "If I weren't a witch, David would still be alive."

No, Sarah said softly, relieved that Tammy could hear her. *You're not to blame, and neither are your beliefs.* She reached toward Tammy's hand, remembered she couldn't make contact, and smiled sadly. *I'm not sure I even blame the* Old One, *though its certainly responsible. From what I understand of them, they're usually benign, avoiding harm to their believers. Unfortunately, this one has been starving for so long... I'm not sure its sane at this point.*

I cleared my throat to gain their attention. "At any rate, we need your help. If we can exorcise the *Old One,* Sarah will guide it to a point where it can cross over and join its fellows."

Sarah nodded. *I've sent a message that I hope will be received. If it is, another* Old One *will meet us and assist this one in its journey.*

"What about Mr. Adamson?" Tammy asked. "What will happen to him?"

I shook my head. "I'm not sure. So far we haven't found any tangible evidence against him, so the case could simply go cold, but..." I paused and took a deep breath. "It also depends on how he comes out of this experience. We just don't know."

Tammy bit her lower lip, but nodded. "Okay. What's the plan?"

7

I called Gerald Adamson and asked him to meet me at *First Fruits* that night at 11:00 p.m. He thought the hour was strange, but when I explained we were trying to recreate the scene of the crime, he agreed readily enough.

The shop had been released as a crime scene and had undergone a thorough cleaning by a company familiar with removing blood and gore. I was grateful that Tammy wouldn't be faced with entering a room where the blood of someone dear to her stained the floor and display cabinets.

Tammy had shivered when she first arrived, but then had set to work renewing the wards, though she left the one on the back door incomplete. We expected Adamson to enter through that door since he habitually parked just outside it. Once all the players were inside, she'd close that final ward. She had also cleansed the main sales floor with rosemary and sage and had placed candles scented with lavender around floor at the compass points.

We lit the candles, reciting an ancient prayer of thanksgiving to the four winds and invoking the protection of the four elements. When all was in readiness, we waited for Adamson to arrive.

At the stroke of eleven, a key turned in the back door's lock and Adamson stepped over the threshold.

"Detective," he said, nodding to me. "Tammy! I didn't expect you to be here." He appeared to be unaware of Sarah.

"Detective Collier asked me to come," Tammy said, stepping behind him to complete the ward on the door. "I'm happy to do anything I can to solve this horrible crime."

Adamson nodded, though he frowned as he watched her movements at the door. "Of course. What can I do to help, Detective?"

I gestured him onto the sales floor. "If you'll just kneel here," I said indicating the spot where David Howe had knelt on that fateful night. "I want to recreate the scene."

Adamson eyed the floor warily, but knelt facing the front door.

"No. I'm sorry," I said, "but if you'll just turn toward the display counter. I want to get the orientation right. Mr. Howe was facing east."

Adamson scootched around on his knees until Tammy nodded that his position was correct. I held up a hand and said, "Perfect. Now, if you'll just hold still."

Before the man had time to blink, Tammy, Sarah, and I began to chant the words to an ancient rite. Not in English, but in a long forgotten language that Sarah had coached us on. Tammy stood at the north compass point, Sarah at the west, and I held the south. As we chanted, we held our hands in front of us, palms up, and slowly raised them from waist to shoulder height, and then turning them outward, raised them above our heads.

At first, Adamson didn't move, but simply looked bemused by our actions. By the time our hands reached shoulder height, he'd begun to fidget, then he fell forward, writhing on the ritually cleansed floor. His body took on a bluish glow and something appeared to detach itself from the man.

A blue-green mist rose from the body, and Adamson lay deathly still. The mist continued to rise, and as it did so it coalesced into the form of a shimmering, ghostly man. He turned slowly, making eye contact with each of us as our hands reached the pinnacle of our ability to stretch. He stopped when his gaze reached Sarah.

You no longer live, he said in a cool, cultured voice. *Why have you agreed to challenge me?*

Sarah continued to chant without breaking her rhythm. We all knew that no matter what happened, we had to finish the incantation. The *Old One* undoubtedly knew it too.

He turned to Tammy. *You have worshipped me. Would you defy your god?*

Tammy didn't falter, though she did close her eyes. Tears trembled on her lashes.

Finally, he met my gaze. *You have no idea what you are unleashing on your world,* he said, his tone rising and becoming frenzied. *I will rip your limbs from your body. I will devour your soul.*

He turned back to Sarah with a sneer. *And you! You think death protects you? You have no concept of the immortal pain I will cause you to suffer! You think the Christian depiction of Hell is bad? Just wait until you taste the torments I will inflict on you for eternity.*

We were nearing the end of the incantation, and if anything, the *Old One* appeared stronger than he had at the start. A bead of sweat ran down the side of my face as I continued chanting. What if this didn't work? What if I'd led Tammy and Sarah not only to their deaths, but to everlasting torment? Could he really bring devastation to the world at large?

I closed my eyes and completed the incantation. We all clapped a beat after the final syllable had been uttered. Even Sarah. I swear I heard Sarah's clap as well as Tammy's.

Absolute silence descended on the room.

An uncanny silence.

A silence so dense it felt like all sound had fled the universe.

I opened my eyes…

…and saw not one being, but two. So much for the efficacy of Tammy's wards!

The blue-green male had been joined by a golden radiance. A being inhabited the center of that molten gold glow, but I was incapable of assigning a gender to the being. All I knew was that it radiated peace… and acceptance… and a large measure of sorrow.

As I watched, the golden being engulfed the blue-green man, subsuming him into itself. The color of the newly joined pair mutated, ran through all the shades of the rainbow, and quite a few I had no words for, before stabilizing again at gold.

The newly joined being nodded to each of us and a bell-like voice rang through the room.

Well done. We will take our lost one home. Be at peace.

Light flared… and we were alone. Two conscious humans, one unconscious man, and one starry-eyed ghost.

I guess the Old Ones *got my message!* Sarah cried jubilantly.

I knelt beside Adamson. He was still breathing and his pulse felt steady, but I glanced at Tammy and said, "Call 9-1-1. Ask for an ambulance."

8

Gerald Adamson suffered a stroke on the way to the hospital and died without regaining consciousness.

Jack and I closed David Howe's murder investigation without making an arrest. How could we? Our suspect was dead.

Tammy Wilcox stayed in Portland just long enough to help Adamson's heirs learn the ropes of the marijuana dispensary. Once the new owners had the shop up and running, Tammy relocated to the East Coast where she'd made contact with a coven of witches who were willing to mentor her in her craft.

And Sarah? She and I enjoyed a relaxing dinner at my place, complete with a great recording of her favorite jazz. Well, I enjoyed the dinner, but Sarah appreciated the music... and my company.

She's a great gal. Too bad we didn't meet until after she died.

Ah well. There's always the next homicide to look forward to...

VI

DEATH OF AN ALCHEMIST

Uncollected Anthology

ALCHEMY

ISSUE 24 **UA** APRIL 2021

DEATH OF AN ALCHEMIST

DEBBIE MUMFORD

PROLOGUE

My name is Gus Collier and I'm a homicide detective for the Portland Police Department. Portland, Oregon, that is. My city. My beat.

My partner, Jack Barnes, is a solid detective, though you might not guess it to look at him. His graying hair is thinning, his cheeks are constantly stubbled and a little on the flabby side, and he's got a definite spare tire around his middle, but if you look closely into his gray-blue eyes, you'll see a keen intellect staring back... and taking your measure.

Jack is my official partner. The one Commander Abrams assigned to work with me. If you see me working a case, Jack will be by my side, but we won't be alone. Jack will never acknowledge her (because he has no idea she exists), but Sarah, my other partner, my *ghostly* partner, will be on the case too.

Sarah has been with me for a few months now— ever since I investigated her death at the summer solstice. When her case was solved and her murderer locked away for the rest of his natural life, I expected Sarah to leave. To move on. To *go into the light*. But she didn't. We'd developed a kind of working relationship, a bond of sorts, and she chose to stay on this plane to help me solve other murders.

So how is it that I can see and communicate with Sarah when no one else can?

Well, that's where it gets interesting.

You see, our desire to solve murders isn't our only bond. Sarah and I are both seventh-sevenths. I'm the seventh son of a seventh son, and while I always thought the legends were a bunch of hooey, I discovered I was wrong. Dead wrong, as it turns out. My abilities awoke on the summer solstice as I knelt over Sarah's dead body. That's when the impossible happened. Sarah opened her eyes, grabbed my wrist, and ordered me to find her killer.

To top it all off, it was my twenty-eighth birthday. Seven quadrupled.

I've got to say, I've had better presents than a corpse ordering me around.

So that explains me: seventh son of a seventh son. But what about Sarah? I mean, she's female, right?

Turns out, gender has nothing to do with it, but we're a patriarchal society and have been for thousands of years, so sons are the expected heroes. But the patriarchy is wrong. The definition should be: seventh offspring of a seventh offspring.

Whatever.

I'm not out to change the world's understanding of the supernatural. I'm just here to solve crimes... specifically, murders.

1

Portland's not exactly a hotbed of crime, but it's not always peaceful either. Sometimes the murders assigned to me and Jack are all too familiar patterns of life in a sizable city: drive-by shootings; bar fights gone wrong; domestic violence taken to the extreme. But today was going to be one of the unusual ones.

Not even zero-eight hundred and we'd already been notified that a prominent businessman had been gunned down in his own home. The maid found the body when she arrived for work and let herself in to his upscale home in the West Hills.

Jack parked our department issued dark blue sedan across the street from the crime scene, a beautiful specimen of a Tudor home, complete with steeply pitched gable roof and decorative half-timbering. I said as much to Jack as we studied the property, noting the lush gardens and sweeping views of the city and nearby hills.

He quirked an eyebrow at me. "You been studying architecture in your spare time?"

"Hey! I went to college," I said, stung. "And unlike you, I even remember a few things."

He grunted and headed for the nearest uniformed officer.

Sarah snickered softly. *I'm impressed.*

I managed not to jump when her voice whispered through my mind.

Barely.

I'd expected her to join us, but when she pops up out of thin air like that... well it still gives me an adrenaline rush that makes my heart hammer like a drummer in a rock band.

The uniforms had already cordoned off the area around the home with yellow crime scene tape, but even though the work day had begun and the neighbors could be expected to be at their offices in the city, they weren't. Curious onlookers craned their necks from driveways and porches all up and down the street. Experience told me that law-abiding citizens got a vicarious thrill out of being near the scene of a crime. Especially when one of their neighbors had been murdered in his own home. They might profess horror that someone they knew, or at least recognized as living in the area, had been killed, but deep down the experience excited them... a momentary shiver of fear, a brief brush with the seamier side of life.

Jack figured it was a result of too many cop shows on television. Everyone thought they understood police procedure... and knew how to do our jobs better than we did.

I thought their fascination with death was part of human nature. That it had existed long before the advent of TV crime shows, which were probably a symptom of the disease rather than its cause.

Whatever.

The neighbors were there, and we ignored them as we crossed the driveway and ducked under the crime scene tape. Occasionally the perpetrator would join the looky loos, curious about how his work was perceived, but not often. A quick glance confirmed that one of the uniforms was scanning the curious neighbors with a cell phone camera. Just in case.

Jack took the lead, and we flashed our badges as we approached the uniform we'd been told was first on the scene. The man stood about six feet away from the home's entrance, blocking the path to the front door.

"I'm Detective Jack Barnes and this is my partner, Detective Gus Collier," Jack said, pulling a small spiral-bound notebook from his pocket and clicking his pen open. Glancing at the man's name badge, he continued, "What can you tell us, Officer Abernathy?"

The uniform nodded. He stood at ease, relaxed but ready, feet solidly planted, thumbs hooked in his belt. "Dispatch called with the nine-one-one report at zero-seven-fifteen. My partner and I responded, arriving at zero-seven-twenty-two." He nodded toward the house. "The housekeeper was waiting on the front steps. Said she didn't want to be alone with the body. My partner and I cleared the house while she waited outside. Back-up arrived while we were taking her statement."

I nodded, glancing past him to the empty steps. "Where is she now?"

Abernathy hooked a thumb at the front door. "She's in the kitchen with my partner. The vic is in what looks like a home office. Want me to walk you through?"

Jack signaled one of the other uniforms to join us. A petite, dark-haired woman strode to Jack's side. He glanced at her name badge and said, "Officer Herrera, Abernathy here is going to walk us through the scene. Take over his station for him."

She nodded. "Of course, Detective."

Abernathy turned and led us through the open front door and into the house. He paused in the wide, wood floored foyer and pointed to another open door. He didn't have to tell us the vic was in there, the smell nearly knocked us off our feet. And that was with the front door open to the fresh late September air.

I turned toward the open front door, took a deep breath of the less tainted air, and noticed Sarah floating serenely behind me. I grimaced. She could afford to be serene. She could no longer smell the stench of death, the metallic tang of blood mixed with the foul odor of excrement and a lingering dollop of fear.

Not that I envied her being dead, of course. I had no desire to cross over to her side of eternity. Not for many long years to come.

She smiled sadly and nodded toward Jack, who was also working to maintain his professional demeanor in the face of the smell. Violent death in a small space was always harder to deal with than a body discovered out of doors.

It never gets easier, does it? she asked. Sarah had experienced her share of blood and gore. She'd been in her final year of residency as a doctor when a man she'd trusted had ended her earthly life. Since she'd just come off a double shift at the hospital when she died, Sarah was (and always would be) dressed in blue scrubs and white soft-soled shoes. Her long blonde hair was pulled back in a high pony tail. Even in hospital scrubs, Sarah was a beauty.

I sighed, wishing for the thousandth time my friend wasn't dead. If we'd met in life... well, a guy could dream, and I often did.

The opening to the room where the vic's life had ended was secured by French doors which opened into the foyer. Both sides boasted full, frosted glass panels, and each was etched with a large and detailed caduceus.

I raised an eyebrow and glanced at Abernathy. "Was the vic a doctor? What's his name?"

Abernathy pulled out a notebook and checked his notes. "According to the housekeeper, our vic is Dimitri Xanthropolous. A quick scan of that name pulled up this address, so I've no reason to doubt her statement. Not sure of his profession."

Jack nodded and stepped into the room with the body. "Did you take his prints?"

"No, sir. Procedure is to secure the scene and wait for the detectives and the medical examiner."

Abernathy remained in the foyer, but I followed Jack into what turned out to be Xanthropolous' office. The body was slumped against the front of a large walnut executive desk. Blood and excrement stained what had been an expensive Turkish carpet, its red, black, and gray pattern now blurred and indistinct in the area around the corpse. Glancing around, I noted a set of wide diamond pane windows looking out onto one of the front gardens, this one featuring rose bushes. Despite the lateness of the season, a few flowers remained, red, pink, and golden hued. Bookshelves lined the other walls, and a walnut credenza sat beneath the windows.

A younger-looking version of the vic sat in the black leather swivel chair behind the desk.

I was about to ask Abernathy what he was thinking to let a civilian into the crime scene, when Sarah gasped and floated around the desk to join the intruder. That was when my brain caught up with my sight and I realized the guy was almost transparent and he shimmered slightly.

Great. Another ghost.

I knew from my experience with Sarah that Xanthropolous wouldn't be able to tell us who killed him. For some reason beyond my understanding, the universe had decreed that while a ghost might be able to remember all the details of their death, they were unable to articulate them to the living.

However, Sarah wasn't living, and this wasn't *her* death, so it was possible I might get some, shall we say, *inside* information on the crime.

I left the ghost to Sarah and joined Jack in examining the body.

When I knelt across the corpse from him, Jack pointed his pen at the neat hole in the man's forehead. "Looks like a single shot to the head. Guy was dead before he hit the ground."

I nodded and glanced at his hands, which were open and relaxed. "Doesn't look like he struggled. The room's neat as a pin except for the body. No signs of a fight."

"Abernathy!" Jack yelled, and the uniform's face appeared beside the open door. "Did you see any sign of a fight in the other rooms? Anything look disturbed?"

The officer shook his head. "No, sir. The whole house is neat. Even the beds are made in the rooms upstairs." He moved back out of the doorway, and then reappeared a moment later. "Oh! And we found a safe room at the back of the garage. You know, one of those super secure rooms a guy can lock himself into if he feels threatened."

"Huh," Jack grunted. "Thanks, Abernathy. We'll take a look in a minute." He turned to me and cocked his head. "Sounds like Mr. Xanthropolous might've known his killer. No fight, and he sure wasn't shot while running for his safe room."

I nodded. "Why don't I poke around his office here while you check out the rest of the house." I was anxious to get Jack out of the room so I could check in with Sarah. One of the down sides of having a ghost for a partner was that I couldn't talk to her when anyone else was around.

Jack shook his head. "Nah. We can do that in a while. Right now we need to interview the housekeeper. I'm sure the poor woman would like to get as far away from this place as possible... as soon as possible."

"Right," I agreed, since I couldn't tell him I had a ghost to interview. "Housekeeper first, then we'll case the house."

2

The housekeeper, Angela Preston, wasn't much help. But then I hadn't expected her to be. Other than calling in the murder and telling us the dead man's name, she didn't know anything that would advance our search for the killer.

Abernathy's partner, a woman in her mid-thirties by the name of Langston, escorted Ms. Preston out the back door and to her older Subaru sedan, making sure the woman had our contact information just in case she remembered anything. She wouldn't. How could she? She hadn't witnessed anything.

Sarah and Xanthropolous' ghost floated into the breakfast room while Jack and I were finishing up our notes on Ms. Preston's interview. I caught Sarah's eyes and nodded. We needed to talk.

After sending Abernathy and Langston to canvas the neighborhood and take statements from anyone who might have seen anything, I turned to Jack. "Why don't you head upstairs and look around," I suggested. "I'll check out the rest of the downstairs, then we can meet back in Xanthropolous' office and see if we turn up anything interesting in there."

"Sure," he said, "make your aging partner climb the stairs."

I lifted an eyebrow. "You planning to ask the commander for a desk job?"

He scowled and, before stomping off, grumbled, "Not bloody likely."

Once my living partner was out of sight, I gestured to the ghosts. "Join me, please."

Sarah shepherded Xanthropolous over to the breakfast table, a beautifully polished white oak piece surrounded by four matching oak chairs. Diamond pane windows caught the morning sun and scattered refracted rainbow fragments across the table, chairs, and gold-toned slate floor. The ghostly victim looked totally bewildered as he floated beside the table he'd so recently owned.

I studied the man who was now a corpse on his office floor. He'd been a good looking guy. Late forties or early fifties, with a fit but not body-builder overblown physique. His hair had been dark, with silver wings at the temples, and his skin had a Mediterranean tone consistent with his surname. Dark eyes, chiseled cheekbones and chin, and a long, straight nose completed the picture of an adult male in his prime.

Gus, this is Dimitri Xanthropolous, and he has a very interesting story to share. Sarah turned to the vic's ghost. *It's okay, Dimitri. You can talk to Gus. He's not just a police detective, he's also the seventh son of a seventh son, so he has special, uhm, abilities. He can see you and hear you.*

Xanthropolous eyed me skeptically, but shrugged his shimmery shoulders, and said, *I am pleased to meet you, Gus. Though I wish I were still living. After my long centuries of existence, this... transformation... is something of a shock.*

My breath caught and I straightened in my chair. "Hold it," I said, my voice sounding less steady than I liked. I cleared my throat and continued, "Did you say *centuries*?"

The ghost nodded. *I was born in a small village in Greece in 326 B.C. by your reckoning. The name of the village is immaterial as it ceased to exist over a thousand years ago.*

I glanced from Xanthropolous to Sarah and back again. "How is that possible?"

I am, he glanced down at his semi-transparent hands, and amended, *or at least I was, an alchemist. Long ago I was known as Xanthos the Merciful. I was, have always been, a healer. I discovered an alchemical elixir that could cure any human ailment. I could even raise the dead, so long as the body had not sustained irreparable damage.*

He glanced mournfully in the direction of his office. *Alas, even were I to give you access to my panacea, my physical form is beyond repair.*

"So, let me get this straight," I said, making an honest effort not to sound like I thought this guy was a loony, which I did. "You're an immortal who, if you hadn't been shot in the head by an unknown perp, would've been able to heal anyone from anything? Including yourself?"

Xanthropolous nodded. *But the perp, as you call him, is not unknown. It was...*

But no further words came out, only a kind of strangled, gurgling sound. He closed his mouth, cleared his throat, and tried again. With the same result.

Sarah gave him a sad smile and shook her head.

"Don't worry about it," I told him. "It seems to be a rule, though who makes these crazy rules, I have no idea. Sarah couldn't tell me who killed her either. She had to show me."

He reached for my arm, but I threw my hands in the air and scooted my chair away from the table.

"Nope," I said, tempted to yell, but I didn't want Jack to come barreling down the stairs to my rescue. "I'm not doing that again.

Besides, this time we have Sarah to intervene. You won't be able to tell her anything where I can hear it, but I'm betting you'll be able to give her all the details once the two of you are alone."

Xanthropolous nodded. *Very well, but you should know, there is another.*

"Another what?" I asked, hoping we weren't talking ghosts.

Alchemist. Another alchemist. My wife is also a practitioner and knows the secret of my elixir, though she has never been able to reproduce it. He shrugged and examined the fingernails of his right hand. *It seems a certain... talent... is required to produce an efficacious elixir.*

"Wait a minute. If your wife lives here with you, why didn't Ms. Preston mention her?"

His eyebrows flew toward his hairline. *Did I say she lived here? I think not! I merely said she was my wife and in possession of my alchemical formula.*

I frowned. "If she's your wife, why doesn't she live here?"

He shook his head. *You are very young, Gus. Though Korina and I remain fond of each other, living together amicably for over two thousand years is not as easy as the romantics of the world might think.*

"Right. So where do I find this Korina, and if she's not involved, why would you think I should bother?"

She lives across the river in Vancouver, Washington —we like to stay close to each other— and you should bother, as you say, because she will need protection. You see...

The ghost's speech was interrupted by another bout of strangled gargling. He scowled and tried again, *You see 'the perp' is aware that Korina also holds the formula.*

3

Turns out I was wrong about Xanthropolous' ability to communicate the name of his killer to Sarah. He choked with her just like he'd done with me, and since she had no physical body for him to grab hold of, he had no way to force his memories into her head.

Bummer.

Didn't change my decision not to allow him to touch me. I'd lived through Sarah's death, and it hadn't been fun. No way was I going through that again.

That left a trip to Vancouver, which we would've had to make anyway.

"Tell me again why we're driving to Vancouver?" Jack asked as he guided our dark blue sedan across the Glenn Jackson Bridge, over the mighty Columbia River.

"I found the vic's ex-wife listed in his contacts," I said without even a hint of a blush at the lie. "We need to notify her of Xanthropolous' death and find out what she knows... she could be involved."

Since I'd come into my power and Sarah had joined our team, I'd gotten used to misdirecting Jack. I consoled myself with the knowledge that we couldn't use any information I received from a supernatural source anyway, so the misdirections weren't really lies... they were alternate routes to information I already had. Routes that Jack would understand and the courts would accept.

It worked.

Most of the time.

A few minutes later we pulled into the drive of a sprawling riverfront mansion. I studied the graceful beige stone façade, appreciating the fluted pillars supporting the curved portico entrance. Eternal life evidently paid well. Both Dimitri and Korina Xanthropolous had lived well.

We strode to the door, and Jack rang the bell. A few moments later, a young woman wearing a gray dress covered by a starched white apron opened the door.

"May I help you?" she asked, eying us cautiously.

Jack flashed his badge and gave our names. "We'd like to speak to..." he glanced at his notes, "Korina Xanthropolous."

Sarah floated past the young woman and down the hall, disappearing into the home.

"Ms. Xanthropolous is meeting with another visitor at the moment," the maid replied. "Perhaps you could leave your card and I'll ask her to call you later?"

I was about to answer when Sarah reappeared behind the maid. *Come now*, her voice rang in my mind. *Korina is being threatened.*

Before I could say or do anything, a woman's scream sounded. "Sophie! Call the police!"

The maid startled and turned, but Jack and I pushed past her, racing toward the all too familiar sound of bodies in conflict.

We emerged into a spacious, light-filled room and saw a well-dressed man struggling to restrain a golden-haired woman. She screamed again, bit the hand that was trying to silence her, and wrenched herself free.

Jack and I both unholstered our weapons, and Jack yelled, "Stop!" while I circled around to get between the woman and her attacker.

"We're police officers," I said, leveling my gun to aim directly at his heart. I neglected to add that we were from Portland and had no jurisdiction in Vancouver. "We're responding to a call for help."

Jack cuffed the man and, following the maid, escorted him into another room. Jack would stay with the man until the Vancouver police arrived to take custody. Leaving me free to interview Korina Xanthropolous.

Sarah floated beside Korina who had composed herself and now sat regally in a modern overstuffed chair upholstered in a soft blue fabric. Maybe velour? I settled on the matching sofa and glanced around the room. The light I'd noticed earlier came from floor-to-ceiling windows overlooking a wide stretch of lawn leading down to the majestic Columbia River. Lush flower gardens lined both sides of the lawn; available for the owner's enjoyment, but not detracting from the view of the river.

The room itself was spacious, with a river rock fireplace at one end and a cathedral ceiling of light wood. The floors were flagged in beige stone and covered with neutral toned area rugs. The furniture was simple and tasteful in a manner that practically screamed wealth.

"You are a detective?" Korina asked. Her voice was low and melodic. If I hadn't witnessed the altercation, I'd never have guessed that the calm woman sitting across from me had just endured a harrowing experience. She wore a light gray silk shirt, neatly tucked into charcoal gray slacks, and her honey-gold hair was pulled back in a high ponytail, not a lock out of place. Her skin glowed with health, and her dark blue, almond shaped eyes studied me with curiosity.

"Yes," I said, showing her my badge and introducing myself.

Glancing at it, she said, "You arrived awfully quickly."

I nodded. "We're not from Vancouver. Portland Police Department. We'd come across the river to talk to you."

She sighed deeply before replying. "Well, whatever the reason, I'm grateful for your timely arrival."

She won't be when she hears your news, Sarah said quietly.

Korina glanced at her sharply.

I jumped, the hairs on my neck prickling. "Excuse me. This may sound odd, but are you aware of another... presence?"

Korina turned back to me and cocked her head, studying me. "Of course. She was speaking to you?"

I nodded. "This is my unofficial partner, Sarah Allen."

Korina stared at me another moment and then turned to Sarah. "It is not often that I'm visited by a spectre," she said, "and even less often that we're introduced." She turned back to me. "What is it that you have come to tell me, Detective Collier?"

I took a steadying breath and said, "I'm deeply sorry to inform you that your husband, your ex-husband, was found murdered in his home a few hours ago."

The color drained from her face, her eyes widened, and she covered her mouth with her hand.

"Dimitri?"

I nodded.

"No! That's not possible. You don't understand, Dimitri can't be dead."

"I'm afraid he is," I said gently.

And we do understand, Sarah said. *He told us everything.*

"He... he told you?" she asked in a shocked whisper. Her spine straightened, and she said, "Then why isn't he here? Why did you come without him?"

I motioned to Sarah. This was her area of expertise, not mine.

The newly dead are bound to their bodies. Soon he will have a choice: remain in this realm or move on into the light. As you can see, I chose to remain. I doubt that your husband will.

Korina smiled fondly. "No. He will not. Dimitri has seen enough of this world. He will choose to move into the next." She closed her eyes and relaxed into her chair. Suddenly she sat straight again. "That man! The one who attacked me. Did he kill Dimitri?"

"We won't know for sure until we hear his story, but I suspect so. Tell me, who is he and why was he here?"

She reached out to the low table between us, picked up a business card, and handed it to me. "He said he was a pharmaceutical rep and was interested in a chemical formula of mine." She smiled sadly. "I suppose Dimitri told you about it?"

I glanced at the card before nodding. "He did. His house appeared undisturbed, so I assume his killer didn't search for it."

Korina shook her head. "If this man was the killer and he bothered to speak to Dimitri, he would've known that would be useless. Dimitri had mixed his elixir so often over the ages that he had no need for instructions. I possess the only written copy."

Dimitri told us you'd been unable to make an effective version of the elixir.

Korina shrugged. "It seems more than the formula is required. A certain... magical... talent is also necessary." She studied Sarah. "I suspect you might have been able to make it work. You were a healer, were you not?"

Sarah nodded.

"And not just a physician, in the modern sense of the word," Korina continued. "You also had a supernatural ability, I think."

I would have, Sarah said quietly, *if I'd been allowed to live.*

"Ah. A true tragedy. I would gladly give it into your keeping if you were corporeal."

"So," I said, interrupting, "you're saying this formula would be of no value to a pharmaceutical company?"

Korina turned those lovely almond eyes on me. "That is correct. But I doubt they wanted to produce the elixir. I imagine they would want to destroy the formula."

4

Jack made arrangements to exchange information with the Vancouver police since it looked like our cases were related. The Vancouver detectives were willing to give us an opportunity to interview the perp... once they'd had their shot at him.

Jack had tried to get him to talk while I was interviewing Korina, but the guy had clammed up and refused to speak. We wouldn't even know his name if Korina hadn't given me his business card. I snapped a cell phone pic of the card before handing it over to the Vancouver guys. After all, fair is fair, and this was their case.

As we headed back across the river to our territory, I filled Jack in on what Korina had told me. The whitewashed-for-normal-humans version.

"So our vic had some kind of snake oil remedy that a pharmaceutical guy was trying to buy." Jack glanced at me quickly before shifting his eyes back to the road.

"That's what it sounds like." I agreed.

"Sounds like a perfectly legit business transaction," Jack said, frowning in concentration. "So why'd he off him? And why go after the ex-wife? Makes no sense. Either they sell, or they don't. Can't see how killing either of them accomplishes anything."

That's because he doesn't have the whole story, Sarah said, leaning into the back seat so that her blue-scrub clad body disappeared into it. *He wanted to erase all evidence that a panacea had ever existed.*

I cleared my throat; our signal that I'd heard and understood her.

To Jack, I said, "It's a puzzle all right. We'll just have to see what he says once he realizes we have him on murder."

Jack slid a sideways glance my direction. "Do we?"

I shrugged. "We'll have his fingerprints as soon as VPD processes him and sends them over to us, and I'm betting they'll match whatever the crime scene team comes up with from our vic's home."

"Let's just hope he didn't think to wipe everything clean."

"Yeah, but I bet he didn't. That guy didn't strike me as an experienced killer, and amateurs make all kinds of mistakes." I paused as we crossed the imaginary line in the middle of the Columbia River that marked the border between Washington and our home state of Oregon. "Besides, how likely is it for a man and his ex-wife to both be attacked in their homes within a few hours of each other and it not be the same guy?"

Jack grimaced. "True. I just hope the evidence supports that theory. I'd hate for a killer to walk."

Once back in the office, Jack and I filled the time waiting for finger-print analysis by researching both the vic and the perp. As expected, I found that Dimitri Xanthropolous was a well-respected practitioner of alternative medicine. His website was filled with glowing testimonials from patients he'd cured, as well as a number of references from traditional physicians, both medical doctors and osteopaths. I was frankly surprised to find the respectful comments from the MDs.

"Well," Jack said, blowing out a breath to break my concentration and gain my attention, "the perp is who he says he is. Nathan Johnstone. Found his picture on A2Z Chemical's website. It's a multinational pharmaceutical corporation and he's the director of their research and development department." He scrubbed his hands over his stubbly face. "Still makes no sense. If the vic had a promising formula, why kill him?"

I shrugged. "Maybe he wouldn't sell."

Jack glared at me. "Legitimate business men don't kill each other over formulas."

"If they didn't, we'd be out of business," I said. "Come on, Jack. The why isn't our job. We're just supposed to assemble the evidence and arrest the bad guy. We don't always get all the answers."

Jack shook his head and stared at the murder board across from our desks. "I know. But it galls me when the crime doesn't make sense."

I really wished I could explain it to him. But he'd never accept that the vic's ghost had told me he'd been an immortal (well... *almost* immortal) alchemist who could cure any human ailment and a pharmaceutical company had offed him to keep his cure from becoming public.

After all, pharmaceuticals was a huge business... that would no longer exist if a universal panacea existed.

Too bad the perp hadn't realized that only someone with a magic touch could produce the elixir.

After the lab contacted us with a positive match on the fingerprints, Jack contacted VPD to let them know that Portland PD would be charging the man in their custody with murder. No matter what Washington decided, Johnstone would be tried in Oregon.

EPILOGUE

When I finally got home that night, I went straight to the small safe built into the wall of the closet in my bedroom. Pulling an ancient but well preserved scroll from the inside pocket of my jacket, I locked it away carefully.

Nice of Korina to entrust that formula to you, Sarah said when I came out of the closet.

"I guess so," I said, sitting down on the edge of the bed and taking off my shoes, "but I've got to admit it makes me a bit nervous to have it in the apartment. After all, a man was killed for it today."

True, but he was a healer and was using it. You couldn't even if you wanted to.

I nodded. "I get that Korina is hoping I'll find another healer to pass it along to, but what are the odds? You're the only other seventh-seventh I've ever known."

And you didn't find me until I was a corpse, she said with a shrug. *Still, you were her best option.*

"I can't believe a woman who's been alive since before the birth of Christ will now die because of Johnstone. He should face two counts of murder."

Sarah didn't respond, and it occurred to me that I'd just been incredibly insensitive. Korina had lived for thousands of years. Sarah didn't even make it to her twenty-eighth birthday.

Perspective is an important tool, and I needed to use it more often.

"Well," I said into the silence. "At least she'll have plenty of time to put her affairs in order."

Later, while I enjoyed a slice of pepperoni pizza, Sarah popped back into view.

Who'd've ever thought we'd meet a real, live alchemist? she asked with a smile that told me my thoughtless remark was forgiven and we were back to normal.

"We didn't," I said around the gooey mouthful I was chewing.

She frowned and fisted her cute little hands on her blue clad hips.

I swallowed, took a swig of beer, and finished the thought. "The alchemist was dead before we met him." I decided it was the better part of valor to leave Korina out of our currently friendly banter.

Her eyebrows rose in surprise, and then she grinned. *So he was.*

I lifted my beer can in salute. "And we solved the death of an alchemist."

And allowed him to move on... into the light. She nodded and faded from view, but her parting words lingered in my mind, *We make a good team, Gus.*

I took another bite and nodded. "That we do, Sarah. That we do."

VII

SEVENTH: THE SAMHAIN DILEMMA

DEBBIE MUMFORD

SEVENTH:
THE
SAMHAIN
DILEMMA

SPUN YARNS
A *Gus & Ghost* Short Story

1

Once the bastard was incarcerated, I'd never expected to see Jason Morgan again. But here I sat in a bland interview room in the high security ward of the forensic unit of the Oregon State Hospital, waiting for an orderly to bring in the maniac who had killed Sarah Allen and tried to do the same to me.

What a great way to spend a beautiful late October Saturday.

Designed to avoid triggering mental aberrations in patients who were also inmates, the room was more comfortable than a prison interview room, but far more sterile than OSH spaces beyond the forensic unit. No cheery paint jobs on the walls or brightly colored murals for this room. Nope, my navy blue sport coat was the most colorful item to be seen. White walls and ceiling, beige linoleum floor, a light tan over-stuffed sofa and matching chair that had seen too many decades of use, and a slowly spinning ceiling fan whose white pine paddles circulated stale air. The best I could say about the room was that as soon as the interview was over, I'd get to leave it behind.

Why are you here, Gus? The question was a good one, and I'd asked myself the same thing several times as I drove south on I-5 from Portland to Salem, Oregon. But this time, I wasn't the one asking.

"You know why, Sarah," I said to the ghost of the woman Morgan had killed in cold blood. "He said he had information that would save lives."

Right, she said with a cute little snort. Though how she could snort—or talk for that matter—without physical lungs to produce breath, I'll never understand. *He's suddenly concerned with saving lives. Too bad he couldn't have developed that concern a little earlier, like before he killed me and tried to murder you.*

Sarah appeared to perch on the edge of the tired couch. She'd been a pretty young woman, a doctor finishing up her residency at Sisters of Mercy Hospital, before Morgan had blown a hole through her skull in an alley at midnight on the cusp of the summer solstice. Now she was an attractive ghost, manifesting in pale blue scrubs and soft-soled white shoes, with her long blonde hair pulled back in a pony tail.

I'm sorry I never got to meet Sarah while she lived. We had a lot in common, which is why she was able to speak to me when I was called to the scene of her murder in my official capacity as homicide detective, and ultimately why she was still with me even after we arrested Jason Morgan and solved her murder.

You see, Sarah and I were both seventh-sevenths. That little accident of birth is what got her killed and provided me with psychic abilities.

2

The solid core door opened and Jason Morgan shuffled into the room followed by a burly orderly. Once this man had been meticulously groomed, a distinguished university professor with gleaming silver hair and a firm jaw. Now his hair was unkempt, his jaw stubbled and unshaven, but the most noticeable change was his eyes. Once they'd been clear and intelligent, now they held a wild expression as his gaze flitted around the room and came to rest on Sarah. He licked his lips and stared at her, clearly terrified.

"Over there, Morgan," the orderly said, pointing to the couch. Right where Sarah appeared to sit.

Morgan balked, his eyes widening. The orderly gave him a nudge in the direction of the couch. Morgan stood his ground.

I raised an eyebrow at Sarah. She grimaced, but moved to stand behind my chair. Morgan followed her with his eyes, but he shuffled to the seat she'd vacated.

Once he was seated, the guard pulled a metal ring from beneath the cushion and threaded handcuffs through it before locking them onto

Morgan's wrists. When the inmate was secure, the orderly turned to me.

"That ring is welded to the steel frame of the couch. He's not going anywhere unless he drags that thing with him." He paused, glanced at Morgan, and continued, "Are you okay, or do you want me to stay in the room?"

"I'm fine," I said. "I'd prefer to speak privately if the rules permit."

He nodded. "I'll be right outside the door." He pointed to a small white button on the wall to my right. "That's a panic button. Hit it if he gives you any trouble."

I glanced at Morgan who was still staring at Sarah. "Thanks, but I doubt I'll need it."

The orderly turned and left the room. As far as he was concerned, I was now alone with Jason Morgan, a convicted murderer.

Morgan been tried and found *guilty except for insanity* and sentenced to life in prison. The *except for insanity* clause meant he would serve out his sentence in the state hospital instead of the prison. Some people thought his claims of being haunted had been a fake in order to mitigate his sentence, but I knew better. He saw Sarah as clearly as I did, and she took a perverse pleasure in visiting him. She never spoke to him, simply manifested in whatever room he currently occupied and made sure he could see her.

If he wasn't insane when he killed her, she intended to make sure he ended up that way.

"Okay, Morgan," I said. "I'm here. What did you want to tell me?"

His gaze flicked from Sarah to me and back again. "Why did you bring her?"

"Who?" I asked. I liked to support Sarah's work whenever possible.

He turned his attention to me and glared. "Don't play games, Detective Collier. I know you can see her. Remember, I know what you are."

"I remember," I said, my words seething with repressed anger. "You tried to kill me because of it."

He nodded, his gaze drifting back to Sarah. "If I'd succeeded, I wouldn't be here. My knowledge and ability would've made me unstoppable."

"So you've told me. Fortunately, I'm still alive and you're locked up for life. Now, what was so important that I had to drive to Salem to see you?"

"The power I gained from Sarah's untimely demise..."

You mean from my murder, you immoral bastard!

"Semantics," he said and waved her away as though she were an annoying fly. "As you well know, now that your abilities have manifested, the seventh child of a seventh child has particular paranormal powers. Some are gifted healers," he nodded toward Sarah, "some are guard dogs," he glanced at me, "and some are attuned to alternate realities."

I glanced at Sarah in surprise. Her puzzled expression told me she'd never heard of that last one either.

"Even before they come into their particular talents, seventh-sevenths are drawn to fields of study that will compliment their abilities. Sarah was drawn to medicine and excelled in her studies. You were drawn to law enforcement, though many with your affinity turn to the military. The others are often drawn to the theoretical sciences or higher mathematics."

"You're lecturing, Dr. Morgan," I said, hoping to pull him out of academic mode. "What's your point?"

He scowled at me. He'd clearly been enjoying his momentary reversion to professorial posture. "My point," he said, his voice dripping sarcasm, "is that since I wasn't born to seventh-seventh power, but came by it through what might be termed *blood magic*, I am attuned to a rather different set of parameters than you may be aware of without someone like me pointing them out."

Sarah snarled from behind my shoulder. I didn't look at her. I knew how his clinical description of her murder and the usurpation of her power was angering her.

"So, what you're telling me is that when you murdered Sarah for her power, you got more than you bargained for."

He nodded, his gaze flicking around the room. "Because I killed for my power, I see and hear things." He paused and licked his lips, "Evil things." He turned his gaze on Sarah. "Things indescribably more evil than I ever could've imagined.

"I know you think you're scaring me when you show up in my room and just watch me, but you're actually a comfort. I know who and what you are. I know that you're incapable of physically harming me. Not because you're a ghost," he said, his gaze still firmly set on Sarah, "but because of the kind of person you were." He stopped, his gaze traveling to all corners of the room as if to assure himself that we were truly alone. "These other beings," he shuddered, "once they tire of toying with me, they will devour me … and the meager power I stole from Sarah won't be sufficient to protect me."

I frowned, but held my silence.

"That's why I called you here. If I tell you about what I've heard, what I know will happen at Samhain, will you protect me?"

I stared at him. I had no idea what he was talking about. I'd never heard of sow-in and I had no clue how he expected me to protect him.

Sarah spoke up before I could reveal my total ignorance.

I know about the thresholds thinning at Samhain, Morgan. We don't need you to explain that. She moved to my side and glanced at my puzzled expression. *Halloween, Gus. Samhain is the old Celtic term for Halloween.*

"Oh," I said. "Got it. Thresholds thin at Halloween." I frowned. "What thresholds?"

Sarah rolled her eyes. *Between the worlds, Gus. The threshold between the living and the dead thins at Halloween. It's why there are so many stories of haunted houses and witches and ghosts. The threshold thins and things can cross over ... and even normal people can sometimes see them.*

"Correct," said Morgan. "Only this year, the barrier will be unusually thin in one particular place because of an unique astral alignment ... and that place is in the Columbia Gorge. Close enough to Portland to make it your concern. There are plans for an actual invasion. Think zombie apocalypse. Think the end of civilization as we know it."

"You've got to be kidding," I said, glaring at Morgan. "You call me to say you have information that can save lives, talk me into driving all the way down here from Portland and then waste my time with ghost stories? What do you think I am, five?"

Morgan's expression turned icy. "What I think you are is a guardian seventh-seventh whose partner is a ghost."

Sarah glided in front of me and caught my gaze. *I hate to say this, but he's right.* She turned to glare at him, then gazed into my eyes. *If he's telling the truth, you're the only person who can prevent a disaster.*

I looked from one to the other in dismay. Sarah, the ghost I'd come to rely on, and her murderer in firm agreement. Talk about scary.

"Fine," I said. "I'm listening. What do you know and what do you want?"

He nodded and leaned forward as far as his restraints would allow. "Second part first. I want you to contact a practicing witch I know and ask her to come and set wards on this unit. I need protection from the wights. They don't need thin thresholds to reach me. I opened myself up to them by using blood magic."

I inclined my head slightly. "If your information checks out, I'll make that call."

His eyes widened and the terrified look returned. "What do you mean, 'if my information checks out'? How do you plan to check it?"

I can make some inquiries, Sarah said. *My sources are, uhm, otherworldly.*

Relief flashed across his face. "Fine. I can accept that."

"Great," I said. "If your information checks out with Sarah's sources, I'll contact your friend. But that's all. I'm not guaranteeing your friend's willingness to help. So, what have you got?"

Morgan licked his lips again, they were seriously chapped from this nervous habit, and scanned the corners another time. He leaned forward and whispered conspiratorially. "You know where I-205 passes over Government Island?"

I nodded and Sarah frowned.

"There's a good-sized lake east of the bridge, in the center of the island where the public isn't allowed. There's also a much smaller pond west of the lake. About half-way between the two is a magical hotspot where two ley lines cross, you'll be able to feel it when you get close, though normal people wouldn't notice anything except maybe a slight sense of unease. That's where the crossing will take place. Right at …"

His words died and he sat bolt upright, eyes wide.

Sarah shot to his side, but I froze, too astounded to move. A gaseous green fog enveloped Morgan. Slightly more defined tendrils wrapped around his throat; he clawed at them with desperate hands. His eyes bulged and his mouth worked, but emitted no sound.

Gus, Sarah screamed. *Do something!*

I snapped out of my astounded daze, hit the panic button, and leapt to Morgan's side. I couldn't touch the wispy tendrils. Morgan's hands were all I could connect with, and they weren't the problem. Whatever the green gas was, it was choking the life out of the man and I couldn't do a damn thing about it.

The door slammed open and the orderly ran in, Taser drawn. He skidded to a halt when he saw me apparently choking the prisoner.

"He's choking," I yelled. "Do something." I knew he'd be no more effective than I'd been, but I needed to position myself as a good guy.

"Step away, Detective Collier," he ordered before mumbling a code into a hand-held radio. "I'll take it from here."

I stepped back, hands raised. Sarah floated over to stand beside me. We watched helplessly as something neither of us could name drained the life out of Jason Morgan.

He'd been right to be afraid, but of what?

3

The ride home had been a silent, solemn affair. I had a lot of questions, but I didn't feel like speaking them aloud. Of course, I had no one to speak them to, so the point was moot. Sarah had simply vanished from the interview room. I wasn't worried. I knew she'd return when she was ready to talk about what we'd witnessed.

I'd been half afraid that Morgan would manifest as a ghost and try to join our team. That didn't happen. His form started to materialize when the last of his life force flickered out, but before he could manifest properly, the green gas merged with his insubstantial being and both were sucked out of existence.

In his last moments, as the room filled with medical personnel and equipment, Morgan locked eyes with me. I read terror and remorse in his expression, but also acceptance. He had played with fire and now it consumed him.

I hadn't wanted him dead, just incarcerated. Still, I wouldn't mourn his passing. But I sure as hell — maybe not the best phrase under the circumstances — wouldn't have wished that end for him. Especially since I had no idea what I'd witnessed.

I could only hope that he'd told me enough to avert whatever disaster he'd seen coming, because the manner of his death had authenticated his message. Something was coming …. and it was going to be bad.

I sat at the breakfast bar that separated my compact kitchen from the living room of my apartment and studied the map of Government Island I'd pulled up on my laptop computer. Not much to look at, just a long, narrow island covered in trees and pasture land in the middle of the Columbia River. The lake didn't look like much and the pond to the west barely registered on the map, but it did look like it had some nice beaches on the southwest side.

As far as I could tell, access was by boat only and the beaches were pretty much all that was accessible to the public.

Planning a camping trip?

I glanced up to see Sarah coalescing on the upholstered stool beside me.

"I suppose that would be as good an excuse as any as to why I'd be on Government Island on Halloween. Bit late in the season for most folks, but a great way to avoid trick-or-treaters."

She nodded. *Also a good reason to be there for an extended period of time. Morgan wasn't able to tell us exactly when the crossing would take place.*

"Any idea what killed him?" I asked. "Or why we couldn't actually see it?" I frowned as a thought occurred to me. "You couldn't see it, could you? I mean, all I saw was this wispy greenish fog. Did you see anything more defined?"

She glanced away from me, appearing to study the map on my laptop's screen. *I saw it. There are worse things than ghosts on the other side.*

"What was it? Why couldn't I see it? Why could you?"

She shivered and met my gaze. *It was a ghoul. A hideous gray-green crea-ture that consumes humans. As long as the barrier, the veil, is in place they have to be content with eating unwary ghosts or the few live people who open themselves to them through evil, as Morgan did. But if the barrier is suffi- ciently thin, if they manage to cross over in physical form instead of as spir- its,* she shuddered and dropped her gaze to her hands, *well, then they'd be able to feed on anyone. Normal people who have no clue such creatures even exist.*

Sarah looked up, her eyes pleading with mine. *We have to stop them, Gus. We can't let them slaughter innocent people.*

I sucked in a breath and made myself exhale slowly, willing my pounding heart to regulate. "Okay. Ghouls are real and they're plan- ning an invasion of Government Island on Halloween. That's a good thing, right? I mean, it's past camping season, so the island should be deserted. Better there than in downtown Portland."

Yes, but once they've crossed into this world, they won't stay on the island.

A thought niggled at the back of my brain, but I couldn't quite catch it. Something about water. Flowing water.

"Wait," I said, excitement zinging through me like a mild electric shock, "isn't there something about magic and flowing water? Won't the Columbia itself contain them?"

Hope lit her eyes and then faded away. *Well, it would except that the Glen Jackson Bridge crosses the island. There isn't any vehicle access to the island, but the ghouls will be able to swarm up the pillars and use the bridge to cross into both Portland and Vancouver.*

We sat and stared at the map.

I suppose you could blow up the bridge.

I grimaced. "Not without Homeland Security locking me up and throwing away the key for domestic terrorism."

True, but if it's the only way to keep the ghouls on the island ... She left the thought hanging.

Rising to my feet, I paced to the picture window in my living room, then turned and strode back to the kitchen counter. Clenching the back of the upholstered stool, I said, "I never thought I'd say it, but I wish Morgan was still around. He might be able to answer some questions."

Like what?

"Like is this a temporary invasion? Do they have to return to their dimension when the stars or whatever are no longer aligned?"

If it was possible for a ghost to pale, Sarah did. Her eyes widened and she stared at me. *What if ... What if that ghoul killed him so that he couldn't tell us something?*

I frowned. "Like what? I mean, he didn't tell us exactly when the portal would open, but we have an approximate idea."

No, she said, shaking her head so that her cute little pony tail swung back and forth. *I'm thinking something bigger than that. What if they've found a way to maintain the portal once the barrier thins. What if they can keep it open forever?*

I collapsed back into my seat at the counter, stunned. I'd been imagining ways to hold the monsters at bay for an hour or two. Trying to figure out how to keep them on the island where they couldn't hurt anyone but me. Praying that I could survive Halloween night and keep the cities on both sides of the Columbia safe.

There was no way I could do that indefinitely.

I doubted a battalion of military commandos could accomplish that.

"We need more information," I said, as soon as my breathing stabilized enough that I could speak. "If there's a way they can hold the portal open, then there must be a way we can close it. But if we go to the island alone and unprepared, we won't do anything but die."

Sarah snorted, and I amended my last statement. "Okay, *I* won't do anything but die." I leaned forward, forearms on the counter, hands clasped. "But you're in danger too. You said ghouls can eat ghosts. I'm guessing that's not a good thing."

She lowered her head. *No, it's not. I'd be gone forever. No more visiting this world, and no possibility of moving on to the next. Just total annihilation. You're right. We can't face this alone, but who can we turn to? We've got less than a week.*

I stood and paced the perimeter of my small apartment, rubbing my forehead and trying to think. Trying not to allow my terror to block my logical mind. Morgan had said something. He'd given us a clue. I knew he had.

And then it hit me.

I whirled and pointed at Sarah. "What was it Morgan said when he was in lecture mode, telling us about seventh-sevenths?" I strode back to where she appeared to sit at the breakfast bar watching me. "He mentioned three kinds of sevenths. Healers, like you, guardians, like me, and … What was that third one? The one neither of us had heard of before?"

Sarah leaned back so far that she floated right into the center of the breakfast bar counter. She didn't seem to notice. Her eyes were closed and her brow wrinkled in a cute little frown of concentration. I ignored the fact that she was probably sitting in tomorrow morning's cereal box and wracked my own brain. What had he said?

Alternate realities, she said, opening her eyes and looking startled to find herself in the middle of the counter. She moved back to perch on the stool. *He said the third group are attuned to alternate realities and often end up studying theoretical physics or higher mathematics.*

"That's it!" I said, exultation rising in my chest. "We have to find Morgan's seventh-seventh files and see if there are any of the third type in the area. Adults who have come into their power."

Yes, she agreed. *And any of the others as well. We'll need guardians like yourself to defend the theoreticians, and healers to keep us all on our feet.*

I smiled and reached out to hug Sarah, but my arms went right through her, leaving me with a cold, empty feeling. She gave me a chagrined look.

No matter. We had a plan. We didn't know where Morgan's files were, or whether he'd identified any seventh-sevenths who had come into their power, and we didn't have much time. But we did have a plan.

It was better than nothing.

4

W e were lucky. After doing a bit of sleuthing, I discovered that Morgan's files had been confiscated as evidence and then transferred to storage after the completion of his trial. Since I'd been the arresting officer, I had access. Of course, I had to fill out a small mountain of paperwork, but by the next afternoon Sarah and I were ensconced in a concrete storage facility surrounded by ceiling-high shelves crammed full of boxes.

With a print out in hand, we scanned the box labels for Morgan's files. Sarah floated near the ceiling, checking labels above my line of sight. Saved me a lot of climbing. I mean, metal ladders were provided, the ones that looked that portable staircases, but having Sarah do her floaty thing saved me a lot of time and energy. When we finally found Morgan's files, the boxes occupied an entire section — three boxes wide, from floor to ceiling. The man had kept meticulous records.

My stomach was rumbling and my brain was getting mushy by the time we finally narrowed our search to a single box crammed full of files, each with a coded label that started with 7-7.

Bingo!

I checked the box out from the desk sergeant, loaded it into the back seat of my Honda Accord and drove straight to my favorite fast food drive-through. Twenty minutes later, the box rested on the end of my breakfast bar while I scarfed a cheeseburger and fries, and Sarah fumed.

Couldn't you at least pull out a couple of files and flip them open so I could read while you're eating? She was really cute when she was miffed. Floating there beside the box with her hands fisted on her hips.

"Nope," I said, sinking my teeth into the burger and savoring the mix of grilled meat, melted cheese and tangy pickle. I chewed, swallowed, and added, "If I did that, you'd be whining at me to flip the pages for you. You can wait another minute or two. Some of us still need to eat."

Fine, she said with a scowl. *So quit talking and eat. We've got work to do and you're wasting time.*

I stuffed the last of the fries in my mouth, wiped greasy fingers on a cheap paper napkin and pulled the box closer.

Sarah wasn't much help since she couldn't affect material objects. I had to do all the pawing through the files, as well as all the note taking, but by midnight we had a list of names and probable abilities along with the most recent addresses and phone numbers Morgan had known. The names' locations spanned the nation, but there were a few in the Portland and Seattle region. If they really had power and were willing, they could arrive in time to help.

Only seven possibilities, Sarah said in a dejected voice.

"Frankly, that's more than I expected," I replied. "Big families have been out of style for a generation or more, and seventh-sevenths require lots of kids."

She nodded. *But there are oddities. Look at my family, as far as anyone knew, there were only three kids. I knew my eldest sister, Angie, was a twin and that her sister died at birth, but no one ever told me Mom had miscarried triplets before Angie was born. I wonder how many other people are out there who have no idea they're a seventh child, or worse, a seventh-seventh?*

"Still, finding any seventh-sevenths close enough to join us on short notice is a miracle," I said. "We're making good progress, but time is critical." I glanced at the clock. Midnight had come and gone, and I felt the seconds ticking away with each beat of my heart. "It's already Monday and Halloween is Friday. Granted, we only discovered the threat yesterday, but still…"

My words deserted me.

Sarah floated over, coming to rest on the stool at my side. *You need to rest. Tomorrow will be exhausting, mentally and emotionally if not physically.*

I wanted to protest, but she silenced me with a stern glance.

You can't contact anyone at this hour, she said reasonably. *Get some sleep. We'll call the list first thing in the morning.*

I nodded, resisting the urge to rub my eyes like a sleepy toddler. "You think any of them will admit to being a seventh-seventh over the phone?"

She shrugged. *Who knows. But worrying about it won't change the outcome. Go to bed, Gus. You'll be better able to handle their objections if you're rested.*

"Good point." I headed to the bedroom, stripping off my clothes as I walked, and climbed into bed wearing only my birthday suit. Tomorrow would be soon enough to save the world … or at least the Pacific Northwest.

5

Monday morning dawned sunny and clear, an unusual occurrence at any time of year in perpetually rainy Portland, but definitely unexpected in late October. My first task of the day was to contact my partner Jack Barnes and let him know that I was taking the week off.

"You're what?" he asked, disbelief coming through loud and clear. "What's up, Gus? You never take time off."

"I met someone," I said, winking at Sarah. "She's a real outdoor fanatic. We're going camping for a few days."

"Camping," he said, the word dripping with sarcasm. "In October. Come on, Gus. You can do better than that."

"Believe what you want," I said. "That's my story and I'm sticking to it. Let the captain know for me, will you?"

"Sure, sure," he said. "Shouldn't be a problem, but you're going to miss all the weirdos who'll be out on Halloween."

I wish, Sarah murmured.

"Thanks, Jack. See you next week." I didn't add, *I hope*, though it rang through my brain.

"Okay," I said to Sarah after disconnecting with Jack. "Now we call the Seattleites."

I poured myself a cup of liquid courage, freshly brewed black coffee, and settled onto the sofa with my list, a notebook and my favorite ballpoint pen. Time to see if I could get a group of complete strangers to admit to having paranormal abilities. Over the phone, no less.

The first call was over too fast. David Aiken died last year.

I didn't ask for details, though the detective in me ached to know more. The manner of his death was irrelevant to the task at hand and time was limited.

The second call took some time. Ethel Douglass, a canny elderly woman, had lived long enough to know how to hide in plain sight.

Once I'd established my credentials as a Portland homicide detective, we reached the delicate stage of our conversation.

"I'm sure I don't understand, Detective," she said. "What possible difference could the circumstances surrounding my birth make to a murder investigation in Portland? Did you, perhaps, misdial? I do live in Seattle, you know."

I drew a deep breath and glanced at Sarah. She nodded. *Just tell her the truth. If she's one of us, she'll understand. If she's not, what can she do?*

I closed my eyes and took the plunge.

"In all honesty, Mrs. Douglass, I'm not investigating a murder." I paused and licked my lips. "I'm searching for seventh children of seventh children and I have reason to believe you may be such an individual."

Our connection was so silent I almost pulled the phone away to check that she hadn't hung up. Then I heard an inhalation on the other end.

"What makes you think so, Detective?" she asked. "And what difference would it make if you're correct?"

Bingo.

I gave Sarah a quick thumb's up. "My associate and I are also seventh-sevenths," I said. "We've discovered a, well, a paranormal anomaly. Something the normal folks in the police department won't be able to handle. We're looking for help, for other, uhm, gifted people, to assist us in protecting the population.

"Would you be such a person, Mrs. Douglass?"

Silence reigned again.

"What proof do I have that you are who and what you say you are, Detective?"

"I'm twenty-eight years old. I came into my power on my birthday in late June. As you might guess from my profession, I'm a guardian and I'm psychic." I glanced at Sarah and our gazes locked. "My associate wasn't so lucky. She was murdered by a psychopath before she came into her power, she was a healer."

I extended my senses and could almost feel the older woman's agreement through the phone connection. "I remember," she said. "The young doctor who was murdered in late June. The story made the news in Seattle.

"Very well, Detective, I believe you. Telling me you have a ghost for a friend wouldn't be politic for a normal person. Yes. I am one of the people you seek. I'm assuming that the anomaly you have discovered deals with an unusual thinning of the barrier between worlds that will take place on Halloween."

My jaw dropped and my heart raced. "H-how did you know?" I stammered.

"My powers deal with other realities," she said. "I'm a theoretical mathematician, and my recent work has been pointing to a cataclysmic disturbance.

"Is Alexander Davidovich on your list?" she asked with brusque assurance.

"Yes, that's the next name I planned to call."

"Don't bother. Alex is my protégé. I will explain the situation and he will drive me to Portland. Where should we meet you?"

I gave her my address and told her I'd leave a spare key with the doorman.

After disconnecting the call, I sat staring at the phone. I'd done it. I'd found another seventh-seventh. Two in fact.

She's coming? Sarah asked.

"And bringing Alexander Davidovich. He's her protégé," I said, my mouth twisting into a manic grin. "Two for one call! And she's an alternate realities seventh." My grin morphed into a frown. "I forgot to ask what Davidovich's specialty is."

Doesn't matter, Sarah said jubilantly. *We have help. We're not alone!*

Relief whispered through my psyche. We'd just doubled our chances.

I grabbed my list and dialed the final Seattle number. It was a dud. Elaine Carpenter was a minor. Didn't matter whether or not she was a seventh-seventh, at ten years of age, she wasn't old enough to help with this battle.

"Okay. That's the Seattle list. I'm going to grab some lunch and then we can tackle the three names we have in Portland."

Since they're local, why don't we visit them in person? Might be easier to convince than over the phone.

"My thoughts exactly," I agreed. "Give me a few more minutes with my computer. I'm going to use department resources to see if I can determine their work addresses, just in case they're not homebodies."

An hour later, I sat in my Honda Accord finishing the last bite of a pulled pork burrito and watching pedestrians navigate the busy sidewalks of the Lloyd shopping district. An Army recruiting station was right across the street, and if my information was correct, I'd find Captain Luke Young inside. A perfect candidate for the position of guardian seventh-seventh.

I wiped my mouth and hands on a paper napkin, popped a breath mint between my teeth, and climbed out of the car. "Alright," I said to Sarah as she floated to my side, "let's see if we can recruit the recruiter."

We walked to the corner and crossed the street with the light. The day was warm, the sky clear and blue without a trace of clouds or moisture. An unusually fine day for Portland in late October. The sidewalk was busy, but not crowded, and the air smelled of city, a combination of car exhaust, asphalt, and green growing things.

I walked quickly, with a spring in my step, more hopeful than I'd been since I'd watched Morgan be devoured by a ghoul. We had two comrades coming from Seattle, and I was willing to bet Luke Young would also join our team.

Cool air wafted across my face as I opened the glass door to the recruitment office. A middle-aged black man in a crisp Army uniform stood and stepped around his desk, hand extended to greet me. Then his gaze landed on Sarah, and his ebony skin grayed. His hand wavered and dropped to his side.

"Who are you?" he asked in a strained, husky voice.

"I'm the seventh child of a seventh child," I said, "just like you are."

His gaze flicked from Sarah to me and back again. "How do you know?"

You can see me, Sarah responded, and when he flinched, she added, *and hear me as well.*

When we got past the obvious, we sat down with Luke and outlined what we knew. He agreed to help with no hesitation.

He'd served two tours in Afghanistan, but had been reassigned stateside when his psychic vision had become too much for him. The Army thought he was suffering from post traumatic stress disorder; Luke knew he was seeing too many ghosts of fallen heroes. Ghosts he had no way to help. The reassignment had been a good one. Luke continued to serve the living without the need to deal with the dead.

The final two Portland names turned out to be children. An eight year old boy in Gresham, and a twelve year old girl in Beaverton.

For good or ill, we had our team. Four living souls and one ghost. Five seventh-sevenths to stand against the ghouls who planned to ravage the world.

6

The team gathered for dinner in my compact apartment. Mrs. Douglass sat ensconced in my one overstuffed chair, like a queen on her throne. Alex lounged on the floor, leaning back with his arms braced behind him, legs stretched out in front, ankles crossed. Luke sat on the couch, one arm thrown across the back, the other resting lightly on the armrest.

I passed out cold bottles of beer.

Mrs. Douglass arched an eyebrow at me. "Are you trying to get me drunk, young man?"

My cheeks warmed until I caught the twinkle in her eye. "If a single beer is too much for you, I can offer you water."

She nodded and accepted the bottle. "I can handle a beer."

Alex laughed. "Watch out for her, Gus. She likes to use the 'helpless little old lady' ploy on the unwary. Rest assured, she's far from helpless."

Mrs. Douglass huffed. "I notice you didn't negate the 'little old lady' part."

Alex shrugged. "Truth is truth, Ethel."

"So it is, Alex," she agreed. "So it is."

The doorbell rang and I strode down the hall to answer. A pizza delivery guy handed me two boxes in exchange for my signature on the credit card receipt. I carried them to the breakfast bar and threw them open. The delicious aroma of tomato sauce, spices and yeasty bread crust filled the air, making my mouth water in anticipation.

"Okay, everyone. Come and get it," I called to the others.

Luke approached Mrs. Douglass. "What can I bring you, ma'am?"

When everyone was seated again, I broached the reason for our gathering.

"Frankly," I said, "I'm fairly new to this seventh-seventh thing, so I'm not sure what everyone can do ... or see. Mrs. Douglass, Alex, are either of you aware of the fifth member of our team?"

Both of them turned to gaze at Sarah where she perched on one of the upholstered stools beside the breakfast bar.

"You mean the lovely young woman in hospital scrubs?" asked Ethel Douglass.

Sarah beamed. *Oh! Thank heavens! This will be so much easier if you can see me and hear me.*

Alex nodded. "You were a doctor?" When Sarah nodded, he continued, "I'm a healer as well. A naturopath by profession, but my seventh-seventh power is healing."

"So," I said, and all eyes turned back to me, "I guess all seventh-sevenths must be psychic, if everyone is aware of Sarah. That means Luke and I must have additional powers as guardians. Anyone know what those might be?"

Luke looked blank. "I'm a lot older than you, Gus, so I probably should know, but I came into my power in Afghanistan. You people are the only other sevenths I know.

"The psychic thing threw me for a loop with all the dead soldiers showing up. The Army sent me home with a diagnosis of PTSD. That's all I knew about this stuff until you showed up at the recruitment office today."

Mrs. Douglass nodded. "A familiar story, Captain Young. There are too few who have been trained these days. It's hard for those of us who are capable of mentoring to find our young in time, especially when there are predators like Jason Morgan in the world." She turned to Sarah. "I'm so sorry Morgan found you before I did."

Sarah dropped her gaze. *So am I.*

"Well," I said, "we'll never have to worry about Morgan again. He's actually the reason I sought you out. He contacted me with information about a planned invasion from another dimension. Sarah and I were interviewing him when he was killed."

"How horrible," exclaimed Mrs. Douglass. "What killed him?"

A ghoul, Sarah answered.

I nodded. "We believe he was devoured at that moment to prevent him from giving us further details."

"Wait a minute," said Luke, sitting forward with an intense look on his face. "What's a ghoul and what do you mean 'devoured'?"

Mrs. Douglass held up her hand in a silencing gesture. She looked straight at me. "If you don't mind, Gus, I'll take control of this meeting."

I spread my hands in agreement. "As the only trained seventh-seventh in the room, I believe you should."

"Ghouls are foul creatures of the other world. They can materialize in our world only when the barriers are sufficiently thin, often at Halloween. They're incredibly dangerous. Jason Morgan dabbled in black magic, blood magic to be precise, as evidenced by his murder of Sarah. This opened him up to evil influence from the other world. He paid the ultimate price for his terrible choices."

Luke looked slightly bewildered, but nodded.

Mrs. Douglass continued, "The other world is my specialty, my gift. In this realm, I'm drawn to theoretical mathematics. Advanced mathematics helps me define what my gift tells me. Recently, my work has shown that there will be a dangerous thinning of the barrier somewhere in the Columbia River basin on Halloween. I know when, but I've yet to determine exactly where. Because of this, I was receptive to Gus's call this morning."

My eyes widened and my pulse raced. She knew when! "I can tell you where," I blurted. "Morgan got that much out before he was silenced."

All eyes turned to me.

"Well?" prompted Mrs. Douglass.

"Oh. Sorry. Government Island. Where the ley lines cross halfway between the west end of the lake and the pond."

"Excellent," said Mrs. Douglass, "and the portal will be on an island, surrounded by flowing water." She nodded. "That will help."

Yes, said Sarah. *We thought of that. The only problem is that the Glen Jackson Bridge crosses the island. There are buttresses that the ghouls can use to access the highway, leading them straight into both Portland and Vancouver.*

"That's not good. We'll have to devise a plan to hold them back from the bridge."

"Also," I said, "we're concerned about the possibility of them stabilizing the portal. Do you know if they can make the breach permanent?"

Mrs. Douglass frowned and her eyes seemed to glaze for a moment. "I'll need some time to run some calculations," she said. "Let's meet in the morning for breakfast. I've taken a suite at The Benson. Join us at 8:00 in the morning. I'll have breakfast delivered."

When the others were gone, I studied Sarah, wishing I could pull her into my arms. We were in this together. Had been since my power had manifested on my twenty-eighth birthday as I knelt beside her corpse. She'd driven me nearly out of my mind in those first few days as we hunted her murderer, Jason Morgan, but in the months since, she'd come to mean a lot more to me. With her cute little blonde ponytail, beautiful blue eyes, and quick wit and lively intelligence, she was everything I'd ever dreamed of in a woman. Except for one little detail … she was a ghost. Insubstantial. With no ability to affect the material world. Which meant we could never so much as touch each others' hands.

I sighed and pulled my thoughts from the impossibility of my friend-ship for Sarah ever becoming something more substantial to the immediate problem of ghouls invading our world.

"This morning we were alone," I said quietly. "Tonight, we not only have a team, but someone who can teach us what it means to be seventh-sevenths."

Sarah nodded, her pretty lips curving into a cautious smile. *We still have a daunting task ahead, but I agree, we have a better chance now than we did this morning. I hope Mrs. Douglass has good news for us tomorrow.*

"Agreed. There's a lot we don't know, but still … Tuesday looks a lot better than today did. Let's get some rest."

She cocked her head, lifted an eyebrow, and gave me her 'are you seri-ous?' look.

"Fine. You do whatever ghosts do while mere mortals sleep, and *I'll* get some rest."

Sleep well, Gus, she said and blew me a kiss. *I'll see you in the morning.*

7

Mrs. Douglass's suite at The Benson was luxurious. Alex ushered us into a spacious living area with an immaculate cream sofa, two elegant, curved-legged chairs their seats upholstered in matching fabric, an ottoman and a highly polished mahogany coffee table. Breakfast had been arranged on a sideboard beside a wet bar and smelled heavenly. Bacon, scrambled eggs, an assortment of fresh fruit, and steaming hot coffee.

Sarah, hovering at my side, sighed. *What I wouldn't give to be able to smell and taste again.* She shook her head sadly and floated to Mrs. Douglass, who sat in one of the chairs. *Thank you for driving down from Seattle. Having you on our team makes me feel like we have a chance.*

Mrs. Douglass reached out as if to pat Sarah's hand, then remembered herself, curled her fingers, and dropped her fist back into her lap.

"You're very welcome, my dear. I only wish we could've met under different circumstances."

Luke arrived wearing jeans and a green plaid work shirt. As Alex showed him inside, I heard the young healer explain that his room was much more modest, and two floors down.

"Now that we're all here," said Mrs. Douglass, in tones very much like my captain bringing the department to order for our morning staff meeting, "why don't you all fix your plates and have a seat. I'll give you a briefing of the calculations I ran last night while you eat."

Alex raised an eyebrow at her, but she waved him away. "Don't worry about me. I ate earlier."

When everyone was seated with heaping plates, except for Sarah, of course, Mrs. Douglass began. "As you probably remember, Sarah brought up the question of whether or not the ghouls would be able to stabilize their portal once it opens on Halloween night. Unfortunately, my calculations inform me that it is not only possible, it is probable that such is their intention."

Leaning forward, she picked up a small leather bound book and flipped through the pages. "Here are the facts as I know them, thanks to Gus and Sarah's information and my own perceptions of the other world. The barrier will thin at sundown on Samhain. Halloween," she explained, seeing Luke's frown at the unfamiliar word. "The moment when the sun leaves the sky is a threshold in and of itself: no longer day, but not yet night. Samhain is another threshold, the end of one season—in this case the end of the Celtic year—and the beginning of the next. Finally, this year sundown on Samhain in Portland, Oregon will happen during a highly unusual alignment of heavenly bodies important in both our realm and the other world. This conflation of threshold events will result in the opening of a portal between the worlds where the ley lines cross on Government Island."

She paused, replaced the book, picked up her coffee cup and took a sip.

I placed my plate on the coffee table. I'd been enjoying the scrambled eggs and crisp bacon, but my stomach turned queasy as Mrs. Douglass lectured. I'd hoped she'd say our fears were groundless. No such luck.

"On a normal Samhain, a ghost or two might slip through. Perhaps even a ghoul, but not in a corporeal form. Monsters are often seen on

Halloween, it's why the holiday exists, but they're usually insubstantial, incapable of causing physical harm. That will not be true this year, in this place.

"We'll need to be ready, and we'll need reinforcements."

"Reinforcements?" I cried. My stomach clenched as my hopes crashed. "But you three are my reinforcements! We don't have time to search out more seventh-sevenths, and even if we did, they'd have to come from all over the country. We'd never get them here in time."

"You misunderstand me, Detective Collier," Mrs. Douglass said calmly, making eye contact with each of us in turn. "I'm not suggesting we find additional seventh-sevenths. I'm saying that we need to enlist the aid of civilians."

The room erupted in noise as everyone spoke at once. Only Sarah held silent. When I realized I hadn't heard her voice in my mind, I sat back and scanned the room. She had moved to Mrs. Douglass's side, where the two of them waited quietly.

Alex quieted next, and then Luke realized he was the only one still arguing.

We all looked at Mrs. Douglass.

She nodded, then continued as if we'd never interrupted. "Detective Collier, you'll need to enlist as many of your fellow officers as you can convince to join us on Government Island. I don't care if they think you're crazy. Find some way to have them arrive armed and ready to do battle. Once the portal opens, their doubts will disappear. They'll be able to see the enemy as easily as any of us.

I swallowed my fears of ridicule and nodded. She was right. We'd need armed men to stop this invasion. My pride was irrelevant.

"Captain Young, you'll have a similar assignment. Gather whatever men and women you can, convince them in any manner you can dream up, but make sure we have armed forces standing between the portal and the Glen Jackson bridge when the sun leaves the sky on Halloween evening."

"Yes, ma'am," Luke said, eyes hard, jaw set. "We'll be ready to defend the bridge."

She nodded. "Alex, you'll need Sarah's guidance to gather medical supplies. You're our healer. You must keep our men and women on their feet and able to hold the enemy at bay."

Taking another sip of coffee, she closed her eyes for a moment, and then replaced her cup and saucer on the table. "Gus and Luke, the men and women you gather must protect the bridge without your assistance. You two will have another task."

I startled, but then an unexpected calm radiated through my soul. I understood with an instinctive assurance what she would ask. I nodded. "You need us to guard you while you seal the portal behind them."

"Very good, Gus," she said with a curt nod. "I'll prepare the necessary elements to seal the rift. You and Luke must keep me alive long enough to complete the task."

8

---

*Y**ou can do this, Gus,* Sarah whispered as I inhaled deeply and approached my partner, Jack Barnes.

"Hey, Gus," Jack called as I crossed the battered linoleum to our desks. The scarred old wooden war horses were butted together so that we could discuss our cases face-to-face while we worked. "I thought you weren't coming in this week."

"I'm not." I grabbed my desk chair and wheeled it over where I could sit close to my partner. I wasn't ready for this conversation to be overheard. "I'm here to ask a favor, Jack."

My partner caught my mood, his face sobering instantly. Jack's not a great-looking guy. His hair is thinning and going gray, his cheeks are constantly stubbled and a little on the flabby side, and he's got a definite spare tire around his middle, but he's a solid detective and a good friend. Yeah, he can rib me, but he'd stop a bullet for me without a second thought. He's my partner, and that's what partners do.

Still, I'd rather have done nearly anything in the universe than ask Jack to help me battle monsters on Halloween. Unfortunately, it needed to be done and the time was now or never.

"Anything, Gus," he said, as serious as a funeral. "What do you need?"

I glanced at the floor, then stared into my partner's gray-blue eyes. "I need you to listen to me and believe me," I said with all the sincerity I could muster. "I'm going to tell you some stuff that's going to make you think I've fallen off the deep end, but I swear to you, it's all true. Portland is in danger and I need help protecting her. Will you listen?"

A frown creased his forehead, but his gaze didn't waver from mine. "I'm listening."

I told him everything. All the seventh-seventh crap. The truth about Jason Morgan's death, and everything I knew or guessed about the monsters that were going to come out from under the bed on Halloween.

His eyes widened a few times and at first his lips started to curl into a 'you're putting me on' kind of smile, but he kept his gaze on my eyes and the ridicule faded. I guess he believed me. Or at least, he believed that I believed what I said.

When I finished, he leaned back in his chair and stroked his stubbled chin for a while. Then he stood up and extended his hand. "I'll be there," he said, "and I'll round up as many of the guys as I can manage. You've got better things to do than try to convince people who don't know you like I do to buy into this. Besides," he added with a grin, "I've got an advantage you don't."

I frowned. "What's that?"

"I can honestly say that my partner's gone over the edge and I need help with an intervention."

"That's an advantage?"

He slapped my shoulder. "Definitely, because if we all show up on that island at sunset on Halloween and no monsters appear, you're really going to *need* an intervention, because I'll be first in line to lock you up in the State Hospital and throw away the key."

I gave him a rueful smile. "Just show up, Jack. The monsters will be there."

When the team gathered that night at The Benson, I discovered that Luke had had a similar experience. Twenty men had agreed to show up, but they didn't believe him. They were coming to prove that he needed psychiatric help.

"Who cares why they're coming?" Alex asked. "As long as they show up. Ethel and I will figure something out if no ghouls show … and wouldn't that be the best case scenario? There's no portal, no monsters, and we just have to figure a way to spring you two from the loony bin. Piece of cake!"

Mrs. Douglass agreed. "This is wonderful news. We have twenty to thirty trained people to help us defeat the ghouls. Alex made great progress gathering his medical supplies, and I've finished my research into what I'll need to seal the portal. We're almost ready."

She smiled at each of us. "Tomorrow, I'll give our guardians a crash course in the magic of seventh-sevenths while Alex arranges for a boat to take us to the island. We'll cross the Columbia Friday morning and make our final preparations."

9

B y late Friday afternoon my nerves were shot. We'd set up camp on Government Island. A four-man tent for Alex and Luke and me and a cabin in the small yacht she'd rented for Mrs. Douglass. The yacht was anchored just off a pristine beach on the southwest end of the island and we'd hiked to the interior to find the place between the lake and the pond where the ley lines crossed.

I'd expected it to be hard to find the exact location. I mean, what did I know about ley lines? I figured they were imaginary constructs like lines of latitude or longitude.

Wrong.

The closer we got to the spot, the weirder I felt. The hairs on my arms stood on end, the back of my neck prickled, my pulse sped up until I thought I might be in danger of a heart attack. Then we found the spot and it was like stepping into the eye of the storm. Complete and utter calm.

Crap. That calm scared me more than the weird stuff.

About an hour before sunset the Army arrived. Literally.

Luke's men came tramping across the meadow and into the small stand of trees that surrounded what would soon be the portal site. Jack and my colleagues were right behind them. All told we had thirty-five heavily armed men and women, most of whom thought they were in the middle of the lamest Halloween prank ever.

Luke took charge. "Okay, people, listen up," he called, using his military-trained instructor's voice. "I don't care whether you believe this shit or not. It's real and you're going to be locked in deadly combat very soon. Your enemy will not be human. They'll be creatures out of your worst nightmares. They will NOT be people dressed up in Halloween costumes. If you make the mistake of thinking they are, YOU WILL DIE."

He paused, letting those words sink in.

"Lieutenant Mason, you're in command of our troops. Detective Barnes, you're in charge of Portland's finest. Deploy your people as you see fit, but remember, if a single ghoul gets past you, men, women, and children in Portland and Vancouver will die."

He nodded to Jack and Lt. Mason. "Good luck, and God speed."

Luke turned and marched back to the event zone to take up position beside Mrs. Douglass. Jack stared at me for a few seconds then huddled with Lt. Mason to work out a strategy.

"Well done, Captain Young," said Mrs. Douglass. "Alex, is your aid station ready?"

"Yes, ma'am," he replied. "Everything is set up over by the pond."

She nodded. "Very well. Take up your place. I don't want you anywhere near here when they come through. You're our only healer and I won't risk you."

He looked like he might argue, but he tightened his jaw, nodded and jogged off toward the pond.

"Sarah," I said, "you should join him."

I don't want to leave you, Gus.

"I know, but you can't help here and you're vulnerable. If I'm worrying about you, I won't be worrying about what I should be."

She nodded, tears shimmering on her cheeks. Stretching out a hand to me, she turned to go, but not before her fingers touched my arm.

I recoiled, and she turned in alarm.

"You touched me," I said.

"I felt your arm," she said.

Mrs. Douglass turned to face the portal that was forming. "Go, Sarah," she called. "You're becoming substantial, that means the portal is opening."

I grabbed my suddenly substantial Sarah and kissed her with all the longing I'd been denying. She fit in my arms perfectly, like we'd been made for each other. The taste of her lips was so sweet, I felt dizzy. This was heaven!

But hell was materializing around us and I had to protect her. Reluctantly, I broke our kiss, noting the love and longing shining in her eyes. I stroked her cheek with trembling fingers, then pushed her toward Alex's aid station. "Go," I said in a voice made harsh by emotion ... and turned to face the horde of ghouls shimmering into existence through a rent in the universe.

10

L uke nodded at me, his face grim, but his eyes were filled with sympathy and pity. "Ready?" he asked.

"As I'll ever be," I answered, fighting the urge to turn and watch Sarah's retreat.

We strode to Mrs. Douglass and took our places, one on each side of her. She smiled at Luke, then reached out and patted my arm. "I'm so sorry, Gus." Straightening her shoulders, she said to both of us, "Remember the plan. We can do this."

Ghouls stampeded through the rent. Some loped on all fours, others stood erect. All were a nasty gray-green that made Army fatigues seem bright and cheery. The ones on two legs were surprisingly tall, most over seven feet. Their heads were misshapen amalgams of human and ram, complete with deadly looking curved horns. Lean and muscular, they wore nothing but loin clothes of ill-tanned leather, and their fingers and toes were tipped with inch-long claws.

The first wave raced across the meager space that separated us from the portal. Mrs. Douglass grasped an ornate silver cross in her right hand and held it before us like a shield. Luke and I pulled energy from the ley lines and, using the cross as a focal point, flung our arms wide. A sphere of blue-white flame enveloped the three of us, and the raging ghouls were forced to separate and flow around us.

Our bubble of safety was engulfed in a mob of slathering monsters. I'd always had an active imagination, but never, even in my most vivid nightmares, had I dreamed of such horrors. They couldn't touch us — not as long as Luke and I held firm — but their red eyes glared at us as they ran past, and their howls and clicking claws and snapping teeth sent waves of primeval fear racing along my nerves.

Gunfire erupted behind us and I heard all too human screams of agony. Concern for Sarah and Alex and Jack blurred my focus and my side of the sphere sparked and wavered.

"Concentrate!" Mrs. Douglass commanded.

I redoubled my efforts. Jack and the other thirty-four volunteers were armed and dangerous. They could take care of themselves. They had to. They were all that stood between the ghouls and the people of Portland and Vancouver.

After what felt like hours, but had probably been only seconds, Mrs. Douglass spoke again. "All right, gentlemen. Let's move forward." She held the cross aloft and stepped forward. Luke and I moved with her, just like we'd practiced yesterday. It had seemed so easy in the safety of her suite at The Benson. Raise the shield, hold it steady, and walk forward in formation. No sweat. The definition of simplicity.

Not so much in the real world.

Ghouls gave way before us. They had to, those that came into contact with our blazing sphere disintegrated into charred flakes of ghoul-dust, but it was slow going. When the rent first opened and I saw the slathering monsters emerge, the distance between them and us had seemed much too small, but now it felt like we had miles to cross and we were moving at an anguished crawl.

And as long as the rent was open more and more ghouls would spew into our world. How long could thirty-five defenders hold the monsters at bay?

I fought to hold up my portion of the shield, but the howling and stamping of the ghouls coupled with blasts of gunfire and screams of terror and anguish from my allies tore at my concentration. I clenched my jaws, heart racing, sweat streaming down my face and back from the sheer effort of harnessing unaccustomed energies.

Gods! I wished I'd had more time to practice! I hadn't even known I possessed this ability until Mrs. Douglass explained the concept yesterday. How could I be expected to wield this power successfully today?

I glanced at Luke. He looked as shaky as I felt. Our eyes met and our resolve firmed. Neither of us intended to let these creatures win. We'd ride this whirlwind ... even if it killed us.

We pushed forward another step. Almost there. I could see the rent shimmering just behind the ghoul directly in front of us. It snarled and snapped, but had to move aside or be destroyed. Our bubble intersected the edge of the portal and flashed out of existence.

Now came the tricky part.

Luke and I whirled to face the horde of ghouls we'd just passed. Mrs. Douglass was on her own. She had to seal the rent before another ghoul stepped through and dissected her. Luke and I were in charge of incinerating any of the already extant ghouls who tried to take advantage of our lack of shield.

I conjured a fireball — now there was a statement I never expected to make.

Luke did the same.

My instinct was to hurl it at the nearest ghoul, but Mrs. Douglass had warned us to resist that urge.

"Just be ready," she'd counseled us. "Don't do anything to call attention to us until the rent is sealed. If they turn and notice, don't hold back, but don't start anything."

Easier said than done, especially now that I was facing my friends and could see what they were battling. Dead ghouls littered the meadow.

Good.

Our weapons were effective against them.

But our troops were badly outnumbered. I couldn't count the ghouls properly, not while they were darting back and forth, weaving around trying to catch our people off balance, but my estimate was an easy three to one in their favor.

I caught sight of Alex and Sarah moving from wounded police officer to wounded soldier. Each time one of them moved on, the defender rose and shouldered his or her weapon. Sarah's transformation to substantial being was a point in our favor.

The last ghoul we'd forced out of our way turned, realized that our shield was down, and howled. Another dozen of those in the rear turned as well, their red eyes gleaming and saliva dripping from exposed teeth.

"Shit," I said. "Here they come."

"I'm on it," Luke responded.

We lobbed fireballs at the advancing ghouls.

My aim sucked, lack of practice can be deadly, but one connected. It didn't disintegrate the monster the way our combined shield had done, but it screamed in pain and dropped to the ground, its shoulder emitting greasy black smoke, the flesh (if that's what it was) turning into a pulpy purple mass.

Interesting. Purple, not blood red.

I cut my observations short and conjured another fireball. Now that I knew I could hurt them, my pulse steadied and my aim improved.

Behind me, I heard Mrs. Douglass chanting. I don't know where she found the information — I mean, I've never run across a library book on the best way to seal a portal to hell — but she was prepared with silver, holy water, several obsidian stones inscribed with runes, and an incantation.

Luke's aim was better than mine. He was dropping ghouls in a perfectly timed cadence. Conjure. Aim. Throw. Repeat. I tried to emulate his technique while avoiding thinking about how our friends were faring.

I'd finally managed to find my rhythm, when I heard Mrs. Douglass give a sharp intake of breath and whisper, "Oh, my." The world blazed white for an instant and someone fell against me.

I turned, caught Mrs. Douglass, and saw the portal disappear from the corner of my eye.

"You're on your own, Luke," I yelled as I eased Mrs. Douglass to the ground. "The portal is sealed, but Mrs. Douglass is down."

"Get her to Alex," he called, his voice tight and labored. "I'll cover your retreat."

I scooped up the elderly woman and sprinted around the edge of the fighting toward the aid station by the pond. Now that the enemy's numbers were finite and Luke had been released from shield duty, our side was making better progress.

Luke blasted ghouls from my path until I reached Alex and Sarah. Once I'd deposited Mrs. Douglass on a blanket, I turned, conjured a fireball, and joined a soldier who was guarding the wounded and the healers. Luke nodded at us and turned to join the fray.

"How is she?" I called over my shoulder.

Sarah floated over to hover beside me. *She was gored in the chest, probably in a last ditch effort to prevent her from sealing the portal, but she'll be fine. Alex has a real talent for healing, even without the supernatural power, but when he's fired up he can do everything except raise the dead.*

I stole a glance at the woman I loved. Yeah. I could admit that now, at least to myself. Sometime during the last few months, I'd come to love Sarah. She was my complement, my perfect mate. Morgan had taken more than her life; he'd stolen our future. "You're insubstantial again."

On your left, she cried.

I let the fireball I'd been holding fly and watched in satisfaction as the ghoul who'd been sneaking up on me dropped and writhed on the ground. I conjured another round and waited.

Sarah sighed. *Yes. As soon as the portal ceased to exist, so did my physical body.*

"Shame we had to waste our opportunity fighting monsters."

She nodded. *Maybe next year?*

I laughed. If it had a bitter edge, Sarah didn't comment. Neither did I.

Once Mrs. Douglass succeeded in sealing the portal, the battle was all over except for the mop-up. Our troops finished off the remaining ghouls with extreme prejudice. I won't say it was easy; it wasn't. But we knew we'd won and we knew Alex could heal our wounded, so we persevered and pounded the monsters into gray-green rubble.

Not a single ghoul reached the Glen Jackson bridge and not a single defender died.

That's not to say we didn't have casualties, we definitely did. Especially in the psychological arena. Alex may have healed their physical wounds, but those thirty-five men and women had had their perception of reality altered. They now knew beyond doubt that monsters existed, that ghosts were real, and that Luke and I weren't loonies to be tolerated with indulgent smirks.

Jack summed it up nicely. "I know I said I wouldn't hassle you any more after Morgan tried to kill you over the seventh-seventh crap," he paused and looked me square in the eyes, "but I still thought it was nonsense. I mean, just because a deranged lunatic believes something enough to kill for it doesn't make it true." He licked his lips and glanced at my hands. "But today I not only saw monsters and fought them, I saw you conjure fire in your hands." He nodded toward Alex. "I saw him heal wounds that should've been fatal."

He stretched out his hand to me, and I took it in a firm grip.

"I'll never doubt you again, Gus," he said. "You're the real deal, and I'm honored you trusted me enough to ask for my help."

"Thanks, Jack," I said, laying my free hand over our clasped ones for a moment before releasing him. I turned to include all the men and women who had fought beside us. "I appreciate the leap of faith all of you made in coming here today. I'm sorry we had to involve you in this. I'm sorry your illusions have been shattered. But I'm also extremely grateful. We couldn't have kept the citizens safe without your assistance."

Luke stepped up beside me and clapped a hand to my shoulder. "Gus and I need to dispose of all these carcasses." He cocked an eyebrow at me. "The shield should incinerate them, don't you think?"

I nodded my agreement.

He looked around at all the weary faces who had helped us save the world. "What say we head into Portland, find a pub, and celebrate Halloween with a round of beers?" he asked.

Smiles and cheers of approval answered him.

"Great. You all head out and find a bar. Mason, text me where to meet you. Gus and I will join you as soon as we've finished cleaning up."

I nodded my approval. Luke was a natural at taking command.

After the civilians left the island, the seventh-sevenths cleaned up the remains of the battle. When our combined shield had turned the bodies into so much ash, we gathered the remnants of our equipment and returned to the yacht.

We gathered on the flying bridge while Alex fired up the engines. Sarah floated over to sit beside me. I reached for her hand, then curled my fingers in regret.

"You know, I never thought I'd think such a thing, let alone say it aloud," I said, smiling ruefully at Sarah, "but Morgan did a good thing. He may have done it for selfish reasons, but he still did it. Without his warning, this might have turned out very differently."

The others nodded. Even Sarah.

Mrs. Douglass, who still looked pale and drawn despite Alex's best efforts, said, "Let's go join our friends ... and maybe raise a glass to Jason Morgan, a monster who remembered his humanity in the end."

VIII

DARK OF THE MOON

UNCOLLECTED ANTHOLOGY

PARANORMAL PIRATES

ISSUE 27 **UA** APRIL 2022

DARK OF THE MOON

DEBBIE MUMFORD

PROLOGUE

Darkness swirled around the demon prince as he paced through the beach grass at the edge of the sandy strip that was the shore of the tiny island. Frustration seethed as he stared east toward the shore of the mainland where electric lights blazed, pushing the night's shadows back toward the prince. So close. His prey was so close. And yet moving water separated him and his horde from the succulent meat to be found on that well-lit coastline.

He threw back his head and roared his rage to the night sky. The curved ram's horns adorning the blood red flesh covering his skull reverberated with the sound; the undergrowth along the shoreline rustled as the horde of minions cowered from his wrath.

All his plans. All his carefully laid plans had come to naught. If he didn't find a way off this island, he and his minions would perish. They required meat. More, they needed human souls to nourish and strengthen them. To provide the power to open a permanent portal to the Otherworld.

His roar of frustration split the night yet again as he remembered the sacrifice he'd made to open the portal at midwinter. His favorite female; his youngest offspring; destroyed at the most auspicious moment of the longest night of the year to open the way to the bountiful meat and power of the mortal world.

And all for naught.

He and his horde of minions had arrived in the mortal world, but on a small, deserted island off the coast of what the humans called North America. Close enough to see the lights of their cities, but separated from that succulent source of sustenance and power by moving water.

Rage built within him yet again. The portal had snapped closed unexpectedly. The sacrifice he had provided had not been enough even to bring all of his horde through the veil. The ones who had managed to make the transition were stranded. No way back to the Otherworld; no way to cross the moving water.

In the months that they'd been imprisoned here, they'd decimated the island's population of small animals. Not even a rat remained. Soon the horde would fall upon each other. He would survive. None would dare to touch him, and he would willingly drink the blood of every one of his minions, but what would it profit him? He would be left to roam the island, bereft of purpose and companions.

He must find a way off this cursed island!

"My lord!"

He turned, eyes fiery, a roar upon his lips. Who dared to disturb his musings?

A minion groveled in the sand, his expression a satisfying mix of terror and... was that hope?

"Prince Rakasha," the low-order demon said, angling his face away from his master. "A ship! A ship approaches from the south."

Fierce joy flooded Rakasha. Meat! And power! And most importantly, a vessel to carry them across the moving water to the mainland!

"Show me!"

1

My cell phone buzzed. I glanced at the readout and sighed. Ethel Douglass. I'd had a long day and the last thing I wanted was for Mrs. D, a seemingly sweet little old lady from Seattle, to tell me we were in for another supernatural invasion from the Otherworld.

My name is Gus Collier, and in addition to being a homicide detective for the city of Portland, Oregon, I'm also a seventh-seventh. The seventh son of a seventh son.

Not that gender has anything to do with it.

Seventh-seventh is a birth order anomaly. The seventh child of a seventh child is hard-wired to come into some form of psychic power. Usually on their twenty-eighth birthday. It's all about the sevens, and since twenty-eight is seven quadrupled, that's when it happens. I suppose putting it off until the seventh-seventh turns forty-nine (seven squared) would make even more sense, but that's not what happens.

Hey, I didn't make the rules, I'm just living this weirdness.

Anyway, Mrs. Douglass is another seventh-seventh, but she's not like me. Her abilities are tied to alternate realities. As far as I understand it, seventh-sevenths come in three flavors: guardians like me and my friend Luke; healers like my ghostly partner Sarah and our friend Alex; and those who are attuned to alternate realities, specifically the Otherworld, like Ethel Douglass. All of us are psychic, so we can all see and hear Sarah, which makes life a whole lot easier when we're on a mission.

A mission.

I so didn't want to experience another mission like the one we'd survived last Halloween. But Mrs. Douglass rarely called, and never without a reason. So I braced myself and answered my cell phone.

"Hey, Mrs. Douglass," I said, using my cheeriest voice. Maybe if I sounded happy and carefree she wouldn't have the heart to spoil my mood. Right. Like that was even a remote possibility.

"Good evening, Gus. Is Sarah with you?"

I rolled my eyes, thankful the elderly woman couldn't see my expression. Of course Sarah was with me. She'd been with me constantly since I'd investigated her murder... and her corpse had dug its well-manicured fingernails into my wrist. All because I'd been called to investigate the murder of a fellow seventh-seventh on my twenty-eighth birthday and my power had manifested as I knelt to examine the body.

Talk about a bizarre birthday gift! But that's another story.

"Yes, ma'am," I said politely. Sassing Mrs. D wasn't a good idea. The woman might look like a sweet little old lady, but she was a powerful psychic and knew how to deal with upstarts like me. "Sarah's right here."

"Excellent. Put this call on speaker, you both need to hear what I have to say."

I motioned Sarah over and did as Mrs. Douglass directed while my hopes for a nice quiet evening watching the game on TV evaporated.

My ghostly partner floated over, a quizzical expression on her pretty face. Sarah was a beauty in life— perfect peaches and cream complexion, large blue eyes, silky blonde hair— and despite being doomed to wearing blue hospital scrubs with her hair pulled back in a pony tail for eternity, she was still my ideal woman.

If only I'd met her before Jason Morgan blew her brains out so he could steal her psychic power. Fate could be a real bitch sometimes.

"All set, Mrs. Douglass. What's up?"

"My work, all my calculations as well as the information my gift has supplied, tells me that there's a problem coming. A big one."

As I said before, Mrs. D's power is attuned to alternate realities. That means that in the real world she's a theoretical mathematician. Advanced mathematics help her define and refine the information her abilities provide. I don't pretend to understand. That's not my gift. I'm a guardian. I just accept her information and come up with a strategy to combat the problem.

"Got any details?" I asked.

"You're not going to like this," she said.

She was right. I already didn't and I hadn't heard the worst yet.

"We're going to need to call in Luke and Alex and head out to the coast. Astoria should do it."

"The coast?" I said in a choked voice. "Can't we wait 'til summer? I mean if I'm heading to the Pacific coast, I'd rather do it in hot, sunny weather."

Mrs. Douglass sighed audibly. "Gus, this won't be a vacation. We'll be fighting off pirates."

"Pirates? You have *got* to be kidding!"

Mrs. D was silent for a few beats of my heart, during which time Sarah glared me into submission.

"Are you ready to listen yet, Gus? If not, I'll call Luke and let him explain the seriousness of the situation to you."

I closed my eyes. The last thing I wanted was for my fellow guardian, Captain Luke Young, army recruiter extraordinaire, to come down on me. Alternate reality seventh-sevenths might be drawn to the sciences, like higher mathematics, but guardians were drawn to law enforcement or the military. Protection. Structure. Justice. Those were our strengths.

Opening my eyes, I nodded to Sarah and forced myself to set my disbelief aside. Mrs. D was serious; I needed to at least sound professional.

"All right, Mrs. Douglass," I said using my best homicide detective voice. "Tell me what we're up against." I could almost see her nodding on the other end of our cell connection.

"According to my work, a portal opened on an island off the Pacific coast at the winter solstice. The demons who came through were contained by the vast quantity of moving water surrounding the island."

I nodded. "That's good news."

"Well," she said, sounding discouraged, "it was. Unfortunately, further calculations and insight from the Otherworld indicates that they've found a way to leave. A group of maritime reenactors landed an old style sailing vessel on the island. Something similar to the pirate ships of the seventeenth century."

She sighed. "The crew was devoured and the ship taken over. Using the power provided by their victims' souls, the demons are learning to sail it and will head to the mouth of the Columbia. They've timed it well. They should arrive at the dark of the moon just prior to the vernal equinox. Their last moment of dark power before the light ascends."

"Let me get this straight," I said, frowning and rubbing my forehead. "You're saying a shipload of demons, corporeal demons, is going to land in Astoria? When exactly will this *dark of the moon* occur?"

"We have a week," Mrs. D said. "But it's not just Astoria. If we don't stop them there, they'll sail down the Columbia to Portland and beyond, devastating everything along their route and growing more powerful with each soul they consume."

And if they make it to Portland, Sarah added, *what's to stop them from reopening the portal on Government Island? The one we fought to close last fall.*

Since I wasn't sure Sarah's voice would carry over the cell phone signal, I relayed her concerns to Mrs. D.

"Sarah makes an excellent point. We could lose the ground we thought we gained at Halloween."

With that sobering thought, we agreed that Mrs. D and Alex would drive down to Portland while I brought Luke up to speed. We'd meet in Mrs. D's favorite suite at The Benson the next evening.

Another supernatural battle was shaping up… and we were going to need help.

Again.

I could hardly wait.

2

The next morning, I enlisted the help of my partner, Detective Jack Barnes.

Jack's a middle-aged guy who's nothing to look at. His hair is thinning and going gray, his cheeks are constantly stubbled and a little on the flabby side, and he's got a definite spare tire around his middle, but he's a solid detective and a good friend. He used to rib me about the seventh-seventh crap, back when we both thought it was nonsense, but then he and a bunch of other cops helped us battle real, live ghouls last Halloween and all teasing stopped.

He didn't believe me when I asked for help—nobody did, but he and more than a dozen other cops showed up on Government Island anyway. They didn't expect the danger to be real; they expected to stage some sort of intervention for me. Instead, they fought for their lives and the lives of every citizen of Portland and Vancouver, because that's what cops do: protect and serve.

And now I had to ask Jack, and as many of the others as were willing, to repeat that performance.

Hell's bell's! Why couldn't I have been born a normal guy?

Taking a deep breath and squaring my shoulders, I crossed the battered linoleum of the homicide bull pen to the pair of desks Jack and I claimed as our own. The scarred old wooden desks were butted together front-to-front so Jack and I could see each other and talk while we worked.

He glanced up, saw me coming, and his eyebrows quirked in a question.

Huh. I must not have been doing as great a job of keeping my features neutral as I thought.

"What's up, Gus?" Jack asked as I yanked my chair out and plopped onto its sturdy seat. "You look like you've lost your best friend." Then he grinned, mischief dancing in his eyes. "Which can't be true since I'm sitting right here."

"Ha ha," I said, adding a grimace for form. "Listen, Jack. I need to ask another favor."

Jack's face sobered. He glanced around the bull pen, leaned forward, and said, "Is this another seventh-seventh thing?"

I nodded. "There's another supernatural invasion on the way." He scowled, but didn't interrupt. "I'd like you and as many of the other cops as you can round up to meet me at The Benson this evening. Mrs. Douglass has a suite there and we're going to lay out our strategy."

"Will Captain Young and that scrawny, curly haired guy—what was his name?—be there?"

I nodded. "Yep. Luke and Alex are coming. And Alex isn't scrawny. He's just not muscular like Luke."

Jack snorted. "Don't kid yourself, partner. Alex makes *you* look brawny, and you can't hold a candle to the captain."

I waved his comment aside. "Whatever. Alex is a healer and we'll need all his talent to keep our side healthy during the fight."

"Yeah, he was amazing at Halloween. Kept everyone alive and kicking, although I have no clue how he accomplished it." Jack paused, looked thoughtful, then added, "Will Sarah be helping him again?"

I glanced at the corner of my desk where Sarah appeared to perch. She shook her head.

"Doubtful," I said quietly. "At Halloween the veils between the worlds were thin and the ghouls had opened a portal to the other side. The combination allowed Sarah to manifest physically. That shouldn't happen this time."

He nodded. "Too bad. That means Alex will be working alone."

I shrugged. "True, but it also means the demons we'll be facing will be limited. They won't just keep coming out of a portal."

"Good enough," Jack said with a curt nod. "Demons, huh? Are they different from the—what'd you call 'em?—ghouls we fought last time?"

I frowned. "Beats me. Guess we'll find out when Mrs. D tells us what's what."

Jack nodded, picked up a pen and pulled a notebook out of his pocket. "Tell me which suite at The Benson and what time. I'll bring along everyone I can round up."

"Thanks, Jack." I hoped Luke was having as much luck with the military contingent.

3

I strode off the elevator on Mrs. D's floor and hurried toward her suite, only to be stopped in the hallway, unable to reach her door.

The group who gathered in and around Mrs. D's suite at The Benson had overwhelmed the room. Elbowing and shouldering my way forward, I reached the door and saw the elderly woman standing beside Alex Davidovich, who acted as her assistant.

"Call the front desk," she directed Alex, "and arrange for a small conference room. Have them provide coffee service and cold cuts for..." she paused, glanced around the room, and estimated the number of people crowding her suite and the hallway beyond, "fifty should do it."

While Alex made the arrangements, Mrs. D raised her hands and the group quieted.

"As soon as we have adequate space," she said in a calm, carrying voice, "I'll explain why I've asked you here tonight."

Alex cleared his throat, and she turned to face him. "Yes, Alex?"

The young man turned to the group. "If you'll all head down to the second floor, we'll gather in the Willamette Room."

I stepped to the side to allow others to move past me into the hall. When the room was empty except for Mrs. D, Alex, and Luke, I moved to join them. Sarah floated silently beside me.

"Looks like we have help," I said after greeting the others.

"We do indeed. You and Luke have done an admirable job gathering forces on short notice." She nodded to us and then fixed her gaze on Sarah. "I'm glad you chose to join us, Sarah."

I wouldn't want to be anywhere else, my ghostly partner whispered into our minds.

"I wondered if you might have chosen to move on after our victory at Halloween."

Sarah shook her head, her semi-transparent blonde ponytail bouncing. *Halloween just served to convince me that I can still be of use here in the mortal realm. I'm not ready to move on.*

Mrs. D nodded. "I understand, and we're glad to have your help."

My help will be limited this time, Sarah said with a shrug. *I doubt I'll be able to materialize, so no 'helping hand,' so to speak.*

"Understood," Alex said with a smile, "but your medical knowledge will still come in handy."

Luke clapped his hands. "This is great and all, but we can catch up later. Right now we've got people waiting downstairs."

Mrs. D nodded and stepped toward the door. "Captain Young is correct, as usual. Let's join the others and get this briefing underway."

When we reached the Willamette Room we discovered that the hotel staff had set it up like a lecture hall. A stage at one end with a podium and microphone; rows of folding chairs; and tables at the back of the room loaded with coffee urns, carafes of water, and platters of sliced meats, cheeses, bread and condiments.

Most of the group hovered around the food while Luke and I muscled the podium off the stage and replaced it with a table and four chairs which Alex had procured from the staff. When everything was ready, Alex handed Mrs. D onto the stage and we took our seats.

"If everyone will find a seat," Luke called, his voice carrying throughout the room even without benefit of amplification, "we'll get this briefing underway."

I watched as police officers and army men and women juggled plates and cups and found seats in short order. At Halloween, we'd had thirty-five heavily armed men and women backing us up, twenty military personnel and fifteen members of Portland's finest. This time, our ranks had grown. I counted twenty-five from each service, with my partner Jack sitting front and center.

Jack nodded and gave me a quick salute with the first two fingers of his right hand. I responded in kind as Mrs. D rapped on the table for attention.

"Thank you all for coming," she said, inclining her head to her audience. "I see quite a few faces I recognize, as well as several who are new to me. To those who were with us at Halloween, thank you again for giving the people of Portland and Vancouver your protection. To those who are new, thank you for suspending disbelief and joining our ranks. As those of you who fought beside us last fall know, we couldn't have prevailed without you. We will need your strength and skill just as much this time around."

With that, she proceeded to give us all an overview of the coming battle. At least, her best guess as to what we'd be facing.

When Mrs. D finished, a tough looking man in an army uniform with sergeant's stripes on his sleeves called out, "So, we'll be facing those same slimy gray-green creatures?"

The woman behind him jerked, obviously startled by his description. One of the new recruits.

Mrs. D shook her head. "I don't believe so. If my calculations are correct, and I believe they are, we'll be facing demons this time."

"What's the difference?" another man asked.

"Last fall we dealt with an incursion of ghouls. They're nasty creatures that love nothing more than to destroy and devour. Human flesh is a delicacy they'd love to consume with gluttony."

I heard several sharp intakes of breath, but no one spoke, so Mrs. D continued.

"But they're not very smart. Their main advantage is strength. They're tall and wiry, and as you said, gray-green in color. Demons on the other hand…"

She paused, bit her lower lip and clenched her fist until her knuckles whitened.

"Demons come in several classes. They're most often red in color, often with horns, and they all possess more intelligence than even the brightest ghoul. We'll be facing a demon prince and his horde. The prince will be highly intelligent, capable of strategic thinking and able to deploy his horde with great effectiveness. It will be up to us to anticipate his moves and break up the formations he sends out."

She paused again, took a deep breath, and released it slowly.

"Probably his greatest strength, and the thing we must guard against assiduously, is his ability to use glamour."

"What?" someone called from the back of the room. "Is he going to make us faint from envy over his pretty clothes?"

Mrs. D's smile was strained. "Not Hollywood glamour," she clarified. "Supernatural glamour. He'll be able to change his appearance, make himself look like anyone or anything."

A wave of muttering washed through the group. Mrs. D waited, allowing everyone to vent their feelings.

"We'll have to be very careful; we'll need to guard our thoughts. He'll be able to pull fear-inducing images from our minds and manifest that image in front of us... and he won't have to be standing right there to do it. He'll be able to cast the image, the glamour, over any member of his horde. Of course, he'll also be able to change his own appearance."

"Crap," someone near the front muttered.

"Exactly," Jack replied.

I stood up. Time to give our troops some hope. Mrs. D was arming them against reality, but they also needed to know we had a chance.

"I know this sounds bad," I said, and everyone quieted down again, "but we do have good news too. Things haven't all gone their way. Their prince miscalculated."

I held up one finger. "One: he opened the portal on an uninhabited island."

A second finger joined the first. "Two: he couldn't maintain the portal. He'd counted on drawing power from the people his horde slaughtered to hold the portal open. Since he didn't have that *resource*, he lost the portal and only has the minions who came through with him. It won't be like last time where they just keep coming until we manage to close the portal."

"And finally," I said as I released my ring finger. "Three: Mrs. D knows he's coming and is raising this defense force to protect and defend the mainland."

I fisted my hand. "They're going to make landfall at Astoria at the dark of the moon... and we're going to be there to make sure they don't make it a single step further."

4

Just before sunset on the evening when the dark of the moon would occur, our team gathered on the beach at Fort Stevens State Park, a narrow spit of land guarding the mouth of the Columbia River. Mrs. D informed us it was the perfect place for our battle since it had once housed a military installation whose purpose was the defense of the mainland. We, the seventh-sevenths in our group, would draw power from that historic intention to serve and protect. Especially me and Luke, the guardians.

Mrs. D also figured that since the campground was already in use, even though it was early in the season, the demons would be drawn to the lure of an easy meal. After all, except for the crew of the sailing vessel they'd swarmed, they'd been starving since midwinter.

So we set our lines of engagement on the beach where the Pacific met the Columbia, just off Jetty Road. Alex and Sarah set up the medical tent in a line of scrub oaks behind us, while Jack and Luke's second, Lieutenant Mason, deployed our non-psychic fighters. Luke and Mrs. D and I stood facing the water. We were the first line of defense. We were the ones who could deal with the demon prince... and we'd also take out as many of his horde as we could manage.

If Luke and I had our way, none of the rest of our people would need to lift a finger.

Of course, that was wishful thinking.

Fortunately, we hadn't based our battle plan on wishful arrogance. Everyone had a job to do, and everyone knew exactly what was expected of them.

Now we just had to do it... defeat a horde of red-skinned, ram-horned demons whose prince could change their appearance at will.

Piece. Of. Cake.

———

WE DIDN'T HAVE long to wait. The sun slid into the Pacific, turning water and sky a deep bloody red, and there— outlined against the horizon— rode a majestic seventeenth century sailing ship. Three tall masts pointed into the darkening sky where no moon would rise.

Of course, the moon would rise, but in its final waning crescent, it would remain all but invisible, casting no light to protect the world of men against the monsters who rode those bloody waves.

The ship's sails billowed, stained pink and orange by the light of the dying sun, and drove the vessel straight for the beach where the defenders waited. As it drew near, an eerie silence descended on both land and water. No breeze sighed; no birds called; no small creatures rustled in the beach grass. Even the waves lapping across the sand were unnaturally silent.

Mrs. D whispered, "Hold," her voice raspy and low.

I readied my defenses, running spells through my mind, while my fingers curved, itching to conjure fireballs. I glanced at Luke. He met my gaze with a curt nod, steely determination blazing from his eyes.

The ship dropped anchor. A rowboat was lowered and several creatures clambered down ropes and into its sheltering hull.

"Remember," Mrs. D whispered. "They're at their most vulnerable right now. They cannot swim and moving water defeats them."

Luke and I stepped forward, both conjuring fireballs, and hurled our missiles at the row boat as it slipped toward the shore.

My fireball hit a rower's arm and bounced into the water where it fizzled out of existence. Luke's throw was better aimed. He knocked a demon out of the boat.

The minion screamed with agony and then disintegrated into slimy sludge as the moving water engulfed him.

Cheers rang out behind us, and my heart raced with a fierce joy. They weren't invincible! We could end them.

Luke and I peppered the boat with fireballs while the crew lowered a second, third, and fourth boat to the water. Each small vessel held a dozen minions, while a fifth boat ferried a single, tall figure toward the shore. The demon prince was accompanied by only two of his horde. Lower caste demons whose only responsibility was to row the boat.

A total of fifty minions and a demon prince. And we'd already reduced that number by four.

We could do this!

Before I could get too cocky, Mrs. D stepped between me and Luke and held out the large silver crucifix we'd used in our last battle.

"Shield," she said.

Luke and I each took a half step back so that she and the ornate silver cross were at the apex of our triad and drew energy from the ceaseless motion of the waves. With the cross as our focal point, we flung our arms wide and poured that energy back out, into a sphere of blue-white flame. The sphere surrounded us, protecting us, and the troops behind us, from evil enchantment.

The minions who had managed to jump from the boats to shore, flinched back from the light and radiant warmth.

In unison, the three of us stepped forward.

The minions retreated. Until one moved too far back, his foot landing where a wave could reach it. On the next influx of water, the creature screamed, dropped to the sand (for the water had retreated momentarily) and clutched at his leg, which was smoking and disintegrating as he screamed in agony. When the waves rushed in again, his doom was sealed.

The other demons panicked. Unsure where to go or what to do, they raced along the beach, away from our shield, but focused on staying away from the moving water.

Our troops recognized their advantage and pursued the fleeing demons, harrying them into the water if possible, dropping them with bullets if not. Whether or not guns were used, all defeated demons ended in the relentless arms of the Pacific Ocean.

While our men and women in uniform, whether military or police issue, dealt with the minions, Luke and Mrs. D and I concentrated on the demon prince.

He jumped lightly from his boat, carefully avoiding the ocean's grasp. He smiled at us, rearranging his visage into that of seasoned sailor. A man with a ready smile, sun-bleached blond hair, and skin leathered by long exposure to wind, salt, and sun.

A happy man. One who was glad to see us. Delighted to be among humans again; away from the foul creatures who had overrun his ship.

If Mrs. D hadn't warned us about the glamour, Luke and I might have lowered our defenses. After all, rescuing humans from supernatural evil was our reason for existence, our mission in life.

But she *had* warned us, and so I saw the man this monster had murdered, devoured, and soul-razed. And righteous anger made our shield burn even more brightly with the pure light of justice.

In perfect unison, we stepped closer to the prince, pinning him between the brilliance of our shield and the destruction of the moving water.

Something gray and misty flashed at the edge of my vision as I focused on the prince.

Sarah! I'd forgotten the two minions who'd been with the prince and one of them had Sarah!

I faltered, but Mrs. D and Luke called my name, holding me to my purpose. With regret, a deep and soul-crushing regret, I remembered that the woman I loved was already dead, that there were living souls who required my protection. I renewed my focus, cast a wordless cry for forgiveness to Sarah, and pushed on.

Mrs. D and Luke and I were as relentless and implacable as the Pacific. The demon prince and his last two minions succumbed to the ocean's watery depths. Their brief stint as pirates at a blessed end.

EPILOGUE

When the clean-up was complete and we were sure everyone was safe and no demons had escaped to wreak havoc in the campgrounds, Luke and Mrs. D and I sank into camp chairs in Alex's medical tent.

Mrs. D leaned over and touched my arm, her wrinkled fingers gentle against my skin. "What happened, Gus? What broke your concentration?"

I sighed, leaning forward, elbows on knees, and cradled my head in my hands.

"Sarah," I said quietly, trying desperately to ignore the aching chasm that had opened where my heart had been. "She's gone. He took her."

"What?" Alex yelled. "When?"

"Near the end of the battle. After we broke his illusion of being the ship's captain."

Alex laughed, hard and loud.

I jumped to my feet. How dare he laugh at my devastating loss! Sarah might be a ghost, she might already be dead, but she was still the only woman I'd ever loved. The only woman I *would* ever love!

When Alex saw my face, he stopped laughing. Quickly. His face drained of color and he held out his hands as if to push me away.

"Hey, c'mon, man," he said. "You're serious! But Sarah's fine. She was with me here in the tent the whole time you were pushing that bastard into the waves. He didn't do anything to her."

I scowled at him. "Sure. Right. Then where the hell is she?"

Gus? What's wrong? I can feel your anguish all the way across the park? Are you hurt? Do you need me?

"You're okay?" I yelled into the night. "You're still here? He didn't send you... I don't know, somewhere bad?"

Her sweet laugh echoed through my mind. *I'm fine, Gus. Just doing a quick sweep of the park to make sure none of them got away from us. It's about the only thing I've been able to contribute tonight. If you're sure you don't need me, I'll just finish up.*

I breathed a sigh of relief while Luke and Alex and Mrs. D patted my back and assured me that it had just been a deceptive glamour perpetrated by the demon prince. He'd pulled Sarah's image from my mind and cast it onto one of his remaining two minions. If I'd broken, he could've beaten us.

And if he'd done so, it wouldn't have mattered how many of his minions we destroyed... he'd've won. He was on the mainland where he would've slaughtered and pillaged until he had sufficient power to open another portal. And we wouldn't have been around to stop him the next time.

My friends praised me for holding firm in the face of such devastating heartbreak, but I felt no pride. I was too relieved that Sarah was still here.

Because, to answer her implied question: *OF COURSE* I needed her!

I loved her. Simple as that.

Alive or dead, Sarah would always be the only woman for me.

ABOUT DEB LOGAN

Deb Logan specializes in tales for the young – and the young at heart! Author of the popular Faery Chronicles series, Deb loves the unknown, whether it's the lure of space or earthbound mythology. She writes about demon hunters, thunderbirds, and everyday life on a space station for tweens, teens, and anyone who enjoys young adult fiction. Her work has been published in multiple volumes of *Fiction River*, as well as in *2017 Young Explorer's Adventure Guide*, *Feyland Tales*, and other popular anthologies.

Sign up for Deb's newsletter and receive a FREE story!

To learn more, visit Deb at:
debloganwrites.com
Or send her an email at:
debloganwrites@gmail.com

ALSO BY DEB LOGAN

Children's Stories and Chapter Books:

Cinnamon Chou Files:

- The Case of the Missing Inarian
- The Case of the Glittering Hoard
- The Case of the Recreational Thief
- The Case of the Vanishing Puppy
- The Case of the Missing Merchandise

Prentiss Twins Novels:

- Thunderbird
- Coyote
- White Buffalo
- The Twelve Days of Tricksters (Short Story)
- A Trickster Halloween (Short Story)

"Read-to-Me" Stories:

- Chattermaster
- Deirdre's Dragon
- The Fox and the Fleas
- Mom's Helper
- Read-to-Me Stories (Collection)

Short Story Collections:

- Galactic Cadets: Kids in Space
- Read-to-Me Stories

Short Stories:

- ANGELIC VOICES
- LILAH'S GHOST

Young Adult Stories and Novels:

Dani Erickson Stories:

- DEMON DAZE
- SCHOOL DAZE
- FAMILY DAZE
- CHALLENGING DAZE
- DANGEROUS DAZE
- DANI'S DEMONS (COLLECTION)

Faery Chronicles:

- FAERY UNEXPECTED (NOVEL)
- FAERY BEAUTIFUL (SHORT STORY)
- FAERY UNPREDICTABLE (NOVELETTE)
- LEXIE'S CHOICE (SHORT STORY)
- OF DRAGONS AND CENTAURS (SHORT STORY)
- FAERY COLLECTIBLE (COLLECTION)

Feyland Tie-Ins:

- EMMA: A FEYLAND DRYAD
- ON GUARD: A FEYLAND STORY

Seer Chronicles:

- THE SEER CHRONICLES: VOLUME 1 (COLLECTION)
- TERRORS (SHORT STORY)
- TO HAVE...AND TO HOLD (SHORT STORY)
- SELKIES IN PARADISE (SHORT STORY)

- The Journal (short story)
- Paladin Shield (short story)

Siren Tales:

- Salt Water
- Siren Surf

Short Story Collections:

- Ghosts and Ghoulies
- More Ghosts and Ghoulies

Short Fiction:

- Amelia Fox: Spy in Training
- Beauty or Butterface?
- Flutterbies and French Toast
- Rush!
- That Lake House Summer

"WDM Presents" Anthologies:

- Spun Yarns Unwound, Vol. 1
- Spun Yarns Unwound: Vol. 2
- Spun Yarns Unwound: Vol. 3
- Tales of Mystery & Mayhem
- 2016: A Year of Short Fiction
- 2017: A Year of Short Fiction
- WDM Presents: Short Fiction from 2018
- WDM Presents: Short Fiction from 2019
- WDM Presents: Short Fiction from 2020
- WDM Presents: Short Fiction from 2021

ABOUT DEBBIE MUMFORD

Debbie Mumford specializes in speculative fiction (fantasy, paranormal romance, and science fiction) as well as mystery and historical fiction. Author of the popular *Sorcha's Children* series, Debbie loves the unknown, whether it's the lure of space or earthbound mythology. Her work has been published in multiple volumes of *Fiction River*, as well as in *Heart's Kiss Magazine*, *Amazing Monster Tales*, and many other popular anthologies. She writes about dragon-shifters, time-traveling lovers, and detectives—whether amateur or professional—for adults as Debbie Mumford, and science fiction and fantasy for tweens and young adults as Deb Logan.

Join Debbie's special announcement newsletter list and receive a FREE story!

To learn more, visit Debbie at:
debbiemumford.com/
Or send her an email at:
deborah.mumford@gmail.com

facebook.com/DebbieMumfordWrites
amazon.com/author/debbiemumford
bookbub.com/authors/debbie-mumford
twitter.com/deborah_mumford

ALSO BY DEBBIE MUMFORD

Kristi Lundrigan Mysteries:

- DELECTABLE MOUNTAIN QUILTING (NOVEL)
- IN A PICKLE (NOVEL)
- FOOL'S PUZZLE (SHORT STORY)
- WILDFIRE! (SHORT STORY)

Gus and Ghost Short Story Series:

- SEVENTH
- SEVENTH: FIRST FRUITS
- DEATH OF AN ALCHEMIST (UNCOLLECTED ANTHOLOGY)
- SEVENTH: THE SAMHAIN DILEMMA
- DARK OF THE MOON (UNCOLLECTED ANTHOLOGY)

Logans of Lastalrig Series:

- HER HIGHLAND LAIRD (NOVELLA)
- HER HIGHLAND YULE (SHORT STORY)

Red's Series:

- RED'S MAGICK (SHORT STORY COLLECTION)
- SEEING RED (SHORT STORY)

Signs of the Prophecy Novels:

- YOUNGEST
- SEEKER
- CHOSEN (COMING SOON!)

Sorcha's Children Series:

- Sorcha's Children (Omnibus Edition)
- Sorcha's Heart (Novella)
- Dragons' Choice (Novel)
- Dragons' Flight (Novel)
- Dragons' Desire (Novel)
- Dragons' Destiny (Novel)

Supernatural Yellowstone Short Story Series:

- Reality Bites
- The Cat Lady of Yellowstone

Uncollected Anthology Short Stories:

- Death of an Alchemist (UA Alchemy)
- The Wedding Cake (UA Magical Arts)
- Dark of the Moon (UA Paranormal Pirates)
- In the Banyan Copse (UA Unexpected Histories)
- Old One (UA Magical Quests)
- Have Hoard, Will Seek (UA A Diversity of Dragons)

Universal Star League Short Story Series:

- Voyages Into The Black (Collection)
- The Warbirds of Absaroka
- Awakening the Warrior
- Incident on the Odyssey
- The Queen's Captive
- The Lost Colony
- Freighter Families in Space

Witchling Short Story Series:

- WITCHLING
- THE SOLITARY SORCERESS
- TO PROTECT A PRINCESS

Stand Alone Novels:

- SECOND SIGHT

Historical Fiction:

- HER HIGHLAND LAIRD (NOVELLA)
- HER HIGHLAND YULE
- INCIDENT ON THE HIGH LINE
- MISS BAINBRIDGE'S SUMMER ADVENTURE
- MISS BAINBRIDGE'S CHRISTMAS PARTY
- SISTERS IN SUFFRAGE
- THE TRAIL WHERE WE CRIED
- THE WHITE DRAGON AND THE RED

Short Story Collections:

- LOVE IN A FLASH
- TALES OF BYGONE DAYS
- TALES OF LOVE & MAGICK
- TALES OF THE UNEXPECTED
- TALES OF TOMORROW
- TALES OF DISASTROUS DEEDS

Short Fiction:

- A GROVE OF MOUNTAIN ASH
- A WALK WITH GEORGIA
- AN ALIEN ADVENTURE
- ASTROMANCER
- BECAUSE OF THE CHRISTMAS STROLL

"WDM Presents" Anthologies: